Jill Mansell lives with her family in Bristol. She used to work in the field of Clinical Neurophysiology but now writes full time. She watches far too much TV and would love to be one of those super-sporty types but basically can't be bothered. Nor can she cook — having once attempted to bake a cake for the hospital's Christmas Fair, she was forced to watch while her co-workers played frisbee with it. But she's good at Twitter!

Just *Heavenly*. Just *Jill*.

'Bursting with humour, brimming with intrigue and full of characters you'll adore — we can't think of a better literary remedy' ***** *Heat*

'To read it is to devour it' *Company*

'A warm, witty and romantic read that you won't be able to put down' *Daily Mail*

'Slick, sexy, funny' *Daily Telegraph*

'Mansell's fiction is a happy leap away from the troubles of today' *Sunday Express*

'Jill Mansell is in a different league' *Sun*

By Jill Mansell

Jill Mansell

THREE AMAZING
THINGS ABOUT YOU

headline
review

First published in Great Britain in 2015
by HEADLINE REVIEW
An imprint of HEADLINE PUBLISHING GROUP

First published in paperback in 2015
by HEADLINE REVIEW

8

Cataloguing in Publication Data is available from the British Library

ISBN 978 1 4722 2695 2 (A-Format)
ISBN 978 1 4722 0886 6 (B-Format)

Typeset in Bembo by Palimpsest Book Production Limited, Falkirk, Stirlingshire

Printed and bound in Great Britain by Clays Ltd, Elcograf S.p.A.

Headline's policy is to use papers that are natural, renewable and recyclable
products and made from wood grown in well-managed forests and other
controlled sources. The logging and manufacturing processes are expected to
conform to the environmental regulations of the country of origin.

HEADLINE PUBLISHING GROUP
An Hachette UK Company
Carmelite House
50 Victoria Embankment
London EC4Y 0DZ

www.headline.co.uk
www.hachette.co.uk

Acknowledgements

I am hugely grateful to Dr Joanna Cannon for reading this book while it was still in manuscript form, in order to reassure me that I hadn't made any embarrassing medical errors. Thanks are also due to Dr Keir Shiels, who generously answered medical questions, and to Helen Davies for her advice on inheritance issues.

Finally, I would like to thank the inspirational Oli Lewington whose autobiography *Smile Through It*, about living with cystic fibrosis, was invaluable while I was writing this book. Any mistakes, needless to say, are mine alone.

Chapter 1

Now

OK, this is it, confession time. For the last two years I've asked all of you to tell me three things about you. And in return I've never told you anything about me. Which probably hasn't seemed very fair, has it?

But it's currently one o'clock in the morning, I'm in the back of a car being driven down to London and I've decided to come clean.

So here we go:

1. I'm twenty-eight, I have cystic fibrosis and I never actually expected to live this long.
2. The hospital transplant coordinator called two hours ago – they have a new pair of lungs for me.
3. I've never been so scared in my life. Also, excited. But mainly scared. Because this is a big thing that's about to happen and since I'm a coward I can't help picturing the worst-case scenario.

So now you know the reason for the full disclosure. Basically, if this turns out to be the final entry on the website, you'll understand why. Needless to say, I really hope it won't be.

One more thing. Thank you, thank you, THANK YOU to the wonderful family of the donor for giving me this gift, this incredible chance. I'll be grateful until the day I die and

Hallie paused, reread what she'd written and deleted the last sentence. In its place she typed: I hope you know how amazing you are. Your courage, kindness and generosity will always be remembered.

Droplets of light summer rain speckled the windscreen of the car. Hallie gazed out into the warm night as a sign saying *London 25 miles* loomed out of the darkness towards them and slid past. Street lamps glowed amber and houses showed only occasional lights in their windows; almost everyone at this time was asleep. Soon, though, dawn would lighten the sky, alarm clocks would wake them and they'd carry on living their normal lives without even pausing to think how miraculous their normal lives were.

Just being able to breathe in and out, that was pretty miraculous . . .

The finality of it all hit her afresh. There was still a chance, of course, that the tissue match would turn out not to be good enough and the transplant wouldn't go ahead. Which was why she wasn't uploading her post to the website just yet. But a few short hours from now, she could be in the operating theatre receiving another person's lungs. And who knew what might happen after that?

How many people would read what she'd written? What would they think?

Sitting back, Hallie thought of the line she'd deleted and wished she could as easily erase the song now playing in her head. It was a great song, one that people loved to sing during karaoke sessions. Everyone always joined in enthusiastically with the chorus.

She wasn't sure of the exact lyrics, but the last line of the chorus went something like: *This could be the day that I die . . . this could be the day that I die . . .*

Oh well. Seemed like her brain still had a sense of humour, at least.

Before

'Hey, hi, how's things? What are you up to?'

Hallie brightened at the sound of Bea's voice. 'You really want to know? OK, I'll tell you. But I'm warning you now, you're going to be *so* jealous.'

'Fire away.'

'I'm in Venice, sitting at a table outside Caffè Florian in St Mark's Square. The sun is shining, church bells are ringing and the waiter's just opened a bottle of ice-cold prosecco.'

'Is the waiter handsome?'

'What do you think? This is Venice! Of course he's handsome. He's giving me one of those handsome-waiter looks,' said Hallie. 'With his *eyes*.'

'Hmm, and is he listening to you saying this?'

'It's fine, he doesn't speak a word of English. I may seduce him later. He has a look of Bradley Cooper about him.'

'Sure you don't mean Tommy Cooper?'

'Shut *up*.'

'Are there pigeons there?'

'Yes, loads.'

'My mum went to St Mark's Square once. A pigeon did a poo on her head.'

'Lovely.'

'She was so mad,' said Bea. 'She'd had her hair done specially for the trip. I wouldn't stick around there if I were you. Get out while you can. Those Italian pigeons are evil.'

'Fine, you've convinced me. I'm going to jump into my helicopter now and fly home.'

'I think you should. Shall I come over after work this evening?'

'That'd be good.'

'Around seven then. See you later. Bye-eee!'

Hallie put down the phone and straightened her duvet, which had gone crooked again. She pulled herself into a more comfortable sitting position and did her best to adjust the pillows too. There was a definite art to staying in bed and not having to endlessly rearrange yourself, and she'd yet to master it. Back-arching, shoulder-stretching, bottom-wiggling and neck-tilting all played their part.

Having stretched and wriggled and got herself half sorted, Hallie looked out at the indigo sky as darkness fell. It was the week before Christmas, and multicoloured fairy lights were being switched on. From here, she had arguably the best view of the village: to the left, the high street; to the right, the River Windrush with its low stone bridge and the row of honey-coloured shops, hotels and houses on the other side of the water. She could watch everyone coming and going, keep track of people she knew, and also view the progress of tourists making their way around Carranford, the self-styled jewel in the north Cotswolds' crown.

Not so many visitors during the winter months, of course, but still enough to keep the people-watching interesting and the tourist-friendly shops open. A coachload were currently milling around, taking endless photographs, diving in and out of shops and buying souvenirs they didn't need, as well as Christmas presents for friends and relatives back home. By the looks of things, plenty of them would be opening a festively wrapped umbrella this year, printed with scenes of Carranford. Bea must have sold over a dozen today alone.

Eight days to Christmas. Hallie tried not to wonder if this one might be her last, basically because such thoughts were unanswerable and never helpful. Apart from anything else, the answer was always *possibly*.

Then again, that applied to everyone on the planet.

Banishing the question from her mind, Hallie switched on

the iPad and checked her emails instead. Several more had arrived this afternoon from visitors to the website. Brilliant, something to keep her occupied until Bea turned up. Never mind wondering if this Christmas would be her last; there were far more important problems to be sorted out, like how a girl should handle the discovery that she's inadvertently been dating twin boys, and the best way for a middle-aged man to divide his time over the festive season between his dull wife and his enthralling mistress.

Hallie had set up the website during a prolonged and particularly tedious hospital stay. Didn't everyone enjoy reading advice columns? She always had. She loved them, and loved coming up with solutions to problems too. When the columnist neglected to mention a useful suggestion, it always killed her not to be able to jump in and add a reply of her own.

The answer to this particular dilemma had, therefore, been to create the web page and begin dispensing advice herself.

She hadn't done it as poor-tragic-Hallie-with-the-manky-lungs-and-limited-lifespan either. This would only have inhibited questions; she'd known that from the word go. No, when people had problems in their lives, those problems were overwhelmingly important to them and everyone simply had to respect that. They certainly mustn't feel as if they couldn't compete with the person doling out the advice.

So she'd been anonymous from the start, and had remained so. All her readers knew was that she was female. The website was called www.threethingsaboutyou.com, and everyone writing in for advice with a dilemma was asked to include three things about themselves. Whether they chose to reveal big or small details was entirely up to them, but it was always an interesting indicator of character, and Hallie used them to more fully understand the people who were asking her to advise them.

Of course, for the first few weeks there hadn't been any readers, nor any problems being sent in, simply because no one knew the

5

website existed. She'd had to make up dilemmas, borrow and adapt some from old magazines and reply in her own words to people who'd never confided in her in the first place.

But before long, interest had started to grow. Thanks to the power of social networking, people slowly discovered the website and, deciding they liked it, spread the word to their friends. The number of hits steadily increased, and readers began submitting their own problems, which was good of them and freed Hallie up to spend more time researching the relevant issues and compiling the best possible answers.

Since then, the popularity of the website had continued to grow. Hallie was known to her readers as Rose, which was her middle name. Visitors to the site were welcome to contribute their own advice, but she was the one who decided whether or not it was posted. It was generally agreed that Rose's replies were great and her rapport with the contributors second to none. She had warmth, wit and compassion, and the readers appreciated this.

Almost as much as Hallie appreciated them in return.

She clicked on the first email:

Dear Rose,

1. I'm a fireman.
2. I play rugby.
3. I'm afraid of the dark.

I'm forty-six, married for almost twenty years, and my wife doesn't know I like to wear women's underwear. Well, no one does. My problem is that last week my mother-in-law took it upon herself to wash and clean my car while I was out at a works event. Being the thorough type, she took out the spare tyre in the boot and found the bra and knickers underneath.

She has now accused me of having an affair and is demanding I confess all to my wife. I know what my mother-in-law is like – she won't rest until I do. So which do you think I should admit to being, Rose? An unfaithful husband or a transvestite? I honestly don't know which option she'd find easier to accept.

Okaaaaay.
The second email said:

Dear Rose,

1. I'm ugly.
2. I'm fat.
3. I hate my life.

There's this boy in my class and I really like him but he never looks at me. I thought it was because I wasn't skinny enough because he seems to like only thin girls, so in October I stopped eating and now I've lost three stone but he still isn't interested.

What's wrong with me and how can I make him fall in love with me? I just want to be happy. Do you think it'll happen if I lose more weight? Help me, Rose, I'm so miserable I just want to die. Please please tell me what to do.

Hallie's heart went out to the desperately unhappy teenager. She would answer this one first. Poor girl, a bit of love-bombing probably wouldn't go amiss.

Chapter 2

It was Christmas Eve, and Tasha Sykes was discovering that coming out shopping three hours before she was due at the airport possibly wasn't the brightest idea she'd ever had.

But there were last-minute things she'd needed to buy, and she hadn't expected *quite* so many people to be as disorganised as herself. The shops were hot and heaving, the biting cold outside was making her nose sting and her phone kept buzzing with texts from friends demanding to know why she'd left the party early last night.

Tasha was ignoring the texts; it wasn't as if her friends weren't used to her by now. They seemed far more bothered by her single status than she was and were endlessly attempting to set her up with men she wasn't remotely interested in being set up with. Last night had been more of the same, a smart drinks party in Hampstead full of couples, apart from one unsuspecting person who'd been lured there on her behalf.

Poor chap.

God, it had been a nightmare. And he'd seemed so *nice*, that was the thing. His name had been Tom, he was decent looking and he worked as an accountant, which would come in incredibly handy. He'd been polite, interested in her, good company and well dressed.

She could almost – *almost* – have contemplated going out on a date with him, if not for one thing.

'His what?' hissed Jeannie in the kitchen. 'His *ears*? What's *wrong* with his ears?'

'They're hairy.' Tasha hated saying the words; she knew just how she sounded.

Jeannie gave a so-what gesture. 'He's a man. These things happen.'

'Yes, but it's a bit yuck. I don't like looking at them.'

'So don't look at them!'

'But I'd still know they were there.'

'And that's the only thing wrong with him?'

Tasha shrugged helplessly; it probably wasn't, but it was all she could concentrate on right now. 'I can't help the way I feel.'

'Once you get to know him, though, you could make him shave them,' Jeannie suggested. 'You could treat him to a lovely pampering session and do it yourself with Veet!'

'Do you have any idea how revolting that sounds?' Just the thought of it made Tasha squirm.

'I used to feel the same way about Barry's toenails, and they don't even bother me now!'

Worse and worse. Tasha said, 'I need an early night anyway. I'm just going to sneak off.'

'You're way too fussy, that's your problem. We find you all these lovely men and you don't even give them a chance. There's always something wrong with them.'

'I'm not too fussy. They just have to be . . . right.'

'You mean perfect.' Jeannie was blunt. 'And that's your problem right there. You're not perfect. No one is. If you're holding out for a man with nothing at all wrong with him . . . well, you may as well give up now, because he doesn't exist.'

Which was undoubtedly true, but Tasha still couldn't help the way she felt.

Also, hairy ears. *Yeurgh*.

By midday, she was almost done; all but a couple of items had been crossed off her list. Leaving Marks & Spencer loaded up like a donkey, Tasha almost got her armfuls of bags squashed in the revolving door. She was overheated and feeling pretty claustrophobic in her big pink coat. As for her arms, well, two simply weren't enough. Holding this much stuff was making them ache, and now she was such a cumbersome wide load, the bags and packages were inadvertently bashing into other people . . .

Right, this needed to be sorted out. Three of the items, ordered online and picked up in store, were far smaller than the boxes they'd been delivered in. Making an executive decision, Tasha put down the mountain of shopping, removed all the excess packaging and rearranged everything into a smaller number of bags. There, that was *much* better. Delighted with her organisational skills, she crammed the discarded cardboard into a nearby litter bin and shovelled the empty carriers in after them. Then, after flexing her aching shoulders, she gathered up the remaining full bags. OK, still heavy, but far easier to carry and less likely to knock small children to the ground.

And . . . back in control. All that remained to be picked up now was a box of Christmas crackers and the silver scarf for her mum and she was all done.

Pleased with herself, Tasha turned left and headed for the last shop. As she pushed open the door, her favourite Christmas song was playing and a blast of cool, deliciously scented air filled her lungs. She overheard a small girl say, 'Mummy, look at that lady in the pink coat, she's pretty,' and quite suddenly all was right with the world. A wave of joy enveloped her. This afternoon she was flying off to see her mum in the South of France and they would spend Christmas together . . . what could be more perfect than that?

Twenty minutes later, all was no longer right with the world and icy fingers appeared to be closing around her heart, whilst her own fingers scrabbled desperately for the third time through her handbag and pockets.

'It's here somewhere. It has to be here, I had it in the last shop . . .'

The queue behind her had already begun to tut with irritation at the delay.

'Better see if you left it there, then,' said the singularly unsympathetic girl manning the payment desk.

'But I know I didn't leave it behind, I had it in my hand . . .' It was impossible to mentally retrace your steps when Slade were bellowing MERRY CHRIIIIIIIISSSTMAAAAAS out of the tannoy and you were gripped with panic.

The man behind her in the queue said loudly, 'Excuse me, my parking meter's about to run out, can I pay for my stuff?'

'Yes.' The girl behind the till pushed Tasha's items to one side and reached for the next customer's basket.

Oh God, where was her credit card? What had she done with it? Feeling sick, Tasha searched through her pockets again. Three days ago, her debit card had snapped in half when she'd stupidly used it to clear ice from the car windscreen, and the replacement hadn't arrived yet.

And now her credit card had vanished. Nightmare, *nightmare.*

'If it's been stolen, you need to cancel it,' a woman in the queue reminded her.

Stolen . . .

Images of the card falling to the ground and being stealthily pocketed filled Tasha's brain. They could rack up so much money on it, even in just twenty minutes. She nodded and said, 'I don't know the number to ring to report it stolen.'

'Nor me,' said the woman, adding helpfully, 'But I know it's printed on the back of your card.'

Gathering up her bags, Tasha turned and hurried out of the shop. When she'd been struggling to carry everything in M&S, she'd given up trying to fit the card back into her overstuffed purse. It was all coming back to her now; she'd slid it into one of the plastic carriers instead. Her heart galloped into optimistic overdrive at the realisation that the carrier bag was one of those she'd discarded during her Tetris-style reorganisation.

11

Which meant, fingers crossed . . . it *should* still be in the litter bin.

Out of breath and panting, Tasha stood and stared at the bin, relieved that it hadn't been emptied but slightly put off by the amount of junk that had been crammed in since she'd left it, not least the upended polystyrene container now dripping the remains of an unwanted doner kebab over the items beneath it.

Life would be easier, too, if it could have been one of those topless bins that were open to the elements. But no, this was the rectangular kind with an enclosed roof and letter-box openings around the side. Although luckily a bit wider than an actual letter box.

Oh well, better get on with it. Tasha put her many bags down on the pavement, removed her pink woollen coat and rolled up the sleeves of her black dress . . .

Eurgh, this was truly gross. Within seconds her hand was gluey with chilli sauce, there were bits of shredded lettuce stuck to her bare arm and an upside-down McDonald's cup was spilling melted ice cream over her too. There were cigarette butts in there, vinegar-soaked chips, and something repulsively slimy and unidentifiable.

'Hungry, are we? If you're that desperate, I'll buy you a burger!'

Fabulous, just what she needed. A gaggle of teenage boys with skateboards and micro-scooters had gathered round to watch.

'I saw an old drunk bloke puking up in that bin earlier,' one of the boys called out.

'He had a piss in it too.' His friend, joining in, caused the rest of them to crack up.

OK, that wasn't true, they were just saying it to wind her up. Pointedly ignoring them, Tasha knelt down and leaned against the icy cast-iron bin, pushing her arm further into its grim depths. The boys were still sniggering, other shoppers were stopping to stare and she was floundering helplessly in the dark, trying to *feel* for a lone credit card inside a scrunched-up plastic bag . . .

12

'Could you get your hand out of there?' barked a hatchet-faced woman holding a coffee cup.

'I'm just looking for something.'

'Well I need to throw this in the bin and I'm in a hurry.'

'Sorry, but—'

Too late: the woman had already lobbed the cardboard cup into the bin, leaving Tasha with an arm drenched in lukewarm cappuccino.

Under her breath she muttered, 'And a very merry Christmas to you too.'

'I bet there's dog crap in there an' all.' The boys were by this time helpless with laughter, competing to come up with more and more stomach-churning ideas. One of them had started skateboarding in circles around the bin, and the sound of the wheels whizzing menacingly round her feet, missing her by inches, was making it all that much harder to bear.

'Right, you lot, that's enough. Off you go now.'

It was an in-control voice, belonging to someone not remotely fazed by a bunch of hoody-wearing teenagers and effortlessly taking command of the situation. Since it was coming from directly behind her, Tasha couldn't see the owner of the voice, but she was certainly glad he'd turned up.

Chapter 3

'So,' said the male voice when the teens had reluctantly skated off, 'do you want to tell me what's going on here?'

'I missed breakfast, was just looking for some chips.' Pulling out her arm and twisting round to get a look at him, Tasha discovered that the authoritative voice didn't belong to a police constable. Well, not one in uniform, at least. Her rescuer was around her own age, mid to late twenties, and he was actually pretty good-looking in a dressed-down, sporty kind of way.

He was also grinning at her flippant remark.

'You're in luck, found one.' He pointed helpfully to her arm. 'There's a French fry stuck to your elbow.'

Oh, perfect. Tasha held her contaminated arm out in front of her and shook the chip off.

His grin broadened. 'You know what you look like?'

'Like a vet about to stick my hand up a cow's bottom, probably.'

'That's exactly what I was going to say. We've been watching you from the café across the road, by the way. Taking bets on what you're trying to do.'

'And laughing at me.'

He looked wounded. 'Nooo. Well, maybe a bit. That was mainly the others, though. Not me.'

'Well I'm so glad I managed to keep you entertained. It's like all my wildest Christmas dreams come true.'

'Hey, I came out to see if you needed any help.'

Tasha gazed up at him. 'If you're offering to rummage round and see if you can find my credit card, that would be fantastic.' Now that she was paying proper attention, it struck her that he had amazing eyes; they were a clear, light shade of green, with darker rings around the iris. He also had incredibly thick dark lashes, like a girl.

'Note that I didn't actually offer to lend you a *hand*.' His mouth twitched as he pulled a folded black bin bag from his jacket pocket and shook it out. 'But I'm happy to hold this open so you can empty everything into it. Otherwise you could be just feeling your way around in there indefinitely.'

This made sense. It was a good idea. They got to work. Tasha said, 'Do you carry a bin bag around with you wherever you go, in case of emergencies?'

'Always.' He caught her eye. 'OK, I asked the waitress in the café if I could have one.'

'And then you came swooping to the rescue like Superman.'

'Something like that. Thanks,' he added drily as she pulled the polystyrene kebab box out through the gap, splattering his wrist with chilli sauce.

'Sorry.' She wasn't *that* sorry.

'Is your credit card definitely in here, by the way?'

'I really hope so.' The back of Tasha's neck was prickling with perspiration. She dragged out a handful of wet rubbish and managed to splash more sauce over the front of her dress.

'Wouldn't it be easier to cancel the card and order a new one?'

'It would, but I need it. I'm driving straight from here to Luton airport.'

Superman raised an eyebrow. 'You're flying on Christmas Eve? Off on holiday?'

15

'I'm spending the week with my mum in Saint-Tropez. And I managed to break the only other card I have. It all happens when you don't want it to.'

'Definitely going to need a credit card in Saint-Tropez.' He nodded at her, because she'd suddenly gone still. 'Don't stop. Keep looking.'

But Tasha was concentrating on what her fingers had just brushed past. She moved them back and touched the crinkling plastic of a bag with something straight-edged inside . . . Oh please *please* let it be her card . . .

Hardly daring to breathe, she explored the edges, closed her hand around the small rectangle and hauled it up through the detritus inside the bin.

'Yes!' With a whoop of triumph, she dragged the bag out through the opening, pulled out her credit card and . . . well, no, she couldn't quite bring herself to kiss it, but *almost*.

'Brilliant.' Superman grinned as she exhaled with relief and clutched the card to her chest like an Olympic medal. He closed the bag he'd been holding open for her, flattened it out as much as possible and crammed it with some difficulty back into the litter bin.

'Thank *God*.' Fishing a tissue out of her pocket, Tasha did her best to wipe the worst of the gunk from her right hand.

'That's great.' He hesitated. 'Now, can I ask you a question?'

Ooh, was he about to ask for her phone number?

Like someone who definitely *wasn't* wondering this, she looked mystified and said, 'Of course you can! What is it?'

He pointed behind her. 'The people in the café, who've been watching all this going on? Could you give them a quick wave?'

'Oh!' Twisting round, Tasha saw that she did indeed have an audience. To cover up for the disappointment of not having been asked for her phone number, she beamed and waved the credit card in the air to show them it had been found. Rather sweetly, the customers applauded and waved back.

16

'Do you know those people?' She marvelled at their enthusiasm.

'No, never been in there before. I think they're just feeling the festive spirit.' He shrugged. 'Either that, or they're a bit drunk.'

Tasha slotted her card into her purse, securely fastened her shoulder bag, rolled down her sleeve and put on her coat.

'If you want to go and wash your hands, I can look after your bags for you.'

She checked her watch, conscious now of the time. Also, he didn't look the type who'd run off with someone else's last-minute Christmas shopping, but could you ever really know for sure? Untrustworthy men had a habit of appearing trustworthy.

'It's OK, I've got a pack of wipes in my case. And I really need to get going.'

He nodded. 'Don't want to miss your flight. If you like, I could help you carry your stuff back to your car.'

Tasha brightened. 'Oh, well that—' His phone rang before she could say more, and he answered it.

'Hi. Yes, no problem, I'll pick you up. Twenty minutes OK?'

It wasn't eavesdropping; she couldn't help hearing the female voice raised in protest at the other end of the line.

'Right, five minutes. Just wait outside the shop and I'll be there.'

So much for getting her hopes up.

'I'm fine. You'd better go.' Tasha started to gather together her motley collection of bags as he ended the call. 'Thanks for coming to my rescue, anyway. You've done your good deed for the day, Superman.'

Then their eyes locked, and for a split second the look on his face made her think something magical might be about to happen after all. There was electricity sparking in the air between them. She held her breath. The next moment a

17

snowflake landed on her nose, startling her and completely breaking the spell.

'It's starting to snow.' Glancing up, Tasha saw the flakes tumbling out of a pale-grey sky. 'Anyway, thanks again. I really do have to go now.' Nodding at the phone in his hand, she said, 'And so do you.'

'I suppose I do. Have a great time in Saint-Tropez.'

'Thanks, I will.' She picked up the last of her packages, still flustered by what had almost just happened. 'Well, bye. Merry Christmas, Superman!'

He hesitated, fat feathery flakes of snow landing in his dark hair, the expression in his green eyes unreadable. Then, as his phone began to ring impatiently again, he raised his hand in a gesture of farewell. 'Yes. Bye. You too.'

On the flight to Nice, Tasha found herself squashed between an overweight middle-aged Frenchman who appeared to have been gargling with garlic, and an underweight younger one who reeked of stale cigarettes, fell asleep on her shoulder and snored like a backfiring moped.

As far as fantasy Frenchmen sandwiches went, this one was singularly lacking in glamour.

OK, reasons to stop thinking about the man from the café.

For a start, she hadn't even found out his name. Mad as it now seemed, she'd kind of hoped he'd volunteer this information so she wouldn't need to ask him. But he hadn't, so that was that.

He hadn't asked her name either.

He had a nagging, high-maintenance girlfriend. Well, not absolutely definitely, but from the gist of what she'd overheard on the phone, it was certainly on the cards that she was.

For heaven's sake, how could she be obsessing over someone she'd only known for ten *minutes*? She knew nothing whatsoever about him. He could have a million irritating habits she hadn't had time to experience during their brief encounter.

18

Tasha exhaled. She was never going to see him again anyway, which was kind of the main overriding reason. She didn't know who he was, and in return he knew nothing about her.

Never mind that he'd seemed really nice and hadn't had freakishly hairy ears. They'd shared a spark of attraction, that was all. He'd had the opportunity to ask for her phone number and hadn't taken it.

His loss.

Dammit.

Chapter 4

Well, this was awkward.

The last of the mourners had left, and Flo was in the kitchen with her high heels kicked off, doing the washing-up. In the living room, the executor of Elsa's will had just broken the bad news to Elsa's grandchildren, and from the sound of things, they weren't taking it too well.

'What?' Lena's voice through the closed doors was shrill with disbelief. 'Oh please, tell me this is some kind of joke!'

Flo rinsed a long-stemmed glass and placed it on the rack to drain. Hell hath no fury, it seemed, like a woman not being given an airy first-floor flat in the upmarket area of Clifton, in Bristol.

Not yet, at least.

'But that's not FAIR,' Lena bellowed. 'She can't DO that.'

Flo exchanged a look with Jeremy, who was stretched out in his usual spot in front of the radiator. 'Oh dear, brace yourself. Sounds like someone isn't too happy with you.'

Jeremy blinked and lazily swished his tail back and forth. He was the laid-back type who took pretty much everything in his stride.

The kitchen door burst open and Lena Travis appeared, tall and angular in her tailored black suit and resembling a furious preying mantis.

'So you've known about this all along.' Her ice-blue eyes narrowed in disdain. 'It was probably your idea in the first place. My God, people like you make me want to be *sick*.'

Flo dried her hands and said, 'It wasn't my idea.'

Luckily she was used to being shouted at by people who thought they knew better than she did, so Lena's outburst didn't scare her.

Well, not much.

'You'd better come through.' Lena gestured to the living room. 'And just so you know, I'm going to be fighting this all the way.'

In the high-ceilinged living room, Elsa's friend Mary was helping herself to more coffee from the silver pot on the sideboard. Elegant and precise, she was in her late sixties and had known Elsa for over thirty years. Standing beside the sash window overlooking Caledonia Place was Elsa's grandson Zander, two years younger than his sister but eerily similar in looks. With their dark hair, pronounced cheekbones, narrow blue eyes and striking dark brows, they had the air of a couple of vampires about them. Since they lived just across the square, it seemed weird that Flo had never met them in person before, but their paths simply hadn't crossed.

At least the brother seemed calmer and less overwrought, although you couldn't say he was looking exactly thrilled.

'Right,' said Mary, who had been Elsa's solicitor and was sole executor of her will. 'Let me just stress here that Elsa made her own decisions about this property. In no way was she coerced or persuaded by anyone. Flo, how long ago did you first meet Elsa?'

'It was two years ago. Just over two years,' said Flo. 'In the October.'

'And Elsa told me five years ago that this was what she wanted to happen. Her mind was made up, even then.'

'But she's only known my grandmother for two years! And now she's got this place! How can that be fair?'

21

'Sshh.' Zander shook his head irritably. 'Stop screeching.'

'I'll screech if I want to,' Lena snapped. 'This is the most ridiculous situation EVER.'

What a couple of charmers. Flo raked her fingers through her hair, painstakingly blow-dried before the funeral but now, thanks to the rain, back to its natural state of out-of-control corkscrew curls. 'Look, I haven't *got* this place—'

'Oh really?' Lena retorted. 'Certainly looks like you've got it to me.'

'Enough.' Zander was glaring across the room at her.

'I'm going to speak to a lawyer about this. A *proper* one.'

'You're most welcome to do that,' said Mary. 'But I'm telling you now, it won't change anything. I'm quite capable of drawing up a legally binding will. And this one is watertight.'

'Well it doesn't stop it being ridiculous.' Lena grabbed her handbag and pulled out her phone. 'For God's sake, how can she do this to me? It's only a fucking cat!'

Time to zone out. Flo remembered instead the very first time she'd met Elsa Travis, after responding to the advertisement she'd placed in the local post office.

'The trouble with being eighty-two is I *know* everything,' Elsa had explained. 'I just can't *do* everything any more. I'm no longer . . . spry. Basically, I want someone I can call on whenever I need a hand with anything.'

'Like a really good neighbour,' Flo had suggested.

'Exactly. Got it in one. And my neighbours are fine, they're perfectly nice people. But they're always busy, they have their own lives to lead and even if they were happy to help me, they wouldn't have the time.' Elsa's eyes were bright and unsentimental. 'The last thing I want is to become a nuisance. I'd far rather pay someone to run errands and do odd jobs for me.'

'Makes sense.' Flo had nodded sympathetically.

'Of course it makes sense. That's why I'm doing it. Where do you live?'

'Barrow Street. Three minutes away on my bike.'

'How old are you?'

'Thirty.'

'And you've been working in the retirement home for the last five years. Why?'

'Why not? I love it there.'

'Really?' Elsa raised an eyebrow. 'What does Flo stand for?'

'Florence.'

'Funny sort of name for a thirty-year-old.'

'Wait till you hear my middle name.'

'What's your middle name?'

'If you give me this job,' said Flo, 'I'll tell you.'

Elsa stared at her for a long second, then burst out laughing. 'Go on, then. You're hired. Now tell me.'

Flo kept a straight face. 'It's Elsa.'

'Good lord.'

'I know. My mum was two hundred years old when she had me.'

'It's a wonder you didn't run away from home.'

That had been their first encounter, and it had gone on from there. Elsa had her moments; she could be irascible and impatient, but they'd fallen into an easy relationship studded with humour. Twice a day, when her shifts at the retirement home allowed, Flo called in to check up on her, bring the shopping she'd asked for, carry out any odd jobs that needed doing, pick up prescriptions from the chemist and hoover up after the incredible moulting Jeremy.

Jeremy was the great love of Elsa's life and the reason she'd flatly refused to consider moving into a retirement home herself.

'But there are plenty of places that allow pets,' Flo had protested, the first time the subject had been raised.

'Maybe so,' Elsa sniffed. 'But Jeremy wouldn't like it.'

They were two of a kind, a match made in heaven, both of them prickly and aloof. Jeremy didn't care to mingle with other cats, and Elsa found other old people profoundly tedious. They were quite happy as they were, thank you very much.

Luckily Flo had liked Jeremy, finding his air of world-weary disdain amusing, and Jeremy had in turn just about tolerated her. Until a year into her time there, when Jeremy went out one evening and didn't reappear for his dinner. He was such a creature of habit that it was obvious something had happened. After seven hours of searching throughout a windy, rain-swept night, Flo found him mewing weakly beneath a hedge on Sion Hill.

Hit by a car and left for dead, Jeremy had sustained multiple fractures and severe internal injuries. Another hour or two, they were told, and it would have been too late. The vet warned them that he still might not pull through, but Elsa, utterly distraught, insisted on everything possible being done to save him. Money was no object. Jeremy couldn't – *mustn't* – be allowed to die.

He'd survived, obviously. It had taken time, a lot of care and more money than some people earned in a year. But slowly, he recovered. And Elsa had taken note of the love and devotion Flo had lavished on her most beloved pet.

'I have a proposition for you.' She had broached the subject with typical bluntness. 'If I die before Jeremy, will you look after him?'

'Of course I will.' Touched that she'd been deemed worthy of such an honour, Flo said, 'I'll have to check with my landlord. I know we aren't allowed to have dogs, but I'm sure he'd be fine about—'

'Good grief, are you mad?' Elsa recoiled in horror. 'Jeremy wouldn't want to live in some ghastly damp basement flat. I meant you'd move in here with him.'

'Here? Oh! For how long?'

'For as long as he's still alive, of course. This is his home. He's happy here.'

'Right. So I'd be Jeremy's . . . lodger.'

'Exactly. This place has to be nicer than where you are now. And you'd be living here rent-free. How does that sound?'

Well, she was certainly right about the huge Georgian flat in Caledonia Place being a cut above her damp basement bedsit in Barrow Street.

'And Jeremy's only nine years old,' Elsa pointed out. 'If I drop dead tomorrow, you could be here for the next ten years. I call that a good deal.'

Flo considered the offer. It actually was pretty good.

'I'm only offering because I know you'd take good care of him,' Elsa went on. 'You might not love him as much as I do, but you'd be the next best thing once I'm gone.'

'OK, fine, I'll do it.' Flo nodded and smiled. Think of the money she'd save in rent.

'After Jeremy dies, the flat will go to my grandchildren. You'd have to move out then, obviously.'

'Obviously.' Amused, Flo envisaged herself staying on, refusing to leave, shackling herself to a radiator.

'Good girl. That's settled, then.' Satisfied with this, Elsa said, 'I'll call Mary and arrange for her to put it in the will.'

Which she had.

Flo tuned back in to the current drama; Lena was on the phone now to some hapless legal expert who basically wasn't telling her what she wanted to hear. Infuriated all over again, she snapped, 'Oh Marcus, you're such a pompous arse, no wonder Arabella left you,' and abruptly hung up.

'So I'm guessing that means Marcus agrees with me.' Mary's tone was dry.

'He's a pathetic wimp.' Lena was still simmering with resentment. 'What gets me is the way Elsa kept us in the dark about this ridiculous plan of hers. I mean, for God's sake, why didn't she *tell* us?'

Her brother drawled, 'Are you seriously asking that question? Just listen to yourself.'

'Well, this has been a bloody awful day and I've had enough of it.' Lena snatched up her expensive black handbag. 'Come on, there's no point staying here. Let's go.'

Flo watched from the window as the two of them made their way along the pavement in the direction of their own flat on the other side of the Mall Gardens.

When they'd disappeared from view, Mary said, 'That went well, then. Let me know if they give you any more trouble.'

'I will. Hopefully she'll calm down.' Jeremy had joined them in the living room; he rubbed his flank against Flo's leg and she bent down to pick him up. 'Poor boy, are you missing Elsa, hmm?'

Jeremy blinked haughtily and turned his face away.

Mary said, 'I should leave too. Are you going to be all right here?'

'We'll be fine.' Flo stroked the cat's velvety head. 'But just to be on the safe side, I think I might buy him a bulletproof vest.'

Chapter 5

The doorbell rang at eight o'clock that evening.

'Hi, it's Zander.'

'Oh.' Flo waited, her finger on the intercom.

'Can I come up?'

'That depends. Are you going to shout at me?'

'No. God, no. I promise.'

'OK.' She buzzed him in, opened the door and watched Zander Travis run up the flight of stairs towards her. He'd changed out of his funeral suit into jeans and a pale grey shirt, which lessened the similarity to a vampire. But the haughty cheekbones and electric-blue eyes were still unnerving.

'So. Hello again.' He paused. 'I thought I should come over and apologise.'

Flo tilted her head to one side. 'You thought you should?'

Zander smiled briefly, acknowledging the poor choice of words. 'I wanted to. I'm sorry. My sister is too.'

'Is she really?'

Another telling pause. 'She'll calm down. It came as a shock. If you don't know my sister, it's hard to explain what she's like.'

Flo said, 'Oh, I think she's given me a rough idea.'

'Yes, well. Lena's always been a bit . . . highly strung.' He shrugged. 'When Elsa died . . . well, of course she was upset . . .'

'Mmm.' Flo's response was non-committal.

'But she did rather assume that the flat would be left to her.'

'And to you.'

He nodded in agreement. 'OK, to both of us. But I already have my flat across the road. Lena doesn't have one.'

'You seemed a bit fed up too, when Mary explained the conditions of the will.'

'Yes, well, that could have something to do with the fact that my sister's been living in my flat for the last year.' Zander raked his fingers through his hair. 'It hasn't been easy, let me tell you. I was kind of looking forward to her moving out so I could have the place to myself again.'

Flo said, 'She's a grown-up. All you need to do is tell her she has to find somewhere else to live.'

'You'd think so, wouldn't you? But it isn't that easy.'

'Well I'm sorry, but there's not a lot I can do about that.'

With a flicker of humour, Zander said, 'I don't suppose you fancy a lodger?'

'Funnily enough, you're absolutely right.'

'Well, if you change your mind, let me know.' He looked around the living room. 'Where is Jeremy, anyway?'

'In the bedroom, watching *EastEnders*. It's true,' said Flo when Zander smiled. 'As soon as he hears the theme tune, he's glued to the screen.'

'Really? May I?' He indicated the bedroom door.

'Go ahead.'

Flo followed him across the hall to Elsa's bedroom. He pushed the door open and silently observed Jeremy sitting in state in the centre of the king-sized bed. Jeremy glanced over at them, did one of his slow-motion cat blinks and returned his attention to the television, where a ferocious cockney showdown was going full pelt.

'What a racket,' said Zander.

'He likes it.'

'And what Jeremy likes, Jeremy gets.' After a moment, Zander said, 'So how is he, health-wise?'

'Fine. Really well.'

'Right.' He didn't sound thrilled.

'Sorry, was that the wrong answer?'

'Look, I'm not a complete monster. I quite like cats. If Elsa had left Jeremy to me, I'd have been happy to take him in.' Zander shrugged. 'It would have made all this a hell of a lot easier.'

Quite like cats. There was your answer, right there.

'Maybe. But she didn't.' Flo pulled the bedroom door to, leaving Jeremy in peace to watch the rest of his programme.

'Luckily for you.' His tone was neutral, his direct gaze eerily reminiscent of Jeremy's.

The way he was looking at her was making her feel . . . odd. He was like a smooth-talking character in a film, the kind you didn't know whether or not you could trust.

'Yes, luckily for me,' said Flo. 'And I'll be taking very good care of him, too.'

The more charming the smile, the less she trusted him. As he turned to leave the flat, Zander said, 'Oh, I'm sure you will.'

In Carranford, the biggest and best New Year's Eve party was being held at the White Hart. There was a band, and a comedian, and a fancy dress competition and a disco. The marquee at the back of the pub was pulsating with loud music, and an assortment of dogs and hyped-up children of all ages were racing around the dance floor.

Hallie's wheelchair was being whizzed around too, but Hallie wasn't occupying it. She was sitting at a bench drinking cider and eating crisps, watching as Bea took her cousin for a spin.

'You're a shocking driver,' she told Bea as they zoomed up to her. 'You need L-plates.'

'Bloody cheek. And you'd better hide that drink,' said Bea. 'There's a doctor watching you.'

'Oh hell, really? Which one?' Hallie couldn't help it; she was twenty-eight years old and still terrified of Dr West. Ridiculously, it was one of those Pavlovian reactions that refused to go away. Dr Jennifer West, in her forties, had an air of Jeremy Paxman about her; she liked to scold and interrogate and her bedside manner was enough to make grown men quake in their boots.

'Don't worry.' Bea was grinning at the look on her face. 'It's only Luke.'

Thank God for that. Hallie relaxed and didn't tip her drink into the plant pot behind her after all. Adrenalin raced through her veins for quite a different reason; not that she would admit it to a living soul, but for some months now she'd had a bit of a crush on Dr Luke Hilton. It was a pointless, never-going-to-happen kind of crush, obviously; harmless enough. Luke was so nice, and seeing him always brightened her day.

He was also far less likely than Dr West to give her a long, boring New Year's Eve diatribe on the perils of alcohol-inflicted dehydration.

Spotting Luke through the crowd, Hallie waved and watched him zigzag his way across the dance floor. He was wearing a striped green and white shirt, dark trousers and a black leather jacket. His hair was fair and cut short in a neat, doctory sort of way, and he was carrying a bottle of alcohol-free lager, which, presumably, meant he was on call.

'Hi. You made it down here, then.'

'I did.' Hallie smiled; he had such lovely eyes, grey and warm and sympathetic. 'I wasn't sure if I'd be up to it, but thought I should give it a go.' She showed him her glass. 'This is my first drink, by the way.'

Luke shrugged. 'I'm not going to lecture you.'

'Thanks. I've got my chair with me, anyway. I might leave at nine, have a bit of a rest at home then come back later if

I'm still awake.' Hallie pulled a face. 'I know, right? Rock and roll.'

'Nothing wrong with pacing yourself.' He nodded at the bag in her left hand. 'Are you going to offer me one of those crisps or not?'

Hallie held out the packet, but just as he reached in, his phone rang.

'Yes . . . yes . . .' He listened to the voice at the other end. Finally he said, 'No problem, on my way now.'

'Selfish patients,' said Hallie as he put down his drink. 'Being ill and spoiling your evening. Hope it doesn't take too long.'

'Never can tell. Anyway, I'm off.' He pinched a few crisps to keep him going. 'If I don't make it back, happy new year.'

'Thanks.' Would it be? Who knew? Hallie smiled and said, 'You too.'

Chapter 6

OK, this was turning into one hell of a New Year's Eve. And so far, not in a good way.

Rory McAndrew was by nature impatient. He hated to queue for anything. He hated to wait. It was all so pointless, such a waste of time; why be waiting when you could be doing something interesting or fun or constructive instead?

This time, though, he was waiting for a reason. The process itself might be mind-crushingly boring, but if he stuck it out, the end result would hopefully be worth it.

And he was going to stick it out; after fourteen hours, there was no way on earth he'd give up now. Even though the mixture of boredom and anticipation was playing havoc with his system.

But if this was the only chance he had to find her again, he wasn't going to miss out on it.

Rory drummed his fingers against the side of his takeaway coffee cup, looked again at the arrivals board and saw that the delayed flight from Nice was finally about to land. It was his best chance, and the one he'd spent the evening pinning his hopes on, although there was always the possibility that she'd been forced to catch an indirect flight.

He absolutely refused to countenance the idea that she could be travelling back to a different airport. Or that when she's said a week, she'd actually meant six days, or eight . . .

Right, no more coffee; he didn't want to risk not being here in pole position at the exact moment she appeared through the doors before promptly disappearing within a matter of seconds in the direction of the car park.

One of the women who worked in WHSmith came past and said chattily, 'You still here, love? Bless, it's no way to spend New Year's Eve, is it?'

Rory smiled at her; she'd spent the day on the till selling him cans of Coke, packets of chewing gum and bags of Jelly Babies. Furthermore, she had a point. He just hoped none of the other men hanging around the arrivals gate were here to meet the same girl as he was.

When the glass doors slid open thirty minutes later and there she was, Rory felt as if he'd been hit in the chest with a medicine ball; delight that his mad plan had worked mingled with relief that the unbearable wait was at last over. He hadn't been hanging around the wrong airport on the wrong day after all.

She was here.

Better still, no one else was flinging their arms around her yelling, 'Welcome home, darling, me and the kids have missed you *so much*!'

Rory watched from his position ten metres from the exit as she stopped to unzip her suitcase and pull out a scarf and gloves. She was going to need them, too; it was icy outside.

Oh, but look at her, just look at her: she had a face he knew he would never tire of looking at. She was wearing a black beret, black sweater, black tights and a swingy purple skirt, the kind an ice skater might wear. And low-heeled black suede boots. She looked fantastic. Comfortable, too. And now that she'd pulled on her gloves, she was about to leave the airport . . .

OK, action. He headed towards the exit at the same time she did, two arrows set to converge at the revolving door. When he reached her, he knocked his foot against the wheels of her suitcase and said – completely convincingly – 'Oh, sorry . . . hey, *hello*!'

She turned, her mouth falling open as she recognised him. 'Wow. It's you! Hi!'

'I don't believe it. Talk about a coincidence.' Rory shook his head in disbelief. 'This is amazing. Have you just got back from your holiday in . . . where did you say you were off to? Was it Paris?'

See? Super-casual, super-cool.

'Saint-Tropez.' She was smiling, similarly astounded by the coincidence. 'This is so weird! And what are you doing here?'

'Just dropped a friend off. He's catching a flight to Frankfurt.'

'Well, isn't that nice of you? Especially on New Year's Eve!'

'What can I say?' Rory gave a modest shrug. 'I'm a kind and thoughtful person.'

'I already knew that. Always happy to help others.'

'How's the credit card? Been looking after it?' They'd moved to the right of the revolving doors now, to avoid getting in other people's way.

'I've been taking very good care of it.' Her blue eyes sparkled. 'No more bins, you'll be glad to hear.'

'Excellent. And how was your Christmas?'

'We had a great time, thanks. You?'

See how she was keeping the conversation going? Asking a question in return? This was progressing well, really well. He nodded, encouraged by how brilliantly he was doing. 'Yes, fantastic. I didn't introduce myself last time, by the way. Rory. Rory McAndrew.'

'And I'm Natasha. Tasha. Tash.' She shrugged generously. 'Whichever. Take your pick.'

'I like any of those. All good names.' Just the sound of her voice was mesmerising.

'Well, fancy bumping into you again like this. I still can't get over it.'

'I know. Maybe it's fate.' He'd practised saying this in his head *so* many times. 'Look, how about we—'

'Oh that's lovely, she turned up at last! I'm so pleased for you.' The garrulous woman from WHSmith was right in front of them, now wearing a thick coat and carrying a handbag. Beaming at Natasha, she said, 'He was here when I started my shift first thing this morning and he's been waiting for you all day. Must be love!'

And with a cheery wave, the woman disappeared through the revolving glass doors, leaving Rory to drown in a sea of his own mortification.

He couldn't look at Tasha, but was burningly aware that she was looking at him.

'All day? Really?'

He nodded. *Oh God*.

'Are you like Tom Hanks in that film, *Terminal*? Do you live here at the airport?'

He forced himself to meet her gaze. She was trying not to smile.

'That bloody woman. OK, here's the thing. I'm not a stalker and I'm not weird. My name's Rory McAndrew, I live in Hampstead and I'm a financial investment adviser. I'm normal, I promise.' The words weren't flowing quite as easily now that he was having to improvise. 'I've never done anything like this before, but after last week . . . with you and the bin . . . well, after you'd left, I just couldn't stop thinking about you. And I was kicking myself because I hadn't taken your number. There was no way of getting in touch with you again . . . and it just kind of felt like it could be the biggest mistake of my life.'

'Wow,' said Tasha.

'But you'd said you were going away for a week, so I thought if I came here today, with a bit of luck I might see you again. It wasn't ideal, but it was better than nothing at all.' Rory shrugged. 'So I went for it; I took the chance.'

35

'And it worked. I'm here.' She pulled a face. 'Sorry I'm late.'

'That's OK. Are you seeing anyone?' He held his breath; this was the other possible stumbling block. Just because she hadn't mentioned a boyfriend didn't mean she didn't have one.

'Um, I'm not sure,' said Tasha. 'I think so.'

'Oh.' *Oh*.

Fuck.

'How about you?'

Rory shook his head. 'No. No one.'

'Who was it who called you last week? Made you go and pick her up?'

'That was my Aunt Mel. She broke her leg in November and we have to keep giving her lifts all the time. She's pretty bossy.'

'Right. So would you like my phone number?'

'Yes.' But what about the possible bastard boyfriend?

'Would you like us to go out on a date?'

Rory nodded. 'Yes.' Was this some kind of *trick*?

'Fantastic,' said Tasha. 'How about now?'

'What? You mean . . . tonight?'

'Tonight is now. So, yes. Only if you want to, though.'

'I do want to.' He had to ask. 'Except, what about this boyfriend you think you might have?'

And now she was hooking a strand of hair behind her ear, properly smiling and giving him a keep-up look. 'Well, this may be jumping the gun a little bit, but I'm kind of hoping he might be you.'

Rory had to replay the sentence in his mind to make sure she meant what he thought she meant. Not slow as a rule, he said, 'Are you serious?'

Tasha's grin broadened. 'You tried to play it so cool, pretending that us meeting up here was a coincidence. Then that woman came along and blew your cover. So I'm returning the favour and not playing it cool either. Everything you said about how you felt after last week . . . you know, kicking yourself and wishing you'd got my number and wondering if you'd ever see me again?'

'Yes?' Rory held his breath; was this how it felt to have five numbers on the lottery and the final ball teetering, about to fall into place?

Tasha moved closer to him and rested the palm of her hand lightly against his chest. Her blue eyes were shining up at him. 'Me too.' She nodded for emphasis. 'It was exactly the same for me.'

Chapter 7

At twelve minutes to midnight, the doorbell went. Upstairs, Hallie pressed the intercom and said, 'Yes?'

'I saw your light was on.' It was Luke's voice, friendly and laid-back. 'Not going back to the pub?'

'No, I decided not to bother. Too much effort.'

'I can wheel you there if you want.'

'Thanks, but it's fine.' She smiled, touched by the offer. 'I'm comfortable here now.'

He hesitated. 'In that case, would you like some company?'

'Brilliant! Can I have Leonardo DiCaprio?'

'Well . . .'

'Joke,' said Hallie. 'Buzzing you in. Come on up.'

She was sitting on the bed rather than in it, still wearing her red dress. When Luke appeared in the bedroom doorway, she said, 'How was the patient?'

'He'll be fine.' Luke wouldn't go into details, she knew that. He was far too discreet.

'Take a seat. Pull the chair round.' Hallie indicated the full-length windows. 'We've got the best view of the fireworks from up here.'

'Perfect.'

'And we have this to toast the New Year.' She held up an unopened mini bottle of Moët decorated with Swarovski crystals. 'Bea gave it to me for Christmas, isn't it fab? We can share it!'

Outside, people were beginning to gather in front of the White Hart, ready for the fireworks that would shortly be set off on the centre of the low stone bridge across the river. Hallie switched on the TV so they could see and hear the celebrations in London too.

'So how about New Year's resolutions?' She tilted her head at Luke. 'Made any?'

'Just the usual, I suppose. Do the best job I can, try to save a few lives.' He shrugged. 'Try not to kill too many people off.'

Hallie grinned. 'Most people are too scared to joke about death in front of me. It's so boring, knowing they're editing themselves the whole time.'

'Go on then,' said Luke. 'What about your resolutions?'

'Well, I've been giving this some serious thought, and I reckon I really need to *start* killing people off. So long as they've definitely registered themselves on the organ donor list.' She shrugged. 'Otherwise it might all be a bit pointless.'

He nodded in agreement. 'And they'd have to be a good match.'

'Obviously.'

'Try not to get caught, though. Mass murderers probably have a hard time getting to the top of the transplant list.'

'And I'm so clumsy I'd be bound to leave clues and give myself away. I won't bother. Too much effort.' Hallie pulled a face. 'OK, my resolution is to make it through the next twelve months and get to see the fireworks a year from now.' She paused and looked over at Luke. 'Do you think I will?'

He didn't flinch. 'Will any of us? There's no answer to that. Obviously we hope so.'

'When was the last time you saved someone's life?'

Luke thought about it. 'Actually resuscitating them? A couple of years ago. Spotting a symptom and making sure the patient gets the right treatment . . . well, that happens more often.'

'How does it feel to know you've saved someone?'

'Honestly? Pretty fantastic.'

'Must be amazing. I'd love to have the chance to do that.' Leaning over, Hallie opened her bedside drawer, reached inside and pulled out a bag of liquorice allsorts. 'If you swallowed one of these and got it stuck in your throat, I could do the Heimlich manoeuvre on you and make it shoot out of your mouth. Want to give it a go?'

'So you can save my life?'

'Yes!'

'How do I know it isn't all part of your evil master plan to bump me off so you can harvest my organs?'

'Honestly, you're so *suspicious*. Ooh, nearly midnight, here we go. Open the window a bit so we can hear everything . . .'

The crowd outside the pub had grown to a couple of hundred. On the TV, Trafalgar Square was jammed with many thousands of revellers. The countdown began and the noise levels increased.

Eight.

'Oh *nooo*.' Hallie was struggling to release the wire around the cork of her mini bottle of champagne. 'I can't get it undone . . .'

Seven.

'Here, give it to me.' Luke took the bottle from her.

Six.

'You're twisting the wire the wrong way!'

Five.

'The foil won't tear, I can't see which way to – ah, got it!'

Four.

'Good job you're not a surgeon. Ooh, glasses . . .'

Three.

'The cork won't come out!'

Two.

40

'Let me do it!' Hallie grabbed the bottle back and twisted the cork with all her might.

One.

Pop went the cork as the new year began and the cheers outside rose to a crescendo. Hallie gave a whoop of delight as champagne foam fountained out of the bottle and the cork, having ricocheted off the ceiling, landed on the bed. On the TV, everyone was yelling and laughing and kissing each other. Through the open window they could see and hear the inhabitants of Carranford carousing in similar fashion. In her bedroom, since exchanging a celebratory kiss with your doctor clearly *wasn't* the done thing – even if you did have a crush on him – Hallie splashed the remainder of the Moët into two glasses and said, 'Cheers. Happy new year!'

'Happy new year.' Luke clinked his glass against hers as, on the TV and below them on the bridge, the firework displays punctuated the energetic singing of 'Auld Lang Syne'.

'To the best year possible.' Hallie clinked again, the side of her hand brushing against his fingers.

'Definitely,' said Luke.

'Their fireworks might be bigger,' she pointed to the TV, alive with the spectacular display lighting up London, 'but I like ours better.'

There were oohs and aahs from the onlookers outside as rockets shot into the darkness, rising high above the trees and illuminating the inky Gloucestershire sky. Squiggly white serpents mingled with fizzing red and yellow Roman candles, machine-gun bursts of green light rat-tat-tatted like gunfire and – *boom* – a fabulous blue and orange chrysanthemum exploded overhead, causing the onlookers to cheer and applaud.

The display on TV was still in full flow, but fireworks were expensive and the one in Carranford was now over.

'Ours were best,' said Luke.

'Goes without saying.' Hallie took another sip of champagne. 'Well, thanks for keeping me company.'

He smiled. 'No problem. Where's your mum this evening?'

'Friends invited her to a party in Tetbury. I told her I'd be over at the pub, otherwise she'd never have agreed to go.'

'Is the smoke bothering you? Shall I close the window now?'

Hallie shook her head. 'I love the smell of fireworks. Makes me feel young again.'

'You're still young,' said Luke.

'I know. I just act like an old person. Look at us, sat here now like a couple of geriatrics.' Except she was never going to *be* an actual geriatric, was she? Would never get to have a face mapped with saggy skin, wrinkles and unexpected whiskers. Ha, not that anyone looked forward to *that*.

'Don't worry about it.' Luke was watching her again, evidently reading her mind. His voice softening, he said, 'One day at a time.'

What would it be like to kiss him? How would his mouth feel against hers? The thought had crossed her mind before, but the longing to discover the answer was growing stronger.

Not that she would ever find out, of course. This was strictly a fantasy and there was no way in the world she'd ever act upon it. Feeling a bit hot, Hallie reminded herself that Luke was her doctor and, as such, was completely and utterly off-limits . . .

No, it was never going to happen. Before he'd come to Carranford and joined the practice, she'd been stuck with Jennifer West as her GP, and that was a situation she definitely didn't want to return to. Besides, her little crush was a secret for another very good reason: basically, she was hardly what you'd call a catch. It wasn't as if Luke would be even remotely interested in any kind of involvement.

42

Let's face it, when you were a manky-lunged twenty-eight-year-old perilously close to your sell-by date . . . well, you weren't exactly overwhelmed with lustful attention from the opposite sex.

'What are you thinking?' said Luke.

Ha, no chance.

'Just wondering what I'd look like if I was eighty-three. I really hope I wouldn't wear wrinkly old tights and ugly slippers.'

'Me too. Especially the tights.' As he said it, they both heard the sound of rapid clattery footsteps on the pavement outside. The next moment the doorbell rang: DINGDINGDINGDINGDINNGGG . . .

Hallie pressed the intercom. 'Hello?'

'Happy new yeeeear! It's us! Are you asleep?'

'Well I was, but some idiots just rang the doorbell.'

'Let us in! Let us in!'

'Is this how old people feel when their noisy grandchildren come to visit?' Luke's tone was dry as they listened to what sounded like a herd of cows galloping up the stairs.

'It's worse. Noisy grandchildren haven't usually downed seven pints of cider and a load of shots.'

'Ta-daaah!' The door flew open and six of her friends burst into the room. Bea, swaying on her high heels, held her arms out wide. 'You said you'd come back to the party and you didn't! So we thought we'd bring the party to you! Happy new yeeeeeaar!'

When she'd hugged and kissed everyone, Hallie said, 'There's wine in the fridge downstairs if you want to go and get it. And more glasses in the cupboard next to the sink.'

'Why's Luke here? Are you OK?'

'I'm fine. He's just been keeping me company. We watched the fireworks together.'

'And I'd better be going.' Luke rose to his feet. 'I'm still on call. Getting a couple of hours' sleep might be an idea.'

'Bye. Thanks.' Hallie gave a little wave while her stomach did a secret backflip. 'See you again soon.'

'Oh, you opened it!' Bea had spotted the mini bottle of Moët. 'And it's empty – you drank it all!'

Confused, Hallie said, 'Was it not meant to be drunk?'

'It was really expensive,' Bea wailed. 'You were supposed to save it for a special occasion!'

'Sorry.' Hallie loved Bea to bits, even if she did sometimes fail to think things through. *Because who knows how many special occasions some of us have left?*

'That's OK, I forgive you. Don't do it again, though.' As Luke attempted to squeeze past her, Bea's arm shot out, barring his exit. 'Hey-hey-hey, not so fast, Dr Hilton. I think there's something important you're forgetting, don't you?'

'What?' Luke looked baffled.

'This!' Throwing both arms around his neck, Bea planted a kiss on his unsuspecting mouth, and this time Hallie's stomach did a much bigger and frankly jealous triple somersault.

'*Mwah*.' Beaming and swaying, Bea let him go. 'Happy new year. Sorry, just had to do that! Couldn't resist!'

Chapter 8

'Look at this.' Rory showed Tasha the text that had just come through on his phone: *Mate, where are you? You're missing a bloody brilliant party. Get yourself down here NOW!!!*

'Who's it from?'

'My oldest friend, Joe. Now watch this.'

Tasha watched as he began to compose his reply. It was five o'clock in the morning, and she was still struggling to believe the last seven hours had actually happened. What she'd expected to be an entirely uneventful New Year's Eve had turned out to be the most eventful, most extraordinary, most utterly *magical* one ever. She felt as if she were in a dream.

OK, this really had better not be a dream. That would be too cruel.

Superstitiously, she pinched her left wrist, just to make sure. *Ow*, good.

Rory finished writing the text and angled the phone so she could read it: *Joe, I'm not missing out on anything. I'm with an amazing, incredible girl. This is it, she's the one I want to spend the rest of my life with. Will you be my best man?*

Every centimetre of Tasha's skin tingled as she read it. OK, the best man bit was a joke . . . maybe the third sentence was a joke too, but that didn't matter. It was enough that he thought she was amazing and incredible.

Aloud, she said, 'You're going to frighten the life out of him.'

45

'True.' Rory pressed send.

'Poor Joe.'

'And I meant it.' He looked at her. 'In case you were wondering.'

'You did?' *Zinnnggg* . . .

'Every word. I don't even know how I know. I just know.'

'Men don't usually come out and say that kind of stuff.'

'I *know*.' His eyes crinkled at the corners. 'I've never done anything like this before in my life. I can't believe it isn't freaking me out.'

His phone beeped and together they read Joe's text: *Shit, are you completely smashed? Do you need rescuing?*

Rory messaged back: *Haven't had anything to drink. Definitely don't need rescuing.*

Less than twenty seconds later, his mobile rang.

'Here we go.' Rory switched on speakerphone so she could hear it too. 'Brace yourself.'

Tasha clutched his hand. 'I'm braced.'

'Oh man, what is going *on*?' Joe's voice was raised over the noise of the party continuing in the background.

'Like I told you,' said Rory. 'It's happened. I found her.'

'Found her where? And who the hell is she? Are you telling me this is someone you just met tonight? Have you had sex with her yet?'

OK, *slightly* embarrassing.

'No,' said Rory. 'I haven't.'

'Ha! So, are you even sure she's female?'

Rory mouthed, *Sorry* at Tasha, who nodded reassuringly and mouthed back, *I am female.*

'I'm pretty sure she is. Joe, listen, it's the one I told you about. From last week. I found her again.'

There was a long silence. For several seconds, all they could hear in the background was music and laughter from the party. Then Joe said, 'You mean Bin Girl?'

Tasha looked at Rory. Bin Girl? Oh, the glamour . . .

'Yes.' Rory grimaced apologetically. 'Her name's Tasha.'

'And you found her again. How?'

'I staked out the airport until she came home. Didn't have to wait long,' said Rory. 'Only fourteen hours.'

'You hung out at the airport for fourteen *hours*? You're mad.'

'No I'm not. It's the best thing I ever did.'

'You're still missing a cracking party. And she's there with you now?'

'She is.'

'Let me speak to her.'

Rory handed over the phone.

'Hi, Joe,' said Tasha. 'It's me, Bin Girl.'

He laughed. 'Hey, Bin Girl. What the hell have you done to my boy?'

'I have no idea. It's been quite a night.'

'And you're not a bloke?'

'Definitely not a bloke.'

'Any other guilty secrets you might want to share with me? It's OK, I won't breathe a word.'

'Do you promise?'

'Absolutely.'

'OK. I do have a secret,' said Tasha.

'Six kids? Scary husband? Serious drug habit?'

'Nope.'

'Go ahead then. Tell me,' said Joe.

'I think I've found the man I've been waiting for.' As she said the words, Tasha's gaze met Rory's and a smile spread across his face.

'Ah Jesus, you're a pair of hopeless cases, both as bad as each other.' With mock disgust, Joe said, 'I'm going to leave you to it and head back to the party. Happy new year, Bin Girl.'

Tasha grinned. 'Thanks, Joe. You too.'

Chapter 9

'This is scary,' said Tasha. 'I can't believe how nervous I am.'

'I know.' Rory held her hand under the table. 'Me too. It's never bothered me before.' He took another drink. 'Basically because it didn't matter.'

The door to the pub swung open and Tasha's fingers tightened around his. 'OK, here we go. Here's Carmel now.'

It was like a cross between a fait accompli and a really important job interview. Falling in love with Rory had been the easy bit; now they had to meet each other's best friends and hope that went well too. Everyone knew there was nothing worse than your oldest friends not getting on with your new partner. Occasionally they couldn't stand them. And sometimes the best friends downright hated each other too.

It had seemed like a good idea at the time to get the whole thing over with in one go. It was now eight o'clock in the evening on Wednesday the third of January, and Rory had arranged for Joe to meet them here at the Frog and Shovel in Hampstead. Tasha had done the same with Carmel. Talk about kill or cure; it was either going to go brilliantly or turn into the night of a thousand knives.

Tasha rose to her feet and waved, and Carmel made her way over towards them. Then the door opened again and Rory said, 'Well that's a first; Joe's turned up on time too.'

Carmel was tall and narrow-hipped, with a curtain of Scandinavian white-blond hair falling down her back; she wore black flicky eyeliner, pale pinky-beige lipstick and an impractical cream coat over jeans and a black sweater. They'd been best friends since school and had met all of each other's boyfriends over the years, with varying degrees of success.

Tasha mentally crossed her fingers that this evening's meet-up would go well. She couldn't think, offhand, of any reason why Carmel might not like Rory, but you never knew; before now, Carmel had taken against one boyfriend purely because she didn't like the way he stroked his chin. But that had been Colin, who'd turned out to be a complete dick anyway. And to be fair, Tasha remembered, she'd once had a similarly strong aversion to one of Carmel's boyfriends because he'd worn Cornish-pasty-style shoes.

Honestly, between the two of them and their peccadilloes, was it any wonder she was nervous?

The four of them sat down, everyone was introduced – 'Hello, Bin Girl!' – drinks were ordered and the serious business of getting to know each other began.

'So you must be incredibly sporty.' Kicking off proceedings, Joe turned to Tasha. 'What are you into? Snowboarding? Paragliding? Marathon running?'

Carmel spluttered with laughter. 'You're asking Tasha? Marathon lying down, more like. Marathon TV watching with a packet of crisps—'

'OK,' Tasha hastily cut in, 'that's enough.'

'Ha ha.' Carmel's eyes danced. 'I'm just trying to imagine you being sporty.'

'No, but seriously.' Joe was looking genuinely taken aback. 'You must do something.'

Tasha shrugged. 'I do plenty. Just not necessarily . . . those kinds of things.' Was this going to put him off her?

'Do you swim?'

'I *can* swim. I prefer to sunbathe. I'll jump into the water to cool down, but I wouldn't do fifty lengths of the pool.'

'Did you know about this?' Joe switched his attention to Rory.

'Yes, she told me.'

'And?'

Rory shrugged. 'It's fine.'

'So let me get this straight. You're an adrenalin junkie.' Joe tapped his friend on the forearm. 'A non-stop action man. And you're completely crazy about this girl here, but she's inaction girl.' He tilted his head apologetically in Tasha's direction. 'No offence, I'm sure you're a lovely person, but you're not remotely sporty and you don't do any of the stuff Rory likes doing.' The look on his face was frankly dubious as he sat back and took a gulp of his pint.

'Hey,' Carmel said heatedly, leaping to Tasha's defence. 'Why are you making it sound like it's all *her* fault? Is your precious friend interested in literary festivals and art galleries and Ancient Egypt? No, I'm guessing he probably isn't, but that doesn't make him a lesser person, or a better one. They're just different. Opposites attract, OK? And these two opposites are attracted to each other.' Her gaze narrowed. 'So we're just going to have to make the best of it.'

Oh dear, imminent warfare.

'Where did *that* come from?' Joe was instantly on the defensive. 'You were the one who started it,' he pointed out, 'making fun of her marathon TV watching.'

'Tasha's my oldest friend.' Carmel gave him a withering, don't-you-understand? look. 'I'm allowed to make fun of her. You don't get to do that until you've known her a lot longer than this, OK?'

For a few seconds they glared at each other. Finally Joe said, 'When, then?'

'Another year,' said Carmel. 'At least.'

He shook his head. 'No way. I can't wait that long. At the

rate these two have been carrying on, they could be married with kids by then.'

Tasha held her breath. *Imagine* . . .

'Just be nice to my friend, that's all I'm saying.' Carmel still had the proprietorial light of combat about her. 'Or you'll have me to answer to.'

'Right.' Joe raised his hands in defeat. 'I'm sorry, OK? God, you're terrifying.' But there was a twinkle in his eye as he said it. Returning his attention to Tasha, he added, 'Bin Girl, I apologise, OK? Most sincerely.'

'And don't call her Bin Girl any more either.'

'Actually,' said Tasha, 'I'm starting to quite like it.'

Joe said solemnly, 'You'll always be Bin Girl to me.'

'So how would we say this is going, then?' Rory enquired.

'They want us to get on well together,' Joe told Carmel. 'It means a lot to them.'

'You're right.' Carmel nodded. 'We should probably be nice to each other, for their sakes.'

'Give us a kiss then,' said Joe.

He'd been joking, but Carmel reached across the table, grabbed his face between her hands and fastened her lips on his.

'Blimey,' said Joe when she let him go and sat back in her chair. 'Well, that defused the sexual tension.'

Carmel grinned. 'There is no sexual tension. I don't fancy you one bit and you don't fancy me. But I like you. I think we can be friends, don't you?'

Tasha hid a smile as Joe, still knocked for six by the kiss, raked his rugby player's fingers through his tufty reddish-gold hair. 'We could probably manage that. Uhh . . . those eyelashes of yours. Are they real?'

'Of course they're not real, you plank. Even a monkey could tell they were fake.'

'And are you always this polite?'

'I like to call it refreshingly frank,' said Carmel.

'You're certainly that.' Joe raised his glass and clinked it against hers. 'Cheers, Frank.'

'Cheers. Will I like your friend Rory, do you think?'

'I can't see why you wouldn't. He's a good guy.'

'Ah, but will he break my friend's heart?'

'Hello, excuse me?' Tasha cleared her throat. 'We are here, you know. Within . . . what's it called? Oh yes, *earshot*.'

Joe and Carmel completely ignored her. 'Honestly?' said Joe. 'Well, he's had his share of girls and played his share of games in the past. But the way he's been talking about this one . . . she's definitely in a whole different league. I've never seen him like this before.'

'If he gives her any grief,' Carmel said pointedly, 'he'll have me to answer to.'

His breath warm on her cheek, Rory murmured in Tasha's ear, 'I wasn't planning on giving you any grief.'

'Just as well.' Tasha was tingling all over at his proximity. 'Carmel has a black belt in karate.'

Overhearing this, Joe turned and regarded Carmel with new respect. 'You do? Wow.'

'I can be quite annoying,' said Carmel. 'It makes sense to be able to defend myself.'

'Ha.' He was clearly impressed. 'I have a feeling you'd win.'

'Oh yes.' Carmel crossed her long legs and surveyed him with cool amusement. 'I always do.'

Was she being deliberately ambiguous? Most probably. Tasha watched as Joe, caught off guard, visibly wondered the same thing. After a second or two, he turned to her and said, 'How about you then, Bin Girl? Are you a martial artist too?'

'I'm a make-up artist.' Tasha added flippantly, 'If anyone tried to attack me, I'd jab them in the eye with a mascara brush.'

Twenty minutes later, Rory and Joe went over to queue at the bar for more drinks.

The moment they were alone, Tasha said, 'They'll be talking about us now.'

'That's OK. We're going to be talking about them too.'

'And?' Tasha had been bursting to know. 'What's the verdict?'

'I like him! He's great.' Carmel's eyes were bright. 'I really like him a *lot*.'

'I knew it, I knew it, I'm so glad!' *Phew*. Beaming with relief, Tasha said, 'Thank goodness for that. And how about Joe?'

'Oh.' Carmel looked confused. 'I thought we were talking about Joe.'

'No, you dingbat! Never mind him – I want to know what you think of Rory!'

Carmel shrugged. 'Well, I like him too. He's really nice. Good-looking, fun, I can see why you're so keen . . .'

'But,' Tasha prompted, feeling sick. 'There's a *but* coming. Tell me what it is.'

'Oh come on, you already know what it is. Don't look at me like that . . . oh please, not the Bambi eyes. But Joe said it too, didn't he?' Carmel lowered her voice. 'I know you're crazy about each other and it's all new and exciting, but the two of you are kind of polar opposites. All those extreme sports he's addicted to . . . I mean, it's not as if you're ever going to do anything like that.'

'Does it really matter? You said opposites attract.' The panicky sensation was rising up inside her ribcage now; she had been working so hard to keep it squashed down. 'People don't have to be exactly like each other to make a good couple . . . we *laugh* at married people who wear matching outfits and end up turning into one person . . .'

'I know, I know, and I do understand how you feel about him. I'm just a bit worried that you two are *so* completely different . . . Oh God, sorry, just ignore me.' Carmel flapped her hands by way of apology. 'He's great and I do like him. I'm sure you'll be able to work things out. And I haven't spotted any annoying habits like stroking his chin in a creepy way or laughing like a camel with hiccups.'

The camel laugh had belonged to Harry, the stockbroker Tasha had gone out with for a couple of weeks last year; cunningly, he'd managed to hide it at first. But once apparent, it had been a definite deal breaker. He'd had to go.

'And he doesn't wear Cornish pasty shoes.' Tasha joined in to show she wasn't offended by Carmel's bluntness. 'Look, I know we're different, but it'll be OK. Maybe I'll learn to like extreme sports.'

'*What?*' Carmel boggled in shock and fell back in her chair.

'I mean watching them. Not doing them.' Tasha pulled a face. 'Obviously. So, you like Joe too. That's good.'

'I do.'

'As a friend? Or more?'

'Just as a friend.'

'Really? But you kissed him.'

'I know. That was just for fun, though. He's not my type.'

'You see, I think he *could* be your type.'

Carmel shrugged. 'Let's leave things as they are for now. If I change my mind about him . . . well, all kinds of stuff could have happened by then . . .'

They'd known each other for fifteen years. Tasha raised an eyebrow. 'You mean me and Rory could have broken up by then? Is that what you're thinking?'

'Possibly.' Carmel's grin was unrepentant.

'Except we're not going to break up.' Tasha didn't expect Carmel to believe her, but she knew it was true. 'Really.' She nodded at her oldest friend. 'I promise. It's not going to happen.'

Over at the crowded bar, still waiting to be served, Joe said, 'So how long d'you think this thing with you and Bin Girl is going to last?'

Rory gave him a pitying look. 'Trust me. It's going to last.'

'I mean, don't get me wrong, I like her a lot. But she's so not your type. She isn't sporty *at all*.'

'I really don't care.'

'Blimey, you've got it bad.'

'I have.' Rory nodded happily in agreement. 'What do you think of her friend?'

'Carmel? Fancies me rotten.'

'Does that mean you're going to sleep with her?'

'Might do, might not. See how we go.' Joe paused. 'Is that OK with you?'

'Do whatever you like.' With a shrug, Rory said, 'Probably best not to upset her, though, what with her black belt in karate.'

When they left the bar at midnight, Rory and Tasha led the way down the side street, heading for the main road where there would be cabs to flag down.

'Hey.' Joe drew Carmel to the side of the pavement, his breath visible in the icy night air. 'Do you want to come back to my place for a drink?'

Carmel stopped walking. 'You mean sex?'

'Well, OK then.' His mouth curved up at the corners. 'If you absolutely insist.'

'Listen to me.' Patiently, Carmel pointed to Rory and Tasha, ahead of them. 'See them? Love's young dream. Now see us? *Not* love's young dream. Absolutely nothing of a romantic nature is ever going to happen between us, I can promise you that.'

'Oh.' He looked crestfallen, then hopeful. 'Are you playing hard to get?'

'No.'

'That's disappointing, then.'

'I can see that it would be. Don't worry, you'll survive. We're just going to be friends and make life easier for those two.'

'They're not going to last five minutes. You do realise that, don't you?'

'Of course,' said Carmel. 'But we're going to humour them. It's called being kind. Like when little kids get all excited about Father Christmas. You don't spoil things for them.'

'OK.' Joe nodded. 'Yes, you're right.'

'I'm always right,' said Carmel.

At the end of the road, Rory and Tasha had managed to flag down a cab and were yelling at them to hurry up if they wanted a lift.

'Actually, I'm going in the other direction,' said Joe. He stuck out his hand and solemnly shook hers. 'Friendly enough for you?'

Carmel smiled. 'Perfect. See you again.'

As she caught up with the others, Joe yelled down the road after her, 'Carmel!'

She turned. 'Yes?'

'He's OK, isn't he?'

'Who?'

'Father Christmas.'

He was completely mad. Carmel smiled and called back, 'Don't worry. He's fine.'

Chapter 10

In the seven years since Flo had started working as a care assistant at Nairn House retirement home, overlooking the Clifton Downs, there had been one noticeable change in the habits of the residents.

Before, they'd read newspapers and books when they weren't socialising with each other, playing whip-smart games of racing demon and canasta, watching TV or listening to music.

Then technology had entered their lives, following the installation of lightning-fast Wi-Fi, and nowadays, more than fifty per cent of the residents had their own tablets.

And not the kind you swilled down with a cup of tea either.

It never failed to entertain Flo to see ninety-year-olds overcoming their fear of the unknown and launching themselves into the brave new electronic world of the internet.

Margot, one of her favourite residents, was simultaneously chatting on Skype with a retired Italian archaeologist, completing a cryptic crossword online and debating the merits of Bombay Sapphire gin versus Tanqueray London Dry with a history professor in Zagreb on Twitter.

If only Elsa could have been persuaded to come and live here in one of Nairn House's stunning garden apartments. Flo just knew she and Margot would have got on like a house on fire.

'Seven across. Switched palms, illuminating. Five letters.' As she said it, Margot glanced up at Flo. 'Any ideas, darling?'

'Oh God, you know how hopeless I am with crosswords.' Flo was busy changing the water in the crystal vase and preparing to rearrange the out-of-season white roses. 'Um, something to do with light?'

'I know ze answer to zat.' The Italian archaeologist with the deliciously accented voice came to the rescue via Skype's audio feed on Margot's trusty iPad. 'Eet ees lamps.'

'Of course. Thanks, Paolo. OK now, twelve down, seven letters. Sheepish puff is violent.'

Honestly, how did people *do* these things? Flo was completely lacking in the cryptic gene.

'Ha, too easy,' said Paolo from his villa in Florence. 'Eet is rampant.'

And it wasn't even his first language.

'You know, you're not bad at this, for a foreigner!' Having chuckled and tapped in the answer on the screen, Margot switched back to her Twitter conversation with Erik in Zagreb and deftly typed: *You've just reminded me, I once drank martinis with David Niven at the Hotel du Cap. Such a charming man. #happydays*

For the next twenty minutes, Flo tidied the apartment, washed dishes and made up the bed with new sheets Margot had ordered online from Liberty. She listened as Margot finished the crossword, concluded her conversation with Paolo and signed out of Twitter.

'He sounds lovely.'

'Paolo? I know. Great fun to chat to. Not so great in the looks department, sadly. Bit of an old bullfrog. That's why I stick to audio.' Margot pulled a not-very-apologetic face. 'Still, nobody's perfect. I'm no oil painting myself these days.'

Margot wore her silver hair pulled back in a sleek bun; her eyes were hooded but bright, she had an elegant aquiline nose and a narrow, clever mouth. Her outfits were flowing, her taste in jewellery baroque. Flo said honestly, 'When I'm ninety, I'd love to look like you.'

'Oh darling, aren't you kind? Sometimes I completely forget how old I am, then get the most terrible shock when I catch sight of myself in the mirror.'

'Oh well, I get that too. Did you really drink martinis with David Niven?'

'I did! Back when life was full of adventure. Here, I've been uploading some photos from around that time . . .'

The photos showed Margot in her thirties, as leggy and glamorous as a movie star herself. When she'd finished skimming through them on her iPad, a *ting* announced the arrival of a new email in her inbox.

'Ooh, lovely, our favourite. Now, have a listen to this.' With great relish, Margot began to read aloud:

Dear Rose,

OK, three things about me. I'm twenty-six, my wedding is in six weeks and my mum is trying to ruin *everything*.

You should see the dress she's bought to wear . . . Rose, she's the mother of the bride and she's going to make a mockery of the whole show. I have spent *months* planning every last detail and our colour palette is ivory, palest heather and duck-egg blue. I told my mum to make sure she chose something to tone in with these colours. I also stressed that it had to be elegant and appropriate for the occasion. Well, she came home with an above-the-knee orange dress and the cheapest-looking pair of shoes you ever saw. It's a complete nightmare. She's always had hideous taste in clothes and I've told her a million times how much she shows me up. When I said she wasn't wearing that dress, she actually burst into tears. Rose, is it OK to ban my embarrassing mother from my wedding? If she comes along,

59

she's just going to wreck the whole day *and* all the photographs. And please don't tell me to ask my dad to have a word with her – he walked out before I was born and she hasn't had another boyfriend since.

Stressed of Southampton

'Go on then,' said Flo. 'What's the answer?' Since Margot had begun subscribing to www.threethingsaboutyou.com, reading the problems aloud and debating the replies had become a regular ritual between the two of them.

'I hope she gives her a piece of her mind,' Margot snorted. 'Right, here we go:

Dear Stressed,

I see you didn't bother putting much thought into your three things about you. Luckily, the rest of your letter told me pretty much all I needed to know about your character.

Oh dear, poor you, how *dare* your mum turn up at your wedding in cheap shoes? It's almost as if she's been trying to scrimp and save all these years so that someone else can afford to have everything they want!

How lucky your mum is to have a daughter as loving and thoughtful as you. What does your fiancé think of this situation? If he agrees with you that your mother should be banned from the wedding because her dress is the wrong colour, then you two truly deserve each other.

If your mother was the one writing to me, I would urge her to sew neon-yellow fringing around the hem of that orange dress and kick off her cheap shoes when she dances on the table at your wedding. After all, she's going to be in the mood to celebrate, having succeeded in offloading her selfish, ungrateful daughter on to someone else.

Seriously, you need to apologise to your mum, tell her you love her and let her wear whatever she likes to the wedding. Then maybe you should thank her for spending the last twenty-odd years single-handedly bringing you up.

'Good answer,' said Flo.

'Great answer.' Margot nodded with satisfaction. She was quite the connoisseur when it came to advice columns; she subscribed to half a dozen, but this was the one she liked best. 'Rose always gets it right.'

'I wish we knew what she looked like. In my head she's all soft and cuddly, in her sixties, with rosy cheeks and a kind face.'

'But not afraid to say what's on her mind. Tells the grand-children off when they're naughty. She could be Irish.' Margot paused to consider this possibility. 'Or Cornish.'

'Or a big burly truck driver calling himself Rose.' Flo checked her watch; she was due off duty in five minutes. 'I have to leave soon, Margot. Anything else you need me to do before I head off?'

'No thank you, my darling, I'm fine. Oh, but I'm almost out of Tabasco . . . next time you're in the supermarket, could you be an angel and pick me up a couple more bottles?'

'No problem. I'm not in again until Sunday, though. Can you last until then?' Margot's addiction to splashing Tabasco over almost everything she ate meant she carried the little bottles in her handbag wherever she went and lived in terror of running out.

'I can. Ah, you're a good girl.' Margot smiled at her over the top of her elegant silver-framed reading glasses. 'Make it three bottles. That'll be perfect.'

Chapter 11

'Ta-daaaa!' Bea burst into the living room, where Hallie was engaged in painting her toenails bright coral. 'Guess what I'm doing for my thirtieth birthday?'

Hallie straightened up. 'You've already told me. You're having a party at the White Hart.'

'That *was* the plan. But now I have a new plan. I'm going to Paris.'

'Really? Wow, fantastic. And so perfect for you,' said Hallie. 'I hear the men in France prefer older women.'

'Cheek.' Bea aimed a playful swipe at the plastic tubing snaking between Hallie's nasal cannulae and her oxygen tank. 'I could always unplug you, you know. Anyway, guess who's coming along with me?'

'Bradley Cooper again? Poor boy, hasn't he suffered enough?'

'This time it's girls only. Sarah's coming.' Bea began counting off on her fingers. 'And Jen. And Poppy and Carla. And me, obviously.'

'You'll have an amazing time.'

Bea carried on counting on her fingers. 'And you.'

Hallie's heart sank. 'Oh Bea, no. I can't.'

'You can.'

How to explain? 'Look, thanks for thinking of me, but it just wouldn't . . . work.'

'It would. I've checked with Luke. And I asked your mum too. There's no reason why you can't come along with us.'

'It's just so . . . complicated.'

'But not impossible. People with cystic fibrosis can travel abroad; they do it all the time. You *know* that.'

Hallie sat back, bare legs stretched out before her, toes splayed in order not to smudge the glossy polish. 'I know, and it's really kind of you to invite me, but I don't want to be the one who spoils things for everyone else. I'd just hold you back and then I'd feel guilty—'

'Whoa. Stop it. Look at it from my point of view.' Bea shook her head at her. 'You're my best friend, and if you refuse to come to Paris you *will* spoil things. I mean it,' she went on when Hallie opened her mouth to protest. 'My birthday will be ruined and it'll be all *your* fault.'

She actually meant it. 'Are you sure?'

'Of course I'm sure. You have to be there. I don't want to turn thirty without you.'

Hallie was an infrequent crier, but her eyes were brimming now. Moved, she said, 'OK. If you really mean it, I'll come to Paris.'

'I really *really* mean it. Come here, you.' Careful not to dislodge the transparent oxygen tubing, or trigger a bout of coughing, Bea gave her a hug.

'And the others don't mind? You're sure they're OK with it too?'

'Completely sure. You're the must-have accessory of the season.'

'I'll have to get travel insurance.' Which would probably cost a fortune.

'There are specialist companies. It's not a problem.'

Well, not quite true. It was easy for Bea to be airily dismissive, but Hallie knew it was going to involve travelling with a wheelchair, oxygen tank, nebuliser and assorted other vital bits and pieces. But if Bea was determined to have her there . . . well, she could make the effort.

'OK, let's do this thing.' Paris! How glamorous! 'Have you decided where you want to stay?'

'I have brochures. I have chocolate.' Bea withdrew both from her huge glittery shoulder bag. 'And now I have you to help me choose a hotel. So,' her eyes gleamed, 'shall we make a start on it now?'

It was midday and there still hadn't been any word from Rory. Tasha checked her phone for the fiftieth time to make sure a message hadn't arrived and somehow been missed.

No, still nothing, even though he'd promised faithfully to keep her updated. Unable to help herself, she sent a text: *Please call and let me know you're still alive. Xxx*

'You're looking worried.' Moira, a TV chef who was being made up for today's photo shoot, was watching her in the mirror. 'Everything OK?'

'It's just my boyfriend. He should have been in touch by now and he hasn't been.' Did she sound hopelessly neurotic? 'He's on his way up to Edinburgh.'

'Ah well, maybe there isn't any signal.' Moira, in her forties, was sympathetic, chatty and good company. 'Is he flying?'

Tasha shook her head. 'No. Riding up there on a Harley-Davidson motorbike.'

'What? Oh God!' Pulling a horrified face, Moira said, 'No wonder you're all of a faff. All that way? And bikes are so *dangerous*. My neighbour's son had the most dreadful accident last year, came off his motorbike and nearly died. Ended up having to have both legs amputated.'

'Oh dear.' Sometimes Moira could be a bit *too* chatty. Tasha felt her insides curdle at the thought.

'Then there was my friend's auntie, she crashed her moped into a wall and she's had a withered arm ever since!'

'Right.'

'And Alan from the golf club went under a bus on his motorbike. Killed outright. Oh, sorry.' Moira clapped a hand over her mouth, evidently realising that her comments might have been less than tactful. Belatedly she said, 'I'm sure your boyfriend's *fine*.'

The shoot, for a women's magazine, dragged on interminably. First one o'clock, then two o'clock went by, with still no word from Rory. Tasha's stomach continued to tighten with fear. On the outside she carried on applying make-up to models, while on the inside her brain conjured up terrifying images of an accident on the motorway . . . bits of broken motorbike strewn across three lanes . . . blue flashing lights . . . sombre-faced paramedics shaking their heads at each other . . .

'Tash! Has my forehead gone shiny? Could you sort me out with some powder?'

Moira again. Tasha went over to deal with the shine.

'Any news from your boyfriend?'

'Not yet.'

'Oh well, I'm sure he's OK!' Eager to make up for her earlier faux pas, Moira patted her arm. 'Don't you worry about a thing.'

'Why?' The photographer was busy setting up a different backdrop. 'Is he in hospital?'

'We hope not!' Moira shook her head vigorously at the photographer. 'No, definitely not! He was riding his motorbike up to Edinburgh this morning and poor Tasha hasn't heard from him since he set off. Not a word! She's worried sick that he's had a terrible accident!

Only because you practically told me he had. Tasha resisted the urge to bop Moira on the head with the powder brush.

'Ah, don't panic, love, he'll be all right.' The photographer picked up his camera and winked at Tasha. 'If he's too busy to call you, it's probably because he's in bed with another woman.'

'Great, thanks, that makes me feel so much better.' Tasha

marvelled at his lack of subtlety; luckily, she wasn't the jealous type.

He grinned. 'Or another man.'

Which had been, to give him his due, quite funny.

By five o'clock, Tasha had long stopped laughing. This was ridiculous. In the last few hours, she'd used up a week's worth of heartbeats. Convinced that Rory must be dead, she tracked down the number of Joe's dental practice and insisted on being put through to him.

'Look, have you heard from Rory? He said he'd call me, but he hasn't. And I know it's ridiculous, but I can't stop wondering if he's had an accident.'

'Let me try his phone.' Evidently taking out his mobile, Joe pressed buttons. 'No,' he said a few seconds later, 'it's gone straight to answerphone. Maybe his battery's flat.'

'Do you think I'm being neurotic?'

'Honestly? A bit,' said Joe. But in a kind way.

'I'm worried.' Tasha took a deep breath; was it just her? 'Really worried. What if he's in hospital on life support?'

'OK, just a thought,' said Joe, 'but don't hospitals go through phones and contact the next of kin?'

'But I'm not next of kin! They wouldn't call me!'

'Whoa, calm down. They'd call his next of kin and then *they'd* call me. But nobody has. So I think you should stop panicking and relax.'

'Unless he's unconscious in hospital and his phone flew out of his pocket and got run over on the motorway by a ten-ton truck.'

There was silence for a moment as Joe considered this possibility. At last he said, 'Hey. I'm sure he'll be in touch when he can.'

'Are you laughing at me?'

'Just a little bit.'

And really, who could blame him?

'I'm not usually like this, I promise.'

'If you say so.' He definitely sounded as if he were smiling. 'OK, can I go now? Only I've left a patient with a drill hanging out of his mouth.'

Whoops. 'Sorry,' said Tasha. 'Bye.'

An hour later, her doorbell rang. As she went to answer it, Tasha pictured Joe on the doorstep, grave-faced and accompanied by two here-to-break-the-bad-news policemen, one of whom was holding the remains of Rory's smashed-up phone . . .

She took a deep breath and opened the door.

'Hey!' Rory was wearing his leathers and holding his bike helmet under one arm. He was beaming from ear to ear. 'What an amazing trip that was. *Amazing.* Give me a kiss.' He moved forward to embrace her. 'How was your day?'

Tasha had reached the stage where she'd actually hoped he *had* been in an accident – just a minor one – because then at least he'd have a valid excuse for having put her through all those hours of torment. Now that she knew he was alive, she could yell at him.

OK, not yell. But make him understand.

'Where's your phone?'

'Can you believe it? Forgot to take it with me . . . just didn't remember to pick it up. I haven't been home yet . . . it's still lying on the bed in my flat. Why, did you try to call me?'

He was telling the truth, Tasha knew. He actually didn't have a clue what he'd put her through.

'Yes, I called.' Only about three hundred and fifty times. 'You said you'd call me.'

'I know I did, but I couldn't, could I? Not without my phone.' Rory shrugged. Genuinely no clue.

'I was worried.' Tasha forced herself to stay calm. 'I've been worried sick. Motorbikes are *dangerous*.'

They were in the hallway now, and he was still looking

bemused. 'Look, I've never once come off a motorbike. You don't have to worry about me.'

'Don't I? Am I allowed to worry about all the other idiots on the road who could crash their cars into you? I've been picturing it all day,' Tasha blurted out. 'And I'm sorry if this sounds crazy, but I've only just found you.' Her voice cracked as she struggled to explain. 'I'm terrified something's going to happen to take you away.'

'Oh God, I'm sorry.' Rory wrapped his arms around her. 'Nothing's going to happen to me, I promise.'

Did he think she was a complete madwoman? Had she managed to scare him off completely? 'I'm sorry too. I can't help being like this. I hate it.' Tasha held him tightly, inhaling the mingled smells of leather, engine oil and warm skin. 'I worry too much and I have too much imagination.' She didn't say it, but she'd even envisaged his funeral; if he knew that, he'd definitely dump her.

Oh, but when all the old feelings came rushing back, it was hard to ignore them. She was going to have to explain. Helplessly she said, 'You know I told you my mum and dad split up when I was six? Well the thing is, my mum didn't know how to tell me he'd gone, so she pretended he was working abroad. And I kept waiting for him to come back but it just didn't happen . . . I had *months* of feeling all knotted up inside, wondering if I'd done something wrong or if he was even still alive . . .' She trailed off, embarrassed by the admission. 'Of course he *was* still alive. He was just far too busy being besotted with his new girlfriend to bother with his old family.'

'What a bastard. Jesus. Now listen to me.' Rory exhaled. 'I'm selfish and I don't stop to think things through. It honestly didn't occur to me that you'd be worried.' He gazed deep into her eyes. 'I'll never do that to you again, I promise. I'm going to learn your number off by heart, so I can always get hold of you. And I'll keep in touch so you don't have to get yourself into a state.'

'Thank you.' Tasha tilted her face back, reaching up to kiss him. 'Has this put you off me? You can say it.'

'Honestly? No.' He was smiling again now. 'Play your cards right and you're still in with a chance.'

'That's good news. Are you staying tonight?'

'I'd like to. Very much.' Rory stroked the side of her face. 'But I need to go home first, have a shower and change. I'll be back in an hour, OK?'

He left. Twenty-five minutes later, Tasha's phone rang.

'It's me. I've had my shower. I'm getting dressed now.'

'Great.'

'Just putting a clean shirt on.'

'Excellent.'

'I'll be there by ten past nine.' Pause. 'Maybe twelve minutes past. Definitely no later than nine fifteen.'

'Don't make fun of me,' said Tasha. 'I know I'm a hopeless case.'

'There was a message on my phone from Joe saying you were worried about me.'

'I know, I phoned him. I was desperate.'

Rory sounded amused. 'I also had another forty-six missed calls.'

That many? Alone in her flat, Tasha's cheeks burned; this was definitely a neurosis she was going to have to overcome. 'Just some nutter, I expect. Ignore them.'

'I'm heading back now in the car. Want me to give you a call when I'm halfway?'

'Just get yourself over here and stop taking the mickey,' said Tasha. 'Or you might find yourself waking up tomorrow with your eyebrows waxed off.'

Chapter 12

There was a homeless man sitting on the cold pavement, middle-aged and resigned, with a hat in front of him containing a few scattered coins. It was growing dark as Flo made her way past him on Saturday afternoon, but light from the street lamp and from the windows of the pub spilled over him, illuminating his messy greying hair and his shoulders hunched in defeat. She paused, searched in her coat pockets and found a stray pound coin.

'Thanks very much.' The man gave a nod of appreciation.

Flo hoped he wouldn't spend it on lager or drugs.

At that moment, a huge roar went up in the pub, practically rattling the windows. Inside, the bar was heaving with rugby fans following the big game on the TV.

'Is it frustrating, having to listen to the match and not being able to watch it?'

The man shook his head. 'Not a rugby fan. But if they're happy with the way it's going, that's hopefully good news for me.'

Flo nodded; it was worth putting up with the racket if it meant that cheerful punters with a few drinks inside them came out of the pub and chucked a bit of extra cash into the hat. She said, 'Bye then,' and made her way down the street as more shouts and yells of approval emanated from inside. From the sound of it, everyone was supporting the winning team.

In the supermarket, she picked up the little bottles of Tabasco for Margot, then added soup and a bag of toffees, and some of the tins of tuna Jeremy liked best. Followed by a baguette, a ripe Camembert, red grapes and a tub of honeycomb ice cream. For her, not Jeremy. Tonight was going to be a staying-in-and-being-blissfully-lazy night, just the two of them and a pile of DVDs.

Having paid at the checkout, Flo headed back up the street. She could see that a group of men had spilled out of the pub on to the pavement, presumably to get their nicotine fix.

As she neared them, she observed their posh-boy clothes, heard their posh-boy voices and identified the type. Clifton was the Bristol equivalent of London's Chelsea; there were plenty of privileged characters from wealthy families who liked to speak that much more LOUDLY and CONFIDENTLY than normal people. Some, in particular, liked to watch rugby matches with their collars turned up and shirt tails dangling beneath their expensive designer sweaters, whilst knocking back vast quantities of alcohol, preferably bottled lager alternating with champagne. Having lived in the area for several years, Flo knew the breed well.

They also brayed like donkeys whenever something was amusing them. Like now.

Hopefully the homeless man, currently hidden from view, was reaping the benefit of their cheery high spirits.

As she neared the pub, Flo heard several of the braying voices set up a chant of 'Do it . . . do it . . . *do it*', followed by another voice exclaiming, 'Jesus Christ, give me a second, someone's just knocked my bloody drink over. Who wants to lick it up?'

'Come orn, Giles, get your wallet out and let's do this thing, shall we? Bit fucking chilly out here!'

'Yah, fucking freezing! Get a move orn, Giles!'

Flo hid a smile, because they were *so* posh they were all pronouncing it *Jaaahls*. Still, at least he was opening his wallet. Wow, and look at what he was taking out; it wasn't even a twenty-pound note. In the light from the street lamp, and now that she was only a few metres away, she could see that it was unmistakably a fifty. Say what you like about braying posh boys, but they could be wildly generous when the alcohol-fuelled fancy took them.

'Come on then, Henry, do the honours, old chap!'

One of his companions began rummaging in the pockets of his jeans – Armani, no less. Giles was now holding the fifty-pound note aloft, waving it in front of the man sitting on the ground. Flo shifted her carrier bag to her other hand and watched as Armani Henry handed Giles something small. She experienced a warm glow of affection; men like this sometimes came across as complete tosspots, but their hearts were actually in the right place.

Except . . . it wasn't money that Henry had contributed. There was a click, and a small flame sprang to life. The other men were laughing and urging Giles on. And now Giles was waggling the fifty-pound note, bringing it closer to the cigarette lighter.

What? *What?*

'Do it! Do it! Do it!'

Flo moved forward to get a closer look. Was she hallucinating? It was like watching someone rush over to rescue a person who was about to fall off a cliff . . . then seeing them push that person over the edge.

And now the flame brightened and expanded as it caught the bottom edge of the note. Within seconds it was merrily ablaze, and Giles was dangling it in front of the homeless man, roaring with laughter and saying, 'Bet you wish you had money to burn, don't you, old chap? HahahahaHA.'

'Why? Why's he doing that?' Flo demanded as one of the other men noticed her for the first time.

'Just a bit of fun, yah?' He shrugged and sniggered. 'Drinking club rules. If someone dares you to do something, you do it.'

Flo was shaking with fury. Worst of all was the closed-down

look of resignation on the homeless man's face. There was one of him and six of them; what could he possibly do? Just as she knew that any argument she might put forward would have no effect whatsoever. If she shouted at Giles, he would simply laugh at her too.

The possibilities flashed through Flo's mind in a millisecond. She took the can out of the carrier and ripped off the lid with the ring pull. Calling out, 'Hey, Giles!' she moved towards him as he turned in surprise to see who had shouted his name.

SWOOOOSH went the contents of the can of Heinz tomato soup, arcing in a great orange wave through the air and landing in pleasingly splattery fashion over Giles, covering him from head to foot.

'Whoa!' Sensing danger, his friends backed away. Flo, who had never done anything remotely like this before, braced herself for the fallout.

Which could be spectacular.

'What the *fuck* . . .?' Giles was staring at her like a cartoon character, soup dripping gloopily from his face and shirt front. 'What the actual fuck do you think you're *doing*?'

'Sorry.' She pointed to the still-smouldering banknote in his left hand. 'Thought you were on fire. I was just trying to put out the flames.'

'*Bullshit.*' He spat the word out. 'Don't give me that.'

'Fine then, I won't.' Still quivering with outrage, Flo shook back her hair and said, 'I did it because I couldn't believe what I was seeing. You're actually a disgusting human being. How can you do something so vile?'

'Look.' He took a step towards her, his jaw taut and jutting. 'It's my own money. I earned it and I can do whatever I like with it. Are you able to comprehend that?'

'Legally, you're right. Morally, that just makes you a pig.'

'Oh Jesus, listen to yourself. What are you, some kind of God-botherer in your spare time?' He was towering over her

73

now, reeking of alcohol and practically spitting with anger. 'Or are you one of those types who pesters people in the streets to buy copies of the *Socialist Worker*? People like you make me sick.'

'Well *that's* a coincidence,' Flo retorted, squaring up to him and simultaneously wondering if she were completely mad to be doing so.

'*Fuck*, look what you've done to my shirt.' Giles gestured down at himself. 'It's Dolce and Gabbana, for fucking crying out loud. It cost me four hundred pounds.'

It was a plain white shirt. Flo snorted with slightly hysterical laughter. Enraged, he reached out and wiped the palm of his hand across her front, from collarbone to collarbone. Now she had tomato soup smeared over her own pale blue sweatshirt.

'My top's from Primark. It cost five pounds fifty.' Unable to resist it, Flo added, 'I win.'

'Fucking communist,' sneered Giles. 'And nobody wins against me. I'm calling the police.'

OK, less funny now. Outwardly Flo was standing her ground, but inwardly she was wondering if he could actually have her arrested. It wouldn't do wonders for her CV.

'Leave it, Jaaahls.' One of his friends, thank God, was shaking his head. 'Probably not a good idea, old chap. We don't need the hassle.'

Wiping the splattered soup from his face, Giles snarled, 'Fuck it, I'm orf,' and stormed off up the street towards the taxi rank. *Phew.*

'And if any of you lot have even an ounce of decency, you'll make up for what your charming friend just did.' Back to feeling brave again, Flo pulled out her purse, took out a tenner and gave it to the homeless man on the pavement.

Shamefaced, a couple of them did the same before sloping off down the road to the next pub.

'Bastards,' she muttered under her breath.

'Thanks. Sorry I didn't join in.' The homeless man shook his head by way of apology. 'They'd have just . . . well . . .'

'It's OK, I know.' He couldn't afford to get involved; she understood that. 'I'm sorry they were so awful.'

'Here. You don't have to give me this.' He held the tenner out to her insistently. 'You shamed the others into it, that's enough.'

Realising that he meant it, and secretly relieved, Flo took the money back. 'OK, but—'

'My God, it's *you*.'

Startled, she swung round to see who'd just crossed the road behind her, and came face to face with the vampire brother.

OK, don't call him that. His name was Zander Travis. 'Oh. Hi.'

'What was *that* all about?' He gestured in the direction of the taxi rank, where Giles was currently doing his best to persuade the waiting drivers to let him – in his tomatoey state – into one of their cabs.

Could she be bothered to explain? No. She shook her head and said, 'Nothing important.'

'Sure about that?' Zander was frowning at her. 'Didn't look like nothing to me. Is he your boyfriend?'

OK, *now* she could be bothered. *Yeurch*, just imagine. 'Definitely not,' she said with a shudder.

The man sitting on the pavement chipped in: 'She was sticking up for me. He was burning a fifty-pound note in front of me. For fun.'

'And he *wiped* something on you?' Zander was staring incredulously at the stains on her sweatshirt. 'That's assault, for a start.'

Honestly, these Travises and their fondness for legal action. Did they all keep their solicitors on speed-dial?

'It's probably best if we don't call the police,' said Flo. 'Technically, I did throw a can of soup over him first.'

Zander's face was a picture. She pointed to the irregular trail of gleaming orange droplets along the pavement. 'Heinz tomato.' Only the very best for her victims.

A glimmer of a smile softened the angular features of Zander Travis's face. 'Better than blood, I suppose. Do you know who he is?'

Flo shook her head. 'Never seen him before.' She shivered as a blast of icy wind curled around her too-thin coat. 'Quite hoping I never see him again.' A glance in the direction of the taxi rank showed that Giles had disappeared from view – had a cab taken him away, or was he lurking in a darkened side street?

'Are you on your way home?' Having followed the line of her gaze, Zander was evidently thinking the same thing. 'Come on, I'll walk you back to the flat.'

Chapter 13

Within minutes, they'd reached Caledonia Place. The fact that it was still only five thirty in the afternoon for some reason made it easier for Flo to say, 'If you'd like to come in for a coffee . . .?'

It seemed equally natural for Zander to say, 'Thanks, that'd be great.'

And now, several cups of coffee and a packet of biscuits later, it was nine o'clock. Flo shook her head in disbelief. They'd been talking non-stop about pretty much everything, and her and Jeremy's planned quiet evening *à deux* had somehow, instead, turned into a jolly *ménage à trois*.

Not that kind of *ménage*, obviously. But the ease with which they'd connected had taken her by surprise. The atmosphere between them was completely comfortable. Zander was on the sofa and Jeremy was stretched out on the rug at his feet, which for Jeremy was high praise indeed.

She'd learned about Zander and he was learning about her. They'd both lost their parents in their twenties. He'd since found himself in charge of his sister, older than him by two years but less able to look after herself. Lena, she now understood, was a tricky mixture of bossy but needy, helpless but opinionated.

'I used to wish I had a sister.' Flo pulled a sympathetic face. 'Maybe being an only child isn't so bad after all.'

'Luck of the draw.' Zander broke the last biscuit in half. 'Did your mum and dad want you to go to university?'

'Yes, they did.'

'Why didn't you go?'

'I did go.'

'Really?' He looked surprised. 'What did you study?'

'French.'

'You have a French degree? But you work as a care assistant in a retirement home?' Now he sounded downright astonished.

'I was living in Normandy, working for a pharmaceutical company in Rouen, when my mum was taken ill. I gave up my job and came back to look after her. After she died, it wasn't so easy to land another job in France. I started temping at Nairn House just to tide me over, then discovered I really liked it.' She tilted her head. 'Seven years later, I'm still there.'

'But it must pay peanuts.'

'Does your job pay peanuts?' He worked for an international property lettings company.

'No, of course not.'

'And do you absolutely *totally* love your work, every minute of every day?'

'Well, no . . .'

'See?' said Flo. 'There you go. I do, which means I win.'

Zander nodded and accepted defeat. 'Touché. Maybe you do.'

At that moment, Jeremy stretched, jumped up on to the sofa and settled himself on their visitor's lap.

'Well *that's* a first,' Zander commented. 'I'm honoured.'

'You should be. It's the equivalent of winning an Oscar.'

He left at ten fifteen, returning half an hour later with takeaway from the Chinese on Regent Street. Flo felt her heart skip a beat as she pressed the buzzer and let him back into the flat. And he'd brought wine, too. Was it her imagination, or was he actually far nicer than she'd expected?

Or was he only pretending to be nice? Maybe the plan was to get her drunk, then subtly persuade her to sign guardianship of Jeremy over to him.

Special fried rice. Szechuan king prawns. Tom Yum squid. Singapore noodles. Beef with cashews in yellow bean sauce. And prawn crackers.

Flo raised her eyebrows. 'Sure you got enough?'

'Sorry.' He shrugged good-naturedly. 'I didn't know what you'd want. So I ordered a few things. Take your pick.'

'I love all of it. Can I have some of everything?'

Zander gave a nod of approval. 'Help yourself.'

Together they piled food from the foil containers on to their plates. Carrying everything through to the living room, he said, 'I went out with a girl last year who only liked chicken. She had it every day. In all the restaurants we ever went to.'

'And she didn't get bored? I'm too greedy,' said Flo. 'I like too many different kinds of food. I'd panic if I had to narrow it down. This squid is *amazing*, by the way.'

'Good.' He was smiling as he watched her eat, which hopefully meant he didn't think she was a complete gannet.

'How long did you go out with her for?'

'Four months? Five?'

'And what went wrong? Was it the chicken thing?'

'More the sister thing. Lena didn't like her. She didn't like Lena, either. After a while, it just seemed easier to break up.'

'Can I say something? You shouldn't let your sister dictate who you see. It's your business, not hers.'

'I know. But it wasn't just Lena. It was the chicken thing too.' He paused. 'And the fact that she used to call herself practically-a-vegetarian.'

'Ha, we had a resident at the home like that. Went on and on about being a vegan, then every Sunday morning he'd slope off to the local café and have a bacon sandwich.'

'Quite. Anyway, as you can probably tell, no great loss. I wasn't

79

heartbroken. That was last year.' He added soy sauce to his Singapore noodles. 'How about you? Seeing anyone at the moment?'

Did he think she'd be sitting here sharing a Chinese with him on a Saturday evening if she were? OK, this wasn't a date, but still.

'No.' Flo took a gulp of wine – it was delicious, an icy New Zealand Sauvignon Blanc – and shook her head.

'So what happened with you and your last boyfriend?'

'Are we sharing tragic stories?'

'Seems only fair.' Zander speared a king prawn with his fork, then stopped with it halfway to his mouth. 'Oh. Is yours really tragic?'

She grinned. 'Not tragic. Just one of those boring break-ups for the usual reasons.'

'He cheated on you?'

'Not that reason.'

'Now I'm curious. Do you want to talk about it? Or would you rather not?'

Flo wondered if she should quickly make up some other story, one less likely to send shivers of terror down any man's spine. She could say they'd grown apart, become bored with each other, the magic had simply faded and died away, blah-de-blah . . .

Ah, sod it. Why not tell the truth?

'His name was Marcus. He was the same age as me. We were together for two years and everything was great . . . well, I thought it was great.' One more glug of wine for good luck. 'Then one night we were out with friends, chatting about various things, and someone asked me if I wanted to have children. So I said yes, eventually, one day. Well, Marcus stopped talking and looked at me . . . and that was pretty much it. He announced that he didn't want kids *ever*. And I said I did, but not for ages. And one of the other guys said jokingly, "Careful,

80

women in their thirties are like time bombs, those eggs don't last for ever." And everyone laughed.'

Flo paused, remembering the way Marcus had reacted towards her after that.

'Anyway, he decided he couldn't trust me, said how did he know I wasn't going to trick him and trap him and deliberately get pregnant? And that was when I realised we were over. There was no way in the world I would ever have done that. But if he thought I was capable of it, we didn't have much of a relationship.'

'And that was it,' said Zander.

'It was. After two happy years, we fell out of love with each other in the space of two minutes. The next day, we broke up.'

'Wow.' Since her wine glass was now empty, Zander offered her a refill.

'Yep. Funny how quickly life can change.'

'And were you devastated?'

'Surprisingly not. Bit shocked at first. But it was like turning off a light switch.' Flo shrugged. 'Once it happened, I knew I was never going back.'

'And do you know what he's doing now?'

'Oh yes, he's going out with a twenty-three-year-old. The really horrible part of me is dying for her to get accidentally pregnant.'

Zander laughed. 'That's very honest.'

'I'm always honest. Otherwise I wouldn't have told you the reason we broke up.'

'And that was a year ago?'

'Just over. I was thirty-one then. Now I'm thirty-*two*.' Flo pulled a face at him. 'Imagine how few eggs I have left.'

'Thirty-two isn't old.'

'It is when men are scared that it's making you desperate. Funny how I'm still single.'

He helped himself to the last of the fried rice. 'You aren't desperate.'

'I know that. But they don't.'

Zander's phone began to ring and he pulled it out of his shirt pocket. When he saw who was calling, his jaw tightened.

'Who is it?' Not that it was any of her business, but she was nosy.

'Lena. I'll let it ring. If it's urgent, she'll leave a message.'

The ringing stopped. Zander put the phone down on the coffee table as gingerly as if it were a small grenade.

Five seconds later, they both jumped as it began to ring again.

'Better answer it,' said Flo. Answering phones was a particular weakness of hers.

'Hi, what is it?' Zander listened to the garbled words on the other end of the line. Finally he said, 'OK, calm down, I'm on my way. I'll be there in ten minutes.' There was another garbled bit, then, 'I'm having dinner. With a friend.' Pause. 'Never mind who. I'm leaving now.'

He ended the call and looked at Flo. 'She's locked out. Forgot to take her key with her. Again.'

'It's freezing out there. You have to go.'

'She's *always* forgetting her key.' Zander glanced at the remains of the food as he rose to his feet.

'Just as well we'd pretty much finished here.' There was hardly anything left in the cartons, and only an inch of wine in the bottle.'

He checked his watch. 'Unless . . . well, it's only eleven fifteen. I could go and let her in, then come back . . .?'

'OK, you really want to be careful what you say to a thirty-two-year-old female desperate to have a baby.' The moment the words were out of her mouth, Flo wished she could cram them back in. Oh God, what had *possessed* her?

Except the practically empty bottle on the table was giving her one of those who-are-you-kidding? looks.

'Eurgh, sorry about that,' said Flo. 'It was meant to be funny, not scare the life out of you. Just one of those things that accidentally bursts out.' As if her brain was *so* full to the brim with lustful thoughts about him that she'd simply been unable to contain herself.

'No problem.' Zander was pushing his fingers through his hair, looking taken aback and somewhat embarrassed too. 'So . . . um, should I let my sister into the flat and come back for a coffee, or shall we just leave it?'

OK, officially awkward. The poor man was undoubtedly terrified of her now.

'Probably better leave it. I mean, it's gone eleven and I have to be up at six tomorrow . . .' Which made her sound even more hopelessly geriatric than the residents of Nairn House.

'Right, yes, that makes sense. That's fine. I'll be off then.' Zander reached for his jacket and put it on.

Downstairs at the front door, he paused and gave Flo a polite kiss on the cheek, which made her face tingle and her heart quicken. And it was still beating at quite a rate, thanks to her earlier faux pas.

Plus, his eyes were so incredibly *blue*.

'Thanks. It's been a nice evening.' Zander paused. 'I've enjoyed myself.'

And now she was super-aware of his left hand resting lightly on her shoulder. Her cheeks heating up, Flo nodded and said, 'It was good fun.'

She opened the door and let him out, shivering as a blast of icy air enveloped them both. 'Bye then.'

Zander raised his hand in farewell. 'Bye.'

Flo closed the door, made her way back upstairs and crossed the living room to the window. There he was, walking away up Caledonia Place with a purposeful stride. She touched the side of her face where he'd kissed it, reimagining the sensation of—

Whoops, and now he'd stopped, turned round and was looking up at her window. Torn between leaping back and ducking down, Flo did both, lost her balance and toppled backwards on to the carpet.

Like an ungainly upturned beetle.

From his position on the sofa, Jeremy looked on impassively, too underwhelmed to even bother swishing his tail. Flo grinned at how she must appear to him; at least no one human was here to witness her shame. Spotting a couple of stray grains of rice on the carpet, she rolled into a sitting position, picked them up and levered herself to her feet.

The doorbell shrilled and she froze. What? *What?* Heart thumping, she crossed the room, pressed the intercom and said, 'Who is it?'

'Me. I forgot something.'

What could he have forgotten? She buzzed open the front door and heard Zander's footsteps on the stairs.

And then he was standing before her. She gazed up at him, feeling the cold air emanating from his body, simultaneously breathing in the scent of his skin.

He drew her to him and kissed her on the mouth. Oh, oh wow, this was amazing . . . the cool, firm pressure of his lips and the warmth of his tongue were having a mesmerising effect, his hand was cupping the back of her head and she could feel his own heart beating against her chest . . .

He pulled away at last, the side of his thumb gently stroking her cheek. 'I didn't have the nerve to do that before. It wasn't until I turned round and saw you watching me from the window that I plucked up the courage to come back.'

To look at him, who would ever think he could be lacking in self-confidence? People with carved cheekbones and perfect eyebrows should never be shy.

'I'm glad you did.' *Oh my word, just listen to me; what a brazen hussy!*

'But now I really do have to go.' He gave her one more brief kiss. 'Before my sister dies of frostbite on our doorstep. What's this?'

'What's what?' Flo turned to try and see what he was looking at, but his hand stayed in her hair at the back of her head.

'Don't move, there's something in here . . . OK, got it . . .'

They both looked at what he'd found: two grains of fried rice and a bit of noodle.

From the carpet. God, *nits* would have been less embarrassing. At least nits had a reason to *be* in her hair.

'How did those get in there?' Zander frowned, genuinely baffled.

'I have no idea. I picked Jeremy up just before you rang the bell. He must have been stealing food off my plate and got some on his whiskers.' Flo gave Jeremy a stern look and said, 'No more leaving rice in my hair, OK? That's gross.'

Jeremy twitched his ears at her. Blaming him was low, but Flo was sure he didn't mind being her scapecat.

'I'm going now.' Zander put the offending items in one of the empty containers. 'Definitely leaving this time.'

'OK.'

He smiled. 'Quite a night. Look, I have to fly to Toronto tomorrow on business. I'm going to be there for a couple of weeks. But as soon as I get back, I'll be in touch.'

What was it she'd said earlier, about life taking an unexpected turn? Who would ever have predicted something like this happening? Best of all, when he said he'd be in touch, Flo knew he wouldn't let her down.

Feeling all pink and glowy, she said, 'Good.'

Chapter 14

Dear Rose,

    Three things about me:

    I adore my husband.

    I can't stand my mother-in-law.

    I don't look great in a bikini.

    The truth is, my mother-in-law wishes I was prettier, more like her. She's super-glamorous and I'm not. Her Christmas present to me was a cosmetic surgery voucher, and she's already told me that once I've had the liposuction, she'll give me another voucher for a nose job. (You can't say she's not generous!)

    I'm happy with the way I look but fed up with the constant digs. Every year my in-laws pay for us to fly out to Barbados and join them at their holiday villa. I'm quite sporty and enjoy being active, but we're expected to spend all our time with them just lying by the pool. By day we sunbathe, by night we eat and drink . . . and that's it. I wish we didn't have to go, but my husband says we'll hurt their feelings if we refuse, and he doesn't want to do that. Nor can we afford any kind of holiday ourselves.

    Please help. I just don't know what to do.

    Love, Laura

Dear Laura,

Oh dear, I kind of feel sorry for all of you. It can't be much fun for your mother-in-law, having to put up with a guest who is clearly bored out of her mind. Maybe she's just being polite, inviting you to join them on their holiday, and would be secretly relieved if you said you couldn't go.

Obviously her choice of gift is awful, but maybe it isn't a personal dig; in her mind, she may genuinely be trying to help. Yes, I'm giving your mother-in-law the benefit of the doubt here, but some people just have different priorities in life.

Here's my suggestion: tell your in-laws that you're only able to take two weeks off work, and you've decided to use the time to have the plastic surgery. Then get a refund on the voucher and spend the money on a brilliant holiday for you and your husband. Tell your mother-in-law that you had the lipo, wait a few weeks, then proudly show off your new body. Tell her you're thrilled with it. If she says she can't see any difference . . . well, that's her problem, not yours. (If she says she can't see any scars, tell her that's because the plastic surgeon was a genius.)

Have a great holiday!

Love, Rose

The queue for the check-in desk at the airport was ridiculously long, snaking like a maze and composed of hundreds of travellers in various stages of impatience.

Rory, already checked in for his brief flight to Zurich on a two-day business trip, was waiting to meet up with his colleagues. He watched as a small child took a bite of an egg sandwich, pulled a face and shoved it, unwrapped, into his Thomas the Tank Engine knapsack.

A group of men heading off on a stag weekend and keen to reach the bar in Departures were complaining noisily about the queue. Teenagers attempting not to look as if they were with their parents were plugged into their headphones and lost in a world of music. An overly loved-up couple, possibly on their honeymoon, were passing the time with their arms wrapped around each other, locked in an emotional embrace. Which wouldn't have been so bad if they hadn't also been kissing. Noisily.

Rather like a couple of camels.

Oh well, each to his own. The corners of Rory's mouth twitched as the pair pulled apart for a moment and the woman, gazing dreamily into the man's eyes, murmured, 'Wuv you.'

Oh God, don't do it, don't say it . . .

The man nuzzled her, nose to nose. 'Wuv you too.'

Eurgh, he said it. And no one else in the queue had even noticed.

Then he realised he wasn't the only one after all; at the very end of the check-in queue was a group of girls in their late twenties, one of whom was in a wheelchair. She had cropped wavy dark-red hair and plastic tubing across her face, mask-style, feeding her oxygen. She was chalk-pale beneath a scattering of freckles and there were violet shadows beneath her huge dark eyes, but she was watching the couple and trying hard not to laugh as well. The next moment, her gaze met Rory's and they silently shared the comedy-gold moment that everyone else had been too distracted to witness.

She looked so unwell, so thin and frail, that Rory wondered if she were actually fit enough to travel. But she was there in the queue, so she must be. And despite the obvious fragility, she was evidently still capable of retaining her sense of fun. As the couple ahead of her in the queue exchanged another noisy kiss – *mwahhh!* – the girl discreetly mouthed the words *Wuv you* and mimed sticking her thin fingers down her throat.

Wuv you too, Rory mouthed back, and she started to laugh, provoking a helpless coughing fit.

One of the officials from the airline approached the girl with a clipboard. 'Hello, you don't need to queue here! If you'd like to come with me, we can fast-track you through.'

'Really? Fantastic.' The girl's friend swivelled the chair round and detoured out of the snaking line, to the considerable annoyance of a group of people halfway along the queue.

'Hey, hold on! Just 'cos she's in a wheelchair, how come she gets better treatment than we do? We've been stuck here waiting for half an hour . . .'

The girl coughed, looked at them and said with a half-smile, 'I know, it's so unfair. I'm just lucky, I guess.'

What a bunch of imbeciles. They carried on whingeing and complaining as the girl was whisked up to the desk. When she lifted herself briefly out of the wheelchair in order to disentangle the strap on her shoulder bag from the plastic oxygen tubing, they howled with fresh outrage because she wasn't completely paralysed and *could* stand up.

'She'd better not be on our flight,' snorted one of the angry family. 'I saw someone who looked like that on one of those hospital programmes the other week. Turned out they had Aids.'

Jesus.

'Look, and now she's got someone pushing her along, taking her up to Departures in a lift. She's probably only pretending to be ill for the special treatment.'

Rory marvelled at the morons' staggering lack of empathy. He had no idea what was wrong with the girl, but she was clearly very unwell. Imagine feeling that ill *and* having to deal with the ignorance of people like that.

Maybe he'd stop for a chat with her if they happened to bump into each other again.

Meanwhile, here came Den and Ehjaz now . . .

The others were so thrilled to be here at the airport, about to fly to Paris for three days to celebrate Bea's birthday. Hallie had been looking forward to it too; having made the decision to go,

89

she'd found herself getting more and more excited about the prospect. Their rooms in Montmartre were all booked, she'd pored over the website for so long she practically knew every inch of the hotel off by heart, and people had recommended all sorts of brilliant restaurants to visit and fantastic places to go. Tomorrow they were taking a trip down the Seine on a Bateau Mouche . . .

Everything had seemed to be going so well. For the last week, praying that she'd be OK for the trip, Hallie had actually felt fine, if anything a bit better than usual.

Until this morning, when she'd woken up feeling just that bit *less* well and, deep down, had recognised the early symptoms and realised she was harbouring the beginnings of yet another infection. Whether her immune system would be up to the task of fighting it off was another matter.

Maybe in her heart she'd known the truth, but desperation had led her to deny it. Like waking up in the night feeling sick and trying hard to go back to sleep in the hope that the nausea might somehow magically disappear, Hallie had resolutely ignored the signs.

But that had been five hours ago, and the infection evidently had no intention of going anywhere. Rather than fighting it off, her hopeless, feeble body appeared to be surrendering completely. She was feeling shivery and weak all over, the backs of her eyes hurt and her chest was already tightening in that oh-so-familiar way.

In the confines of the disabled cubicle in the ladies' loo, Hallie took the thermometer out of her medical bag, uncapped it and put it under her tongue. She already knew she was running a temperature. At a guess, 38.5°C.

OK, and take a look . . .

Damn, 39.2°C.

She took out her mobile, called the surgery and asked Mary on reception to see if Luke could possibly come to the phone.

He knew what she was doing today, obviously. Within twenty seconds she heard his voice.

'Hallie. What is it?'

'I'm at the airport. Feeling pretty rough. Just took my temp and it's thirty nine point two.'

A pause at the other end, then. 'Well, you can ask to be seen by a first-aider, but I think you already know the answer.'

'Yes.' There was no point getting upset and all why-me? about it. She wasn't fit to travel, and even if she made it to Paris, she wouldn't be well enough to enjoy the trip.

'I'm sorry.' Luke's tone was compassionate.

'I know. Me too.' Such a waste of anticipation; all that looking forward to something that was no longer going to happen.

'Have you told the others yet?'

'No.' Hallie coughed weakly. 'Nor my mum. Oh God, I'm going to be messing up her plans too.' Her mother, taking advantage of her absence, had booked a weekend away in Edinburgh. Which she would cancel in a heartbeat, naturally, but it all contributed to Hallie's feelings of guilt. Her poor mum had little enough free time as it was.

Luke, who knew this too, said, 'Look, don't call Fay yet. Let's see if we can work something out. I may be able to help.'

'OK. Thanks. I'll tell the girls now.'

Emerging from the disabled loo, she made her way back through Departures to the champagne bar, where Bea and the others were starting as they meant to go on.

'Here she is! You've been *ages*. Come on, catch up, get this down you.' Bea held out a brimming fizzing glass.

'I'm so sorry, I have an infection.' Hallie's voice cracked; how she hated always having to be the bearer of bad news. 'You're going to have to have a brilliant time without me. I can't fly.'

Oh well, at least the extortionate travel insurance meant she wouldn't miss out financially too. Apart from the extortionate taxi back to Carranford, obviously. Once she'd been seen by the airport first-aider, who confirmed that she wasn't fit to travel, Hallie completed the necessary paperwork and let the airline staff take her and her belongings along the covered walkway to the taxi office.

As they waited for the next cab to become available, Hallie's phone rang. Answering it, she assumed a cheerful holiday voice. 'Hi, Mum! Everything OK?'

'Just wondering how it's all going, darling. Checking you haven't forgotten anything. Not that there's much you can do about it now if you have!'

Hallie's heart went out to her mum, who had worried about her her whole life. As any parent would, obviously, under their particular circumstances. But when it was just the two of them, Fay and Hallie Kingsley against the world, maybe the worry was that much more intense.

Luke was right: she couldn't let her mother cancel her own plans for a weekend away from Carranford. More than anyone, she deserved a break.

'I have everything I need. We've all had a glass of champagne.' Well, she'd forced herself to take a couple of sips. 'And they've just called our flight, so we'll be getting on the plane any minute. I've got priority boarding!' Chirpily she added, 'Because I'm extra special!'

'Of course you are. Have a fantastic time, sweetheart.'

'We will. What time are you leaving for Edinburgh?'

'Not until six. Pete can't get away before then.'

Six? Bugger. Hallie looked up at the ticking clock on the wall. Subterfuge wasn't so much fun when you were shivery and feverish and it was still only two o'clock. But her mum had been so looking forward to this weekend away with Pete, her boyfriend; nothing must be allowed to spoil it.

Aloud she said, 'Ooh, better go, they're calling for me to board. I'll see you on Sunday night, OK? Have fun!'

Chapter 15

It was fine, Luke told himself. It was *completely* fine and there was no need whatsoever to feel guilty. He wasn't doing anything wrong. Hallie was a friend. She currently happened to be a friend in need, and all he was doing was offering to help her out.

The fact that she was also his patient was entirely irrelevant. It wasn't as if anything untoward was going to happen.

He left the surgery at three and drove back to the cottage he'd been renting on the edge of the village since moving to Carranford. Hallie had texted to let him know she was twenty minutes away. Panicking slightly, he'd pictured the place through her eyes. Not having been expecting a visitor, he needed to do a speedy tidy-up. He unlocked the front door, gazed wildly around and headed for the kitchen. Right, OK, *go*.

For fifteen minutes he worked like lightning. Stuff was shoved back into cupboards and windows were flung open to dispel the lingering smell of last night's fish and chips. Not wanting to irritate Hallie's lungs, he didn't risk spraying air freshener but splashed a bit of his best aftershave on to the curtains instead. Magazines were collected up and cleared away, coffee mugs and a couple of plates were thrown into the sink, and in the living room the cushions he never bothered with were retrieved from behind the sofa and placed at jaunty angles next to each arm. No time to vacuum, but he picked a few crumbs off the carpet and did a bit of emergency dusting with a J Cloth. Gym clothes and trainers were stuffed into his sports bag and hidden in the utility room. The empty tube of paprika Pringles he'd finished last night went into the bin. God, preparing the place for unexpected guests was *exhausting*.

Just as he was finishing, he heard the sound of tyres on gravel and looked out of the window – great, a bird had left its calling card *all* the way down the glass – to see the airport cab pulling up outside.

Hallie was here.

He went outside to greet her. She was looking pale, feverish and exhausted.

'Thanks so much. Sorry to be a pain. I feel like a right Nellie No-Mates.' Hallie coughed into a tissue and managed a weak smile.

'Hey, no problem, happy to help.' He lifted her wheelchair out of the cab, followed by the boxes of equipment and her suitcase. 'And you do have mates. They just all happen to be in Paris for the next three days.'

'But you stepped up. Like a complete star. And as soon as my mum's left, I can go home.'

'You don't have to. You're welcome to stay.'

'I know. I hate to be a nuisance, though.' She shrugged and coughed again. 'You don't want your weekend messed up too.'

Luke shook his head. 'Come on, let's get you inside for now. You're not well. We can argue about the rest later.'

He carried everything into the cottage, closed the windows, settled Hallie on the cushion-strewn sofa and fixed up the oxygen feed. She administered her next dose of IV medication via the portacath in her chest.

'Now, what can I get you? Coffee? Tea? Anything to eat?'

'Actually, don't worry. I'm feeling a bit wiped out. All that pretending to be well earlier . . . it's pretty exhausting.' She half smiled. 'Whatever it is you're cooking, by the way, I think it's done.'

'What? Oh God . . .' In his desperation to cover up the fish-and-chip smell, he'd switched the oven up high and thrown in a slice of bread because an estate agent had once recommended it for giving potential properties that fresh baked air of homeliness.

In the kitchen, he discovered that the bread was now charcoal. Feeling like a complete idiot, he flung open the windows once more and energetically dispersed the billowing clouds of smoke with a tea towel.

By the time he'd finished fumigating the kitchen, making tea, unwrapping a cake from the village store — because he wasn't Superman — and carrying everything through to the living room — Hallie was fast asleep.

He paused in the doorway, holding the tray in front of him. She was lying on her side on the faded red sofa, her breathing shallow but regular. The nasal specs were in place, boosting her oxygen intake by a couple of litres a minute. If she needed it, she could switch to the portable non-invasive ventilator he'd unpacked and left on the table beside her.

But for now he'd leave her in peace, to sleep and regain some energy.

She looked beautiful, with her cheek resting on her hand and her other arm dangling over the edge of the sofa. Those dark lashes covered the shadows beneath her eyes, and her delicate bone structure was accentuated by the glow of the fringed table lamp behind her. She was wearing a navy jersey top and skirt, navy tights and a deep purple wraparound cardigan-type thing. She'd taken off her boots. Were her feet cold? Her circulation wasn't good . . .

And look at me, standing here in the doorway like Mrs Overall. Luke glanced down at the tray in his hands, turned around and took it back to the kitchen. He would get on with some paper-work in the office, leave Hallie to sleep for now and check up on her in an hour.

At nine o'clock, she was still sound asleep. Luke had checked on her regularly, in between catching up on admin, cooking a roast dinner and watching a mind-boggling documentary on the tiny kitchen TV about extreme cosmetic surgery in Beverly Hills. God, some people were weird. The pain they chose to put themselves through. One woman was undergoing her seventh procedure in order to correct her slightly asymmetric toes.

The chicken was resting and was ready to be carved, gravy made, vegetables keeping warm in the oven. He returned to the living room and saw Hallie's lashes flicker as the door creaked open.

It wasn't wrong, was it, to have her staying here?

But the flicker of guilt was still there, because no matter that he would never dream of acting on his feelings for her, they still existed. And if she weren't his patient, if they were simply two friends who lived in the same village and enjoyed each other's company . . . well, then of course at some stage he would let her know how he felt.

Luke felt his stomach muscles tighten at the thought of it. Whether Hallie would ever be interested in him in return was quite another matter, but since it was never going to happen anyway, it was irrelevant.

He was a GP and Hallie Kingsley was his patient. Apart from a single visit to his colleague Jennifer for a gynae concern, since his arrival in Carranford she'd always been seen by him. Furthermore, he knew from her mother how relieved Hallie was to no longer have to cope with Jennifer's brusque attitude. His partner in the practice might be an excellent doctor, but her manner was unfortunate.

Anyway, that was the situation and nothing was going to change it. Luke exhaled. For the sake of all involved, he'd learned to keep his emotions absolutely in check. She would never know how much she—

'What time is it?' Hallie's dark eyes were open and she was blinking, getting her bearings.

'Nine.'

'Wow. I was tired.' She flexed her shoulders and sat up. 'Sorry.'

'Don't be sorry. You needed the rest. How are you feeling now?'

'Bit better.' She smiled. 'Hungry.'

'Excellent. I have food.'

'I know, I can tell. My amazing super-powers tell me it's roast chicken.'

He shrugged modestly. 'My signature dish.'

'Really?' Her gaze was innocent. 'I thought your signature dish was charcoal toast.'

Wow, Luke did actually know how to cook. By eleven o'clock, Hallie was finishing her second plateful of food.

'These roast potatoes are fantastic,' she marvelled. 'And that's a compliment, because I'm a connoisseur. Seriously, these are almost as good as mine.'

'I'm honoured.' Amused, Luke put the last potato on her plate. 'Try this one, it might be even better.'

'Oh God, it's Mum again.' Hallie's phone was beeping with yet another message. She pulled a face; she'd diverted all calls to voicemail so the dialling tone wouldn't give away the fact that she wasn't in France, but she couldn't put it off any longer. 'I'll have to call her back.'

She rang the number, coughing first to clear her throat and prepare to sound well.

'There you are!' her mum exclaimed. 'Why didn't you answer before? I was worried about you!'

'Mum, everything's fine. We were out at a bistro. Now we're back at the hotel.'

Years of worry had fine-tuned Fay's ears to the sound of her voice. 'Are you sure you're OK? You sound chesty.'

'I'm great. Just tired. That's why I'm in bed.' To divert attention away from her lungs, Hallie said, 'The hotel's fantastic and my room's really nice!'

Well, it had looked good on the website.

'Oh darling, I'd love to see it! I know, why don't we Skype? Then you can show me everything!'

Aaarrgh. 'I'd love to, but I can't. Bea tried earlier and there isn't enough signal.'

'Oh that's a shame. But at least you can send photos! Take a picture and email it to me now!'

'Um . . .' Shit, shit. Hallie switched to speakerphone so Luke could hear what was going on too.

'You can do it while you're talking to me.' Fay's tone was eager. 'Go on, sweetie, take a photo so I can see your room!'

Chapter 16

'OK, hang on.' Thinking fast, Hallie gazed around Luke's living room and found a section that was safe to photograph. Switching to the camera and holding up the phone, she directed the lens at the area with the comfortable blue sofa to the left, the coffee table in front of it and the curtained window to the right. There were a couple of framed paintings on the wall. Whoops, and a medical journal was visible on the shelf next to the window. Hastily gesturing for Luke to remove it, she took the photo and emailed it to her mother. 'Right, sent. How's Edinburgh?'

'Wonderful, darling. Bit rainy, but so beautiful. Pete sends his love, by the way; we're having such fun . . . wow, the photo's here already, that was quick. I thought there wasn't much signal. Oh dear, you said your room was really nice!'

'Mum! It *is*.' Bugger, speakerphones had their downside.

'Sorry, didn't mean it like that. I just thought the hotel was really modern. I suppose I was expecting a bit more glitz and glamour.'

'I know, and the rest of it is like that, but I'm in the annexe because of my wheelchair. And it's *lovely*,' Hallie stressed. 'All cosy and warm. I much prefer this kind of room.'

'Well as long as you're happy.' Sounding doubtful, her mother said, 'But it doesn't look terribly French. Is the bed OK?'

'Of course it's OK!'

'I mean, is it clean?'

'Mum . . .' Hallie broke into a cough.

'Oh darling, you do sound chesty. Take a photo of yourself and let me see you. Is it a French-looking bed? I *love* those ones with the carved headboards.'

Luckily, Luke knew what a worrier her mum was. Already ahead of her, he was pointing to the staircase and lifting the oxygen cylinder. Hallie nodded and rose to her feet, and together, connected by the clear plastic tubing of her nasal cannulae, they silently ascended the stairs.

Luke's bedroom was small but pretty tidy. The duvet was deep red, the pillowcases blue and white striped, the bed a standard double. He placed the cylinder on the floor next to the bed, threw back the duvet and helped Hallie into it. Her mum was chattering on about Edinburgh and Princes Street now, as Luke plumped up the pillows and she arranged herself accordingly.

Holding up the camera, Hallie took a photo of herself cosily ensconced in Luke's bed. *Ooh, Matron . . .*

'This one's taking longer to get through,' said her mother. 'Oh, here it comes now.' There was silence as she studied the photograph. 'Hmm, well if you say it's all right. Bit quirky, though, having striped pillowcases in a hotel.'

All right, Miss Marple. In a firm voice, Hallie said, 'I like quirky. And it's red, white and blue, like the French flag.'

'Where are the other girls?'

'Down in the bar. I'm having an early night, ready for tomorrow. I'll be the smug one without a hangover.'

'Well make sure you don't overtire yourself. Night, sweetheart, I'll give you another call tomorrow, see how you're doing. Make sure you keep your phone switched on.'

With the call over, Luke carried the oxygen cylinder back downstairs and Hallie followed him. Reinstated on the sofa, she said, 'Sorry, I know it's stupid. She's my mum, though.'

'It's fine.'

'I'm twenty-eight.' Hallie shrugged good-naturedly. 'Sometimes you'd think I was six.'

'She's never going to stop worrying about you.'

'Because she doesn't know how long she has left to worry about me.' As Hallie said it, another message pinged up on her phone and she glanced at the screen.

'Your mum again?'

'No. It's from Nick.'

'Ex-boyfriend Nick?' Luke knew the name; they'd talked about him before. 'Where is he now?'

'Melbourne. Crewing on a yacht. Swimming with dolphins, snorkelling with seals. Having fun.'

Nick had sent a photo as well, of himself and his friends celebrating the end of a perfect day on the yacht. Their faces were the epitome of happiness, their bodies lithe and tanned as they beamed and raised their bottles of beer to the camera, whilst behind them the sun began to set, its rippled reflection bright in the glittering cobalt sea . . .

Hallie tilted the phone so Luke could see it too. 'And unlike our faked photos, his are the real deal.'

'How does that feel?'

She paused, then said drily, 'It's nice of him to keep in touch. But sometimes . . . well, I could do without the reminders.'

Luke went into the kitchen to make coffee and Hallie took one last look at the picture of Nick on her phone. What was the famous quote: don't be sad that it's over, be glad that it happened?

Something like that, anyway.

And yes, she did do her best to live by that mantra, but just sometimes the reality of her own life made it hard to stay positive.

Nick's message said: *Hey, you! How's everything? Haven't caught a single kangaroo today — don't know WHAT I'm doing wrong! Maybe a different kind of fishing line needed?? Xxx*

Hallie typed: *Glad you're having a great time. All good here. Yes, you need to put Tim Tams on your fishing hooks — kangaroos love them. Xxx*

Having replied to his breezy message, using the same number of kisses he had, she duly deleted his text and photo.

Luke, back from the kitchen, watched her do it. 'What happened with you two? Can I ask that question?'

'Of course you can ask. You want the whole story?' She waited for him to settle down with his coffee. 'Nick was my first proper boyfriend. His family moved to Carranford . . . God, must have been eight years ago now. I was twenty, Nick was nineteen. We met in the pub one night and it was just . . . wow. Lust at first sight.' Hallie smiled at the memory of that long hot summer; she didn't have to explain to Luke that her lungs hadn't been as bad then as they were now. The limitations on physical activities had been far fewer and the spark between her and Nick had been mutual and instantaneous. 'He was so carefree and enthusiastic about everything. We fell in love. We didn't actually have too much in common, but who cared about that?' She paused and pulled a face. 'Well, apart from Nick's family and my mum. They didn't want their perfect son getting himself involved with someone in my situation. And my mum just knew I was the one who'd end up getting hurt. She was desperate to protect me. Except I was twenty, so obviously I wasn't going to listen to *her*. As far as Nick and I were concerned, we were Romeo and Juliet. Everyone was trying to split us up, which just made us that much more determined to make it work. Nick's mum was terrified I was going to get pregnant and trap him that way. She couldn't understand why he would want to be tied down with someone with CF when there were so many completely *normal* girls to choose from.'

Luke didn't bother with the usual platitudes. 'And how long did you stay together?'

'Two years. Then the novelty began to wear off, I suppose.

Nick was at Bath University, being a student and doing all the normal student things. He was sporty, he wanted to travel . . . I'm guessing it began to sink in that I was never going to miraculously get better. Then after his degree his parents paid for him to take a year off and go travelling around the world. Well, that was pretty much it. Travelling was what he wanted to do and I couldn't stop him. That was when we broke up. And a few weeks after he left, his parents put their house up for sale and moved to Manchester.'

Luke whistled. 'To make sure you two didn't get back together when he came home?'

'Who knows? Everyone in Carranford felt really sorry for me, anyway.' Hallie's dark eyes gleamed with mischief. 'And we were all delighted when they had to sell the house for twenty grand less than they'd paid for it.'

'And how did you cope?'

'What, once Nick was gone? I wasn't brave, if that's what you're asking. Made a right show of myself for a while. Drank too much, cried a *lot*, even slept with one of Nick's friends, just to punish him. Except it didn't help and I still felt like a bit of old rubbish.' Reaching for her coffee and shrugging, Hallie said, 'So I decided life would be easier if I didn't get involved with anyone else. Basically, it wasn't worth the hassle. I'd be better off staying single.'

Luke frowned slightly. 'And you still think that?'

'It's not so difficult. I'm hardly the catch of the year.' Hallie shook her head dismissively; it was time to change the subject. 'Go on then, enough about me. Your turn now. Why aren't you settled down?'

He looked amused. 'I'm busy. I put in a lot of hours.'

'Is that why you and Christina broke up?' *Wow, listen to me, asking the question I've wanted to know the answer to for months.* But here in Luke's cottage, at this time of night, it somehow seemed OK. Belatedly Hallie added, 'You don't have to say if you don't want to. I'm just nosy.'

Because he was looking a bit embarrassed now. God, how awful if there'd been some humiliating sexual reason for the break-up.

'It's fine. There's no big secret. We got together because we liked each other and everyone told us what a great couple we made. And life was easy and we never argued, and it was all just *fine*.' Luke shrugged. 'But it needs to be more than fine, doesn't it? It wasn't the . . . you know, the love affair of the century. We *weren't* Romeo and Juliet.'

'It just wasn't enough,' said Hallie.

'Pretty much.' He paused. 'And then there were the snakes.'

'You what?'

'Well, quite.' Luke smiled briefly at the expression on her face. 'She kept them as pets. A Burmese python, a royal python and two corn snakes. The spare room was full of vivariums. And Christina loved them. Probably far more than she loved me.' His tone was wry. 'Basically, it was hard to relax in that house. I'm not terrified of snakes, but I was never going to like them. Never understood the appeal.'

'And it was one more reason why you split up.'

'Let's say it didn't help. After we'd been seeing each other for a year, she suggested we move in together, and I realised then that my first thought was *No*. Well, it was *Oh God, not with those bloody snakes*. But if I'd loved her enough, I could have coped with them. After that, we both kind of realised it was never going to work out. She's still living in Cheltenham,' said Luke. 'With Audrey and Daniel and Artemis and Trevor.'

'Those were their names?'

'Yes.'

'Blimey. And none of us ever knew about them,' Hallie marvelled. 'It just goes to show, you never can tell what's happening behind other people's closed doors.'

'In Christina's case, she's usually feeding dead mice and rats to her pythons. Not the loveliest sight in the world. You're

104

looking tired,' said Luke. 'Time to take your meds. And I've made an executive decision,' he added. 'I'm not letting you go home. You're staying here.'

Hallie nodded. He was right: the virus was wiping her out. Despite having slept for hours this afternoon, she was now exhausted and ready to crash out again. She needed to do her IVs and use the NIV if she wanted to avoid CO_2 build-up and the inevitable banging headache tomorrow morning. *Oh, the endless joys of being ill.*

'I feel bad, leaving you with the washing-up. If you can bear to let it sit in the sink, I'll do it in the morning.'

'Don't even think about it. You just concentrate on getting better. Look, I'm going to leave you in peace now. Bathroom's through there. You've got everything else you need here in this room. And you have your mobile,' said Luke. 'Any problems at all, just shout. If you can't shout, call.' He picked up his own phone, rose to his feet and headed for the kitchen.

The rear view was great; in jeans, you could see what a nice bum he had. 'Thanks so much for this,' said Hallie.

He halted in the doorway and turned to look at her. 'Will you stop thanking me? There's no need.' Another pause. 'And can I say something else?'

'Go ahead.'

'Not all men are like Nick. They don't all run away. Plenty of people with CF have normal, happy relationships.'

He was so kind, so compassionate. Hallie's chest gave a secret squeeze of emotion; imagine if Luke weren't her doctor and liked her as much as she liked him. He would, she instinctively knew, be one of the good guys, the trustworthy kind who would never break your heart and run away.

But how many men could you ever really trust? Even if you were fit and healthy? Not many. Add in the fact that she *did* have a life-limiting illness and the odds of actually being able to find someone were just about infinitesimal. Falling in love and being abandoned – again – held no appeal whatsoever. Maybe if you were expecting to live for another sixty years, the prospect of being miserable and heartbroken for a few months was bearable.

The thing was, if a few months was possibly all the time you had left here on this earth . . . well. It wasn't high on her list of must-have experiences.

Basically, who'd want to be utterly miserable for the rest of their life?

Hallie looked at Luke and allowed herself a brief fantasy. What would he do if she were to beckon him over now, wrap her arms around his neck and pull his mouth down to meet hers? What would he say if she whispered, 'Will you carry me upstairs? Can we sleep together? If I promise never to tell anyone, could we do that? Just for tonight?'

OK, get a grip. End of fantasy.

Apart from anything else, what if he backed away in horror, holding up his hands and saying, 'You're kidding, right?'

God, being rejected in a fantasy was the absolute pits.

Hallie braced herself and nodded. 'I know they do. Ignore me, it's just the way I feel. I'm a complete wimp.'

Luke regarded her steadily for several seconds before shaking his head. 'No, not true. You're anything but that.' He reached for the door handle. 'Night.'

In the kitchen, doing the mountain of washing-up, Luke heard Hallie moving around in the living room. She would be getting ready for bed, doing her meds, setting up the portable ventilator and settling down for the night. Luckily the old sofa was big and comfortable enough to stretch out on; he would have offered her his own bed like a shot, but since the bathroom was down-stairs, it made sense for her to stay down here too.

This evening had been simultaneously one of the best and most frustrating of his life. Somehow he'd even managed to end up telling Hallie she shouldn't give up on love, and encouraging her to search for someone special who could make her happy.

Someone else special, obviously. Not him. Even though just the thought of Hallie with another man made his chest tighten with envy.

Luke picked up the wine glass she'd drunk out of and tipped the last dregs down the sink. And if she *did* find someone, he would have to pretend to be happy for her . . .

God, I must be some kind of masochist.

Chapter 17

When you make the discovery that someone you like has never seen your all-time favourite film, there's only one thing to do. And that is to force them to sit down with you and watch it.

'Are you *serious*? How can you never have seen *The Shawshank Redemption*? It's a classic!'

'Man gets life in prison for a murder he didn't commit. I don't know.' Luke shrugged. 'I suppose it just didn't sound that cheery.'

'But it's so amazing. Tim Robbins is brilliant. Morgan Freeman's brilliant too. Come on.' Hallie pointed to the other end of the sofa. 'I've downloaded it now. You're going to love it, I promise.'

And really, was there any better way to spend a Saturday evening? She was feeling better today, still under the weather, but fully rested and not nearly as grim and feverish as yesterday. She had texted her mum and told her she was having a wonderful time being pushed along the Champs-Élysées in her wheelchair. In reality, Luke had made pancakes for lunch and this evening they were going to be ordering a pizza delivery from the new Italian restaurant in Stow-on-the-Wold.

Outside, it was dark and icy cold. Inside, the cottage was toasty warm and comfortable, a bright fire crackling in the grate and the scent of lemons from the pancakes still lingering in the air. As they watched the film together, Hallie kept a covert eye on Luke. It was truly one of life's pleasures, introducing someone to something you knew they were going to love.

And really, how could he not? Luke had kindness, strength and compassion; he was as perfect as the film itself. It couldn't fail to touch his soul.

'Can you pass me a tissue?' she murmured as, on screen, Andy Dufresne found himself alone in the Governor's office overlooking the exercise yard.

Luke reached across for the box on the table in front of him. 'Are you OK?'

Oh, the glamour: he thought she needed a good old chest-clearing cough.

'I'm fine.' Hallie braced herself; this part of the film always made her cry. She couldn't wait to see if it had the same effect on Luke.

Andy Dufresne had found the record and taken it out of its dusty sleeve. He carefully placed it on the record player and listened as the first glorious bars of the Letter Duet from Mozart's *Marriage of Figaro* began to play. Then he plugged the record player into the main speakers that broadcast throughout the prison and sat back with his hands clasped behind his head, transported along with the rest of the incredulous inmates by the beauty of the aria.

And when the warden hammered furiously on the door, yelling at him to stop it, Andy turned the music up. For those few magical minutes he was no longer a prisoner . . .

Under cover of wiping her eyes, Hallie glanced sideways at Luke and saw that he was breathing in that juddery way people do when they're struggling to control their emotions. His jaw was rigid and his own eyes were glistening . . . oh yes, it had got to him too.

Unable to resist it, she reached across, gave his arm a gentle nudge and whispered, 'You OK?'

'Great, thanks. Absolutely fine.' As he murmured his reply, Luke kept his gaze fixed on the screen. 'Not remotely affected.'

She grinned. 'Don't worry, it gets better. This is just the start.'

DDDDDRRRINNNGGGGG.

The shrill of the doorbell shattered the moment. They both jumped a mile.

'What should I do?' Hallie looked at him. 'Hide?' They weren't doing anything wrong, but she *was* supposed to be in Paris.

'Let me go and see who it is. It's OK, I won't let anyone in.' Already on his feet, Luke went to answer the front door. Reaching over for the remote control, Hallie pressed Pause and listened. Hopefully he'd get rid of whoever it was and they could carry on watching the rest of the film. If he was loving it so far, just wait till he got to the bit at the end where—

'Oh.' She heard Luke sounding genuinely startled. 'Hello . . .'

What if it's Christina?

Then she heard the visitor say, 'Hello, Luke, can I come in?' and the shock caused the remote control to slip out of Hallie's hand. It clattered on to the glass-topped coffee table, then bounced on to the carpet at her feet.

'You may as well let me in,' the visitor continued. 'I know she's here.'

Hallie heard them coming through to the living room. Luke and her mother.

OK, this is mad . . .

'There you are.' Her mother wasn't looking remotely amused. 'What's going on?'

'Nothing, I just—'

'You lied to me! I can't believe you *did* that. Hallie, listen to me, this is serious. Luke's your doctor, and if you're having an affair with him, he could get struck off!'

'Mum, stop it!' Oh God, talk about mortifying; Hallie could feel herself going bright red. If there was anything worse than

110

being wrongly accused of having an affair with someone, it was being wrongly accused right in front of them.

And if there was anything worse than *that*, it was having it all happen when you secretly fancied the person rotten and wished more than anything that you *could* have an affair with him.

'Fay, there's nothing going on,' Luke said evenly. 'I'm not having any kind of affair with your daughter.'

Fay stared at him. 'So what's she doing here, then? Why would she tell me she was going to Paris . . . why would she pretend she was there?'

'Because I didn't want to spoil your weekend away,' Hallie blurted out. 'Because I knew you'd come home if you found out I hadn't gone to France. Mum, don't look at me like that, it's the truth. We got to the airport but I was feeling too ill to travel and there wasn't anyone else to stay with me because my friends were all in Paris. So I called Luke and he said I could come here . . . and yes, I could have gone home, but it's actually been quite nice having a change of scenery.' She gestured around the cosy firelit living room. 'But you have to believe me, there's nothing going on, and the fact that you're even thinking that is *really* embarrassing.'

'Oh.' Her mother's fury abruptly subsided. 'You promise that's true?'

Together Hallie and Luke chorused, '*Yes.*'

Fay bit her lip. 'OK. Well I'd better tell you now, I'm not the only one thinking it.'

'What?' Hallie sat up.

'Don't look at me like that. It's your fault for sending me those photos.'

'Why? What did you do?'

'Well, Marilyn called me this morning for a chat and I told her we were having a lovely time in Edinburgh but I was a bit worried that the hotel people in Paris were ripping *you* off, dumping you in a room that wasn't as nice as the others. So Marilyn asked to see the photos and I showed them to her. And the moment she saw them, she said that was no Paris hotel room you were in, it was Luke Hilton's cottage.'

Oh God, of all the people her mother could have shown the photos to, she'd had to choose Marilyn, who had lived here in this very cottage before Luke had come to Carranford. How typical. And Marilyn, who now lived above the pub since taking over the running of it, was a brilliant person, but she did love to gossip.

Hallie said firmly, 'You're going to have to tell her the truth and ask her not to spread rumours. You know what people are like around here. It wouldn't be fair on Luke.'

'Right. I'll do that.' Fay nodded, apparently less than reassured. 'OK, the thing is, when I say I showed Marilyn the photos . . . well, I kind of put them on Facebook.'

Hallie briefly closed her eyes. 'Seriously? You told me you didn't know how to put photos on Facebook!'

'I know, I didn't, but Marilyn showed me how to do it last week. It's really easy. I had no idea!'

'So everyone saw them,' said Hallie.

'Well, yes. That's how we knew you were in Luke's bed. Lynette recognised the pillows and that duvet cover straight away.'

'I don't believe this.' Hallie winced and turned to stare at Luke. 'How does *she* know what your bedding looks like?'

Because not being judgemental, but curly-permed Lynette was in her fifties and Hallie really wouldn't have had her down as Luke's type.

'Lynette does all my laundry.' Luke sighed. 'Washing and ironing, once a week.'

'When she isn't busy on Facebook,' said Hallie. Honestly, what were people like her mum and Lynette even doing on social networking sites? Didn't they know they were too old to be meddling with such things?

112

'Well I didn't know, did I?' Fay was defensive. 'I thought you were in Paris!'

'You'll have to delete the photos,' said Hallie.

'OK, I'll do that.'

From the look on her face it wasn't hard to guess what was going through her mother's mind.

'But this all happened this morning, so it's basically too late now,' Hallie guessed. 'Everyone's already seen them.'

Fay pulled a face. 'Pretty much. We'll just tell them the truth, though. It'll be fine.'

'Yeah.'

'Well,' Fay said brightly, 'at least you two *aren't* having an affair. That's good!'

And yes, it was still embarrassing, too. Hallie said, 'Mum, could you please stop saying it?'

'OK. Anyway, we'd better get your stuff together and make a move.'

'What, *now*? But we're watching a film. *Shawshank*!'

'Oh, *that* one. You've seen it a million times already.' Morphing into bossy mode, Fay jangled her car keys at them. 'And I'm back now, so you need to come home with me if you don't want the whole village to explode with gossip. Luke, it was very kind of you to look after her, but we'll leave you in peace now. You can have the rest of your weekend back. Oh, and by the way, guess who Marilyn bumped into the other day in Cheltenham? Christina!'

'She did?' Luke looked suitably interested and polite.

'In the hairdresser's. Marilyn said she was looking fantastic. *And* she's still single,' Fay went on as she started throwing stuff into Hallie's suitcase. 'You know, you two really should get back together. We all liked her so much!'

And that was it. Within ten minutes, everything had been loaded into her mother's car and Hallie found herself being driven back to her own home. No more *Shawshank*, no cosy crackling fire, no takeaway pizza, good company and easy conversation . . .

113

OK, maybe that wasn't fair. She still had her mum, who had cut short her own mini break in order to race back and rescue her from the clutches of their unscrupulous and dastardly local GP. They would have a nice evening together, she was sure.

But she'd been looking forward to spending the next twenty-four hours with Luke, and now it wasn't going to happen.

Hallie twisted her fingers together in her lap. She was only human; in a life with fewer than usual highlights and more than its share of restrictions, it was a disappointing change of plan, that was all.

Chapter 18

'Oh hi, is that Tasha? This is Joe, Rory's friend. Just calling to let you know he's absolutely *fine*.'

'Hello, Joe, you're lucky this is my favourite scarf,' Tasha replied patiently. 'Otherwise I might wrap it round your neck and strangle you with it.'

Joe cackled with laughter into his phone. The four of them were in the car heading down the M4 to Bristol. Rory was driving, Joe was in the passenger seat directly in front of Tasha, and Carmel was to her right, rolling her eyes and smiling despite herself, because although Joe's endless capacity for silly pranks drove her demented, he could be quite funny sometimes.

'*Aarrrghh*.' Joe clutched his throat as if Tasha had thrown her scarf around his neck and was pulling it tight, Bond-villain style.

'Bristol fifteen miles.' She pointed to the sign as it flashed by. 'Nearly there.'

'Great,' said Carmel. 'Just enough time to saw *almost* all the way through Joe's climbing rope.'

Some people had the oddest ideas of what constituted a good time. It was a freezing day in early February, with remnants of snow and frost on the ground, yet Rory and Joe were planning to spend the day climbing up the Avon Gorge and abseiling back down it.

The mad fools.

Tasha quelled her inner anxieties. Ah well, it took all sorts. She was determined to be brave this time, and at least she wouldn't have to watch. While the two boys were out in the cold, risking life and limb, she and Carmel were going to spend the day exploring Bristol, shopping in Clifton and enjoying a fantastic lunch.

When they reached the centre of Clifton, Rory pulled up to let them out before he and Joe headed off to the lay-by on the Portway where they were meeting up with the rest of the rock climbers. As Rory jumped out of the car, Tasha's phone began to ring with yet another unknown number.

'Hello?'

'Hi, this is Joe, just letting you know that Rory's jumped out of the car. *Ow*,' he added as Carmel leaned in and gave him a playful swipe around the ear.

'OK, have a good time.' Tasha lifted her face for a kiss from Rory. 'We'll see you in a bit.' Then, giving Joe a meaningful look, 'And no more prank calls, OK? Promise. Otherwise I'll never be able to relax.'

'OK.' Joe nodded, because beneath the teasing, he knew what she was like.

'Don't worry, I won't let him do it. We'll phone you when we're finished.' Rory gave her another hug and a kiss. 'You two have fun as well.'

Joe blew Carmel a teasing kiss. 'Don't forget, they do great food at the Town House on Whiteladies Road. You won't regret it if you go there.'

Carmel shrugged. 'Maybe we will, maybe we won't. We might find somewhere else we'd rather eat.'

Joe was grinning. 'I love it when you play hard to get.'

'And you have fun with your rock climbing,' Carmel replied smoothly. 'Break a leg. In fact, break as many as you like.'

'Honestly, you two.' Tasha shook her head at Carmel as the car disappeared from view. The bickering and sparring between them was endless, despite Carmel still insisting she wasn't attracted to Joe.

'I know. Let's not go to that restaurant, though. If we do, he'll just think he's won.'

Two hours later, having walked across the suspension bridge and back, explored Clifton village and the Downs and made their way down Blackboy Hill and Whiteladies Road, they came across the Town House restaurant.

The menu pinned up outside sounded fantastic. The smell was enticing. It was one o'clock, and the place was busy.

'Looks great,' said Tasha. Her stomach rumbled in agreement.

'There are loads of other restaurants,' Carmel pointed to one across the road. 'That one might be better.'

'This place might be booked up anyway. Shall I just see if they have a table?' When Carmel hesitated, Tasha said, 'We could always eat here and tell Joe we went somewhere else, if that'll make you happy.'

Honestly, mad or what? It was like being seventeen again.

There was a free table for two. There were seared scallops – Tasha's favourite – on the menu, and the lunchtime atmosphere was fun and buzzy. They ordered a bottle of wine.

'Cheers.' She clinked glasses with Carmel. 'While we're here, Rory and Joe are out in the cold, clinging to a sheer rock face. I know where I'd rather be.'

Carmel grinned. 'We win.'

An hour and a half later, they asked the waiter for the bill.

'No need to do that,' he told Tasha as she took out her credit card. 'The bill's been taken care of.'

'What? By who?' Carmel's head swivelled round as she searched the restaurant for a likely admirer.

'I believe it's a friend of yours, a gentleman called Joseph James.'

'Are you serious? Where *is* he?'

'He called the restaurant earlier, described what you were

both wearing and asked us to call him back if you turned up. We did, and he was delighted you had. He also gave us his card details to settle the bill.'

'Oh God,' wailed Carmel. 'That's so *annoying*.'

Tasha marvelled at her friend's definition of annoying. 'He bought us lunch. Is that so bad?'

'He'll think we came here because he told us to! He'll be so *smug*.'

'He's smug anyway,' said Tasha. 'But we're going shopping now, and it means we'll have more money to spend on clothes.'

They caught a cab back to Clifton village, ready to hit the shops with a vengeance. As Carmel paid the driver on Princess Victoria Street, Tasha's attention was caught by a girl with long auburn ringlets making her way past, lugging a red pet carrier. A tirade of outraged yowling was clearly audible from inside it. The girl, wearing jeans and a pink jacket, paused to lift the carrier to eye level and in a firm voice said, 'Jeremy, you're being embarrassing. Stop it.'

'They don't like being carted around in those things.' Her tongue loosened by unaccustomed lunchtime wine, Tasha added, 'My mum's cat was just the same. He once yowled in the car all the way from London to Manchester.'

The girl laughed. 'Jeremy would make a racket all the way from here to Timbuktu, he hates it so much. Don't you, sweetie?'

With his snub nose pressed against the plastic bars of the pet carrier and his green eyes radiating hatred, Jeremy hissed at them murderously.

'Come on, the quicker we get you to the vet, the quicker you can take your fury out on him.' The girl lowered the carrier and said with amusement, 'The joy of cats, eh?'

But she loved hers, you could tell. 'Good luck,' said Tasha.

'Thanks, I'm going to need it.' And with Jeremy still howling like a banshee inside his cage, the girl headed off down the street.

Carmel, having paid the taxi driver, was now gazing with rapt attention at the gorgeously lit display in the window right next to them. 'And now the shopping starts. Oh God, *look* at that amazing velvet scarf . . .'

The call came forty minutes later, while Tasha was in a changing cubicle trying on a midnight-blue silk dress. The cubicle was small and Carmel was standing outside it holding all their belongings when Tasha heard her own phone begin to ring.

'Can you get that? Is it Rory?' The zip on the side of this dress was tricky to do up. Twisting round and holding the edges together, Tasha wished she had three hands.

'Number unknown,' Carmel called back. 'Want me to answer it anyway?'

'Yes, go on. But if it's Joe, just hang up. He promised not to do it again.' If it was Joe messing about, she'd be furious.

'And if he's calling to gloat about the restaurant, I'll tell him we put three bottles of vintage champagne on his bill.' Pressing Answer, Carmel said, 'Hello?'

Two seconds later, she said, 'What the *hell*?'

Tasha opened the cubicle door. 'Is it Joe?'

'I don't know. I don't know who it is.' Baffled, Carmel turned on speakerphone so they could both hear what was going on. Tasha's first thought was that the noises sounded like the cat she'd heard earlier, but the human version.

'Could be some kids messing around,' Carmel suggested.

Maybe it was. Tasha took hold of the phone. 'Hello, who's there? What's going on?'

The muffled yells and shouts continued, interspersed with irregular crashes and scuffling sounds. Then someone bellowed, 'For fuck's sake, get me down, get me *down*. Is he OK?'

Tasha's blood ran cold, because that was unmistakably Joe's voice. And he was sounding frantic. Oh God, what had happened? Was he talking about Rory? Had something terr—

'Hold him, hold on to him, don't let him swing . . . someone call an ambulance . . .'

'Hello? *Hello!*' Grabbing the phone back from Tasha, Carmel shouted into it without success; with all the commotion going on, no one at the other end could hear them.

Nauseous and faint with terror, still half in and half out of the changing cubicle, Tasha listened to the sounds of yelling, scuffles and panic. Her overactive imagination was picturing Rory unconscious and dangling by a rope while blood poured from his head and splashed on to the rocks below. Something had clearly gone horribly wrong. He could even be dead. Oh God, this was more than she could *bear* . . .

Chapter 19

The pain was agonising, close to unbearable. Rory struggled to stay calm. One minute everything had been great, they'd been climbing the gorge and it was all going according to plan. Then one of the climbers above him slipped, dislodging a small piece of rock and letting out an inadvertent shout of alarm. If he hadn't looked up, Rory now knew, he would have been fine; the rock would have bounced off his safety helmet. Instead it had landed on his cheekbone and he'd simultaneously lost his own footing, saved by the climbing ropes from plunging a couple of hundred feet to the ground but not from slipping sideways beneath the overhang and crashing into the section of rock he'd just climbed.

Dazed and dangling, he felt the pain radiating through his body and knew at once what had happened. He'd experienced it before, following a ferocious rugby tackle at school. And if it hurt like hell now, this was nothing compared with the remedy.

People were yelling, calling instructions as the rescue team swung into action around him. Within minutes Rory found himself lowered to the ground, being efficiently checked over by a medic. The ambulance, they assured him, would be here any minute now. Behind the medic, he could see Joe saying to one of the other climbers, 'Fuck, I don't believe it.'

The other climber, visibly shaken, said, 'Look at his *face*.'

Rory knew only that there was some blood, not how much. Oh God, what had happened to his face?

The medic, crouched over him, murmured reassuringly, 'Don't worry, it's not as bad as it looks. You're just bleeding like a burst balloon. Ever dislocated your shoulder before?'

'When I was eighteen. Rugby tackle.' He sucked in the gas and air from the mask over his face.

'I'm going to try and put it back now. You OK with that?'

Rory took a couple of extra-deep breaths, nodded and braced himself. 'Go ahead.' It was going to hurt like hell, but the sooner it was done, the sooner it would be over.

'All right, here we go. Grit your teeth.'

Rory found himself enveloped in a whole new world of pain. He let out a gut-wrenching yell as the agony intensified, only dimly aware of his surroundings for the next few seconds as every synapse in his body reached its physical limit. In the furthest recesses of his mind he was grateful that at least Tasha wasn't here to witness the spectacle and hear him making noises like a wild animal caught in a trap.

'There, done,' said the medic.

And like magic, the pain was gone. Unbelievably, the ball had popped back into the socket and his shoulder was normal again. Well, sore obviously. But he was in one piece.

'Fuuuuuuuck,' Joe exhaled.

'Yep.' Weak with relief that the worst of it was over, Rory nodded. Fuck indeed. The sound of an ambulance siren grew louder and he closed his eyes.

Twenty minutes later, Rory had been checked over by the paramedics and was being helped into the ambulance. 'We need to let the girls know we'll be late picking them up. Can you call Tash?'

'OK.' Joe pulled his mobile out of the back pocket of his jeans.

'Don't scare her. When she answers, don't say straight away

122

that I've had an accident. Tell her I'm fine but I just need to go to the hospital for a check-up.'

'Right.' But Joe was frowning at his phone, evidently puzzled by something. As a faint noise emerged from it, he jumped and put it cautiously to his ear. 'Hello? Who's that?'

He was greeted by the sound of faint tinny shrieking.

'What? But I *didn't* call you. How long have you been listening? Well it's not my fault, my phone must have done it. Calm down, for crying out loud. Of course he's all right. Pass me over to Tasha.' Pulling a face at Rory, he said, 'God, that girl drives me nuts. You'd think I'd done it on purpose.'

'You're telling me they heard everything?' Rory winced at the thought of it.

'Yeah.' Now that the adrenalin-inducing panic was over, Joe broke into a grin. 'Including you screaming like a girl.'

It was midnight by the time they arrived home, marking the end of one of the most fraught days of Tasha's life. Joe had driven them back to London, dropping Carmel off first, then Rory and herself.

In the bathroom of her flat, Rory studied his reflection in the mirror.

'Does it hurt?' Next to him, Tasha surveyed the damage. If it had looked bad before, it was worse now. Over the last few hours, the side of his face had ballooned, the bruises already livid cranberry and purple. His left eye was swollen shut, the stitches holding together the cut on his cheekbone looked tight and spiky, and the collar of his shirt on that side was soaked in dried blood. His popped-back left shoulder was in a sling to make sure it stayed that way.

'No.' Rory shook his head.

'That's not true.' Did he think she was stupid?

'It hurts a bit. Compared with getting the shoulder sorted, this is nothing.'

123

She gave him a look. 'So at least you'll never go rock climbing again. That's something.'

'I might. I probably will.' Rory's gaze met hers in the mirror. 'Until this happened, it was brilliant. I was loving every minute.'

'Seriously?' Tasha didn't know whether to laugh or cry. Having to listen in on the phone to the yelling and panic surrounding the accident had almost finished her off; at one stage in the clothes shop, the terror and sense of helplessness had caused her legs to give way.

'It was a one-off accident. There's no reason why anything like that would ever happen again.' His tone reassuring, Rory put his good arm around her waist. 'You're only upset because Joe's mobile called you by mistake.'

The irony of the situation hadn't escaped Tasha. Last time, she'd given him grief because he hadn't bothered to keep in touch. This time, she'd been kept too much in touch.

Either way, it seemed, her overactive imagination was destined to keep her in a state of terror.

'You still could have died,' she pointed out.

'Hey. We were out *doing* something. I could have stayed at home and not got out of bed all day. It'd be safer.' He shrugged. 'But that's not what living's about, is it?'

'You're an adrenalin junkie.'

Rory nodded. 'I am.'

'And you're never going to give up doing all this . . . stuff.'

'True.' He searched her face. 'Can you handle that?'

Tasha quaked inwardly, because this was what it was all about, wasn't it? Basically, she had two choices. Either stop seeing Rory and consequently stop worrying about him, or carry on seeing him and accept the associated terms and conditions.

'I'm not going to stop seeing you,' she told him. She saw the relief on the undamaged side of his face. 'I can't.'

'Good.' His expression softened. 'Well, thank God for that.'

'Wouldn't it be just the height of irony, though, if worrying myself sick about you caused *me* to have some kind of stress-related stroke or heart attack?'

Rory kissed her. 'It would, but it's never going to happen.'

'It had better not.' Forcing herself to relax, Tasha smiled and kissed him on the mouth. 'Because I'm telling you now, if it does happen and I end up dead, I'll be *so cross*.'

Chapter 20

'OK, so we got all excited when you told us about this new man of yours, and that was four weeks ago now.' Bridget leaned across the restaurant table and gave Flo a you-can-tell-us eyebrow raise. 'So why haven't you seen him since?'

'You know what I think?' said Annie. 'I reckon he doesn't exist. He's Flo's fantasy boyfriend, she just made him up.'

Flo was used to being single and teased about it by her workmates. Bridget had a husband, five children and many grandchildren. Annie, divorced, was having the time of her life internet dating, and Mavis had just married for the third time. The four of them had come out tonight to this restaurant in Redland to celebrate Bridget's upcoming sixtieth birthday.

When Bridget had first invited all her colleagues at Nairn House, the younger contingent had hastily made their excuses, preferring to spend their precious Friday night out clubbing and drinking themselves senseless with people their own age. Flo, who had actually been invited to a party in Bath, had felt sorry for poor Bridget when she'd seen how many of the others were dropping out.

Which was how she'd come to find herself here this evening instead. With three women all old enough to have given birth to her.

Oh well, maybe not a wild party night, but still quite fun and nice in its own way. And at least the food was good.

'He had to go to Toronto,' she explained patiently. 'On business. He thought it would only be for a couple of weeks, but it's taken longer than they expected.' She'd told them this before, but her workmates liked to make fun of her.

'He's found himself another girlfriend over there,' Annie gleefully announced. 'That's what happened, I reckon.'

'Maybe he has. And I'm not his girlfriend anyway,' said Flo. 'We just spent one evening together. I liked him. And he seemed to like me. But that's all it is.'

Inside her brain, a little voice whispered hopefully, *So far . . .*

'Did you sleep with him?' Bridget, who was nothing if not blunt, wagged an admonishing finger. 'You should never sleep with 'em on a first date. That's just giving it away.'

'I didn't sleep with him! And it wasn't a date.' *Honestly, these women.*

'Was there kissing?'

'I'm not going to say.' Flo felt her cheeks heat up.

'There was kissing,' Mavis cackled. 'Tongues?'

'Mavis!'

'Ah, look at her, she's gone all red. Bless!' Predictably they found this hilarious.

Ever the optimist, Annie said, 'Perhaps he came back from Toronto two weeks ago and just hasn't told you.'

'That could be it.' Flo smiled. Zander had texted her yesterday to say he would definitely be coming home on Wednesday, and they'd already arranged to meet up that evening. Although she wouldn't share this bit of news with them, seeing as their nosiness and capacity for asking intimate questions would only go into overdrive.

'I've forgotten his name now.' Bridget frowned. 'Ooh, what was it? I know it's something posh . . .'

'Percival. Quentin. Boris! Ooh, I love a posh name, I do,' Mavis said with relish. 'Peregrine! Tarquin!'

'*Zander.*' Annie had remembered it. Triumphantly, she put on a posh voice. 'Oh *Zaaaarnder*, what are you doing hiding away in Toronto? Do you have any idea how long Flo's been waiting for a boyfriend? She's *desperate* for you!'

A Bristolian born and bred, Annie had a strong local accent but a gift for mimicry, and her voices always made them laugh. Bridget was spluttering wine and Mavis was whacking her on the back when the door to the restaurant swung open, bringing in a gust of cold air and two more diners.

Flo stopped laughing abruptly when she saw who had just come in.

Oh God, *Lena*.

'What's up?' Annie was following the line of her horrified gaze. 'Who are you looking at? Don't tell me that's Zaaarnder?'

'*Sshhh.*' Flo shook her head and pulled an anguished face at the three women. 'Don't say anything. *It's his sister.*'

Like Wimbledon spectators, three heads turned to look at Lena, who was removing her black coat and handing it to the waiter. She was wearing a slim-fitting emerald-green dress and black suede stilettos; with her make-up perfectly applied and her hair pulled back in a sleek ballerina bun, she looked amazing.

'Wow.' Evidently thinking the same, Annie murmured under her breath, 'Does Zander look like that?'

'Well, he doesn't wear high heels and make-up,' Flo murmured back. 'But otherwise, yes.'

And she couldn't help feeling a bit proud of the fact that they were visibly impressed.

'So hang on, is this the nutty one who wants to kill Jeremy?' said Mavis.

'Yes.' Flo pressed a finger to her lips, because the waiter was now leading Lena and her dinner date into the dining room. 'Sshh.'

Then she looked at Lena's companion for the first time, and almost dropped her fork.

What, really?

128

No way.

But it was, it *was* him. And how ironic, when they'd just been making fun of Zander's posh name.

Because who should Lena be having dinner with? Why, none other than tomato-soup Giles. And typically, the waiter was leading them to the table right next to their own.

Flo held her breath. It wasn't until she'd been seated and had made herself comfortable that Lena glanced across and saw her.

Talk about a double-take.

'Good lord, it's you. What are you doing here?'

What did she seriously expect by way of an answer? *Oh, this is where we come to do our aerobics class . . .*

'Just having dinner with my friends,' replied Flo.

Lena's pale blue gaze took in every detail, from Bridget's hand-knitted peach cardigan to Annie's wrinkled cleavage to Mavis's overenthusiastic application of shimmery violet eyeshadow.

'Right. I see.' She turned to address Giles, lowering her voice but not enough. 'I thought it might be some kind of geriatric hen night.'

Annie raised her eyebrows in disbelief. Flo shook her head fractionally, indicating that a stand-up fight here in their favourite restaurant might not be ideal. Luckily, her friends had heard all about Lena, and thanks to their jobs were capable of handling rudeness with humour and grace.

'I see what you mean,' Mavis murmured under her breath. 'What a charmer.'

'She's the one I told you about,' Lena was now explaining to Giles. 'The one looking after that damn cat.'

'Right.' Giles, Flo realised, was giving her a speculative look. 'You know, I'm sure I know her from somewhere. I've definitely seen her before.'

Whoops, this could be interesting. Flo turned her attention to the food on her plate. She'd been sober that evening, so recognising Jaaahls had been easy. Whereas he'd been drinking, which had presumably reduced his own memories to a murky haze.

Oh, but awful though she was in her own way, surely even Lena would be appalled if she knew what an obnoxious lowlife her dining companion really was.

'We'll kick off with a bottle of Saint-Émilion,' Giles told the waiter. 'And I'll have a lager too. Bring them both straight away, yeah?'

'*Please,*' Mavis prompted under her breath, marvelling at his lack of manners.

'You.' Giles clicked his fingers, and Flo realised he was doing it to attract her attention. 'It's bugging me now. Do you work in one of the pubs in Clifton?'

'Me? No.' Flo shook her head.

'Are you in business banking?'

'Of course she isn't.' Lena said it with a mixture of amusement and scorn. 'I told you before, she wipes old people's backsides for a living in a care home. Eurgh.' She shuddered with revulsion. 'I don't know how people can bear to do that. Turns my stomach just to think of it.'

Next to Flo, Annie said, 'Just as well we aren't all as sensitive as you, then, isn't it? There's always going to be people whose backsides need wiping.' Flashing Lena and Giles a sunny smile, she added, 'Could be you one day.'

Lena grimaced at the awfulness of this prospect. Giles said, 'True, true, and good for you. We're grateful to people like you for doing those sorts of jobs.'

'I know.' Annie nodded pleasantly, but there was an edge to her voice. 'And aren't we lucky? Sometimes our employers even pay us minimum wage.'

'Mesdames? M'sieur? Ees everything all right?' Having noticed the interaction between the tables, the maître d' had materialised to ensure all was well.

'*Bof, ça va,*' Flo replied politely. '*Ils manquent un peu de charme*

130

*et des manières mais vous inquiétez pas, nous pouvons le surmonter.
Il est simplement ignorant et condescendant; pourtant nous habituons
aux personnes comme ça. Aussi nous avons presque fini notre dîner,
vingt minutes de plus et nous allons partir.'*

Basically, she'd told him all was well, they could easily cope
with two people lacking in charm and manners, and in twenty
minutes they'd be out of here anyway. Saying it fast hopefully
meant Lena and Giles wouldn't be able to work out what she'd
said.

'*Ah, oui. Merci, madame, merci beaucoup.* And I completely agree
with you about the manners.' The maitre d' smiled, tilted his
head at Flo and moved away. He hadn't indiscreetly said the
final sentence in English, of course; he'd still been speaking
French.

And the look on Lena and Giles's faces was gratifying.

'Are you *French*?' Lena was now staring at Flo in disbelief.

'No.'

'So how do you know how to speak it?'

'I learned at school. Then learned a bit more at university.'

Lena looked as if she'd swallowed a hedgehog.

'And what did you just say to that bloke?'

'Nothing much, just told him everything was fine and how
much we were enjoying our evening. The food's great here.
Such a brilliant chef . . .'

Giles was still watching her, clearly puzzling over where he
knew her from. Flo turned back to Bridget, Annie and Mavis,
and the waiter approached Lena and Giles's table with their
menus.

Only half listening, Flo heard him say to them, 'I can recom-
mend the mussels, which are excellent tonight and are cooked
in either white wine and cream or a marinara sauce. And the
soup of the day is cauliflower with toasted almonds.'

'Ugh,' said Lena, her mouth shrivelling in disgust. 'That sounds
awful, I can't stand cauliflower. Cauliflower is rank.'

Such lovely diners. Honestly, this restaurant's so lucky to have them.

Then Flo saw the expression on Giles's pudgy face; he was frowning into his drink, lost in thought, his memory inadvertently nudged by the waiter into almost remembering what had been troubling him up until now.

'Soup . . .' Muttering the word, he raised his head.

'Oh Jaaahls, don't have the soup, just the smell of it'll make me want to be sick!'

Almost there now. Flo readied herself. Finally Giles was staring directly at her once more, like a bull.

'It was you,' he said slowly. 'It was you, wasn't it? Who threw the soup at me.'

'What?' Lena put down her menu. 'What in God's name are you talking about?'

'Yes.' Flo nodded at Giles. 'It was me.'

'OK, I don't know what's going on here. When did she throw soup at you? Was this in another restaurant?' Lena glared at Flo as if she might have had the temerity to be working as a waitress.

'Not in a restaurant. Out in the street,' said Giles. 'I'd never seen her before in my life. She just turned into a complete madwoman and started yelling abuse at me. Next thing I knew, she'd ripped the lid off a can of soup and fucking chucked it all over me. Tomato, it was. My Dolce and Gabbana shirt was completely fucked. Five hundred quid, that shirt cost me.'

Flo raised her eyebrows. 'You said four hundred last time.'

'Are you serious?' Her eyes out on stalks, Lena was quivering with outrage. 'She just did that to you in the street for no reason at all? When did this happen? I hope you called the police and had her arrested.' Shaking her head, she turned to Flo. 'What are you, completely deranged? My God, and you're living in our flat – it's *so* unfair! If my grandmother had known what you were like, she'd *never* have let you move in!'

Luckily it wasn't the kind of restaurant where all the diners

132

suddenly fell silent; other conversations were carrying on and there was enough noise in the room to ensure they weren't the centre of attention. Which made it possible for Flo to say evenly, 'It happened a few weeks ago and I didn't do it for no reason at all. There was a homeless man outside the pub and your friend here thought it would be amusing to stand in front of him burning a fifty-pound note.'

There, she'd said it. Lena deserved to know the ugly truth about her dining companion. So what if Giles was mortified at being publicly outed? He deserved it. And yes, Lena's eyes were widening in disbelief and—

'Bwahahahahaha, bloody funny.' Spluttering into his drink, Giles grinned at Lena. 'Always good for a laugh, that one. The old jokes are the best. *Bloody* funny . . .'

So much for being mortified. But surely by now even Lena would be ashamed of him.

Except she didn't appear to be. The momentary flicker of dismay − a suggestion of actual humanity − had vanished, and she was now back to gazing adoringly at Giles, a smile playing on her lips. When he burst out laughing once more, she said brightly, 'Oh, I know that one, Peregrine Hamilton-Carr did it the morning after the Blue Moon Ball . . . *hilarious*!'

'I know, right?' Giles rocked back in his chair, eyes streaming with mirth. 'Comedy gold!'

Flo shook her head; Lena was evidently one of those yes girls, the kind that would never dream of criticising their boyfriend, choosing instead to go along with anything and everything he said.

'Oh my God, what a dick,' said Annie.

'And she's acting like he just won an Olympic medal,' said Bridget.

'For prize dickery,' Mavis snorted.

'I just thought of something.' Annie clutched Flo's arm. 'If you and Zander end up getting married, that means—'

'What?' Lena had jerked round to stare at them. '*What* did you just say? OK, how do you even know about my brother, and why would he ever end up marrying *her*?'

Whoops. Flo froze. OK, this definitely wasn't meant to be happening. Was there any way out of it?

But she'd underestimated Annie, who was speedy when it counted.

'Excuse me? What are you talking about? I have no idea who your brother is.' She shook her head at Lena, signalling bafflement. 'I'm talking about how brilliant it'd be if Flo marries my son.'

'Your son.' Lena had already noted Annie's overbleached hair, exuberant dress sense and purple nail polish. Having listened to her strong Bristolian accent and cackling laugh, she was evidently sceptical, to say the least. 'You're seriously telling me your son is called Zander?'

'Only my eldest son,' said Annie. 'The others are called Tristram and Tarquin.' She glanced down at her cleavage and brushed away a few focaccia crumbs before returning her attention to Lena. 'You can't call them all Zander, can you? That would be stupid.'

'Oh my God, how much of a wally is that guy? And what a cow *she* is!' They'd spilled out of the restaurant, laughing and clutching each other in hysterics. Gasping for breath, Bridget said, 'Did you see her face when Annie reeled off those names? I thought I was going to wet myself.'

'D'you reckon she believed me?' Annie, whose sons were actually called Lee, Dennis and Jason, mimicked Lena's voice. 'But how can your children *possibly* have names like that when you're so *common*?'

Flo said, 'She doesn't know what to think now, not after you told her your real dad was an earl. You were so convincing. Even I almost believed you.'

'My mum used to be in service. She worked as an under

housemaid at Kilburton Castle.' Annie snorted with laughter. 'She used to say I was the earl's daughter, making out it was a joke, but knowing her, I reckon it was true.'

'You should wear a tiara,' said Bridget. 'All day, every day.'

'While I'm busy wiping other people's bums.' Annie pulled a face at the memory of Lena's disgust. 'Bloody hell, Flo, I hope this Zander bloke's nicer than his sister.'

'He is.' Flo nodded as they made their way towards the taxi rank on Whiteladies Road. 'Much nicer.'

'Well, good, but you're going to have your work cut out if you two carry on seeing each other. How will you cope? That sister of his doesn't like you one bit.'

'It's early days.' There was a fluttery sensation in Flo's throat. 'Way too soon to be worrying about things getting serious.' She added flippantly, 'Like you said, he might already have found someone else in Canada.'

'I know, but I'm just saying. She's a piece of work, that one.'

'Except she doesn't *do* any work.' Flo grinned, briefly imagining herself and Zander getting married, with Lena dressed as a bridesmaid with a malevolent gleam in her eye and a gun hidden behind her back.

'Well, good luck. But I don't envy you,' said Annie. 'She's not going to make life easy for you. That one's a witch.'

Chapter 21

Dear Rose,

    I love gardening.

    I'm shy with strangers.

    One day I want to surprise everyone by doing something unexpected and amazing, so I can be proud of myself.

    My husband was the love of my life until he left me suddenly three years ago for another woman. I was devastated and thought I'd never get over it, but I kind of have. I'd like to meet a new man but can't see that ever happening, because who would want me? I'm hardly a catch. So my life is quite boring, but it's OK, I'm used to being on my own now.

    The thing is, I bumped into him in town yesterday and we ended up going for a coffee. He's not happy with his girlfriend and says he misses me. He wants to come over to my flat on Friday night. Just for sex, basically. I know, not very romantic, is it? I should really tell him to get lost. I don't love him any more, I know that now, but I do miss being intimate with a man and it would kind of make up for the fact that when he left me three years ago I had no warning it was going to happen.

    Rose, I'm so tempted, but would it make me feel miserable all over again? He's already hinted that it could become a regular arrangement (his girlfriend thinks he goes out to play darts every Friday night, but he doesn't).

Help me, please. What should I do?

Julia

Dear Julia,

You sound strong to me. Your ex-husband sounds weak. He knocked your self-confidence and it took a while for you to get back on your feet.

Now, I'm sure most advice-givers would tell you to turn him down flat because you're better than he is and he doesn't deserve the opportunity to hurt you again. Nor does he deserve sex.

This is all true, but I think you *do* deserve sex. You deserve closure. He took your love life away from you without warning. If you can make a pact with yourself that it will only happen once, I really do think you should sleep with him for that one last time. Then, afterwards, tell him it's over for good. Use him like he hoped to use you. Get your own back on him and grow in confidence as a result. You already know he's a pathetic excuse for a man and you deserve better. Hammer that last nail into the coffin of your relationship. It's what Madonna would do, isn't it? Oh, and make sure he uses a condom too.

Do the unexpected, be amazing and surprise yourself. Set yourself free.

Then move on triumphantly with your new life!

Love,

Rose xxx

'Spot on. Couldn't agree more,' announced Margot, having finished reading. 'What a snake. Get your own back on him, girl!' Her dark eyes were glittering. 'Can't beat a bit of closure.'

'I hope we get an update.' Flo was watering the house plants lined up along the windowsill of Margot's apartment; sometimes people got back in touch to let Rose and her readers know what was now happening in their lives.

'Sooner rather than later, preferably. Don't want to pop my clogs and still be waiting to hear how she's doing.' Margot tilted her head to one side like a bird, surveying Flo with interest. 'Have you had a haircut?'

'Just a trim.'

'And a colour?'

'Semi-permanent. It's called Autumn Leaves.' Pleased, Flo swished her ringlets from side to side. 'D'you like it?'

'I do, very much. And you've had your eyebrows tinted too.'

'It was the hairdresser's idea.'

'Nice. This is for a special occasion, I take it.'

'Possibly.' Flo smiled and put down the watering can.

'Your chap back from Toronto at last, is he?'

My chap . . .

'His plane landed this morning. I'm seeing him tonight.'

Margot said, 'D'you suppose he'll have had his eyebrows tinted to impress you too?'

'His are black already.' Unable to help herself, Flo said, 'Honestly, you should see them. He has amazing eyebrows.'

'Ah, look at you. You're glowing.' Margot added cheerfully, 'And you're lovely too, never forget that. He's a lucky chap.'

'Hi,' said Zander when Flo pulled open the front door.

'Hi.' Was she beaming like an idiot? Oh, but it was so wonderful to see him again.

'I'm back.'

'I noticed.'

He was nodding admiringly. 'You look great.'

'Thanks. I had my eyebrows tinted and I'm still getting used to them. Every time I catch sight of myself in the mirror I get

138

a shock.' OK, babbling now, time to stop before she heard herself blurting out that she'd had her legs waxed too.

'I like your eyebrows.' Zander was smiling. 'I like you. I've missed you.'

His words made her quiver; it was the perfect thing to say. Her skin prickling with anticipation, she breathed in the scent of Zander's body, his aftershave, his leather jacket. And then he kissed her and all was right with the world . . .

Well, almost all.

Drawing away a minute later, she rested her hands on his shoulders. 'Sorry, but I have to ask. Have you spoken to Lena yet?'

'Yes. She told me what happened last week. Was it awful?'

'Put it this way, she's not happy with me. Is Giles her new boyfriend?'

Zander looked resigned. 'Seems like it.'

'He's pretty ghastly.'

'Ah well, that's my sister for you. Line up a row of potential men and you can guarantee Lena'll go for the most obnoxious one. It's like a moth to a flame.'

'Did she manage to lock herself out of the flat while you were away?'

Zander grimaced. 'A couple of times. I had to leave spare keys with all the neighbours. Anyway, can we not talk about my sister just now? I've been looking forward to this evening. Let's not spoil it.'

When the clock struck midnight, they were lying wrapped in each other's arms in Flo's bed. Was this too soon? It probably was, but it didn't feel too soon. This had been one of the most magical evenings of her life.

'What are you thinking?' said Zander.

'I'm thinking I'm really glad I had my legs waxed.'

He laughed. 'Most girls wouldn't say that.'

'I know. It's why I'm still single.'

Still laughing, Zander pulled her to him and kissed her on the nose. 'They wouldn't say that either.'

At that moment they heard a peremptory scratching at the door, followed by a series of miaows.

'It's Jeremy's bedtime,' said Flo. 'He won't give up until we let him in.'

She watched as Zander got out of bed, crossed the room and opened the door. *Nice body.*

Jeremy stalked past him, jumped up on to the end of the bed and settled himself down, facing Flo and radiating disapproval.

'Looks like our time's up,' Zander observed as he climbed back in.

Jeremy blinked and slowly swished his tail.

Flo said, 'It's like having Ann Widdecombe sitting on your bed, making sure there's no hanky-panky going on.'

'He's spent his whole life living with my grandmother. He doesn't know what hanky-panky is.'

Beneath the duvet, Flo jiggled her foot and gave the cat a playful nudge. 'Come on, Jeremy, cheer up, no need to be so grumpy.'

Jeremy's baleful gaze was unwavering. He clearly had no intention of forgiving her.

'We'll work something out,' said Zander.

'It may involve moving into the spare room.'

'Well we can't go to my flat, that's for sure. If it's a toss-up between having to cope with Jeremy's disapproval or Lena's, I know which I'd prefer.'

'Are you going to tell her about . . . us?' Oh help, was that horrifically presumptuous? Was there even an *us*? Who knew, maybe now that he'd effortlessly seduced her, she wouldn't see him for dust.

'Don't look like that. I'm not going anywhere.' Reading her mind, Zander lifted her hand to his mouth and kissed the back of it. 'This is just the beginning. But we both know what Lena's like. When she finds out, she isn't going to make things easy. For now, I'd rather keep it just between us. Trust me, it'll be more relaxed all round.'

Flo nodded and said fervently, 'I think so too.'

But inside her chest, happiness was bubbling up like a garden fountain. *Look, it's me and Zander, we're a couple . . . we're an us!*

Chapter 22

When making yourself a bacon sandwich really took it out of you, you knew you were in a bad way.

Although Hallie was already aware of that. Last week she'd gone into hospital for yet another routine check-up and had seen her figures. Full blood count, oxygen saturation and lung function tests, X-rays and IV assessments . . . basically, all the results were worse.

At least it hadn't come as a surprise. When you lived with cystic fibrosis, you knew you were never going to wake up in the morning miraculously cured.

But to see the numbers and understand the degree to which you'd deteriorated wasn't a cheery experience. Her exercise tolerance was markedly reduced. Her sats were 90 per cent. Extra physio had been less effective than before. The insides of her lungs felt spiky and sore, and the stealthy, depressing inevitability of it all caused her to be ambushed, sometimes, by great waves of sadness.

Don't be a whiner, she told herself. *Concentrate on the good things in life, even if there don't seem to be too many of them left.*

Luckily, a bacon sandwich definitely counted as a good thing. Disconnecting herself from the oxygen supply in the kitchen, Hallie carried the plate through to the living room, reconnected her nasal specs to the oxygen supply in there and sat down on the sofa to watch the rest of *Starter for 10*.

The heat from the crispy bacon had melted the butter, giving the fresh white bread just the right amount of squidginess. Oh yes, this was a world-class sandwich. As she picked it up and prepared to take that heavenly first bite, the doorbell rang.

Oh please. Did people like to spy on her with binoculars and do it on purpose?

Just ignore the door and eat the sandwich.

But the moment would be spoiled, Hallie knew; she wouldn't be able to enjoy it if all she was doing was waiting for the bell to ring a second time.

Ooh, and it might be the postman with those new ankle boots she'd ordered from ASOS.

She put the sandwich down, disconnected the oxygen tubing once more and got slowly to her feet.

The doorbell rang again.

OK, after all this it had *better* be her ankle boots.

It wasn't.

It was even browner than the ankle boots.

It was Nick.

He was grinning, holding his arms out to her, his teeth dazzling white in contrast with his ridiculously deep tan. In an over-the-top stab at an Australian accent he said, 'Hey, sport, how ya doin'? Ya got a face on ya like a wallaby on a tightrope.'

Amazed, Hallie said, 'I don't believe it.'

'It's true! Have ya never *seen* a wallaby on a tightrope?' Dropping the accent, he stepped forward and enveloped her in a hug. 'How are you? Surprised to see me?'

'Just a bit. And you want to watch it; I'm an invalid, you know. I could drop dead from this kind of shock.'

'Sorry, I wanted to see the look on your face. Oh Hal . . .' Ushering her inside, out of the cold, he touched her cheek and stroked an index finger along the line of her jaw. 'It's so good to see you again.'

'Well I'm still here. Just about. Come on, I need my oxygen.'

143

Hallie led the way into the living room and plugged herself back in. 'What are you doing back in the UK?'

It was six years since they'd broken up, two years since she'd last seen him.

'Flying visit to the parents. Dad's had a gall bladder op and Mum wanted me to come back for a few days. But I flew into Birmingham so I thought I'd swing by and see you before shooting on up to Manchester.'

'It's out of your way.' He was going to have to double back to Birmingham before heading home.

'Hey, I've hired a fast car. And once you've lived in Australia, you get used to long journeys. Anything less than a six-hour drive is nothing at all . . . Jesus, what is *that* thing out there?'

He was pointing at something through the window. By the time Hallie realised she'd succumbed to the oldest trick in the book, the bacon sandwich was in his hand.

'I can't believe you fell for it.' Nick shook his head pityingly.

'Me neither.' Distraction followed by food theft had always been a game they'd played. 'I'm out of practice.'

'Here.' He offered her the sandwich back. 'To be honest, if you were about to eat this, I'm amazed you even came to the door.'

'I nearly didn't. It's OK, you can have a bite. Seeing as you've come all the way from Australia.'

Nick shook his head. 'You have first bite. It's your sandwich.'

'Correct answer.' Hallie bit into it with relish whilst Nick watched her with a smile on his face. And maybe the bacon was no longer as hot as it might have been, but it was still delicious.

When it was time for Nick to eat his share, she sat and watched him in turn. His lean, rangy limbs were the same, his blond hair as messy as it had always been. He'd just flown from

144

the other side of the world, but you wouldn't know it; in his white T-shirt, soft grey sweater and battered old jeans he looked just as he always had. Only the smell of him was different.

Aware of her gaze, Nick said, 'What?'

'You've changed your aftershave.'

'This?' He sniffed his wrist and pulled a face. 'I tried it in duty-free. Makes me smell like a used car salesman. Seems like it's got stronger since I put it on.'

'That's what happens. The more you don't like it, the stronger it smells.' Hallie smiled. 'But you look just the same.'

'So do you.' Having finished off the sandwich, he put down the empty plate and gave her hand a squeeze.

'Thanks.' Touched, Hallie added, 'But we both know that's not true.'

'OK, maybe not, but when I look at you, I just see . . . *you*.' He reached up and lightly touched her nose. 'I see your freckles, the shape of your cheeks, the way your eyelashes curl at the corners, the way your mouth moves when you smile. And as for your eyes . . . they're never going to change. You still have the best eyes I've ever seen.'

'If this is your way of telling me you'd like another bacon sandwich,' said Hallie, 'you're going to have to make it yourself.'

'That's not why I said those things.' He winked at her. 'But now you come to mention it . . .'

In the kitchen, she sat at the table while Nick made them both mugs of tea and fried up the rest of the bacon. He told her stories about his adventures in Australia. She told him less exciting ones about her life in Carranford. Nick called home and told his parents he'd be with them by nine o'clock.

At two thirty, Hallie said, 'It's time for me to do my meds and physio.'

'No problem.' He sniffed his wrist and the sleeve of his sweater

145

again. 'Actually, can I ask a favour? Would it be OK if I had a shower while I'm here? Clean myself up a bit and get rid of this bloody awful aftershave?'

'No problem. You know where the bathroom is,' said Hallie. 'Help yourself.'

Nick went out to the car, collected his wash bag and a change of clothes from his suitcase and disappeared upstairs while Hallie set out her meds. She also made the discovery that once an idea had worked its way into your brain, it was next to impossible to think about anything else.

It was like being haunted by the catchiest tune ever.

OK, stop thinking about it.

But I just caaaaan't.

It was, she knew, partly to do with the last letter she'd replied to on the website. Poor rejected Julia, abandoned by her husband and in need of closure.

And sex.

And revenge.

But mainly closure.

And sex.

Hallie got on with doing her meds, but the idea was still refusing to go away. Who knew how long she had left to live? Not long, the way things were going and if time ran out before a suitable donor could be found.

For the last year, the only man she could have imagined sleeping with was the one man she couldn't have a relationship with. Basically she'd kind of assumed that, given her situation, that was it on the sex front. There wouldn't be any more. The window of opportunity had passed her by without her even realising that the last time had indeed been *the* last time.

Sad, but it couldn't be helped.

Except, except . . . what if the window of opportunity had just unexpectedly opened again?

Upstairs, the shower was still running. A handsome man was

currently standing under it naked, shampoo and soap suds sliding down his beautiful tanned body.

Better still, it was a body she already knew and was familiar with, belonging to a good friend who in turn was familiar with hers.

Chapter 23

It took Hallie another hour to pluck up the courage to say it.
In the end, she just blurted the words out.

'I have a favour to ask you. It's OK, you can say no if you
want. I won't be offended.'

'Anything.' Nick didn't hesitate. 'What is it? Do you need
money?'

'No, it's more personal than that. This is to do with me . . .'
she gestured helplessly, 'and my . . . situation.'

Nick seized her hand and gazed into her eyes. 'Go ahead.
Don't look so nervous.' He lowered his voice. 'Is it to do with
your funeral? Do you want me to stand up and speak? Because
that's fine, of course I'll do it—'

'Whoa, stop, that's not what I wanted to ask you. *Sshh.*'
Hallie put her other hand up to his mouth as he opened it
to hazard another guess. 'Stop interrupting and listen. You're
leaving at six. My mum's out at work and won't be back
before six thirty. We're home alone. There's no one else I
could ask to do this, but there's something I just miss so
much. Do you remember how we used to lie in bed together,
skin to skin . . . don't worry, I'm not talking about sex now,
just the being together thing, because, you know, it would
feel so nice . . . and it'd make me feel normal again, just for

148

a bit . . . but it's OK, you don't have to if you don't want to. I'll understand.'

Halfway through the garbled explanation, her eyes had begun to fill up and tears were sliding down her face. Hallie, who hardly ever cried, brushed them away and knew that it was due to embarrassment. That was why she'd changed the request to just lying in bed together. Begging for sex, it turned out, was just too much to ask. Poor Nick, was he frantically trying to come up with some kind of reasonable excuse for not having to do it?

Then she saw that his eyes were glistening too. The next moment, he was on his feet, reaching out for her, unplugging her oxygen and lifting her into his strong arms. 'You have all the best ideas,' he said simply. 'Come on. There's nothing I'd like more.'

Upstairs, he laid her down on the bed and closed the curtains. Hallie reconnected herself to her bedroom oxygen supply and slowly undressed down to her knickers. Nick helped her, then removed his own clothes, keeping on only his Calvin Klein trunks.

Then he climbed into bed beside her, pulled the duvet over them both and, mindful of the plastic tubing, wrapped his arms around her.

Hallie felt as if she were on fire; her whole body had become hypersensitive now. The sensation of his warm skin touching hers was just indescribably wonderful. This, *this* was what she'd been missing out on for so long. Simple, honest-to-goodness physical contact, taken completely for granted by so many people, yet almost more perfect in its own way than anything else.

She traced her fingertips over his back, his shoulders, his arms, and felt Nick's hands doing the same. It was heavenly. This was how happiness felt. A never-ending embrace, the scent of freshly soaped skin, the heat emanating from his body and warming hers, like the sun . . .

Nick's mouth brushed against her ear as he murmured, 'Is this the kind of thing you meant?'

'Exactly the kind of thing I meant. Thank you.'

'Hallie, listen, don't thank me. But there's something I need to tell you.'

Her hands were still hypnotically stroking his chest. 'Go on.'

'I don't know if you wanted to carry on further, but I just have to say, I have a girlfriend.'

Hallie blinked. 'Oh. Right. You didn't mention her before.' And she stupidly hadn't asked.

'I know. I didn't want to sound . . . well, you know, as if I was boasting about my great life while yours isn't so great. Her name's Emma and we've been seeing each other for the last couple of months. She's a lovely girl. I suppose what I'm trying to say is, I've been faithful to her and I wouldn't want to upset her, but if you want us to continue . . . well, I will.'

'You would? You'd do that for me?'

Nick exhaled. 'Oh Hallie. It's not like I wouldn't enjoy it too. But it's your choice.'

She smiled and brushed his cheek, touched by the offer and by his honesty. 'Thanks, but it's fine, really. Just this is fine. And it wouldn't feel right, making you do that to Emma.'

To her surprise, it was the truth. At the back of her mind, too, she'd kind of wondered if sleeping with Nick might feel like cheating on Luke.

Yes, it was a weird thing to think, but she couldn't help the way her brain worked.

'You know, Emma's such a nice person, she might even understand,' said Nick. 'I've told her all about you. She knew I was coming to see you today.'

'I think that would be a really big ask. Don't worry. This is enough.' In all honesty, poor Emma-in-Australia probably wouldn't be thrilled about the fact that they were lying practically naked together in bed.

'OK. We can just stay here like this.' Sliding his arm around her, Nick said, 'Rest your head on my shoulder. Just relax. I'm not going to let you go. Remember this is how we used to fall asleep?'

Smiling, Hallie nodded. Now that she knew nothing more was going to happen, she was actually far more relaxed. This was nice, this was what she'd missed, the sheer comfort of physical contact. She closed her eyes and nodded again, feeling Nick's hands gently stroking her shoulders and the back of her neck as she drifted off to sleep . . .

Luke knocked on Hallie's front door. It was five o'clock and dark outside, and the house seemed silent too. There was no sign of movement. Had she gone out? Maybe he should just slide the book through the letter box . . .

Above him, curtains were pulled back, and silhouetted against the dim light in Hallie's bedroom he saw a figure that . . . well, it wasn't Hallie. Taken aback, Luke saw that it was male. More to the point, it wasn't wearing many clothes. OK, he certainly hadn't been expecting *this*.

The figure indicated that he was coming down. There was the sound of footsteps descending the stairs, then the door was pulled open and Luke saw that he'd at least bothered to fling on a T-shirt and jeans. His hair was tousled – he'd evidently been asleep – and his face was distantly familiar.

'Hi.' His expression was questioning, his tanned feet bare.

Luke swallowed. 'Hello. Is Hallie here?'

'She's upstairs. Asleep. Do you want me to wake her?'

Luke hesitated, then shook his head. 'It's OK, don't worry. I just dropped by to return this.' He held up the paperback with the pale blue cover. 'Hallie lent it to me last week.'

151

'Right. Well, no problem, you can leave it here. I'll make sure she gets it.'

'Fine. Tell her I thought it was excellent. Really informative.'

Hallie's visitor took the paperback and looked at the cover, which featured sand running through a glass egg-timer. The title of the book was *Smile Through It: A year on the transplant list*.

'Can I ask?' said Luke. 'Are you Nick?'

'Yes, I am.'

'From Australia?'

'I came back.' Nick was clearly wondering if he should recognise him. 'Have we met before?'

Luke shook his head. 'No. Hallie showed me a photo of you, that's all. I'm Dr Hilton, her GP.'

'Oh right, I get it now. Hallie's told me about you.' Breaking into a grin, Nick said, 'You're the nice one. As opposed to the bossy, scary one.'

'Hopefully,' said Luke.

'So it's a good book, is it?' Nick scanned the back cover; it had been written by a young cystic fibrosis sufferer waiting for a double lung transplant. 'Does it have a happy ending?'

'Yes.' Luke nodded. 'It does.'

It also mentioned on the back cover that a thousand people a year died waiting for their transplant. And the author of the book – his name was Oli Lewington – had only been twenty-three when he'd received his new lungs. Hallie was twenty-eight now.

Nick said, 'She's getting worse, isn't she?'

Luke hesitated. 'It happens, unfortunately.' Their eyes met. 'You know that.'

Of course he did; they both knew. Nick hesitated, then said, 'So, what are the odds on Hallie getting her transplant?'

Luke shook his head. 'You never can tell. It could happen at any time. The more people who sign the organ donor register, the better the chances.' He raised an eyebrow. 'Are you on the register?'

Nick gave him a look tinged with disbelief. 'I've known Hallie for years. Of course I've signed the register. I tell everyone to do it.'

'Good. Well, I'll be off. It was nice to meet you.' It hadn't been, of course, but sometimes you just had to say these things. 'How long are you back for?' he added, and held his breath.

'Just a flying visit. I'm heading up to see my family this evening. Thought I'd call in on Hallie on my way.'

Telling himself he had no business feeling jealous, Luke nodded. 'Well, bye.'

But inwardly he was thinking: *Just a flying visit. Good.*

It had been lovely to have Nick come and visit her, but how were you meant to say goodbye to someone you might never see again?

The same way as if it hadn't crossed your mind for one moment that this could be a possibility.

Well, on the outside at least.

In the living room, Hallie hugged Nick, breathed in the scent of his skin and gave him a kiss on each cheek. Followed by one on the mouth, but a *mwah* kiss, not a romantic one.

'Bye. Thanks for coming to see me.' She pulled back just far enough to be able to look at him without going cross-eyed. 'And thanks for everything else too. Above and beyond the call of duty.'

'Wouldn't have missed it for the world.' He smiled. 'You take care.'

'I hope everything works out for you and Emma. She sounds great.'

'She is.'

'But just to be on the safe side, don't tell her about the nearly naked thing this afternoon. Easier all round if she doesn't know.'

153

'Whatever you say.' Nick stroked the side of her face. 'But I'll never forget it.'

'Nor me. OK, your mum and dad are waiting for you and you have a long drive ahead. Be careful on the motorway.' Releasing him and stepping back, Hallie kissed her fingers then pressed them against his warm mouth, deliberately refusing to think that this could be the last time she'd do it. 'Off you go.'

Chapter 24

'Go on,' said Rory, 'admit it. You didn't completely believe me.'

Tasha grinned. 'Of course I didn't believe you.'

'See? You should have more faith in your boyfriend. I always keep my promises.'

'To be fair, it didn't help when Joe kept dropping all those hints about hang-gliding.'

'Ah well, that's Joe. You never want to believe a word *he* says.'

Tasha prodded him playfully with the stick in her hand. 'Unless you're saving it until last.'

But he wasn't, she knew that. It was Sunday afternoon, the first week of March, and it had been a dream weekend. Better still, it had all been Rory's idea. She'd thought they were spending the weekend in London, but on Friday afternoon he'd told her to pack a small case. Then he'd brought her down to this stunning country house hotel on the outskirts of Bath. Their room had incredible views over the hotel grounds and the wooded hills beyond. It also had a velvet-canopied four-poster bed.

Completely overcome by the gesture, Tasha had gazed around the room. 'Why have you done this?'

And Rory had replied with an easy shrug, 'Because you deserve it. It's your turn.'

'Really? Oh my God . . .' OK, this was the kind of talk that could make you *seriously* fall in love with someone.

'No potholing, no rugby, no wild swimming, no waterskiing, no motorbikes. This is your weekend. We're just going to relax and do whatever you want to do.'

She'd searched his face, the face that had only just recovered from being battered by part of the Avon Gorge. 'Won't you be horribly bored?'

'No. I'll be with you.' He wrapped his arms around her and rocked her from side to side. 'And you'll be happy. That's good enough for me.'

'Sure?'

'Will you stop worrying? We're going to have a fantastic time. Will we have great sex?'

'Definitely. Great sex, great food, lots of fun.'

'Well then, there you go. Sounds pretty perfect to me.'

Tasha had still secretly worried that he might be bored, but her fears had been groundless. They'd had a brilliant weekend, filled with laughter, love and increasing closeness. The connection between them was like nothing she'd ever known before, strengthening and deepening almost by the hour. The meals they'd eaten in the hotel restaurant had been flawless. Better still, the blustery rainstorms and near-freezing temperatures of the last couple of weeks had given way just in time to the onset of spring. The sun had shone in a cloudless duck-egg sky, the air was warm, and gently swaying carpets of crocuses, snowdrops and daffodils had swathed the valley with colour.

Yesterday they had walked all afternoon, discovering picturesque villages and friendly dog-walkers along the way. Today they were exploring the woodland pathways to the south of the hotel. Tasha had never been a great fan of walking before, unless it was around the shops, but it had been her decision that they should give it a go, and to her amazement she was really enjoying it. It wasn't boring at all; there were a million things to see and listen to. The birds sang and swooped across the sky, a haze of just-emerged green softened the finer outer branches of the trees, there was an infinite variety of bark and leaves, and they saw a pair of foxes gazing at them from the edge of a field.

There were also smaller creatures: beetles scuttling between mounds of last year's dead leaves, a mouse racing across the path in front of them at one stage, and a whole party of spiders on a huge mottled tree trunk.

'Ach!' Realising that one of the bigger spiders had landed on his desert boot, Rory leapt back and attempted to shake it off. 'Oh *God*.' He grimaced; the spider was staying put.

'Keep still.' Trying not to laugh at the look of horror on his face, Tasha knelt in the pile of leaves at the base of the tree and carefully coaxed the spider into the palm of her hand. 'OK, got him.'

'Eeeeeurrgh.' Rory shuddered as she gently deposited it back on the rough tree trunk with the rest of its social circle. 'How can you *do* that?'

'I like spiders. Look at their gorgeous legs. They're beautiful.'

'You're beautiful.' He drew her to him for a kiss. 'Also, weird. How can spiders not bother you when you're scared of every-thing else?'

'You mean rock climbing and bungee jumping and extreme water sports?' Tasha shook her head; did he really not understand? 'I'm not scared of those things. I just don't want to do them.'

'Because you're scared.'

'No, because I have zero interest in them. The small risk of injury doesn't outweigh the amount of work involved. I don't like being in cold water or wearing uncomfortable outfits. But I promise you I'm not scared.'

Rory brushed a stray strand of hair out of her eyes and kissed her on the end of her nose. 'I love you.'

Just hearing him say the words made her whole body fizz with happiness. 'I love you too. Even if you are scared of spiders.'

His eyes glinted with amusement. 'Oh, I'm not *scared* of spiders. I just have no interest in them, that's all.'

They carried on walking, slightly lost but not disastrously so, just following narrow paths and lanes as the mood took them and enjoying the rest of their final sunny afternoon in the countryside.

Tasha heard it first. A frail-sounding female voice was calling, 'Blackie . . . Blackie . . .'

'What?' said Rory when she stopped walking.

'Listen.' She raised a finger and pointed down the hill. 'It's coming from that direction.'

They waited, then the voice came again. It sounded like an elderly woman searching for a lost pet. 'Blackie? Blackie! Oh, where *are* you?'

'Poor thing,' said Rory.

'This is why I love you,' Tasha told him as they instinctively altered course and followed the sound of the voice. 'You're a kind person. You try to help people.'

'She sounds upset. Wouldn't anyone do the same?'

'What if Blackie's a massive spider?'

'Then I'll run a mile, obviously. And leave you to deal with it.'

She grinned. 'My superhero.'

They followed an overgrown path downhill, eventually reaching a narrow winding lane. A hundred yards further along, they came to a tiny cottage in a clearing surrounded by trees.

And there in the front garden was a little old lady in a floral print dress, a chunky grey cardigan and green Hunter wellies. Her gnarled hands were cupped around her mouth as she carried on calling.

Not having heard their footsteps in the lane, she jumped a bit when she turned and saw them coming up behind her.

'Hi,' said Rory. 'Who have you lost?'

'What?'

'Who's Blackie?'

'Oh, my cat.' The woman had to be in her early eighties. 'He

158

went out on Friday and there's been no sign of him since. I'm so worried, he's never done this before . . . I've been through the woods searching for him all day yesterday and today. Oh my poor Blackie, what's happened to him? I can't bear it . . .'

'And how many cats do you have?' said Rory.

'What?'

He raised his voice and said, 'How many other cats do you have?'

'None, just Blackie. He's the only one.' The old lady's voice broke and her chin began to wobble like a toddler's. 'Oh *Blackie* . . .'

'Are you a bit deaf?' said Rory.

'What?'

'Are you A BIT DEAF?'

She glared at him. 'Of course I'm not deaf. Don't be so rude.'

Tasha and Rory exchanged a look; she'd heard it too. Somewhere nearby, a cat was miaowing. It sounded as if it was coming from above them. Loudly and clearly, Tasha said to the woman, 'We can hear a cat miaowing. Can you hear it?'

'What? You can hear a cat? *Where?*'

'Up there.' She and Rory were both pointing towards the trees. Glancing over at the old lady, Tasha noticed the hearing aid in her left ear. 'Have you forgotten to switch your hearing aid on?'

'What? Oh no, I keep it turned off to save the batteries. But it's OK, I don't need it. I'm not deaf.'

The mewing continued, feeble and resigned. Shielding her eyes with her hands, Tasha gazed up into the branches of the trees, searching for Blackie.

'Got it,' Rory said suddenly, pointing to a huge chestnut tree to the right of the house. He turned to the old lady. 'What colour is Blackie?'

'Eh?' The woman switched on her hearing aid and Rory repeated the question. 'Oh, he's a ginger.'

159

'But it didn't occur to you to call him Ginger?'

She shot him a look that signalled that he must be deranged. 'I don't like that name. I've always called all my cats Blackie.'

'Right. Well, he's up there.'

The woman lifted her head, following his pointing finger, and clasped her gnarled hands together. 'Oh look, there he is! Has he been up there the whole time?'

'I'd imagine so,' said Rory.

'Oh, poor Blackie! I can hear him!'

Tasha could see Rory biting his tongue, resisting the urge to remind the woman that if she'd just switched on her hearing aid, she would have heard her cat's piteous mewing two days ago. But never mind, they'd located him now. God, and he was *so* high up, perched precariously on a narrow branch with his ginger tail dangling beneath him.

She took out her mobile. 'We'll call the fire brigade, they'll be able to get him down.'

'No signal.' Rory, who had already checked his own phone, held it up to show her.

'Me neither.' Well, it was hardly surprising; they were in a deep valley. 'Look, do you have a phone here?'

'No. I don't like phones.'

'So we don't have any choice. We'll head back to the hotel,' Tasha told the woman, 'and call the fire brigade from there. Tell me your address so they know where to find you.'

'Oh Blackie! What if he falls out of the tree before they get here? He's been up there for two days with nothing to eat or drink!' The woman spread her arms. 'What if he *faints*?'

'I'm sure he'll be fine,' Tasha assured her. Next to her, Rory was taking off his jacket and speculatively eyeing up the enormous tree.

'I think I might be able to do it, you know.'

Was he mad? 'Seriously, don't even try.'

'Why can't he try?' demanded the old lady. 'If he reckons he can do it, he should give it a go.'

OK, maybe having that hearing aid switched on wasn't such a great idea after all.

'And if he falls, he'll kill himself,' said Tasha.

'I definitely think I can get up there.' Rory was facing the tree with his hands on his hips, visibly planning how to do it.

'No,' said Tasha. 'Look at what happened last time.' She turned to the old lady. 'He was rock climbing and he dislocated his shoulder. His face was cut open by a rock. He's only just recovered.'

High above them on a swaying branch, Blackie emitted a desperate wailing cry.

'I used to climb trees all the time when I was a kid,' said Rory.

'Go on, lad, get yourself up there.' The old woman's tone was combative. 'What are you, a man or a mouse?'

Oh for crying out loud, what kind of sweet little old lady was this? Offer to do her a favour and she starts *goading* you?

'No ropes, no safety harness,' Tasha reminded Rory. 'If you fall, you fall.'

'I won't fall.' He was pushing up the sleeves of his sweater now.

'Let me run to the nearest house and use their phone.' She gave it one last go, already aware that this was a lost cause, like trying to persuade a fox not to chase a chicken. Rory's mind was made up. Basically, he couldn't resist the challenge.

He turned to her and broke into a grin. 'Hey, I'll be fine.'

And that was it; the next moment he was leaping to reach the first branch, hauling himself up like a gymnast on the asymmetric bars. Tasha watched, her heart in her mouth, gripped with apprehension. Who knew how slippery the bark was? As if in answer, Rory briefly lost his grip before regaining it.

God, this was torture; she couldn't watch.

Beside her, the erstwhile sweet little old lady bellowed, 'Come on, stop buggering about and get on with it!'

Tasha felt sick. 'He'll break both his legs if he falls.'

'Hmmph, well he'd better not drop Blackie, that's all I can say. Or I'll be the one who breaks his legs.'

It was like being greeted at the front door by Red Riding Hood's grandmother, who was now revealing herself to be the wolf.

'*Mew*,' squeaked Blackie, beadily eyeing the goings-on from his terrifyingly high viewpoint.

Rory was climbing up and out now, grabbing at increasingly bendy branches. Tasha flinched as one of them made a cracking noise before he moved on to the next; she wanted to close her eyes but couldn't bear to stop watching just in case it was her willpower alone keeping him up there. What if she looked away and he crashed to the ground?

Worst of all, she could see how he was relishing the challenge, loving every second of it. The greater the risk, the happier he was.

And yes, it *was* an attractive quality in a man, but it was also a petrifying one.

It's me, though. It's my fault for being like this. I'm going to have to get used to it.

Her mouth dry, Tasha watched as Rory continued to climb. He'd drawn level with the cat now, but the narrower branches were bending beneath his weight and Blackie was crouching just out of reach. He inched towards him, calling his name in a low, reassuring voice, and was summarily ignored.

Bloody animal.

At last he was close enough to scoop the cat into his left hand. Blackie let out an indignant yowl and attempted to lash out. Hanging on to him for dear life, clutching him to his chest, Rory somehow managed to make his way back to a stable fork in the branches and sit with his back to the trunk. Then, still murmuring words of comfort to the cat, he used his free hand to pull his sweater off over his head. The next moment, he'd wrapped it securely around Blackie, swaddling him like a baby so he could no longer lash out with his claws.

Then it was time for Tasha to hold her breath all over again while he climbed slowly back down the tree, this time clutching a less than amused gift-wrapped cat. When at last he reached the lowest branch, he leaned over to pass Blackie down to her. Tasha in turn handed him across to his owner.

The little old lady said with a touch of irritation, 'You shouldn't have done that thing with the jumper. My Blackie doesn't like being wrapped up.'

Amused, Rory jumped down the last six feet to the ground. 'I don't like having my face ripped to shreds by razor-sharp claws.'

'Oh Blackie, you naughty boy. Come on, let's get you inside and give you a drink.' Having unravelled him, the old woman thrust the sweater back at Rory. 'There's a couple of holes in it, but that's your own fault for scaring him. Bye.'

She turned, crossed the garden and stomped back inside the cottage without another word.

Slam went the front door.

'Not even a thank you,' Tasha marvelled, filled with indignation. 'Bet you're glad you risked your life to help *her* out.'

But Rory, as she'd known he would, simply laughed. 'I didn't risk my life; all I did was climb a tree.'

'She's an ungrateful old bat,' said Tasha.

'No.' He shook his head. 'She's grateful. She just forgot to say it.'

Tasha looked at him. 'You genuinely don't mind, do you?'

'Of course I don't mind.'

She reached for him and pulled him close so that the holey, now-ruined sweater was squashed between them. 'I love you for that. You're the nicest person I know.'

'I love you too.' His green eyes glittered with warmth.

'Just think.' Tasha picked a tiny twig out of his hair. 'If you weren't scared of spiders, you'd be perfect.'

Behind them, the window of the cottage was flung open, interrupting their kiss. The old lady eyed them with disgust. 'What are you two still doing in my garden? This is private property. Go on, bloody *clear off.*'

Chapter 25

Was their relationship made more thrilling by the fact that it was a secret? Like having an illicit extramarital affair, minus the marital bit?

Flo took a sip of coffee and covertly watched Zander as he read an article in the business section of the *Sunday Times*. She loved the tiny frown that bisected his eyebrows when he was concentrating, the way his straight dark hair fell over his forehead when his head was tilted, and the way he could be completely engrossed in the words but still capable of idly stroking the inside of her wrist with his thumb, as if to silently let her know he hadn't forgotten she was there.

Oh this was the life, a gloriously lazy Sunday morning in the company of your new boyfriend, with spring sunshine pouring through the windows of the flat. Could anything be nicer? Crikey, and Jeremy was lying on Zander's lap, utterly relaxed and purring contentedly . . . talk about a turn-up for the books.

So of course it stood to reason that something had to happen to disturb the peace.

The doorbell rang, causing Flo to jump and Jeremy to give her his *whoever they are, kill them* look.

'Expecting anyone?' said Zander.

'It's probably just my other boyfriend.'

'Well send him away. Today's my day. Want me to have a word with him, tell him to stop being so clingy?'

'Don't worry, I'll do it.' Easing herself off the sofa, Flo crossed the living room and pretended to press the button on the intercom. 'Hi, Sebastian, look, I'm sorry, but my *other* boyfriend's here. What? Yes, I know you're richer and better-looking than he is, but you still can't come in, so just jump back into your Lamborghini and leave us in peace. I'll see you tomorrow, OK?'

'A Lamborghini?' Horrified, Zander put down the business section. 'Lamborghinis are *so* naff.'

'I know,' said Flo. 'But it's navy blue to match his helicopter.' This time actually pressing the intercom button, she said, 'Hello?'

Then jumped back in dismay as an all-too-familiar voice said, 'Hello, Florence, it's Lena. Can you please let me in?'

'Um, well . . . the thing is, I'm not dressed.'

'No problem, I'll just wait here. Throw some clothes on and buzz me in when you're ready. And you *should* be dressed,' Lena added, her tone crisp. 'It's almost midday.'

Flo released the button and pulled a face at Zander, who shrugged and said, 'I have no idea what she wants.'

'Nor me, but she's not going to go away. So what do we do?'

He was already lifting Jeremy off his legs, getting to his feet. 'I'll wait in the bedroom. Try and get rid of her as soon as you can.'

God, what could possibly go wrong? But they didn't have any other choice.

Flo waited until Zander was safely out of sight in the bedroom. Then, having checked the living room, removed his half-empty tea mug from the coffee table and rinsed it in the kitchen sink, she pressed the buzzer to unlock the front door downstairs.

Oh well, as soon as Lena was out of here, they could carry on enjoying their lazy, happy Sunday in peace.

'Hi,' said Flo when Lena reached the top of the staircase; in

166

a tight-fitting leaf-green sweater and matching narrow jeans, she resembled an elegant grasshopper. 'Is something wrong?'

'You mean apart from the fact that I'm the one who should be living in this flat? Apart from that, everything's just great. How's the cat?'

'Jeremy? He's fine.'

'Can I see him?'

'Why?'

'*Why?*' Lena's perfectly groomed eyebrows rose. 'Because I want to make sure he's all right. I was talking about the situation last night, and my friend said I should check up on him regularly. Otherwise who's to say the cat hasn't died and you're just pretending he's still alive so you can carry on living here rent-free?'

At a guess, the 'friend' was Giles. 'Except I'd never do that,' said Flo.

'Wouldn't you?' said Lena, who evidently would. 'You're looking a bit nervous.'

Was it any wonder? Flo moved to one side, gesturing for her to go through into the living room. 'I'm not nervous. And Jeremy isn't dead. He's right here.'

Jeremy hadn't moved; he was still sitting on the sofa where Zander had placed him. He submitted impassively to Lena's beady gaze and twitched his whiskers when she reached out to stroke him.

Clearly disappointed that he was looking so well, Lena said, 'He's quite thin.'

'He's always been thin. His weight hasn't changed. The vet checked him over a couple of weeks ago,' said Flo. 'He's fine.'

'Anyway, from now on, I'm going to be coming over and checking up on him every couple of weeks.'

'Not a problem.' It might be a problem, but Flo shrugged, outwardly unconcerned.

'And if he does get ill, you have to do the right thing by

him. No ridiculous treatments keeping him alive just so you can stay here longer. If the cat's suffering, he needs to be put to sleep. Otherwise it's just cruel.'

Such compassion and concern for a helpless animal. Flo nodded and said, 'I know, don't worry. Anyway, it'll be up to the vet, not me.'

'God, they're even worse.' Lena grimaced. 'All they care about is getting you to spend as much money as possible . . . they'll do *anything* to keep an animal hanging on. I went out with a vet once. Complete sadist.'

Tempting though it was to comment that Lena wasn't having much luck with men, Flo didn't say it. Hopeful that the inspection was now over, she moved back towards the door. 'Well, now that you've seen him . . .'

'Not so fast. I haven't finished yet. There's something else I need to ask you.' Lena stood with her hands on her narrow hips. 'Have you seen my brother recently?'

Bugger.

'No.'

'Been in touch in any way? On the phone, perhaps?'

Flo shook her head. 'No. Why?'

'He doesn't approve of Giles and Giles hasn't done anything to deserve it. He says he's heard things about him, but he won't tell me what those things are or who they came from.' Lena's gaze was unwavering. 'And I've asked everyone else I know, but they've all said it's nothing to do with them. Which makes me wonder if the spiteful bad-mouthing came from you.'

How could such a nice brother have such an awful sister?

'Well it didn't,' said Flo. 'So you're just going to have to ask around a bit more. But you heard what he did to that homeless man.' It was no good, she simply had to try and get through to Lena. 'It wasn't kind, was it? You could see why your brother might worry about you getting involved with someone who's capable of doing something like that.'

'Oh my God, are you *ever* going to stop banging on about it? The boys were out having a bit of fun! It was just a joke! Giles is really nice and I *really* like him, OK? He's the best boyfriend I've had in years and I just want us to be happy together. Is that too much to ask?'

Feeling a tiny bit sorry for her, Flo said, 'Well, if he's nice, I'm sure he'll be able to win your brother round.'

'Except Zander won't let him stay at the flat.' Lena exhaled, visibly annoyed. 'Which is kind of inconvenient, not to mention bloody unfair.'

'Well, it's his flat. I suppose it's up to him. Can't you stay at Giles's place?' Flo knew that Zander had been under pressure to allow Giles to spend a few nights a week at the flat.

'But it's so *selfish*. And no, I can't stay at Giles's place.'

'Why not?'

'Because his wife wouldn't like it.' Lena gestured with exasperation. 'OK, happy now? You made me say it. And no, I'm not a marriage wrecker; they broke up months ago.'

'They're still living together?'

'No, they're *not*. But she's directly opposite his mother's house, because the property belongs to the family . . . you know, part of the estate. And Giles is living with his mother, who's being completely unreasonable and refusing to let him take me there because she's trying to force him to get back together with his wife. And *she's* just a spiteful bitch who won't move out because she's happy in the family home with the kids, living the life of Riley and bleeding her husband dry.'

Wow, it had all come tumbling out. A wife *and* kids.

'Gosh,' said Flo. 'Couldn't he rent a flat, move in there?' This was, after all, the man who had set fire to a fifty-pound note purely for entertainment purposes. *Because it was fun.*

'No, he can't, because she's making him pay for everything . . . and I mean *everything*. Horse-riding lessons for his daughter,' Lena spat. 'Guitar tuition for the son. Even a skiing holiday, can you believe it? Money money money . . . I swear to God that woman's doing it on purpose, taking him for everything she can get.' She spread her arms in despair. 'So you can see how unfair it all is. Giles's hideous wife is living in his house, you're here living in my flat . . . my God, is it any wonder I'm stressed out?'

The brief silence following this tirade was broken by a sneeze. And it hadn't come from anyone in the living room.

'You've got someone here,' said Lena.

Flo nodded. 'Yes.'

'Hiding a man in your room?'

'I wouldn't call it hiding.'

'So you've got yourself a boyfriend.' Lena's ice-blue eyes narrowed. 'He'd better not be living here. That's not allowed.'

'He doesn't live here,' said Flo. 'I promise.'

'Well, anyway, I'm off. No wonder you weren't dressed when I rang the doorbell. It's all right for some people.' Her tone was pointed as they left the living room. Out in the hallway, she paused beside the kitchen, then turned to look at Flo.

'Have you been honest with me?'

'Yes.' Flo nodded.

Lena's jaw was taut. 'Hmm.'

Chapter 26

'Phew.' Flo threw open the bedroom door. 'I thought she was going to come bursting in here.'

'Me too. I can't believe I sneezed.' Zander shook his head. 'I'd make a rubbish secret agent.'

Back in the kitchen, they began frying bacon and tomatoes. Flo told him about his sister's grievances and Giles's wife and children.

'Why am I not surprised? What a mess. Lena never does anything the easy way.'

Five minutes later, Zander's phone rang. He looked at the screen and sighed. 'Oh God, what now?'

Flo, standing beside him, didn't need it to be on speakerphone to hear Lena's voice, shrill with panic.

'Zander? *Zander!* I just got home and someone's smashed in the front door . . . there's glass everywhere and loads of stuff's gone . . .'

'Fuck.' Zander went pale. 'OK, wait outside, I'm on my way. I'll be there in two minutes.'

He raced down to the ground floor, pulled open the front door and stopped dead in his tracks. Flo, at the top of the stairs, heard him say, 'Oh, fuck,' for the second time.

'Well, quite,' retorted Lena, pushing past him and stomping back up the staircase so ferociously it was a wonder her spiked heels didn't go through the wood.

Which might have held her there and proven useful, to be honest.

Instead, Flo found herself on the receiving end of an arctic glare.

God, Lena was good at that.

Behind her, Zander said, 'So I take it the flat hasn't been broken into.'

'Of course it hasn't. I lied. Seems to be a lot of it about.' Lena was still gazing fixedly at Flo. 'My word, you're a sly one, aren't you? More than my brother realises, that's for sure. I know *exactly* what you're up to.'

'Lena, stop it. Flo hasn't done anything wrong.'

'Trust me, you don't have a clue.' Pointing at Flo, Lena said triumphantly, 'And that trashy friend of yours in the restaurant? I knew she was lying, too. As if her kids would ever have names like that.'

OK, this conversation was in danger of veering in an embarrassing direction . . .

Zander was getting annoyed now. 'What are you talking about?'

'Ah, didn't she mention that bit to you? You've got yourself involved with a real player now. It's all planned out in advance, you know. She's going to *marry* you.'

Zander, understandably, looked pretty stunned. 'What?'

And there it was. Flo's toes were tightly curled under with mortification. 'It was a joke . . .'

'Didn't sound like a joke to me. You'd clearly discussed it with your friends. The tarty one said *When you marry Zander*, as if it was all decided.'

Had Annie really come out with those exact words? Flo couldn't remember, but she definitely knew she'd gone bright red. And all she could do – again – was protest, 'She was *joking*.'

'Sure, you can keep saying that. But I was there.' Turning her attention back to her brother, Lena went on, 'Trust me, they were serious. If you believe her, you're an idiot. She wants this flat for herself and she'll stop at nothing to get it.'

Exasperated, Flo said, 'You seriously think I'd marry someone for a *flat?*'

'Why not? I bet you can't believe your luck, throwing yourself at my brother and actually managing to get him interested. Next thing we know, you'll have accidentally got yourself knocked up. By the time he's bored with you, it'll be too late, you'll have your legal rights. And that's it, bang goes this flat. My brother wouldn't think of this, but I do, because I'm smart and I know what women are like.'

Women like Giles's wife, presumably.

'OK, that's enough,' said Zander. 'You have to leave now.'

'You're so gullible.' Lena's words dripped with derision. 'And she's not too bright either. Have either of you even worked out how I knew it was you hiding in the bedroom?'

This was greeted with silence. Evidently delighted, Lena said smugly, 'See? You have no idea. Maybe I shouldn't tell you.'

OK, talk about frustrating.

'Really not bothered.' Shaking his head, Zander turned away.

'You're dying to know,' Lena jeered.

Flo, who definitely was, forced herself not to ask.

'You didn't know for sure.' Zander's tone was dismissive. 'It was just a lucky guess. Off you go.'

Lena turned and stalked towards the stairs. In the hallway, she halted and looked at them.

'In there.' Unable to resist it, she pointed through the half-open kitchen door. 'Next time, you might want to hide the tin.'

And with a satisfied smirk, she headed back down the stairs.

Once the front door had slammed shut, Zander clasped his hands together behind his head and closed his eyes. A few moments later he said, 'Now you start to see what my sister's like.'

'Well, I kind of already knew,' said Flo.

'I'm warning you now, she's going to get worse.'

'She was right about the tin, though.' In the kitchen, Flo picked up the printed silver canister of Lost Malawi tea from the Rare Tea Company. This was Zander's favourite blend; he ordered a regular supply online and had brought this tin over with him the other evening. 'Dead giveaway. Didn't even occur to me to hide it. All my fault.'

'Or mine, for being fussy about what I drink.'

Flo tried to smile, because last week she'd teased him about his inability to tolerate the ordinary tea bags she used. But the elephant was right there in the room between them and she needed to address it.

'Look, you have to believe me. Lena's wrong about what she overheard at the restaurant.'

Zander wanted to trust her, she could tell, but there was a wary expression in his blue eyes.

'Your friend didn't say it?'

'Well, she kind of said it. But it was only a joke, I promise. I definitely haven't hatched an evil plan to get pregnant, force you to marry me, then divorce you and live happily ever after in this flat.'

'Right. Well, that's a relief.' He nodded briefly, then put his arm around her shoulders. 'Anyway, not a great start to the day. Shall we change the subject?'

'Might be an idea,' said Flo.

But as the day wore on, although Lena wasn't mentioned again, the elephant remained indelibly in the room, and Flo knew that a tiny percentage of Zander's brain was wondering if what his sister had told him might contain an element of truth.

* * *

Dearest Rose,

I do love your way of answering questions. Hopefully you'll be able to help me with mine.

Here are my three things:

1. I was born and raised in Wolverhampton.
2. My hobbies are cake-making and gardening.

3. If that makes me sound incredibly dull, I used to work as an acrobat in a travelling circus. (I'm sixty-five and can still walk a tightrope!)

Now, here we go with my story. My husband died ten years ago. We were *very* happy together and I never imagined I'd meet – or even want to meet – anyone else.

But by some miracle, it happened eighteen months ago, and honestly, it's been so wonderful I can't tell you. His name is Bill, he's sixty-eight, also a widower, and he feels like my soulmate. We love each other's company and would like to move in together, maybe even get married.

Now for the problem – Bill's son and daughter. Basically, I've tried my best, but they disapprove of everything about me. They have money and I don't. I live in a council flat and speak with a Wolverhampton accent. To add insult to injury (apparently!), my name is Tracey.

Bill is wealthy and well-spoken. He loves me but he loves his children too. Nothing I do will ever alter their low opinion of me – they're appalled by his choice and convinced I'm only interested in their father for his money. I'm not; I just wish they could be happy for us. But it's not going to happen, and worrying about it isn't helping Bill's health. (I should say, he has already made a will leaving everything to them, but they are convinced that I'll persuade him to write another without letting them know. Even though I would never dream of doing that!)

I hate being the cause of such conflict. For his sake, should I walk away and leave Bill and his children in peace? If you think so, Rose, I will do it.

Dear Tracey,
Your letter almost moved me to tears. Your personality shines out, you are clearly a lovely person and you and Bill

175

deserve to be happy together. Listen, you aren't the cause of the conflict; his children are. How would they feel if Bill told them he didn't approve of *their* choice of spouse and demanded they end their relationships? Would they do as he asked, do you think? Of course not!

I'm touched that you have asked me to decide your future. Please don't walk away from Bill and a relationship that has brought you both so much unexpected happiness. Carry on seeing each other, move in together, get married if that's what you want. If his children refuse to be civil to you, just don't see them. Of course they're concerned about their father, but they need to learn that in this case they really don't need to be.

I think you should show this web page to Bill. Then I think he should show it to his children. When they see that you were concerned enough about their father to end the relationship, I hope they'll come to their senses and realise how incredibly lucky he's been to find someone as loving and unselfish as you.

I'm sure anyone reading this will be wishing you all the luck in the world. And please do let us know how you get on. We'll all want to know!

Hallie uploaded the post and closed her laptop. There, done. It was one o'clock, and Bea would be arriving at any minute to take her to the pub. By this evening, plenty of people would have read Tracey's letter and sent encouraging replies of their own; she would look at them when she came back and put the best online. If anyone deserved a bit of happiness, it was Tracey and Bill.

Chapter 27

Now that they were into April, the number of tourists visiting Carranford was increasing by the day. There were plenty of people enjoying the sunshine, sitting at tables outside the pub. With morning surgery finally finished – and with his stomach rumbling for the last hour of it – Luke had come over to the White Hart for some long-overdue lunch.

And there were Hallie and Bea, deep in conversation at one of the tables. Waiting for them to spot him and wave, Luke was taken aback when he saw the expression on Hallie's face. Her eyes were red-rimmed, and as he watched, she surreptitiously wiped them with the loose sleeve of her pale denim shirt. Bea, murmuring something in her ear, briefly put her arm around her thin shoulders and gave her a hug.

They hadn't seen him. Luke headed on into the bar. What had that been about? Something to do with Nick, maybe? He hadn't asked Hallie about him, but the knowledge of Nick's visit – minus clothes – continued to haunt his thoughts. Hallie had mentioned the visit but not the lurid details. Those had remained private, between her and the ex-boyfriend who years ago had broken her heart.

Had he done it again now?

Or had someone else?

Luke ordered cottage pie and an orange juice, then carried

his drink outside. Yes, he wanted to know why Hallie was upset. No, he wasn't going to pry.

There were no empty tables, but Hallie and Bea were occupying one with two spare seats. This time they spotted him, and Bea, seeing him hesitate, called out, 'Over here, join us.'

He sat next to Bea and across the table from Hallie, whose eyes were now dry but still pink-tinged.

'Everything OK?' That was as much as he would say; if she didn't want to tell him, that was up to her.

'I'm fine.' Hallie nodded and managed a half-smile, then glanced down at the phone in her left hand. 'Just heard a bit of sad news. Suze died.'

Suze. The name rang a bell. Luke hesitated and said, 'New York Suze?'

'That's the one.' Hallie nodded and showed him the photo on her phone, of a beaming twenty-something girl with a shock of white-blond curls, jokingly cradling an oxygen tank like a proud mother showing off her newborn baby.

'Her brother just emailed me. She died this morning. Didn't manage to get her transplant after all.'

'I'm sorry.' Luke could only imagine how this must make a fellow CF sufferer feel. Suze, who had blogged about her life in New York, was a friend Hallie had known for years yet never met. The internet had brought together so many people around the world who shared the same diagnosis. Together they sympathised with, supported and encouraged each other through bad times and good.

'Poor Suze.' Hallie rubbed at the condensation on the side of her glass of wine. 'She never gave up hope. We used to talk about getting together one day. Either I'd fly to New York or Suze would come over here. She really wanted to meet Prince Harry.' A pause, followed by a gulp of wine. 'And d'you know what? She was so funny and bright, he would have loved her. Poor Harry, really; he'll never get the chance to meet her now.'

178

What was there to say? Luke didn't even try. For a short while they sat together in silence while everyone else laughed and chattered around them. Then Hallie put her phone down on the table and adjusted the oxygen tubing behind her ears. 'Anyway, make the most of every day, that's what I'm going to do. Make more of an effort, stop worrying about what could go wrong, just go ahead and do more things, have a couple of adventures. Before it's too late.'

'What kind of adventures?' said Bea. 'You mean like hang-gliding?'

'Not that. Just . . . I don't know, getting out more. Less staying at home.' Searching for inspiration, Hallie's gaze swept the busy tables surrounding them. 'I could go to London, be a tourist, see all the sights Suze wanted to see. I could visit the theatre . . . sit in the best seats at *Les Misérables* . . . fly in a helicopter down the Thames . . .'

'Oh God, that would be *so* cool.' Bea sat up eagerly. 'I'd do that with you!'

One of the American tourists, in a fit of enthusiasm, had bought a copy of the local paper and was flicking through it with his wife. 'Honey, what's the name of that village where Will Shakespeare hung out?'

'Stratford-upon-the-Avon. Thelma went there last year, she said it was pretty cute. We'll go visit tomorrow, George, then do Bath on Friday.'

'And there's some kind of horse show at the weekend . . . look at this.' George pointed to the next page. 'Where's Denleigh? We could check that out.'

'Oh George, we can't! Saturday's Scotland, Sunday's Ireland, remember? We need to stick to the *schedule*, honey. Otherwise it'll get to Monday and we'll have missed something out.'

Luke saw the spark of interest in Hallie's eyes. Denleigh, only twenty miles from Carranford, was a small village that each year played host to the Denleigh International Horse Trials, a two-day cross-country event attracting competitors and visitors from all over the world. Between one and two hundred thousand people attended the event over the course of the weekend, their cars clogging the narrow lanes for miles around as they made their way to Denleigh Park. As well as the competition itself, there was a huge shopping village on the site, stalls selling everything from luxury cars to riding boots, not to mention dozens of food stands, giant TV screens and a funfair. It was a hugely popular day out.

'I've never been to Denleigh,' said Hallie.

'Never?' Luke was surprised. 'I went two years ago. It was great.'

'I've always wanted to go, but either I've not been well enough or the weather's been too awful.'

'It gets like Glastonbury in the rain.' Bea pulled a face. 'Everyone slipping and sliding around in the mud.' Brightening, she said, 'But the weather forecast's good for this weekend. We should definitely do it!'

'I'd like to, if it isn't going to be pouring with rain.' Hallie looked doubtful. 'You'd still have to push me around, though. It wouldn't be much fun for you.'

'I'd offer to come along and help out,' said Luke, 'but Jennifer's off to a wedding in Dorset and I'm on call all weekend.'

'Hey, no problem, we'll manage. I have muscles.' Bea flexed her biceps with pride. 'I can handle the chair. If she gives me any trouble, I'll tip her out of it into the lake. Ooh . . . I've just realised something!'

Hallie was looking dubious. 'What? You're starting to put me off now.'

But Bea was pointing triumphantly to the photograph of Suze on Hallie's upturned phone. 'Who goes to the Denleigh Horse Trials?'

'Well, quite a lot of people,' said Luke.

'The royals! The princes! Think about it . . . we might bump into *Harry*!'

180

Luke watched the smile edged with sadness on Hallie's face and his heart went out to her; it wasn't the first time she'd lost one of her friends to the disease that was ravaging her own body.

'OK, the odds probably aren't that great,' Bea amended, conceding the unspoken point. 'But you never know.'

Hallie's fragile smile grew in strength. 'You're right. This is true.' She raised her glass in a silent toast. 'For Suze's sake, I think we should definitely give it a go.'

★ ★ ★

'There you are,' Margot exclaimed when Flo let herself into the garden apartment. 'You're late.'

'Sorry, held up in the office discussing care plans with the manager. What is it you need me to do?'

'Nothing urgent. Just wondered how you're fixed on Saturday. Are you working?'

Flo shook her head and pushed up her sleeves, ready to get on with tidying Margot's kitchen. 'Not on Saturday. Why?'

'Fancy doing an old lady a big favour?' Margot's eyes were bright.

'If I can. What does it involve?'

'Well, it's actually a favour for my nephew, Patrick. He's the one with the gift shop in Thornbury, remember?'

'I do remember.' Flo had met Patrick, briefly, a couple of times while he'd been here visiting his aunt. In his late thirties, he was affable, cheery and actually quite attractive in an uncombed, slightly out-of-condition kind of way. His sense of style relied heavily on his love of old checked shirts and corduroy trousers.

'Well, he has a stall at Denleigh Horse Trials this weekend. It costs a fortune to book, but you can make a killing . . . Anyway, the girl who was going to be running it with him can't do it any more. Fell off a table last night and broke her foot. Patrick hasn't been able to find anyone else to step in, so I wondered if you might be up for it. If you've made other plans, it's fine, we'll just keep searching.'

Flo considered the offer. Zander was working this Saturday and she hadn't made any other arrangements. 'I *could* do it,' she told Margot. 'Except I don't know how I'd get there.'

'Oh, no problem. Patrick can pick you up and drop you home afterwards. He lives in Failand so it's practically on his way. And he'll pay you eighty pounds.'

'In that case,' Flo said promptly, 'deal.'

'Excellent. Reaching for her phone, Margot pressed a couple of buttons and waited for her nephew to pick up. 'Darling? Panic over, Flo said yes. I know, I'm brilliant.' Smiling, she added, 'I'll pass you over now so you can make the necessary arrangements.'

When Flo ended the call a couple of minutes later, it was all sorted. A suitably grateful Patrick would be picking her up at six thirty on Saturday morning and dropping her home again twelve or so hours later. It would be a long and busy day, but hopefully an enjoyable one.

'Can't wait,' said Flo. 'I'm looking forward to it.'

'You'll have fun,' Margot assured her. 'Patrick's good company; the customers love him. Just one word of warning, though.'

'What?'

Amused, Margot pointed a manicured finger at Flo's head. 'He'll make you wear a hat.'

Chapter 28

For the first time in years, the weather had stayed fine and Denleigh wasn't awash with mud and rain. Having been directed to the disabled parking area, Bea jumped out of her car and unloaded the wheelchair.

'Thanks for coming with me.' Hallie organised the oxygen bottle, smoothed a couple of kinks out of the plastic tubing and settled herself in. 'Don't panic, you won't have to push me up any hills.'

'No worries,' said Bea. 'If I get tired, we'll swap places. I'll sit in the chair and you can push.'

It was only nine thirty. In order to avoid the queues of traffic, their strategy had been to arrive and leave early. Of course, thousands of other people had had the same idea; rows of cars were already parked in the surrounding fields, and a steady stream of people and their dogs were making their way in through the main gates.

'Haven't spotted Prince Harry yet,' said Hallie.

Bea pointed to the airstrip over to their right, flanked by orange windsocks and stretching between two more fields lined with helicopters and light aircraft. 'He'll be flying in, I bet.'

The cross-country event wasn't due to start until midday. Horsey types were walking the course, striding along purposefully in sludge-coloured country outfits. Inside the showground, the air was rich with cooking smells from various food concessions, sausages and chargrilled steaks vying with Indian and Mexican peppers, spices and garlic. The lake, a glassy pool of silver blue with a complicated set-up of double and triple jumps leading into and out of it, was already surrounded by eventing enthusiasts planning to install themselves there and watch a full day's action from the water's edge.

As for the shopping village . . . well, it was a huge, eclectic sprawl of stalls, some standing on their own, others clustered in tents the size of wedding marquees. From hot tubs to angora socks, from fine diamond jewellery to nylon dog leads, there was something for everyone, and you never knew what you were going to come across next. For the next hour, Hallie and Bea marvelled at stalls selling diamanté-encrusted shoes, luxury summer houses, home-made fudge, life-size wire sculptures of horses, and jars of mustard.

'*Eww*, mustard.' Shaking her head in revulsion, Hallie's eye was caught by a bright stall opposite. 'Let's have a look at that one over there.'

This was better; oh yes, this was her kind of place. The front of the stall was hung with bunting and multicoloured tissue pompoms. Inside, there were art prints, stained-glass lamps, strings of pearl-encrusted fairy lights, velvet gloves, silk scarves, items of bold statement jewellery and a wide selection of hats. The man running the stall was wearing a dashing black fedora with a red ribbon tied around it and was wrapping a pair of candlesticks in silver paper, placing them in a fuchsia-pink cardboard carrier with emerald rope handles.

'It breaks my heart to sell these. I can't believe I'll never see them again.' He handed the bag over to the customer. 'Goodbye, my darlings, you're going to live with a new family now.'

Once the woman had gone, his assistant, who was wearing a purple trilby, reached under the table and with a triumphant 'Ta-daaah!' pulled out two more identical candlesticks.

'Ahh, it's a miracle!' The man applauded her. 'Like the loaves and fishes. Hello, ladies, have you come to make off with more family heirlooms and break my heart too?'

Hallie said to the girl in the purple trilby, 'Is he always like this?'

'Well, it's my first time working with him, but I'm pretty sure the answer's yes.'

'I really like your hat.'

The girl looked amused. 'Another one of his ideas.'

'Why?'

The man chimed in. 'Because we sell hats. If customers see one they like, they don't want to be the only person wearing one. Feel free to try any of them on, by the way. So long as you don't have nits.'

But Hallie's attention had been caught by the silk scarves tied to the branches of a silver tree on the central table inside the tent. 'Oh, look at these, they're just gorgeous.' Wheeling herself over, she lightly touched one of the scarves, feeling the slippery material slide between her fingers. This one had splashes of lime green, fuchsia, deep purple and gold exploding like fireworks over an inky blue background. It reminded her of midnight on New Year's Eve, when she and Luke had watched the celebration in Carranford together from her bedroom window.

'That one's my favourite,' said the girl.

'Mine too.' Hallie found the tiny price tag and turned it over, fingers mentally crossed in the hope that it might by some miracle say £6.50.

Well, you could always dream.

It didn't say £6.50, of course. The scarf cost eighty-five pounds. Which was a crazy amount, even if it was stunningly beautiful.

'Those colours would really suit you.' Joining her, Bea also checked the price tag and pulled a face. 'Ouch.'

'I know.' The girl in the purple trilby was sympathetic. 'They're hand-painted by a designer in Cornwall, so no two scarves are the same.'

'I could let you have it for seventy,' said the man, 'if it helps.'

It was still far too much. Regretfully, Hallie let go of the scarf and turned her attention to the jewellery on the table. The man's phone had begun to ring and he pulled it out of his pocket.

'Margot! Are you calling to find out if I've sacked her yet? No, no, Flo's doing fine, she's just wrestling with a shoplifter at the moment. Flo, put the poor man down, you don't know your own strength!'

'What about this necklace? D'you like it?' Lifting up a long multicoloured string of beads, Bea said encouragingly, 'It's only eighteen pounds.'

Hallie shrugged, because the necklace was pretty but it didn't begin to compare with the scarf.

'Look, you can use it as a lasso.' Twirling it around in the air, Bea said, 'If you spot Prince Harry, you can use it to bring him down. He won't stand a chance.'

Hallie grinned. 'Then I could tie him up with my oxygen tubing.'

'Is he here today?' Flo was interested. 'How exciting!'

'Not sure, but we're going to keep a lookout. It'd be so brilliant to see him, even if it's just from a distance.' Hallie wheeled herself backwards, away from the table. 'Right, let me have a think about the necklace. We might be back later.'

They both knew this was polite customer-speak for *I have no intention of coming back, but this is my way of escaping.*

'No problem,' said Flo, who had wild auburn ringlets and a friendly face. 'Enjoy the rest of your day. And good luck with tracking Harry down. If I hear on the news that he's been lassoed and kidnapped, we'll know who it was.'

'But don't tell anyone, OK?' Hallie waved as she and Bea left the stall. 'Bye!'

By two o'clock, Flo had sold four of the hand-painted silk scarves. It was silly; she knew the girl in the wheelchair wouldn't be back, but she was still hoping no one else would come along and buy her scarf.

The stalls were busier now, thousands of shoppers coming and going, and the tills had been ringing non-stop. Patrick was great at his job, making people smile, winning customers over and relaxing them into opening their wallets. He was entertaining company, charming in a laid-back, unthreatening way and endearingly self-deprecating too. During their van journey this morning, Flo had learned all about his life; divorced three years ago, he and his ex-wife, Dawn, had managed to remain on such good terms that he was invited over to dinner every week or so, regularly played golf with her new husband and had even given her away at the wedding.

'Ah, she's a lovely woman. Just because our marriage didn't work out doesn't mean we can't still be friends.'

'That's really nice.' Flo was moved by his words. And it must surely be an easier way to live, infinitely preferable to Lena's constant sniping, jealousy and challenging behaviour.

She'd continued to think about this as the day progressed. A text arrived from Zander telling her that Lena had evidently had a furious row with the window cleaner, flatly refusing to pay him because he'd woken her up at midday squeegeeing the outside of her bedroom window.

Basically this was a situation that was never going to change. Lena was Lena, and being the way she was meant Flo's own relationship with Zander was guaranteed never to be easy.

Imagine how much simpler and less fraught life would be if she were romantically involved with someone like Patrick instead. Watching him now, interacting easily with a horsey mother and daughter debating which limited-edition print to buy, Flo pictured her and Patrick together, having jolly dinner parties with his ex-wife, having Margot come to stay with them at weekends so they could enjoy each other's company. No stress, no anxiety, no wondering when the next argument might be about to erupt.

Patrick was so nice, the kind of man who was always in a

cheery mood. OK, so he wasn't as handsome as Zander, he probably didn't have a six-pack and he had one of those snub-nosed, friendly faces rather than scimitar cheekbones and thickly fringed Hollywood-blue eyes. But he was a genuinely lovely person . . .

Sometimes wheelchairs had their advantages. One of the kindly event organisers, spotting Hallie and Bea searching without success for a decent position from which to view the jumps at the lake, unfastened a rope and ushered them through to an adjacent cordoned-off area.

'*Result,*' Hallie murmured, eyeing the untrampled grass and elegant white chairs and tables.

'Oh wow.' Bending down behind her, Bea whispered, 'We're in the VIP enclosure. With the *posh people*. This could be our big chance . . .'

There was a white marquee, comfortable seating, men wearing linen jackets and red trousers. There were also leggy blonde girls, waiters serving champagne, and an assortment of dogs noisily slurping water from silver bowls lined up at the side of the marquee.

'If Harry gets a bit thirsty and fancies a drink,' said Hallie, 'this is the place he'll come to.'

'Except hopefully they won't make him drink out of one of those bowls . . . oh my *God*,' Bea squealed in her ear, pointing to a group of glamorous girls and noisy but well-spoken young men. 'The one with his back to us . . . white shirt, orange hair . . . is that *him*?'

'No.' Hopes raised and dashed in the space of a second, Hallie shook her head. But she took out her phone and switched on the camera in readiness, just in case Harry did put in an appearance. It might be naff to take a photo, but compared with these well-to-do types, she was already irredeemably naff.

They had a fantastic view of the jumps, though. Hallie settled down to enjoy it, taking photos of the competing horses instead. Every few minutes a shrill whistle would sound, and the next contestant would come thundering past them, the horse's hooves kicking up turf as it raced along the side of the lake. The rider then steered it around to face a huge fence constructed of wood and barrels before gathering the horse's energy and launching it into the air. Once successfully over, it was down a steep slope and over a second, smaller fence before splashing into the water, cantering across the shallow end of the lake, then leaping back out and over the third fence on the other side while water sprayed into the air and the audience applauded . . . or let out a collective groan of sympathy if it didn't go well.

They'd been watching for twenty minutes when Hallie heard snuffling, and realised that a dog was investigating the right-hand wheel of her chair. Leaning over, she saw a bright-eyed brown and white terrier gazing up at her, the fluffiness of his ears an indication that he was still a puppy.

'Hello!' She reached down to greet him, tickling the little dog under his chin and laughing as he promptly attempted to scramble up the side of her chair. His extendable lead was stretched out behind him, attached to the wrist of his owner. Twisting round, Hallie's mouth dropped open.

Alerted by the sudden movement, Bea turned too. For a couple of seconds they were both stunned into silence.

Then, her eyes widening in disbelief, Bea said, 'No way!'

Chapter 29

'Hallie! And Bea – oh my goodness, fancy bumping into you two here! Hallie, how *are* you?'

Nobody ever wanted the truth when they asked that question; it wasn't an invitation to launch into a list of oxygen saturation percentages.

'I'm good, thanks. You're looking great. Who does this puppy belong to?' Having patted her knees, Hallie had persuaded the little dog to leap up on to her lap. 'He's gorgeous.'

'I know,' Christina said proudly. 'Isn't he perfect? And don't faint, but he's mine!'

Christina, Luke's ex-girlfriend. She'd always been blonde and elegant without needing to try too hard. Today she was looking particularly glamorous in a pale pink dress and matching coat, with flat pink ballerina-style pumps accentuating her slender tanned legs. Her hair was loose and shiny, her make-up light. But it was the look in her eyes as she gazed down at the dog that really made the difference; she was clearly a woman in love.

'Hang on, though,' said Bea. 'I thought you didn't like dogs.'

'I know, I thought so too!' A couple of the Carranford locals had habitually brought their large dogs into the White Hart, and Christina had always shuddered and given them a wide berth. Now, she gave a cheery shrug. 'Turned out I just didn't like other people's big scary dogs. My mum gave me this one for my birthday in January and I couldn't believe it; I told her I didn't want a dog! But she said I should give it a week to see how things went, and if I still didn't want him after that, then she'd keep him for herself.' Christina gazed adoringly into the eyes of her unexpected birthday present. 'Well, that was it. By the end of that first evening, I was completely besotted. His name's Daley, and now I couldn't imagine being without him . . . he's my little darling, aren't you? Oh yes you are!' Blowing ecstatic kisses at Daley, she added cheerily, 'Honestly, I'm a changed person. My mother couldn't be more thrilled!'

A waiter approached, a round of drinks was ordered and Christina pulled up a chair to join them. She'd been invited along today by a couple of horse-mad neighbours who'd had a ticket to spare and who were currently walking the course.

'So do you still have the snakes?' said Hallie.

'No.' Briefly shamefaced, Christina shook her head. 'It's a bit of a crazy story. Audrey died just before Christmas – she was my Burmese python – and I wanted to replace her right away, but my mum got really upset. She told me I was obsessed with snakes and it was no way to live. Then in January she gave me Daley. She did it on purpose, of course, but that's mums for you.' Christina reached over to fondle the dog's ears. 'Plus, she was right: it turns out dogs are a million times more fun than snakes. And it wasn't easy to keep both at the same time – Daley used to bark like mad outside their room, which must have been stressful for them – so the upshot was, I ended up giving them away to a family I knew would give them a good home.' She paused and shrugged. 'And that was it, no more crazy snake-keeping lady. Now I have Daley instead.'

'And your mum's happier,' said Bea cheerily.

'Oh God, *tons* happier. She was starting to panic that no man would ever want me.' Amused, Christina said, 'Which was fair enough, to be honest, seeing as I hadn't been out with anyone since me and Luke broke up.'

191

'Really?' Bea was interested. 'And has it made a difference, having a dog instead? Have you met someone nice?'

The sound of thundering hooves signalled the arrival of the next horse in the competition; conversation halted and all heads swivelled to watch the huge grey leap the first fence, gallop into the water, then stumble and tip its rider into the lake before nonchalantly trotting back out on to dry ground.

'They're both OK,' said Hallie as the rider got to his feet, emptied water out of his hat and set off after his horse.

'And in answer to your question,' Christina continued, 'no, no luck on the man front. Sadly. Although I think I probably know the reason for that.'

A distant warning bell was ringing in Hallie's head; something about the look on Christina's face told her what she might be about to say next.

'Go on, then,' said Bea. 'What's the reason?'

Christina shrugged, and half smiled. 'How's Luke these days?'

There it was. 'He's fine.' Hallie nodded, wishing she hadn't been right.

'Well, that's good. And is he . . . you know, seeing anyone at the moment?'

'No.' Bea shook her head, then let out a yelp of realisation. 'Oh, I get it now, you haven't found someone else because you still like Luke!'

Christina sat back, her expression rueful. 'Well, yes, I guess that's the reason. But this is just between us, OK? You mustn't tell him.'

No we mustn't, no we mustn't . . .

'Why not?' said Bea. 'I'm serious! You two were always brilliant together, everyone said so.'

'Did they really?' Christina brightened.

'God, *yes*. We were all so disappointed when the two of you broke up. You were like the perfect couple!'

'Oh that's so nice of you to say! Yes, we were happy. Sometimes it isn't until afterwards that you realise what a good thing you had.'

'And Luke hasn't been out with anyone else either, which has to mean something. I wonder if he's been thinking exactly the same? You know, we wouldn't be obvious or anything,' said Bea, 'but we could definitely mention that we bumped into you today, say how great you're looking, drop a few subtle hints . . . If he's secretly been missing you like crazy, it could give him just the nudge he needs.'

'That might be interesting.' Christina was definitely looking keen. 'Especially if he hasn't had any other girlfriends in all this time. I hadn't realised that.'

'There hasn't been anyone,' said Bea. 'Well, apart from Hallie, of course.'

Christina sat up and did a double-take. '*What?*'

Oh great, thanks a lot.

'You mean you didn't hear about it? Oh yes, it was the talk of the village!' Bea was grinning. 'Everyone thought Hallie was on holiday in Paris, then her mum found out she was actually holed up with Luke in his cottage . . . well, that was it, and the photos were on Facebook, so *everyone* knew . . .'

'Are you serious?' Christina's eyebrows had by this time disappeared into her hairline. 'Is this true?'

'Ha, it was hilarious.' Bea put down her drink. 'Of course it wasn't true! Hallie was too ill to fly to Paris, and her mum was in Edinburgh and there was no one else she could stay with, so Luke was pretty much forced to put her up. Then her mum turned up on Luke's doorstep and confronted them, can you imagine? Like something out of *EastEnders!* It was all sorted out by the time the rest of us got back from Paris, but just for that weekend everyone actually thought Hallie and Luke were having a secret fling!'

'Oh *no*, how funny!' Christina rested her hand on Hallie's arm and started to laugh along with Bea.'Oh, *bless* you . . .'

Which possibly wasn't meant to come out sounding quite so patronising as it did, but still managed to leave Hallie feeling like the girl least likely to *ever* be physically desired by a member of the opposite sex.

Because let's face it, who in their right mind would fancy her?

She managed a brief smile and adjusted her nasal specs, fiddling with the tubing that hooked over her ears. Then she looked at her watch. 'What time do you think we need to leave if we don't want to get stuck in traffic?'

'As long as we're out of here by four, we'll be fine. Anyway.' Bea turned her attention back to Christina. 'It's decided, then. You and Luke should definitely get back together. We're going to have a word with him, make him realise what he's missing.'

'Go on then. But be subtle,' Christina pleaded.

'Subtle is my middle name. Ha, that's me, *Bea Subtle*.' Cracking up at her own joke, Bea added, 'Don't you worry, leave it to us. We'll work our magic, just you wait and see.'

'OK, I will.' Christina's eyes danced. 'I'm quite looking forward to it now.'

'And when you and Luke get married, you can thank us by letting us be your fabulous bridesmaids.'

Maintaining a carefree smile was starting to make Hallie's cheeks ache. As if sensing she was in need of comfort, Daley rested his soft paws on her chest and attempted to lick her face, but the oxygen tubing got in his way.

Christina raised her glass and clinked it against Bea's. 'If that happens,' she said happily, 'it's a deal.'

As they left the VIP enclosure, Bea said, 'Isn't she lovely? I'm so glad we bumped into her. Honestly, sometimes these things happen out of the blue and you just think it's like fate, it's as if it was meant to be. I feel like a fairy godmother! Wouldn't it be completely amazing if Luke and Christina end up getting back together and it's all down to us?'

'It would.' Hallie was glad Bea was behind her, pushing her wheelchair across the bumpy ground. They were heading past the shopping village, making their way back to the car park. She put out her arm and pointed. 'Five more minutes won't make any difference, will it? Can we call in at that nice stall with the scarves before we go?'

The girl in the purple hat – Flo, that was her name – greeted them with delight. 'Hello! I didn't think you'd be back! Have you decided to buy the necklace?'

No. I have no man in my life, I'm destined to spend the rest of my days as a lonely spinster with nothing to look forward to other than misery and heartache, so I've decided the least I can do is treat myself to a ridiculously expensive scarf.

Wheeling herself over to the table where they fluttered from the branches of the silver tree, Hallie reached up and unfastened *her* scarf.

'I'm going to have this one.'

'Oh, I'm so glad. It's perfect for you.' Flo seemed genuinely pleased.

'And we offered you a discount, didn't we?' The man who ran the stall took it from Hallie's hands. 'Said you could have it for sixty pounds?'

Hallie, already counting out the notes from her purse, said, 'Seventy.'

'No, you're wrong. It was definitely sixty.' The man in the black fedora winked and rang up the amount on the till.

'Any luck with the royal-spotting?' said Flo. 'Did you get to see Prince Harry?'

'No.' Hallie's smile was rueful. 'Would have been fun, but it didn't happen.'

'His loss,' Bea said cheerfully. 'Anyway, we bumped into someone we hadn't seen for a while, which was brilliant.'

Hmm, *had* it been brilliant? Hallie wasn't so sure. Not that she could admit as much to Bea.

195

'There you go.' Flo handed her the scarf in one of the smart rope-handled bags. 'Enjoy. And don't just save it for special occasions. A scarf like that needs to be seen and admired. It'll make you feel fabulous every time you wear it.'

'Thanks.' For a split second, Hallie felt emotional without even knowing why. The girl was right: something so lovely deserved to be worn often. Maybe by someone who went out to more places than she did, but never mind.

'And make sure you come back and see us again next year,' said the cheery man.

Weren't people nice? Touched by his kindness, Hallie smiled and said, 'I will.'

If I'm still here.

Chapter 30

It was six o'clock, the cross-country competition had been completed and people were starting to make their way home. Some were still in the shopping village, looking to buy last-minute items, but the crowds were thinning out now and the stallholders were beginning to pack up.

'Right, quick, I need a present for my next-door neighbour.' The middle-aged woman in the too-tight pink fleece was clearly in a hurry. 'I forgot it's her birthday, and she'll be there when we get home. What have you got for around a tenner?'

'Ooh . . .' Flo scanned the items she'd been selling all day. 'How about one of those mirrored photo frames?'

'Too glitzy.' The woman grimaced and shook her head. 'She only likes boring things. Her house is kind of beige.'

'Well, we have these.' Holding up a notebook with an embossed cream cover and silver-edged pages, Flo said, 'Beige enough?'

'Not sure about the silver . . . Ah, that'll do, I'll have one of those.' The woman had spotted a stack of pale grey tea towels on one of the tables. 'Can you quickly gift-wrap it? Make it look a bit more expensive?'

'Erm . . . maybe you want to check it first. There's writing on it,' Flo explained.

'But I'm in a *hurry*.' The woman was glancing at her watch.

'Here, just take a look.' Flo unfolded the tea towel and held it up. In big capitals it said: IF YOU CAN'T STAND THE HEAT . . .

And then below, in smaller writing: . . . get the fuck out of my kitchen.

'Yes, yes, that's fine, just wrap it up, please.'

Flo glanced at Patrick, who nodded and shrugged. She duly rang up the price, took the woman's money and began gift-wrapping the tea towel in primrose-yellow tissue paper.

As she concentrated on the task in hand, cutting lengths of ivory ribbon and curling the ends with the blade of her scissors, Flo heard a friendly voice say, 'Hey, Patrick! How are you?'

The woman in the tight pink fleece was busy on her phone now, getting annoyed. 'Stop complaining, I'll be there in two minutes . . . Malcolm, if you'd reminded me earlier, I wouldn't be having to buy something now, would I? So just give it a rest.'

Behind them, Patrick was exchanging jovial words with the man who'd greeted him. Working as fast as she could, Flo finished constructing the ribbon curls, handed the gift-wrapped parcel to the woman and watched as she hurried off to catch up with her husband waiting impatiently in the car park.

She turned back to Patrick just as the man he'd been chatting to was leaving with his friends. He glanced briefly over his shoulder, grinned and raised a hand in farewell before heading off in the opposite direction to the woman in the pink fleece.

For a moment Flo wondered if she was the victim of some elaborate practical joke. Were there hidden cameras recording her befuddled reaction? Was it one of those TV shows where they got lookalikes to fool unsuspecting members of the public?

No, surely not.

'Who was that you were talking to just then?' she asked eventually.

Patrick looked the tiniest bit embarrassed. 'You saw, didn't you? Or you wouldn't be asking.'

Still needing to be absolutely sure, Flo said, 'Was it Prince Harry?'

'Well . . . yes.' For the first time, she noticed his cheeks redden. 'You know him?' OK, that was a stupid thing to say. Editing out the question mark, she repeated, 'I mean, you *know* him.'

'Hey, it's not like we're best friends.' Patrick shook his head in protest. 'Really, it's nothing. Before I opened the shop, I ran a pub not far from Tetbury. Quite a few people from Highgrove used to pop in fairly regularly, seeing as we were only a couple of miles down the road. That's all it is. He's a good chap. Always friendly and down to earth.'

'Wow, that's amazing. Oh, the girl in the wheelchair,' Flo exclaimed. 'Didn't you hear her earlier saying how much she wished she could see Prince Harry?'

'Well, yes, I heard her. But he wasn't here then.'

'You could have told her you knew him, though! She'd have been so impressed!'

'Oh no.' Patrick smiled, clearly horrified by the very idea. 'That would have been a bit show-offy. No one likes a name-dropper. Now, shall we make a start on the packing up?'

As they made their way back to Bristol, Patrick's mobile rang. Glancing at the lit-up screen, he said, 'It's Dawn, wondering where I am. Could you answer it?'

Feeling a bit weird, Flo picked up the phone. 'Hi, Patrick's driving at the moment. We're twenty minutes from Bristol. He says he'll be with you by nine.'

'Ah, that's brilliant, thanks so much. Is that Flo?' Dawn sounded friendly. 'Now tell me, what's he wearing? Does he look half-decent?'

Flo hesitated, then said, 'He's fine.'

'Is it the grey corduroy trousers?'

'Dark green corduroy.'

'Red shirt?'

'Red shirt,' Flo confirmed, amused by the hint of eye-roll on Patrick's part.

Keeping his attention on the road ahead, he murmured, 'She thinks she's Gok Wan.'

'I hate that red shirt. The cuffs are frayed. OK, tell him to pop home first, have a shower and change into the black trousers and striped green and white shirt I bought him. I've fixed him up with a hot date and he needs to impress her.'

'OK, got it,' said Flo.

'Thanks. And remind him to put on some cologne, too. The good stuff, not the awful one his sister gave him for Christmas. Thanks, Flo. Have you had a good day?'

'Really good.'

'Excellent. Oh, and tell him her name's Jade. She's an aerobics instructor, thirty-three, lives in Almondsbury. And she's great, so we'll be keeping our fingers crossed – I'm going to get him fixed up with someone lovely if it kills me! OK, bye!'

Flo relayed the details to Patrick, who shook his head in resignation. 'Oh God, she's never going to stop.'

'Jade sounds nice, though.'

'I know. I'm sure she is. It's just . . . an aerobics instructor.' He heaved a sigh. 'Which means she'll eat really healthy food.'

During the course of their long day together, Flo had seen Patrick tuck into an organic bison burger, a sausage sandwich, a chicken burrito and a slice of home-made lemon drizzle cake. Which possibly explained his slight paunch.

OK, more than slight.

'You never know, you might have a great time.'

'True. But it's still a bit of a joke, being set up on blind dates by your ex-wife.'

'So why not find someone yourself?'

'You'd think it'd be easy, wouldn't you?' Patrick's smile was rueful. 'It isn't. Every time I meet someone I like, she turns out to be involved with someone else.'

'Really? *Every* time?'

'Oh yes.' He paused, then reached over to turn up the volume on the radio. 'I like this song. You don't mind if we listen to it, do you?'

They carried on down the motorway to Bristol. When they finally reached Clifton, Patrick turned into Caledonia Place. 'Can I ask you a question?' he said.

Expecting it to be something about Margot, Flo nodded. 'Of course.'

'Are you seeing someone at the moment?'

Well *that* had come out of the blue. Caught off guard, she said, 'Oh! Um . . . well, yes . . . yes, I am.'

Which was eloquent.

'Thought you probably would be.' His tone wry, Patrick half smiled. 'See? There you go, my record remains unbroken.'

He was telling her he liked her. They'd had such a nice day together. He was good company, not unattractive, in a cosy, unthreatening way. He also had a wonderful aunt and a lovely-sounding ex-wife. For a moment Flo was envious of Jade, who would be meeting him tonight for the first time. She almost wished she could be single herself, released from the hassle of having to deal with Lena Travis, allowed instead to relax into a normal, uncomplicated, angst-free relationship . . .

Except then she wouldn't have Zander, which basically wasn't an option. Nightmarish though his sister might be, Flo knew she couldn't bear the prospect of not having him in her life. And since he and Lena came as an inescapable buy-one-get-one-free package, she had no choice in the matter other than to put up with it.

She was in love with Zander Travis. It was as simple as that.

Patrick brought the van to a halt outside her flat and she smiled at him. 'Thanks. And just so you know, if you'd asked me out and I was single, I would have said yes.'

'I honestly don't know if that makes me feel better or worse.'

His eyes crinkled at the corners. 'Ah well, story of my life. Thanks for helping me out today, anyway. It's been fun working with you.'

'Same.' As she climbed out of the van, Flo said, 'And good luck with your blind date tonight.'

Patrick grinned at her. 'Knowing my luck, she'll make me do sit-ups.'

Chapter 31

It was Sunday the twenty-eighth of April, they were a party of ten at the River Restaurant at the Savoy, and through the windows sunlight was bouncing off the surface of the Thames. Boats were making their way up and down the river, tourists were taking photos of the iconic skyline, and on the South Bank, the Millennium Wheel slowly revolved against a cloud-scattered milky-blue sky.

Inside the restaurant, Joe was rising to his feet, tapping a fork against his glass and clearing his throat for attention.

'Ladies and gentlemen, or thereabouts, we're here today to celebrate my best friend Rory McAndrew's birthday, and I feel the need to make a speech.'

'Oh God,' Tasha murmured to Carmel as the rest of the table cheered; there was something about Joe today that was making her nervous.

'Don't worry.' Carmel was in control as always. 'I won't let him say anything embarrassing.'

'Joe?' Tasha needed to just warn him. 'You're not going to tell everyone the story of Rupert's stag do in Amsterdam, are you.' It was a statement rather than a question, to indicate just how serious she was.

'No?'

'No.' It was a funny story, but really not suitable for the Savoy.

'It's OK, I wasn't going to tell them that one.' Joe grinned at her.

'Well, good.'

He winked. 'They already know about that, anyway.'

He was impossible. Tasha smiled, gave in and sat back. Basically, if Joe was up to mischief, there wasn't a damn thing she could do about it; he'd say whatever he liked.

'Right, here we go. Rory is my best friend and we've known each other for some years now. He's an excellent chap, always up for a laugh and a dare, and we've had our fair share of . . . adventures.' Pausing to raise a well-timed eyebrow, Joe added, 'There may have been a few girls involved too, along the way.'

Oh God, what are you about to come out with?

'Then just a few months ago, on Christmas Eve, in fact, he met a girl who was different from the rest. Her name was . . . dammit, her name was . . .' He pretended to rack his brains as laughter erupted around the table. 'OK, got it now, her name was Tasha, and since meeting her, Rory's been a changed man. As we all know, he fell in love with this girl. And to begin with, I'll admit I was worried. Because what if my best friend didn't want to spend time with me any more? What if Tasha didn't want me spending time with her boyfriend? What if she tried to fob me off with *her* best friend and I couldn't stand the sight of her – *ow*.'

'I'm so sorry.' Carmel, having prodded the back of his hand with her fork, smiled sweetly up at him. 'That was an accident.'

'But luckily, *very* luckily, none of those things happened. Tasha is wonderful and I love her like a sister. She and Rory are perfect for each other, as we all know. And Carmel has a huge crush on me, which is perfectly understandable but I'm playing it cool for the moment, because . . . well, just because I'm a pretty cool kind of guy.'

More laughter greeted this statement, because if there was one thing Joe wasn't, it was cool.

'Anyway,' he went on, 'Rory is twenty-six today, and life

204

continues to be a brilliant adventure. So can we all raise our glasses to the birthday boy and wish him well?' Holding his glass aloft, Joe solemnly pronounced the toast: 'Happy birthday to you, and may the next year be even better than the last.'

Everyone at the table clinked glasses and chorused, 'Better than the last.' Then they sang 'Happy Birthday', ending with cheers and a round of applause. Even some of the other diners joined in.

'Thanks,' said Rory when the noise had died down. 'Nice speech. I could kiss you, but I'd rather kiss my girlfriend instead.'

'That's unfair,' said Joe. 'In fact, it's sexist.'

Tasha kissed Rory on the mouth – *mwah* – then said, 'It's because I'm less stubbly.'

'I call it discrimination against men who forgot to shave this morning. Anyway.' Producing an envelope from his jacket pocket, Joe handed it to his friend. 'Here's your birthday present.'

Rory opened the envelope, took a look at what was inside and started to laugh.

'What is it?' Carmel leaned past Joe, trying to get a glimpse.

'I'm going for a skydive. *We're* going for a skydive,' Rory corrected himself. He held the vouchers up so they could all see. 'Joe's bought two, to make sure he doesn't miss out. As if I'd dream of taking anyone else.' Clapping his hand on his friend's shoulder, he said, 'Joe, this is fantastic. Brilliant. It's something I've always wanted to do. Really, thank you.'

'Glad you like it. And of course I'll be coming along with you. But I won't be doing the skydive,' said Joe.

'What? Why not?' Rory laughed. 'Oh God, don't tell me you're pregnant.'

'Don't worry, it's all food and beer.' Joe patted his paunch with pride, then glanced over in Tasha's direction, and in that moment she knew exactly what he was going to say next. 'No, I'm not going to be the one jumping out of the plane with Rory. I think Tasha should do it.'

There it was. She'd been right. *Bastard*.

'No way,' she said.

'You might love it,' said Joe.

'I won't love it, because I'm not going to do it.'

'Come on, you're not even giving yourself a chance. Live a little, feel the adrenalin, experience the buzz. You told Rory you aren't scared to do things, you just don't *want* to do them.'

'True.' Tasha nodded, but beneath the table her palms were prickling with alarm.

'I just think the time has come to give it a go, see if you might have changed your mind. You never know, it could happen. And then you'd be able to share the experience with Rory. Wouldn't that be better than always saying no to everything?'

Joe was evidently a man with a mission. Tasha said, 'You can't make me do something I don't want to do.'

He shrugged. 'I know that. I'm just giving you the opportunity to surprise us. And yourself. OK, here's a thought, you could do it for charity. Raise money for a cause you care about. I'd sponsor you.' He glanced around the table. 'We all would.'

Double bastard.

'Hell, kid, you jump out of a plane and *I'll* sponsor you.' An enormous bearded American at the next table waved an arm in the air. 'Five hundred dollars to start you off, how's that?'

The man's wife chimed in helpfully. 'You need to set up a JustGiving page so people can donate online. Oh honey, don't look so alarmed, it's really easy to do. Only takes a couple of minutes!'

As if the fact that her heart was jackhammering away inside her ribcage was down to fear of setting up a donation page. And now everyone around her was nodding enthusiastically and promising to sponsor her . . . but only if she *wanted* to do it, obviously.

A few seconds later, one of Rory's other friends said happily, 'So we're already up to three thousand pounds. This is brilliant.'

Which wasn't the word currently running through Tasha's mind.

206

Rory gave her hand a squeeze. 'Don't worry, you can just say no. It's fine,' he murmured.

'Let me have a couple of minutes.' Pushing her chair back, Tasha excused herself and headed for the ladies' loo. Once inside, she rested her damp palms on the cool marbled sink and studied her face in the mirror. So much for thinking she'd never taken part in adventure sports simply because they didn't interest her. Because when it came down to it, and the challenge was put to her, it had become blindingly apparent that she'd been kidding herself. What she was feeling now was an overwhelming sense of fear.

Well? What are you going to do?

Say no, of course.

Really? Really-really?

Yes, because I'm not completely insane. Why on earth would I want to throw myself out of a plane?

Fine then. Just say no.

She nodded firmly at her reflection. *Thank you. I will.*

The door swung open and Carmel burst in. 'Honestly, he's such a dick. Are you OK?'

Tasha nodded. 'Yes.'

'I suppose he thought that by doing it like this, you'd be more likely to go along with the idea. But you don't have to at all . . . Just tell him to get lost.'

Tasha's phone beeped. She looked at the text Joe had just sent her: *Sorry, do you hate me? I'm not really a horrible person out to embarrass you. I honestly thought it was a good idea. Rory loves you. I just wondered if this might make him love you even more. Xx*

'Hmm,' said Carmel when she'd read it too.

'Well?'

'Well what?'

Tasha turned to look at her. 'Is he right?'

'Look, just ignore him.'

'Yes, but is he right?'

'I don't know.'

'I think you do,' said Tasha.

'OK, he might be a little bit right. But that still doesn't mean you have to take any notice of him.'

Tasha thought about her current nemesis, with his big brash exterior, loud voice and laddish ways. Last week he'd come over to Rory's flat for supper; when she'd gone into the kitchen, she had found him crouched down, attempting to coax a woodlouse into his hand so he could move it out of the way before it accidentally got stepped on.

Because that was the thing about Joe James. He wasn't always subtle, but he undoubtedly had a kind heart.

He also had a point. Not that she agreed with the idea that Rory would love her more if she did the skydive. But he might respect her more.

Everyone might.

Including herself.

Oh fuck.

Tasha was aware of all eyes upon her as she made her way back to their table. She and Carmel sat themselves down. She took a sip of wine. 'It's all gone quiet. Is everyone all right?' she asked brightly.

Rory's friend Niall said, in a voice loaded with meaning: 'Well?'

If her heart had been thumping before, it was going twice as fast now. Maintaining an entirely false air of calm, she shook back her hair and said, 'Oh, you mean the skydive? I've decided to do it.'

For the second time, everyone erupted in cheers.

Joe was grinning. 'You're a star. Plus we're up to four and a half grand now.'

Rory hugged her. 'You don't have to,' he said again.

'I know. But I want to,' said Tasha.

Which definitely wasn't true.

Chapter 32

Since taking over as landlady of the White Hart, Marilyn had made very sure indeed that none of the residents of Carranford ever missed her birthday. This year was no exception. Waking up late on the morning of Friday the seventeenth of May, Hallie saw from her bedroom window that the front of the pub had already been liberally decorated with banners, bunting and giant balloons. People would be popping in and out all day to wish their vivacious landlady well, and this evening, Marilyn, whose stamina knew no bounds, would be hosting a huge party to celebrate the fact that she might now be fifty-five but in the glamour stakes she could still give the Hollywood movie stars a run for their money.

Well, the more mature ones anyway.

Bea called in at lunchtime to see how Hallie was. 'How are you doing? Feeling better?'

'Feeling better. Don't know about looking it,' said Hallie. Exhausted yesterday, she'd had an early night and slept for twelve hours, which had helped a bit.

'Shut up, you'll be fine. I'll come over after work and we can get ready together. What time d'you want to get there?'

Marilyn's party would carry on until the small hours. Hallie needed to pace herself. 'I was thinking nine, but you can go earlier than me if you like.'

'No way, we're going together. But I think we should head over at eight. Don't want to miss out on anything.'

'Are you talking about the party now? Or the buffet?' It was a standing joke that Bea had once been distraught to discover she'd missed the last of the home-made Scotch eggs.

'How can you even ask that?' Filled with indignation, Bea said, 'Both!'

'Come on then, let's go, we don't want to be late.'

This was especially rich coming from the girl who'd never been on time for anything in her life.

'Two more minutes,' said Hallie. It was still only ten to eight.

'*One* more minute.' Bea emphasised her point with an index finger raised. 'People could be over there finishing the Scotch eggs as we speak.'

Hallie turned back to the mirror above the fireplace, unable to resist admiring her reflection for a few seconds more. God knows, it didn't happen often these days, but this evening was getting off to a good start; by some happy accident, she was actually looking . . . well, not too bad at all. The fitted primrose-yellow dress suited her figure and gave her some shape. The sun had shone for the last week and she'd got a bit of a tan, which definitely helped. Best of all, her short hair had gone right when she'd dried it this evening, and with Bea's assistance her make-up was extra-flattering. BB cream, blusher and mineral powder had made her skin look flawless. Her eyes were huge and luminous, the violet shadows beneath them expertly disguised with concealer, which made a big difference. Together with the smoky eye make-up Bea had proved so adept at applying, the end result was . . . good.

For once, she actually gave the impression of glowing with health.

'Ready?' said Bea.

'I look nice.' It wasn't the kind of thing you could say in front of just anyone, but Bea was her best friend.

Bea's expression softened; she understood. 'Better than nice. You look stunningly beautiful.'

Also, normal. Well, if you took away the oxygen tubing. And the wheelchair.

'OK, let's go.' Tapping her watch and reverting to bossy-boots mode, Bea grabbed the handles of the wheelchair. 'Get in.'

As if she were a harassed mum ordering her naughty toddler into a buggy.

Hallie sprayed herself with scent and did as she was told, disconnecting the tubing from the in-house supply and plugging it into the portable oxygen tank that would be accompanying them to the party. As they left the house, she twisted round in the chair and looked up at Bea. 'Is this really about not missing out on the Scotch eggs, or is something else going on?'

'Ha, can't get anything past you, can we, Sherlock? Anyway, don't bother asking any more questions, because I'm not giving anything away.' Pushing her out on to the pavement and closing the front door behind them, Bea added gleefully, 'It's a surprise!'

The celebrations were already in full swing when they arrived. Marilyn was up on stage with the band, looking like Tina Turner in a fringed silver dress and six-inch heels. Practically everyone in Carranford was there, filling the pub and spilling out into both the connected marquee and the long garden beyond. The noise level was high, the atmosphere buzzing and there were strings of fairy lights everywhere.

Surreally, too, the party was full of Marilyns – dozens of people were wearing masks featuring her face as they chatted, milled about and strutted their stuff on the dance floor.

Hallie spotted Luke at the other side of the bar and felt her heart do its foolish little flip of excitement, the one it always did when she saw him, the one nobody else knew about. Oh, but he was looking extra nice tonight, with his hair slicked back like that. He was wearing a dark blue linen jacket, a cream shirt and jeans. Best of all, he wasn't wearing a Marilyn mask, so she was able to see when he noticed her and broke into a warm smile. Raising a hand in greeting, he made his way over.

'Evening! How are you doing? You look great.'

'So do I,' said Bea before Hallie could open her mouth. 'I'm looking amazing too!'

Luke grinned at her. 'Absolutely. Goes without saying. You both look fantastic. Can I get you a drink?'

'White wine, please,' said Hallie. 'Frascati.'

'Make it two. Ooh . . .' Bea pulled out her phone and read the text that had just arrived. Evidently pleased, she rapidly replied, then watched as Luke threaded his way between a group of cricketers on his way to the bar. She touched Hallie's shoulder. 'Going to be fun tonight.'

'I wish you'd tell me what's happening.'

'I wish you'd stop being so nosy. Just have a bit of patience. It'll be worth it, I promise.'

Hallie knew how Bea's mind worked; she adored springing surprises. Last year she'd organised a reunion of her father's school friends for his sixtieth birthday. From the way she was looking and behaving now, Hallie guessed that she had secretly arranged for some of *their* old friends to turn up tonight. Which would be brilliant, so long as she hadn't invited Martin Ormerod, who had made such merciless fun of Hallie's coughing fits and had called her Fag-Ash Lil all the way through school. For him, the joke had never stopped being hilarious.

Basically, because he was a dick.

Twenty minutes later, Hallie discovered that the down side of brilliant surprises was automatically assuming they were intended for you, when this wasn't necessarily the case.

Like now.

As everyone else partied on around them, Bea had continued to monopolise Luke, chatting away to him as if he were the only man in the room, and doing it with such vivacious intensity that there was no way he could escape.

At first Hallie had been puzzled, wondering what was going on. Then her attention had begun to wander, because the plethora of Marilyns was more entertaining than having to listen to Bea's endless questions about cholesterol.

The moment of realisation came when her gaze drifted from the boisterous group of cricketers demonstrating their twerking skills on the dance floor – really *not* a pretty sight – to the woman who had moved across the room and was now standing just a few feet away from Bea and Luke. She was wearing one of the Marilyn masks and clutching a drink, but it was the legs that gave her away: fine, elegant, shapely . . . and recognisably belonging to—

'Well, hello,' Bea exclaimed, breaking off her conversation and making a poor attempt at pretending to be surprised. She even did an over-the-top double-take. 'Oh my goodness, I don't believe it! Fancy seeing you here!'

Hallie's heart sank as the new arrival lifted the Marilyn mask from her face. She saw Luke's expression change, amazement giving way to delight as he said, 'Wow, this *is* a surprise! Look at you!'

And then she was forced to sit and watch them greet each other with hugs and kisses, trapped and unable to escape because her wheelchair was hemmed in from all directions. Was Luke just being polite, or was it more than that? Was Christina glad she'd taken the plunge and come to the party?

And was this really Bea's idea of a completely brilliant surprise? The answer to this last question was evidently yes, as Bea was now clapping her hands. Beaming down at her, she exclaimed, 'Ha, was this the best plan ever? Isn't it great? I *knew* you'd love it too!'

Hallie, who wasn't loving it at all, marvelled at her own ability to put on a good front. Because somehow she *was* managing to smile and look delighted while inside her ribcage a sensation like slowly setting cement appeared to be pressing down on her lungs.

As if they weren't already useless enough.

And now other people were turning, recognising Christina, nudging each other and pointing to the happy, just-reunited couple. Christina was clutching Luke's shoulder, laughing at something he'd just said and shaking her head in disbelief. Up on the stage, the real Marilyn had spotted what was going on and broke off from singing 'River Deep, Mountain High' in order to yell, 'Ooh, I say, look who's here! Hello, lovely Christina, long time no see!'

Hallie kept the happy expression plastered on her own face as Christina first waved back at Marilyn then turned to smile at other people she recognised and hadn't seen for months. It wasn't just Luke; *everyone* seemed thrilled to see her again.

Oh God.

It was like the prodigal daughter returning home.

Chapter 33

'Come outside.' Slipping her hand into his, Christina whispered in Luke's ear, 'I've got something to show you.'

Together they left the pub by the side door. Christina led him across the crowded car park. In the far corner, he recognised her red Audi. The next moment a volley of high-pitched barks emanated from it and he saw a small dog leaping up and down as if the passenger seat were a particularly bouncy trampoline.

'OK, I don't know how to break this to you, but there appears to be a dog in your car.'

Christina grinned up at him. 'I know.'

'Well, should we dial 999? Or call the zoo? They could probably send out keepers with nets and stun guns.'

She unlocked the car, opened the passenger door and caught the dog as, wriggling with delight, it scrambled into her outstretched arms.

'I don't believe this,' said Luke.

'What can I tell you?' Christina beamed as the little dog licked her cheek. 'I'm a new woman. His name's Daley and he's the best thing that ever happened to me.'

This was definitely a seismic change. 'And he's OK with snakes?'

'No more snakes. They're gone.'

'*Really?*'

'I know.' She laughed at the look on his face. 'It was never going to work. You know I loved my snakes, but I ended up giving them away because I loved Daley more. Basically, he's the light of my life and I couldn't imagine being without him.' Pausing to nuzzle the dog and waggle his hairy paws, Christina said, 'Could I? No I couldn't, because you're my beautiful baby, aren't you? Oh yes you are!'

'He's cute.' Luke stroked Daley's soft, wriggly body; it still seemed nothing short of amazing, but he could see how Christina had been won over. 'Can I ask how Bea came to be involved in you turning up tonight?'

Her eyes sparkled. 'I bumped into Bea and Hallie the other week at Denleigh. We had a lovely chat about all sorts of things . . . Daley . . . life in general . . . *you* . . .'

'Right. And what were you saying about me?'

'It wasn't me, it was Bea! She told me you hadn't been out with anyone since we broke up. And I said I hadn't either. Then they just started saying what a perfect couple we'd always been and wasn't it a shame we weren't still together and did I ever regret what happened?' Christina paused, gazing directly at him. 'And I said yes, I did.'

'Right.' Lost for words, Luke realised he was repeating himself.

'Sorry, you know I'm not usually this blunt, but I thought I may as well come straight out and say it. What with it being the truth, basically.' Tucking a strand of hair behind her left ear, she went on, 'So anyhow, Bea and Hallie seemed to think there was a good chance you might be feeling the same way. They were keen to drop some hints and see if they were right. And because I was kind of curious to know too, I said they could do it, so long as they were subtle. They were so excited about it!' She smiled, shaking her head at the memory. 'And I was too. Until I got a call the next morning telling me my mum was in hospital.'

'Oh no. What happened? Is she OK?' Christina's mother

Annabel was a nice woman who had lived alone in Edinburgh since the death of her husband three years ago.

'She's fine now. Just fell off a ladder clearing her guttering and broke a leg. Nothing too terrible, but she couldn't manage on her own at home. Which meant I had to race up to Scotland and look after her.' Christina pulled a face. 'Which wasn't a problem, except I had to call Bea and tell her and Hallie to put the campaign on hold. It would have been a bit pointless having them drop all those hints about me when I was hundreds of miles away. But I've done my duty now. Mum's on the mend and I'm back home. And when I texted Bea to let her know, she reminded me about Marilyn's birthday bash. She knew you'd be here and it was her idea for me to turn up and surprise you. Then you could see how you felt when you saw me again.' Pause. 'And so could everyone else.'

She stopped, her clear gaze flickering away from him. After briefly burying her face in Daley's neck, she raised her head once more and said, 'So I guess that's the big thing now. *Are* you happy to see me again?'

What a question. What could he say? How was he meant to reply?

'Of course I'm happy to see you again.' Time seemed to slow down as Luke spoke the words, whilst inside his head his thoughts were going at a million miles an hour. It was true: there was no reason at all not to be pleased about seeing Christina again. He'd assumed she would have moved on with her life, met someone else by now, but apparently this hadn't happened. And as far as she was aware, he was in the exact same situation. She had no idea – because nobody had any idea – that he'd developed feelings for another girl. But nothing could ever happen there, so really it was a spectacularly irrelevant situation to be in. And now it seemed that Hallie and Bea had together actively *encouraged* Christina to make the first move in an attempt to resurrect their relationship.

Plus, the snakes had gone. Which, it had to be said, was a pretty big bonus.

'Oh Luke. I've missed you so much.' Christina was exhaling with relief, as if that was it, all sorted.

What?

Then again, maybe this was what he needed to sort himself out. Being single hadn't helped him overcome his feelings for Hallie, had it? Indeed, it might even have encouraged them.

So theoretically, getting back together with Christina could be the answer.

And if that didn't sound hugely romantic . . . well, maybe now that the snakes were out of the picture, the situation might change. They'd had fun together in the early days, after all. There'd been laughter, parties, adventures. They'd shared some great times. And love could return, everyone knew that. There was a chance, wasn't there, that they could get together and create their own happy-ever-after?

He breathed in the flowery scent of the perfume Christina had always worn. It must have taken some courage for her to turn up here this evening, essentially offering herself to him on a plate. It had been a brave thing to do. And the seconds were ticking by, which was making the situation potentially awkward.

Luke took a deep breath and said, 'I've missed you too.'

'Truly?' Christina's eyes lit up. 'So how about it? Shall we get back together? Give it another go?'

Since it appeared to be a fait accompli, and it could just be the answer he'd been searching for, Luke smiled and nodded. 'Let's do it.'

'Oh, thank goodness!' Still clutching Daley so that he was lightly sandwiched between them, she leaned forward for a kiss. A proper one, on the mouth. And Luke found himself kissing her back.

It was nice.

Familiar.

Yes. Familiar was good.

Drawing away eventually, Christina said, 'Wow, and there I was thinking I'd never get the chance to do that again.' Reaching up, she touched the side of his face, stroking his jawline. 'You don't know how happy I am. We can make this work, I know we can.'

Luke nodded. Could they? He hoped so, he really did, for both their sakes.

Woof woof. His tail wagging ecstatically, Daley licked Christina's hand.

'Looks like Daley approves,' said Luke.

'He's a great judge of character. Come on, we should go back to the party.' Christina reached for his hand. 'Hallie and Bea will be waiting to hear if their plan worked.' Her smile broadened. 'Time to let them know we're back together and it's all thanks to them!'

Chapter 34

Hallie had had plenty of practice over the years at hiding her true feelings and presenting a brave face to the world.

And this evening she was getting some more in.

Smile.

Be cheerful.

Be delighted for Christina and Luke.

Appear to be having *the* most fantastic evening.

And yes, she *was* pleased for Luke, because it wasn't as if there could ever be any kind of relationship between them, and he deserved to be happy. But it didn't stop her being envious and wishing it could have been her instead.

She fixed her gaze on the band up on the stage as they launched into their version of Elton John's 'I'm Still Standing'. Which was ironic, seeing as she was currently sitting in her chair and had managed to get herself stuck in a corner again, behind a noisy group of people with their backs to her.

Tempting though it was to simply barge forward into their legs, Hallie detached herself from her oxygen supply and stood up, leaving the coiled plastic tubing on the seat of the chair. She needed the loo, and it was easier just to squeeze past everyone and make her own way through the crowded bar.

Three minutes later, leaving the ladies', she pushed open the door leading out into the corridor, encountered resistance and heard someone say, 'Ow.'

It was a risky business, making your way down this narrow corridor when the doors could unexpectedly open at any moment. Regular customers knew about it, but strangers were apt to get caught out.

'Whoops, sorry.' Easing herself out, Hallie registered three things:

Her victim was carrying a full pint of lager and a glass of lemonade.

By some miracle he'd managed not to spill either of the drinks over himself.

He was absolutely gorgeous.

Phew.

'Well held,' she said. 'No damage. You're OK.' He was *so* much more than OK, but never mind.

'Narrow escape.' His dark blue gaze flickered over her, as if taking in every last detail. 'Unlike you, I'm afraid.'

'What? Why?' Peering down at herself, Hallie checked the front of her dress. It was fine.

'Not there. Here.' Lifting the pint of lager in his right hand, he pointed with his index finger at her left shoulder.

She twisted her neck and saw what he was looking at. An occupational hazard of being a wheelchair user in a crowded pub was the likelihood of finding yourself on the receiving end of other people's spilled drinks. This evening, someone had carelessly deposited two splashes of red wine close to the neck-line of her new primrose-yellow dress. They'd either not noticed or been too embarrassed to point it out.

'Oh great,' Hallie sighed. 'I only bought this last week.'

'Luckily you bumped into the right person. Come with me.' The man with the dark blue eyes and the devastating smile added, 'Trust me, I'm an expert.'

She'd been four minutes without supplementary oxygen and

the effects were just beginning to make themselves felt, but she could cope without it for a bit longer. She followed him down to the end of the corridor and out into the pub garden, beyond the marquee.

'Sit,' said the man when they reached an unoccupied table and chairs at the far end of the garden. 'I'm Ross, by the way.'

'Ross. Hi, I'm—'

'Beautiful.' He pulled a face, shook his head and said, 'Oh God, I can't believe I actually said that; there's no hope for me. I was just thinking it and the word accidentally popped out. I'm so sorry, please don't run away.'

'I'm Hallie.' She couldn't help smiling, because it was so screamingly obvious what Ross was like: forward, unshy, seriously attractive and wildly flirtatious. Just the glint of mischief in his eyes was enough to give it away; he was looking at her as if she were the only girl in the world. This was a naughty boy who loved to overstep the mark and knew he could almost always get away with it.

'Hallie. Nice to meet you. Now, turn your shoulder towards me and let's sort this out.' Taking a clean handkerchief from his pocket, he dipped it into the smaller of the two glasses he'd carried out with him.

'Lemonade?'

He shook his head. 'Soda water. Trust me, it's better than anything else. The carbon dioxide helps to break up the stain.'

She looked around. 'Whose drink was it meant to be?'

'Don't worry, they're both for me. I was late getting here. Marilyn's son invited me . . . we've known each other for years. I haven't even seen him yet.'

Hallie indicated the lit-up marquee. 'He's in there with his friends.'

'That's OK, I'll catch up with them later. I'd much rather stay out here and talk to you.' He was leaning towards her now, patting the soda water into the material with his clean handkerchief, holding it away from her skin and patiently working at the stain left by the red wine. 'If you keep it damp, you'll have more chance of getting the rest out when you get home.'

'Well, you're either a world stain expert or incredibly clumsy,' said Hallie. 'So which is it?'

Ross laughed. 'That's for you to find out. Looks like you need to get to know me a little better. You have incredible eyes.'

'Clumsy with drinks but smooth with the compliments.' Maybe even too smooth, but Hallie was smiling too; when someone was gazing into your eyes like that, it was kind of hard to look away.

'I wish I can be clumsy with compliments too. I once got nervous and told a girl that she had fantastic long teeth and white legs.' He shrugged self-deprecatingly. 'Funny how I'm still single.'

Everyone in the pub was now leaping up and down, dancing and bellowing along to Gloria Gaynor's 'I Will Survive'. It was one of Marilyn's favourite songs. Hallie had always found it hard to sing those lyrics; it felt like tempting fate.

'Are you wishing you could join in?' Ross observed her listening to the music. 'It's fine, if you're desperate to get away from me. I'll understand.'

But he was joking; had any girl ever been desperate to get away from him? When you were that good-looking, it simply didn't happen.

As if she could physically get up and dance at the moment anyway, the effects of doing without the extra oxygen were really making themselves known now.

Still, just ignore it. Mind over matter.

'I'm happy to stay here.' Hallie found herself gazing at his mouth; it was possibly one of the most beautiful mouths she'd ever seen.

'I'm so happy you're happy,' said Ross. 'In fact I'm so very happy you're happy. Can we stay out here all night and get to know each other? Would that be OK with you? Shall we hide away down here at the end of the garden and *really* get to know each other? *Aarrgh.*' He clapped his hand to his head in comical despair. 'See what I mean? It just happened again . . . that sounds so bad. I mean in the gentlemanly, non-physical, just-asking-questions sense, I promise.'

There were garlands of multicoloured fairy lights festooned from the branches of the tree above them, and warm yellow uplighters in the shrubbery bordering the garden. Otherwise they were sitting in near-darkness. If it had been bright daylight, there was a chance that Ross might have been able to make out the faint blue-grey tinge to her mouth – she didn't need a mirror to know that her oxygen saturation levels were decreasing. The sensation of pressure in her lungs and increased difficulty in breathing told her that.

But with the lighting this dim, she was pretty sure she could get away with it. Just this once, she was out of the house and being flirted with by an attractive man who didn't have a clue about her condition. As far as he was concerned, she was just another twenty-something girl. He thought she was normal, was treating her as if she were normal and, given the chance, would probably invite her to do all sorts of completely normal things with him.

Not that she would, of course, but it was doing her ego no end of good to be treated as if she might.

God, it was such a fantastic feeling.

See? And this is par for the course if you're healthy. This is what evenings out can be like.

'What?' Ross tilted his head. 'Why are you smiling like that?'

Because you think I'm normal. Aloud, Hallie said, 'Because I'm having a nice time.' She pointed to her shoulder. 'Thanks for getting the stain out.'

'Well, nearly getting it out.' There was still a faint lilac mark there, but he put down the damp handkerchief. 'Do you have a husband?'

Hallie held up her ringless left hand. 'No.'

'Boyfriend?'

'No.'

'Just checking. I like those answers, by the way. Where d'you live?'

'Right here in Carranford.'

'Cool,' said Ross. 'I'm in Oxford. And what do you do?'

Hmm, let's see. Cough a lot? Lie in bed for days on end with attractive plastic tubes up my nose? Battle against infections and take more antibiotics in a year than some people take in a lifetime? Imagine my own funeral and wonder what people will say about me after I'm gone?

Was that an enticing list of pastimes guaranteed to enthral and entice any potential boyfriend?

No. No, it really wasn't.

Chapter 35

'I work in IT. Kind of . . . problem-solving.' Hallie pictured the home page of www.threethingsaboutyou.com. That counted as IT, didn't it?

'So you're a troubleshooter,' said Ross.

'That's right.' She nodded firmly; a troubleshooter for other people's emotional dilemmas was exactly what she was. 'How about you?'

'Me? Would you hate me if I told you I was an estate agent?' He sat back, holding up his hands in self-defence.

'Are you one of those ruthless ones who strings people along and crushes their dreams?'

'I'm actually one of the nice, helpful ones who tries his level best to make people's dreams come true. Believe it or not,' he confided, 'we don't want property sales to fall through. Mainly because it means we lose our commission.'

'Then I won't hate you,' said Hallie.

'The feeling's mutual.' His smile was playful. 'I won't hate you because you're a computer geek.'

She nodded gravely. 'Thanks.'

'Although you don't look like a geek.'

'Appearances can be deceptive.'

'Anyway, I'm glad I came along here tonight. Imagine if I hadn't. Am I being too forward?'

'Yes, but don't stop.'

'What happened to your last boyfriend?'

'He moved to Australia. I chose to stay here.'

'He made a huge mistake,' said Ross.

'We're still friends.' Hallie shrugged. 'Your turn.'

His eyes lit up. 'My turn to be your boyfriend?'

'You know what I mean.'

'Oh dear. You really want to know?'

'More than ever,' said Hallie, 'now you've said that.'

Ross heaved a sigh. 'It's a very sad story, so you'll have to brace yourself. Her name was Eva and she was beautiful. Perfect. We were getting on so well together.'

'Go on.'

'Then she decided to sell her flat and asked me to put it on the market for her. I showed a potential buyer over the property a week later, while she was there, and he told me he was definitely interested.' Ross raised an eyebrow. 'It wasn't until a few weeks later that I discovered it wasn't the flat he'd been interested in.'

'Oh no. Are they still together?'

He nodded. 'Still together.'

'Was your heart broken?'

'Shattered beyond repair for all eternity. Well,' he amended with a grin, 'for at least the next fortnight.'

'You poor thing.'

'I know.' He nodded bravely.

Hallie said, 'It's not true, though, is it. Didn't really happen.'

Ross burst out laughing. 'How did you know?'

'It's a gift I have. I can always tell when people are lying.'

'That's both impressive and terrifying.'

'Let me guess. You get bored with girlfriends, drop them, move on to the next.'

'This is true.' Ross nodded in agreement. 'Because I'm always looking for something better, someone who really understands me. I always knew that one day I'd meet my match.' His blue eyes crinkled. 'It was just a question of being patient and waiting for her to turn up.'

It had been worth coming to the pub tonight just for this. To feel like a normal girl. Even though it was becoming more and more difficult to suck enough air into her lungs.

Not to mention successfully concealing the fact that it was becoming more difficult.

'And I have to say, you took your time.' His teeth gleaming white in the darkness, Ross leaned forward and murmured, 'But better late than never.'

'THERE SHE IS,' bellowed a voice at the other end of the garden. 'It's OK, I've found her! She's out here!'

And that was the end of feeling normal. Hallie turned to see Bea standing in the doorway to the pub, opening the door wide so that the wheelchair could fit through it.

'My God, you gave us the fright of our lives,' Bea shouted, hair flying as she raced across the grass. 'We were on the dance floor and I thought you were in the corner talking to the Wilkinsons, then they moved away and I saw they'd been standing in front of an empty chair. And nobody knew where you'd got to! You can't *do* this . . .'

Hot on Bea's heels was Luke, pushing the wheelchair at speed over the bumpy ground so that the portable oxygen cylinder clanked against the back of it. And completing the entourage came Christina, wobbling in her elegant stilettos and looking concerned.

It was like a team of paramedics arriving at the scene of an accident. The look on Ross's face was a picture as they came hurtling down the garden towards him.

'Can you stand? Bea, take her other arm. Careful . . .' Luke was lifting her out of her seat, manoeuvring her across into the wheelchair, uncoiling the plastic tubing and fitting the nasal specs on her face. He turned up the oxygen and stood back to watch her intakes of breath.

Hallie knew she'd left it too long. As the minutes had ticked by, each breath had become that little bit harder to draw in, but she'd forced herself to resist the urge to take massive, gasping gulps of air because that would have given the game away and had Ross wondering what on earth she was playing at.

As if he weren't doing that now.

'Don't ever do something so stupid again,' Bea ordered. 'We were so *worried*. Anything could have happened and we wouldn't have known about it!'

Hallie gazed past them and said nothing, concentrating on sucking the oxygen back into her lungs.

'Jesus,' Ross said finally. He looked over at Luke. 'What's *wrong* with her?'

There it was. How many times had she experienced this over the years, since the wheelchair had come into her life? Pair it up with oxygen canisters and tubes across the face and so many people – not everyone, but more than you'd think – automatically assumed you were incapable of answering simple questions.

She looked at Ross. 'I have CF.'

He actually seemed surprised she could still speak. 'What's that?'

'Cystic fibrosis. Have you heard of it?'

'Of course I've heard of it. Lungs, right?' A mixture of horror and sympathy flickered across his face as the information sank in.

'Correct.' Hallie nodded. 'Well done.'

'Wow.' He leaned forward, picked up the pint of lager from the table, then put it down again. 'Why didn't you tell me?'

Did he really not have a clue? She shrugged. 'Sorry. Slipped my mind.'

'How are you feeling?' Luke had his professional face on.

How am I feeling? Disappointed.

Oh well, at least it hadn't come as any great surprise.

Aloud, she said, 'I'm OK.'

There followed a brief awkward silence, broken by Bea saying,

'Well, what are you going to do now? Do you want to come back inside with us? Or stay out here for a bit longer?' She glanced at Ross. 'Because if you do, that's fine . . .'

Ross had the kind of body language going on that indicated he'd been having fun getting flirty with a girl and had just discovered she was his half-sister.

To put him out of his misery, Hallie said to Bea, 'It's all right, I'll come back in with you.'

'Sure?'

'Very sure.' She met Ross's uncomfortable, trying-not-to-look-shifty gaze and managed a brief smile to let him know she understood. 'It's fine. I'd rather be inside. Bye.' She did a little wave as Luke swung her chair round, ready to push her back up the garden. 'It's been nice talking to you.'

'Yes. You too.' Ross nodded; the relief was there in his voice, in the relaxation of his broad shoulders beneath that crisply ironed pink Ralph Lauren shirt.

They were, Hallie noted, physically broad shoulders rather than metaphorical ones.

Ah well, what could you expect? He was an estate agent.

Chapter 36

The party over at the White Hart was still going strong. Hallie could hear the music, the whoops of laughter and other sounds of revelry through her open bedroom window. Everyone was having a great time; yet again Marilyn was celebrating her birthday in style.

And Ross would undoubtedly have found another girl to chat up by now.

She switched on her laptop and concentrated on not feeling as if she were missing out on all the fun. It was an indication of the worsening condition of her lungs that those twenty minutes off oxygen had wiped her out to such an extent. Tomorrow, she knew from experience, she'd be feeling even more exhausted.

Had it been worth all that effort, just to be treated like a normal person for once and receive a bit of attention from someone who, once the truth had come out, couldn't have gone off her quicker if she'd told him she had suppurating leprosy?

Yes, in all honesty it had. Poor Ross, she'd almost felt sorry for him after that. On a couple of occasions, once they were back in the pub, she'd caught him looking over at her, and he'd given her an embarrassed nod and a smile. What he didn't understand was that she hadn't expected anything different, hadn't even secretly yearned for him to say, 'Who cares if you have cystic fibrosis? I want to see you again anyway!'

Because she didn't want to see him again. He had been fun,

but he wasn't her type. He might be physically attractive, but she hadn't *been* attracted to him, either physically or mentally.

That dubious honour – sadly for her and unbeknown to everyone else – appeared to be reserved solely for Luke Hilton.

Hallie gave herself a mental shake. OK, don't even think about it. Luke had Christina now. They were a happily reunited couple. And since there was no point in being jealous of Christina – because it simply wasn't one of those me-or-her situations – she might as well be as pleased for them, as she'd pretended to be earlier.

It might even make a difficult situation easier and put a stop to the hopeless fantasies that could never be more than fantasies anyway.

She turned her attention to her emails; several new letters had come in and she began skimming through them:

Dear Rose,

1. I'm thirty-seven years old and would love to settle down and have a family.
2. I love my three cats more than anything.
3. Six months ago, I met the most wonderful man.

So here's the thing: he's perfect in every way . . . except one.

He really hates all animals, especially cats.

He says we can move in together but only if I get rid of them. Rose, this is so hard for me. It's like asking me to give up my children. He's such a lovely man, I know we could be happy together, but the thought of never having another cat in my life is hard to imagine. (He's not allergic to them, he just doesn't like them.)

This situation is breaking my heart. If we don't move in together, he says we'll have to call it a day. But this could

232

be my last chance to have children. I'm so confused. What do you think I should do?

Yours, Maggie

Sometimes the answers were *so* easy they wrote themselves. Hallie rapidly typed:

Dear Maggie,

Oh dear, I don't mean to doubt your judgement, but are you sure this new boyfriend of yours is wonderful, lovely and perfect in every way? Because I can't say he sounds it. If someone issued those kinds of ultimatums to me, I'm afraid I'd retaliate with one of my own, along the lines of: Please get out of my life and never even *try* to contact me again.

I certainly wouldn't want to hang around in the hope of getting my eggs fertilised by such a charmer – imagine what kind of a father he might turn out to be. If he decides he doesn't much like his children, he might order you to give them away too.

Seriously, you deserve so much better than a man like that.

Was that too harsh? Hallie saved the reply but didn't send it. Tomorrow morning she'd read it again before deciding whether or not to upload it to the site.

OK, next:

Dear Rose,

1. When I was twelve I was involved in a terrible car crash.
2. I know how lucky I am to still be alive.
3. Sometimes when people tell me how lucky I am, I just want to scream at them to shut up.

I suppose that makes me a horrible person. I think I prob-ably am. You see, I'm twenty-three years old now, and last year I met – but didn't go out with – the man of my dreams.

The problem is, he turned out to be the man of my best friend's dreams as well, and now they're really happy together. I'm crying as I'm writing this, because I feel so mean, but just for once I wish someone could fancy me. Except it's never going to happen because of my face. It got badly injured in the car accident and I'll never look normal. I'm so ugly I could burst into tears every time I see myself in the mirror. No one is ever going to look at me and think, Wow, she's nice. Instead, people point and whisper. Some laugh and do Quasimodo impressions. Other people give me sympathetic smiles. (Sometimes that makes me feel even worse.)

So anyway, I suppose there isn't any answer. I am glad to be alive but I wish my face wasn't such a mess. I love my best friend and she has no idea how I feel about her boyfriend. He's nice to me too, because he's a nice person. I wish I could just be happy for them. Do you think it will get easier to bear or am I doomed to feel this way for ever?

Fran x

Dearest Fran,

Oh darling, if only I had a magic wand I could wave, but I don't. As you say, there is no definitive answer, but I want you to know that you're not alone. I know exactly how you feel. And I agree, it's miserable to feel unwanted for reasons beyond your control.

But but but . . . you have to remind yourself that this still happens to those who don't have damaged faces or anything else wrong with them. All over the world, millions of people are secretly in love with their friend's partner. You are not alone!

Secondly, your friend's relationship might not last. It's

perfectly possible that they won't be together for ever. (Yes, this might be sad for her, but it would make things an awful lot easier for you.)

Thirdly, you sound really lovely and I can understand how rejected you feel right now, but there's no reason why you shouldn't fall in love one day and be loved in return by someone wonderful. Search the internet and you'll find hundreds of stories about people whose physical appearance had them worrying they'd never find a partner. But . . . guess what? They did! Because there are plenty of human beings in the world capable of seeing beyond a bit of surface damage. And these human beings are all the better for having been blessed with that ability.

Carry on being your own beautiful self, Fran, and one day it will happen, I know it will.

Promise me you'll let us know when it does!

Love,

Rose xxx

Hallie read through what she'd written, then added: *PS No, in case you're wondering, I don't have facial scars myself. But trust me, I do have a condition that enables me to understand how you feel.*

This time she didn't leave it until the morning. She uploaded Fran's problem and her own reply. Then she shut down the computer and wondered if Fran would let her know when she did eventually find love.

What she deliberately didn't wonder was whether she'd still be around to find out.

Chapter 37

'Ooh, you should have been here yesterday,' Margot exclaimed the moment Flo arrived in her apartment. 'You'll never guess who turned up!'

'Donald Trump,' said Flo. 'Barbara Windsor. Jeremy Paxman.'

'Better than all of those.' Margot put down the glossy magazine she'd been reading and reached for her iPad. 'Patrick brought Jade to meet me. Such a lovely surprise!'

'Really? Great.' Against all the odds, the blind date arranged six weeks ago by Patrick's ex-wife had paid off; the fact that Jade was an aerobics instructor hadn't meant she was a nightmare after all. She'd actually turned out to be a thoroughly nice person who didn't mind a bit if other people weren't as crazy about aerobics as she was.

'She's charming,' Margot said happily. 'I liked her a lot. And she brought me those flowers on the table. Here, come and have a look before you start in the kitchen.'

Flo went over to look at the photos on the iPad. Margot had been keeping her updated on the budding relationship since the first unexpectedly successful dinner party following the day at Denleigh Horse Trials. She'd heard about their subsequent dates and been delighted for Patrick. It just went to show, you never knew who was going to turn out to be a good match or where you might meet them.

She knelt beside the velvet armchair and watched as Margot scrolled back to yesterday's photos of Patrick and Jade outside the apartment. There was Patrick with his tousled hair, beaming smile and favourite baggy green corduroy trousers. And there was Jade in a neat fitted pink sundress and pretty flower-print ballet shoes, her hair tied back in a glossy ponytail. Not the most obviously matched couple, but they were visibly happy together.

'Fingers crossed it'll work out for them,' said Margot. 'He deserves it.'

'He really does.'

'And how about you and your lovely man? All going well?'

'Very well.' Flo smiled, because there had been no more visits from Lena, which had to be a good thing. With a bit of luck, she'd decided to give in gracefully and accept the situation. Well, you could always hope.

'Excellent. Looks like I could be buying myself a new hat, then. Maybe even two.' Margot's dark eyes flashed with mischief. 'I love a good wedding, me.'

Ten hours later, back in her own flat, Flo was lying in the bath when she heard the bathroom door begin to slowly creak open. For a split second she thought of a horror film she'd seen years ago, when a demented-with-jealousy woman had broken into her ex-husband's house and crept into the bathroom where the new wife lay, happily oblivious that the next few moments would be her last.

Goosebumps sprang up on her thighs; what if it was Lena with a bread knife? The next moment, Jeremy's furry face poked around the door and he padded into the bathroom, tail swishing and green eyes gleaming as he met her gaze.

He wasn't carrying a bread knife.

Flo exhaled and shook her head at him as he jumped up and made himself comfortable on the padded lid of the laundry basket. 'You gave me a start. I thought you were Lena.'

Jeremy twitched first one ear then the other, and gave her one of those disdainful looks that said, *For goodness' sake, how can you be so stupid?*

He was right, of course. Lena wouldn't really do something like that. Fingers crossed, she'd had time now to get used to the idea that Flo and Zander were a couple and weren't going to stop seeing each other just because she didn't approve.

You never could tell: as the weeks and months went by, she might even realise that she'd been wrong, that her brother had fallen in love with a nice person. They didn't need to be enemies . . . they could become friends, meet up for girlie lunches, go shopping together . . .

OK, that was taking weird fantasies *too* far. Dismissing the idea, Flo returned to cheerier thoughts of Patrick and Jade and their blossoming relationship. She was genuinely happy for Patrick. You never knew, did you, when a couple might hit it off?

The doorbell rang twenty minutes later. As luck would have it, Flo was out of the bath and wearing her dressing gown. As luck wouldn't have it, she'd just applied a thick layer of moisturiser to her feet, which necessitated waddling like a duck across the wooden floorboards and doing her best to stay upright.

Pressing the intercom, she said, 'Yes?'

'Hello, my name's Julia. I wonder if I could speak with you about Zander Travis?'

Taken aback, Flo said, 'Zander? What about him?'

'Please. I just need a quick word. Or if you don't want to let me in, we could meet in the coffee shop on the corner.'

The coffee shop on the corner would mean getting dressed, drying her hair and putting on at least a modicum of make-up. She would also have to wipe all the moisturiser off her feet. After a brief hesitation, Flo pressed the button to buzz open the door downstairs and said, 'Come on up.'

Julia was slim, pretty, possibly a couple of years younger than herself. She was wearing an expensive blue shirt, cream trousers and a tan suede gilet. Her streaked blond hair swung past her shoulders. She had good teeth.

She also looked slightly – *very* slightly – familiar.

Were they meant to be shaking hands? Unsure, Flo waited for Julia to make the first move.

OK, they weren't going to shake hands.

'Thanks for seeing me,' said Julia. And waited.

'I don't know *why* I am seeing you.' Flo shoved her hands deep into the fluffy pockets of her dressing gown.

'Well . . . you might not want to hear this, but it's only fair that you know.' Lifting her chin, Julia said, 'The thing is, Zander's been cheating on you.'

'He has? Who with?'

'Me.'

'Oh.'

'Sorry. But it's true.'

Flo's heart was racing as she experienced an odd mixture of emotions. On the one hand, this was shocking news, devastating even. On the other hand, a little voice was nudging at her subconscious, whispering that something wasn't quite adding up.

Apart from anything else, Zander simply didn't seem like the cheating type.

'He's been lying to you,' said Julia. 'And to me too. He told me he was single. Then someone told me he'd been playing the two of us off against each other. You didn't see him on Monday night, did you?'

Monday, Monday . . .

'No, I didn't.' Flo shook her head.

'That's because he was seeing me. He's a liar and a cheat,' said Julia. 'I couldn't believe it when I found out, but it's true.'

She knew that face from somewhere, but *where*? Not being able to place her was driving Flo nuts.

'You must be devastated,' Julia continued. 'I was too. Why do men think they can get away with it? Because they always do, don't they! I challenged Zander and he flat-out denied he was seeing anyone else. I bet if you asked him he'd say the same thing. What a bastard. He just wants to have his cake and eat it!'

She was saying the words but they didn't sound completely authentic. Flo stared at her ears, her neck, her earnestly outraged expression. Something was missing, but she still couldn't work out what it was. Julia's hands were tanned, her wrists narrow. She had a well-elocuted voice and was clutching the strap of a small cream leather bag. Something about her was making Flo think of flowers . . .

'How did you know where to find me?'

'I don't think I should say. I wouldn't want to get anyone into trouble. So what are you going to do?' said Julia. 'Once a cheat, always a cheat. You'll never be able to trust him again. I think we should both dump him, don't you? That'd serve him right!'

Flowers . . . flowers . . . and for some reason camels kept sliding into Flo's mind. Honestly, this was infuriating. She cleared her throat. 'Have we met before?'

'What, us? You and me? No, definitely not.' Julia was shaking her head. 'Never.'

'Are you a florist?'

'No.'

OK, in for a penny. 'Do you work at the zoo?'

Now Julia looked offended. 'God, no, I do not!'

It was the squeak of outrage that did it, prompting Flo to realise that it was only the face she recognised, not the voice. The next moment, in a flash, she knew where she'd seen Julia before.

Chapter 38

OK, she was almost completely sure. Maybe best to double-check. Reaching for her phone, Flo checked the time – yes, Margot would be in her room now – and fired off a quick text.

'What are you doing?' said Julia. 'Asking Zander about me? I've already told you, he'll just deny everything. He's a complete *weasel*.'

More to pass the time than anything else, Flo said, 'Tell me how the two of you met,' and Julia began burbling away about the night she'd been chatted up by Zander in a bar on Park Street.

Luckily Margot didn't hang around. The attachments popped up on her phone and Flo opened them.

And there it was, the confirmation she needed. She'd been right after all.

'What?' Julia tried to peer over the top of the phone. 'What are you looking at?'

'Photos of you,' said Flo.

Julia's face instantly flooded with colour. 'I don't know what you mean.'

'No? Maybe it's just someone who looks like you. Ooh,' said Flo, 'or maybe your mum had twins and gave one of you away!'

'Let me see,' said Julia.

'I like this one, of you in Egypt with the pyramids in the background. You're standing next to a camel.'

Julia rubbed the base of her throat, which had gone all blotchy. 'This is ridiculous.'

'And I *really* like this one, taken on your wedding day. Last summer, wasn't it? You look beautiful,' said Flo. 'And your husband seems so nice. Does he know about you and Zander?' She held out the phone to show Julia the wedding photo, taken in the porch of a village church. There were garlands of flowers wound around the wooden posts on each side of the ancient oak door, yellow rosebuds in Julia's headdress and more arrangements of pink and yellow roses in tall silver vases on the deep stone ledges behind her.

Flowers.

And camels.

The brain was indeed a wondrous thing.

'Oh God, I don't believe this.' Julia's haughty demeanour had crumbled. Flushed and mortified, she shook her head. 'Look, I'm sorry. I'm not having an affair with your boyfriend.'

'I know,' said Flo.

'How on earth did you get hold of those pictures?'

'I couldn't work it out at first. I knew I'd seen you somewhere before.' Flo paused, briefly wondering whether to keep her in suspense. But no, she couldn't do it. 'I work at Nairn House.'

'Nairn . . . *oh*.' Julia's face cleared. 'My grandmother's at Nairn House.'

Flo nodded. 'Beryl. She has photos of you in white frames lined up on her living-room wall. I see them every day.'

'Right.' Julia managed a wry smile. 'Busted. I really am sorry.'

'Just a wild guess,' said Flo, 'but was it Lena who put you up to doing this?'

Embarrassed, Julia nodded. 'She's a friend. Well, more a friend of a friend. Her chap Giles plays cricket with my husband. The moment she heard I belonged to an amateur dramatics group, she decided I had to come and see you and pretend I was

Zander's other girlfriend. The thing is, once Lena gets an idea into her head, she doesn't give up. I didn't want to do it, but she isn't an easy person to say no to.'

'I've noticed,' said Flo.

'She can be a bit scary, to be honest.'

'I've noticed that too.'

'I'm so sorry,' Julia said again.

'It's OK.'

'From all the things Lena's been telling us about you, we thought you were a complete monster. But you don't seem . . .'

'Very monstery?'

Julia pulled a face. 'Well, yes.'

'Lena doesn't like me. Nor does Giles,' Flo added.

'Giles is ghastly. I can't stand him.'

A new message popped up on Flo's phone: *Dying of curiosity here! Why did you want the pics?*

Flo smiled; she'd asked Margot to pay a visit to Beryl's flat, take the necessary photos and send them to her. She messaged back: *Bumped into Beryl's granddaughter and recognised her, that's all. Thanks for doing it!*

Seconds later, Margot's reply appeared: *My pleasure! Think I might become an international spy when I grow up.*

A couple of hours after Julia had left, Flo's phone rang.

'Hello,' said Lena. 'Are you OK?'

'I'm great. Why?'

'I just wondered if you'd heard the rumours about Zander. I'm not a great one for spreading gossip, but I thought you should know what people are saying.'

'Gosh. What are they saying?'

'Well, I don't know if it's true, but apparently he's been seeing someone else behind your back.'

'Ah, you mean Julia,' said Flo. 'Yes, she came to see me tonight. It is all true.'

'Oh!' Taken aback, Lena said, 'So . . . that's awful, then. Poor you! You must be *devastated*.'

'Well, I was a bit shocked when she first told me, but then I stopped and thought about it, and I decided it wasn't so bad after all.'

'Are you out of your *mind*?' Lena sounded as if her eyebrows had disappeared into her hairline. 'My God, he's cheating on you! How is that not bad?'

'Yes, but I love him. And I think he loves me. So I'm not going to let it bother me,' said Flo. 'I'm sure he'll get tired of Julia soon, then I'll have him all to myself.'

'So he's sleeping with another woman and you're just going to put up with it? That is ridiculous,' said Lena. 'He's making a fool of you!'

'I don't care,' said Flo. 'I'll win in the end. He's worth it.'

Outraged by the failure of her plan, Lena said, 'Well you're a complete loser,' and furiously hung up.

Flo put the phone down and realised that she was smiling to herself. Was she turning into Lena? Talk about one-upmanship. And telling lies was naughty.

Oh, but sometimes being naughty was fun.

Arriving back at his flat at midnight, Zander unlocked the front door and knew at once from the mingled scents of burnt toast and Chanel No. 5 that Lena was home.

He experienced the familiar sensations of resignation, bafflement and despair. What must it be like to have a sister who didn't perpetually make life difficult?

'Hello! You're late! Does it smell of burnt toast in here? I tried to cover it up with perfume . . . I don't know why the stupid toaster always does that to me. Are you hungry? Would you like some toast? There's a little bit of apricot jam left if you—'

'I've spoken to Flo.' Zander gave her a steady look as he took off his jacket. 'I know it was you.'

As he'd known she would, Lena looked utterly mystified. 'Excuse me? I have *no* idea what you're talking about.'

'Look, this is me. I know I'm not cheating on Flo. Who else would even *want* to make up a story like that?'

And as quickly as she'd denied it, Lena shrugged and said, 'Oh please, she's ridiculous. She wouldn't even care if you did have an affair with someone else. Talk about pathetic. Anyway, I hate her.'

How many times had they gone over this? 'Flo hasn't done anything to you,' said Zander.

'Er, hello? She's living in our flat!'

This was the thing about Lena: listening to the voice of reason simply didn't feature on her radar. The fact that their grandmother had made the relevant specifications in her will was irrelevant as far as his sister was concerned.

'Officially, she's living in Jeremy's flat. It's his for the rest of his life.'

'It's the most ridiculous situation *ever*.' Lena's narrow mouth pursed with irritation. 'Stupid cat.'

Zander raked his fingers through his hair. 'Listen to me. The way you're behaving isn't helping anyone. You can resent Flo all you want, but it's not going to stop me seeing her. I really, really like her. A lot.'

'You don't. You just think you do. You're probably just doing it to spite me.'

'You're not going to ruin this relationship. I won't let you.'

'You're so gullible,' said Lena. 'Can't you see what she's like? You deserve so much better than her.'

'I deserve so much better than *this*.' Zander shook his head at his difficult sister. 'You're living here in my flat. I could tell you to leave.'

'But you can't do that. Where would I go?'

And how many times had they been over this? Dozens? Hundreds? Zander said wearily, 'I could do it. Lena, you're thirty-six years old. You need to stand on your own two feet.'

'I will do, just as soon as that complete bitch moves out of our flat. Anyway, you can't make me leave here. You promised Mum, remember.'

There it was, the argument she always produced as a trump card, the one she knew he didn't have the heart to ignore. When their mother had been dying of cancer, she had begged him to take care of Lena and he'd agreed. Obviously.

It might have worked out a bit better if she hadn't then gone on to share the news of the promise with Lena. On the one hand, it had been closure for their mother. On the other, it had effectively given Lena a get-out-of-jail-free card for the rest of her life.

'I'm going to bed. Good night.' Tired and resigned, Zander left his sister in the living room; there was no point arguing with her any more. Oh, but it was an endless circle of frustration, being responsible for someone older than yourself.

At this rate, he'd still be stuck with her when he was eighty.

Chapter 39

The wind was blasting Tasha's face and she was tumbling through the air. The parachute should have opened by now, but it was still tightly packed into the bag on her back and the toggle to release it had vanished. Having fumbled frantically to find it without success, she gave up and began to flap her arms instead . . . maybe if she flapped them fast enough she could save herself . . . except now the ground was rushing up towards her. Oh God, too late, she was going to crash—

Tasha gulped, gasped and woke up, shuddering with relief because she was at home in bed, not splattered somewhere in a field. God, the *relief*. Still alive, not dead. Although the way her poor overwrought heart was currently crashing around inside her ribcage, it might not hold out too much longer.

Next to her, Rory slept peacefully on, his breathing slow and even. Amazingly, she hadn't woken him up with all her arm-flapping and thrashing about.

Ugh, though. Was there anything worse in the world than that horrific sensation of falling from a great height? No, there wasn't. Her stomach was still knotted at the memory of it, her breathing ragged, her palms tingling and damp with adrenalin-fuelled sweat.

OK, just close your eyes and relax. Stop thinking about it. Go back to sleep.

Ten minutes later, since that clearly wasn't going to happen, Tasha slid out of bed and headed for the kitchen. She boiled the kettle, made herself a mug of tea and sat down in the living room with her laptop.

It was four in the morning on Thursday. Three days from now, the skydive would be over. With a bit of luck, the parachute would open and she wouldn't die. Hopefully too, once the hideous experience was behind her, tonight's recurring dream would stop and she'd be able to sleep like a normal person once more.

'There you are.' Ruffling her bed-head hair, Rory joined her on the sofa. 'I woke up and you were gone. Thought you'd run off with another man.'

'He's picking me up in an hour.' Tasha rested her bare legs across his lap and watched his hand massage her left knee.

'Did you have the dream again?'

'No.' She shook her head, felt him give her knee a gentle squeeze. 'Maybe.' Rory knew about the dreams; last time she'd been flapping her arms so hard she'd whacked him round the head.

'You don't have to do it, you know. You can cancel.'

'Not going to happen.'

'You're terrified.'

This was true. When she'd first said she'd do the jump, she'd been so sure she wouldn't be scared. But that was before Joe had said jokingly, 'Whatever you do, don't Google skydiving accidents.'

Because Googling skydiving accidents *really* hadn't helped.

The recurring dream – except it wasn't a dream, it was a nightmare – had started that same night.

'I can feel your heart racing from here,' Rory said now.

'Seriously, you don't have to put yourself through this. You're allowed to change your mind.'

Tasha shifted the angle of the laptop so he could see the screen showing her fund-raising page. Since setting it up, the donations had kept rolling in, thanks to Joe and Rory shamelessly tapping up their friends and colleagues in the City.

'It's up to eight and a half thousand pounds. I'm not backing out.'

'Is that what's bothering you?' Rory drew her against him so her head was resting on his shoulder. 'Seriously, don't even think about it. If you tell everyone the skydive's cancelled and offer them their money back, I guarantee not one person will accept it.'

Oh God, it was so tempting. The details of the top Google searches were by now pretty much tattooed on Tasha's brain. One man had died when his harness became detached during descent . . . a skydiver had plummeted to her death after her chute failed to open . . . a student and instructor had *both* died during a tandem jump as a result of equipment malfunction . . .

She shook her head. It was no good; she'd said she'd jump out of a plane, and she was going to do it if it killed her.

Although fingers crossed, it wouldn't.

She straightened up, closed the laptop and met Rory's hazel-flecked green eyes. 'Hey, we're doing it. No way am I backing out.'

The deep roar of the engines reverberated in Tasha's ears as the plane soared into the air. Sunlight streamed in through the dusty windows and she had to close her eyes for a moment. It was finally going to happen. When they reached twelve thousand feet, the door would be opened and people would start throwing themselves out through it.

Everything felt the same as it had done before, except this time it wasn't a dream.

Her eyes were still closed when she felt Rory's fingers entwine with hers, and the warmth of his breath in her ear.

'Still time to change your mind.'

Tasha opened her eyes and smiled; he was doing the jump for the sheer thrill of it, because he wanted to. It simply didn't occur to him that he could die. She squeezed his fingers and said, 'Still doing it.'

'It wouldn't make any difference to me. You know that, don't you? I love you whether you jump or not.'

'I love you too.' They were both wearing plastic goggles; it wasn't the most romantic of kisses, what with the sides of the goggles clashing together, but just for a second it made Tasha feel better.

'Look happy,' said one of the instructors, holding up a camera. 'Today's the big day!'

Tasha hoped it didn't turn out to be the day she vomited with fear all over her borrowed blue jumpsuit.

Up and up they went, on their way to twelve thousand feet. Which hadn't actually sounded too bad until someone else remarked cheerily, 'Can you believe it? We're two miles up in the air!'

Two whole *miles*. Ridiculous. Oh God, and now her scalp was starting to prickle with fear . . .

'OK, let's get ready now.' Her designated instructor, the one to whom she would be attached for the tandem jump, moved towards her. His name was Graham, and he looked like a jolly farmer. Tasha let him double-check the safety harness she was already wearing, then fasten her to his front.

'Remember what you have to do?' said Graham.

They'd watched a video and he'd given her all the necessary instructions on the ground. Tasha nodded; she'd never paid so much attention to anything before in her life. A few feet away,

Rory's instructor was clipping and fastening himself to Rory, who grinned and gave him a thumbs-up.

See? Not a care in the world.

Then someone shouted, 'Open the door,' and two people beside the cargo hatch raised it. Without a moment's hesitation, they dived through and vanished from view.

Now the tandem jumpers made their way towards it, walking awkwardly in their tethered pairs, and sitting down as they approached the gaping hole. One woman began to hyperventilate and scream that she couldn't do it, and her instructor moved her out of the queue.

Which didn't help.

Then it was Rory's turn, and he just had time to flash her a smile before his instructor scooted him forward and tipped him out of the plane.

'OK?' Graham rested a hand on Tasha's shoulder.

'I'm good.' Her teeth were chatting uncontrollably. Right now, Rory was tumbling through the air. What if the parachute got tangled and didn't open?

What if mine doesn't?

They'd reached the hatch. Behind her, Tasha could hear the hyperventilating woman sobbing and saying, 'I can't do it, please don't make me do it.' Nudging her forward inch by inch, Graham shouted above the noise of the wind, 'Just relax and cross your arms over your chest.'

Her feet were now dangling down through the hatch, being buffeted sideways by the wind. She felt Graham ease forward, moving her with him. He rocked back, then forward again . . . and then there was no more plane floor to be sitting on. They were tumbling over and over through the air, free-falling. At that point, Tasha knew for sure that her life was over. She was oh so definitely going to die.

Then Graham tapped her smartly on both shoulders, his signal for her to get into the free-fall position. Tasha stretched her body flat and held her arms out wide, arching her back, keeping her head raised and curling her legs up behind her.

Her face was battered by the wind, her hair was tied back but the ends still slapped her cheeks. They were falling, she knew, at 120mph. This was going to carry on for at least the next forty seconds. Since she wasn't going to die for another few minutes, she looked down and saw green grass, hayfields, trees and buildings below. And above and all around her, mesmerising in its vastness, there was clear blue sky.

She didn't even realise it had happened. One minute the anxiety and terror had been all-encompassing; the next minute it had evaporated. They were hurtling through the air together and it felt like the most magical and amazing thing in the world. She was flying. Well, not quite. But the fear was gone.

Then at five thousand feet Graham pulled the ripcord and deployed the parachute. There was a tugging sensation on the harness gripping Tasha's body, and plummeting gave way to gently floating down to earth.

Oh wow, this was incredible. Gazing around, she took in the cars bouncing sunlight off their windscreens, the teeny-tiny people below, the birds flying through the space between up here and down there. And that was the field they'd be landing in; she could see the big white cross laid out on the ground to guide them towards it.

There seemed to be something written on the cross, Tasha saw as she swayed and floated through the warm air. Graham's arm came into view and he pointed over her shoulder.

'Can you make out what it says?'

She shook her head; presumably it would be something along the lines of: 'Please land here, and if you can manage not to break your legs we'd be grateful.'

Thirty seconds later, when they were that much closer, the blurry black letters became recognisable words, and she saw that they said:

```
                    T
                    A
                    S
                    H

WILL   YOU   MARRY
                    M
                    E
                    ?
                    ?
```

Chapter 40

Behind the plastic goggles, Tasha's eyes filled with tears.

Oh wow. Just . . . wow.

Ninety seconds later, the ground came up to meet them and it was time to land. Pulling up her legs and scooting along practically in Graham's lap, Tasha made it without so much as a bump. They'd managed a textbook landing, the white parachute billowing behind them.

'Well?' said Graham, unclipping her and helping her out of the harness.

'It was amazing. Thank you so much. I loved it.'

'Good.' He beamed at her, his jolly farmer's cheeks glowing. 'Although I was actually wondering how you felt about the message on the landing cross.'

He'd known about it all along, had been in on the surprise. Tasha removed her plastic goggles and said, 'Exciting, isn't it? Someone wants to marry me!' Her eyes danced. 'Now we just have to find out who it is.'

Then she turned, because there was Rory waiting at the perimeter of the landing area with Joe and Carmel. And her heart gave a squeeze of love, because he truly made her life complete.

As she reached them, Joe indicated his raised phone. 'I'm videoing this, by the way, for posterity. So keep it clean if you can.'

Tasha shivered as Rory reached out and took hold of her left hand. His gaze unwavering, he said, 'I'm going to do this properly,' and dropped to one knee.

'Oh my God,' Carmel exclaimed, 'this is SO romantic.'

'Don't interrupt.' Joe gave her a nudge.

'I love you more than I thought it was possible to love anyone,' said Rory.

'Thanks,' said Joe. 'It's because I'm such a great guy.'

'*You* shut up,' said Carmel. 'Come on, just let him get on and do it.'

'Tash, you've changed my life. I'm so glad I saw you digging around in that rubbish bin on Christmas Eve. If you hadn't thrown away your credit card, we'd never have met.' Rory shook his head. 'And that just doesn't bear thinking about. I love you and I want to spend the rest of my life with you. So would you make me the happiest man in the world and be my wife?'

Tasha broke into a slow, unstoppable smile. 'Oh yes please. Yes, yes, yes.' She sank to her knees so that she could throw her arms around him. 'Absolutely yes!'

Between kisses, as assorted bystanders whooped and applauded, Rory said, 'And just so you know, I'm not doing this because you jumped out of the plane. It was always going to happen anyway.' He unzipped the top pocket of his blue jumpsuit and took out a small jewellery box tied with white ribbon. When Tasha saw the colour of the box – that distinctive shade of duck-egg blue – her mouth went dry.

Then he opened the lid and she started to laugh, because inside was a ring-shaped Haribo sweet nestled on the bed of white satin.

'Here.' Joe came forward and dropped something into Rory's free hand. 'I made him do that in case his parachute didn't open.' He winked at Tasha. 'Didn't want it getting messy.'

'Good thinking,' said Tasha.

Rory removed the Haribo from the box – predictably, Joe

took it and ate it – and replaced it with the real ring. He held it up to show Tasha, then clasped her hand and slid it on to her finger.

Well, not *slid* exactly. The ring was a slightly tight fit, but after a couple of awkward seconds it went over her knuckle. *Phew.*

'I don't believe this. How did you do it?' The diamond glittered in the sunlight, surely more brightly than any diamond had ever glittered before. The ring was simple and exquisite, exactly what she would have chosen for herself.

'I took Joe along with me to the store on Old Bond Street.'

'They gave us champagne.' Joe was smug. 'At ten o'clock in the morning. It was brilliant!'

'And he tried to chat up the sales girl,' said Rory. 'Without success.'

'Ah, but it was fun trying.'

'Anyway,' Rory went on, 'you can exchange it if there's another style you'd prefer. I don't mind at all – I just want you to be wearing something you love.'

Touched beyond belief by the mental image of Rory and Joe venturing into Tiffany's and setting about choosing a ring for her, Tasha shook her head. 'I love this one, more than anything. I don't want any other style. I'm never taking it off.' She kissed Rory again, then said, 'And I love you too. Right now, I'm the happiest girl in the world.'

Carmel's hands were clasped together against her chest. 'This is so perfect, I think I'm going to cry. Why can't something like this happen to me?'

'Want me to propose to you?' said Joe.

Amused, Carmel rolled her eyes. 'Funny you should ask that. No.'

'OK, that's enough filming.' Joe pressed the stop button on his phone. 'We'll delete that last bit.'

'Good,' said Carmel.

'But one day you'll say yes, I know you will.'

'I won't.' She shook her head and pointed to Tasha and Rory. 'See them? They have it. I want what they have.'

Helping Tasha to her feet, Rory kept his arm around her waist and murmured, 'Hear that? We have *it*.'

The words felt like chocolate melting through her veins, because he was right. Miraculously, they did. Tasha whispered, 'I want us to always have it.'

'Oh we will, trust me.' Rory gave her a squeeze and she felt his breath against her hair. 'This is it now, for better or worse. Till death us do part.'

At midnight, they were in their favourite bar in Belsize Park, still celebrating the events of the day. Friends had joined them, champagne corks had been popped and the videos of Tasha's skydive and Rory's subsequent proposal had been playing on a loop up on the big screen behind the bar.

The Tiffany diamond ring was still glittering away on Tasha's finger. She just couldn't stop looking at it. Every time someone congratulated her, she felt the euphoria bubble up all over again. Asked when the wedding might be, Rory had said, 'Whenever Tash wants it to happen. The sooner the better, if it's up to me.'

It had been such an incredible day. Tasha wanted it to go on for ever. She'd jumped out of a plane and raised over eight thousand pounds for her favourite charity. She'd got herself a fiancé, and not any old fiancé either. Rory McAndrew was everything she'd ever wanted and more. Which meant she was the luckiest girl in the world. Life simply didn't get any better than this.

Although if she were being really finicky, it would be nicer not to have to get up at seven tomorrow morning to go and do the make-up for a wedding in Berkshire.

At half past midnight, Rory said, 'Shall I call a cab?'

'No!' This from Joe, who wasn't nearly ready to end the evening. 'You can't go yet!'

'I'm shattered,' said Rory.

'And I'm working tomorrow,' said Tasha.

Joe looked at her. 'That might be true.' He pointed to Rory. 'But *that* isn't. There's no way you're shattered. You just want to slope off home and have sex with your new fiancée.'

Rory grinned. 'It's a possibility.'

They said their goodbyes. Reaching Joe last, Tasha gave him an extra-big hug. 'Thank you. Really.'

He hugged her back. 'My pleasure, darling. You two are perfect together. I'm so happy for you both.'

She kissed him on the cheek. 'You're brilliant.'

'I *know* I am.' Joe was indignant. 'Could you have a word with that nightmare friend of yours and please tell her that? All this rejection's doing nothing for my self-esteem.'

He'd deliberately said it loudly enough for Carmel to hear. She patted Joe's arm. 'You poor fragile flower.'

'You're making fun of me now, but you just wait,' Joe told her. 'When you're old and all alone in your rocking chair, you'll look back on this and regret not giving me a chance.'

'You could be right.' Carmel nodded. 'Tell you what, if we're both still single thirty years from now, we'll get together.'

'Great. Although we should probably have a practice beforehand, just to make sure we're compatible. If you like,' said Joe, 'we could do that tonight, get it out of the way.'

'You never give up, do you?' Carmel gave him a good-humoured pitying look. 'In your wildest dreams.'

'And he has those most nights,' said Rory with a grin.

Chapter 41

'Hey, what's this? Oh wow, have you just got engaged? Congratulations!' Alice, the bride-to-be whose make-up Tasha was doing for the wedding this afternoon, spotted the ring in the mirror and twisted round in her chair to clasp Tasha's left hand.

Tasha said joyfully, 'It all happened yesterday. I still can't believe it.'

'Well that explains why you're glowing.' Alice's eyes danced with mischief. 'Now we know what you were up to last night!'

Tasha let her think it. In fact, after getting back to Rory's flat, the wild sex everyone had assumed they'd be having hadn't materialised. By the time she'd emerged from the bathroom, ready to celebrate, Rory had been out for the count. Well, it had been a long day; she wasn't offended. And what did it matter anyway? They had the rest of their lives to make up for it.

They'd both slept through until the alarm had gone off at seven. Rory, leaning over for a kiss, had said, 'Sorry about crashing out.'

'No problem.' Smiling, Tasha stroked his chest. 'I was pretty tired too. What are you going to be doing today?'

He stretched experimentally, winced a bit. 'Head to the gym. Maybe go for a run later. My muscles are aching after the jump. What time will you be back?'

'Somewhere around five, I should think.'

'Want me to cook a roast dinner?'

'That sounds fantastic,' said Tasha.

'Roast chicken, roast potatoes, veg, bread sauce and gravy?'

'You know what?' She reached across and kissed him again. 'That's a good enough reason to marry you right there.'

'And after dinner, we'll make up for last night and have loads of really fantastic sex.'

If only they had time for it now. Sadly, they didn't. Tasha slid out of bed. 'Deal.'

But bride-to-be Alice didn't need to know any of these finer details. Tasha said cheerily, 'We had quite a party. And the ring's from Tiffany's, can you believe it?'

'Amazing! Do you have photos? I want to see what he looks like!'

So in the middle of doing Alice's wedding-day make-up, Tasha found herself putting down her brushes and stopping work to show her photographs of Rory.

'He's gorgeous. Looks like so much fun. You'll have beautiful babies.' Producing her own phone, Alice brought up photos of her fiancé Eric and in turn showed them off to Tasha. A human rights lawyer, Eric was thin, fair-haired and geeky.

'Yours looks lovely too.' Tasha *much* preferred hers.

'He is.' Alice nodded happily. 'Ah, I love him to bits. We're so lucky, aren't we?'

Tasha paused at one of the photos she'd taken last night in the wine bar, of Rory with his head thrown back as he laughed at something one of his friends had just said. God, he was perfect. And he was all *hers*.

Aloud, she said with pride, 'Oh yes.'

The wedding had been a triumph. Apart from one bridesmaid having too much to drink and throwing up into a flower arrangement, the whole event had gone without a hitch. Having been asked to stay in order to make sure the bride, her bridesmaids and her mother looked their best for the photographs at the reception, Tasha had been kept busy mattifying faces, redoing lipstick and repairing out-of-control mascara runs.

It had been a happy day, though, and she'd sensed an instant attraction between the best man and the bride's pretty younger sister. As she had been leaving, she'd spotted them sharing a sneaky kiss out in the hotel's car park. And that was the brilliant thing: you never knew what might come of this newest of budding romances. Just think, a year or two from now, she could be asked to do the make-up for another wedding, only to discover it was them.

Driving home, Tasha couldn't wait to see Rory again. Apart from a few hors d'oeuvres, she'd had nothing to eat, so she was also looking forward with a vengeance to her roast dinner. Her fiancé (*ha, get me!*) would be busy in the kitchen now, wearing his favourite blue T-shirt and faded jeans, singing along to the radio as he expertly basted the chicken, turned the crisped-up roast potatoes and flambéed red wine before whisking it into the gravy.

I mean, how many gorgeous adrenalin-junkie thrill-seeking super-sporty types are also capable of making stupendous gravy?

Seriously, they were pretty thin on the ground.

But when she fitted her key into the lock and pushed open the front door, the heavenly scents of roast dinner were sadly lacking. The air in the flat smelled of . . . nothing at all.

Had Rory forgotten about the meal and gone out with Joe? Could he have met up with friends at the gym and decided to join them for a drink or two afterwards? Or had he changed his mind about cooking and decided to take her out to their favourite restaurant instead?

'Hello?' No, the kitchen was empty, as was the living room. 'Are you here?'

The next moment, Tasha heard the creak of the bed. So he *was* here. This made even less sense, unless— She froze, remembering what had happened to one of Carmel's friends the other week. Returning home unexpectedly, she'd burst into the bedroom and caught her boyfriend in bed with the girl from the flat upstairs.

Well, hopefully she wasn't about to walk in on *that* scenario, particularly since Rory's upstairs neighbour was a sixty-year-old history teacher with a vast swollen belly and a ZZ Top beard . . .

Pushing open the bedroom door, she said, 'OK, if you're having sex with Beardy Bernard, you're in big trouble.'

'Huh? Oh God, what's the time?' Rory rolled over and winced as he opened his eyes. 'Is it five o'clock already?'

'Almost half past. You poor thing, are you ill?'

He pulled a face and nodded. 'Sorry, didn't mean to sleep this long. I was going to cook dinner.'

'I've never seen you sick before.' Sitting on the bed next to him, Tasha smoothed his tousled hair back from his forehead.

'That's because I'm never sick. I started feeling a bit rough last night, thought I'd be back to normal today.' He shifted his head against the squashed pillows. 'But I'm not.'

'How rotten.'

'I think it's flu.'

Tasha smiled, because she'd guessed he'd say that. 'It's probably not flu, not at this time of year. You've just caught a bug.'

'This definitely feels like flu,' said Rory.

He looked so sad, how could she not humour him? 'OK, maybe it is.'

'How was the wedding?'

'Great. One puking bridesmaid, otherwise everything was fine. The hotel was amazing; they ran the whole event like clockwork and the staff were lovely.'

'What does that mean?' He broke into a wry smile. 'You wouldn't mind us getting married there?'

'Who knows? It could go on the long-list.' Tasha laced her

262

fingers through his, admiring the look of their clasped hands and the way the diamond flashed light like a tiny sparkler.

'Sorry I didn't get the size right.' Rory touched the narrow platinum band. 'We can have it sorted, no problem.'

Tasha shook her head. 'No way, I'm not giving it back to them, not even for a day. I'd rather stop eating until my fingers get thinner.'

He stroked the back of her hand. 'Sorry about dinner too.'

'Don't be daft, doesn't matter at all. I'll make something quick. How about you, are you hungry?'

Rory coughed and wearily shook his head. 'Wouldn't mind a cup of tea, though.'

Tasha left him to rest and went into the kitchen. But a couple of minutes after she'd started frying bacon and buttering bread, she heard him call out, 'Are you doing bacon sandwiches? I could probably manage one of those.'

Of course he could. Amused, she peeled off extra rashers and added them to the sizzling pan.

Men: they were never quite as ill as they liked to make out.

Chapter 42

Bea hadn't got any better at keeping secrets.

'Is everything OK?' said Hallie, watching with interest as she sat on the end of the bed and fiddled with a toffee eclair wrapper.

'Everything's great.' Bea nodded over-brightly. 'Yes, great!'

She might as well be holding up a placard that said: FEELING GUILTY AND TRYING TO HIDE IT.

'You can have another toffee eclair if you want.' Hallie pushed the bag across the duvet towards her. 'Help yourself.'

Bea had tied the wrapper from the first one into a tight knot. She shook her head.

'Look, something's up,' said Hallie. 'Why don't you tell me what's going on? Just say it.'

'OK, something *is* up.' Bea expelled a long breath and began twisting the bangles on her wrist.

'I know. It's pretty obvious. Also, it's Tuesday and I haven't seen you since Saturday.' Hallie gave her a playful nudge with her foot. 'Have you gone and found yourself a new best friend?'

'*No.*' Bea pulled a regretful face. 'But I've kind of got a boyfriend.'

'You have? Yay, that's brilliant! Why didn't you tell me before?'

There it was again, the guilty grimace. Bea took another deep breath. 'Look, I'm sorry, I feel really bad about this. It's someone you know.'

OK, she hadn't been expecting that. Hallie's heart began to race, because there was only one person she could think of who might be causing Bea to feel bad about the situation.

Luke.

Surely it wasn't him?

Except why would Bea feel bad, when she didn't know about her secret feelings for Luke anyway?

Apart from anything else, Luke was with Christina now. They were a proper couple once more. So it definitely couldn't be him.

'I can't guess.' Hallie shrugged. 'No idea. You'll have to tell me.'

Bea swallowed. 'It's Ross.'

Ross. For a second, Hallie was none the wiser. Then it clicked. 'The one at Marilyn's birthday? Estate agent from Oxford? That Ross?'

'OK, I know, just let me explain what happened,' Bea blurted out. 'I saw what was going on that night and I knew you liked him, so after you left the party I had a bit of a go at him for the way he treated you. And the thing was, he was so *apologetic* . . . he really felt bad about it, but the whole wheelchair and oxygen thing completely freaked him out. Anyway, he *was* sorry, and we carried on chatting and he seemed like a nice guy, but then he asked me if I wanted to meet up some other time and I said no way, because of what he'd done to you, and—'

'Hey,' said Hallie, because Bea was babbling and getting flustered. 'It's fine. Really. He didn't do anything to me.'

'Well anyway, he kept asking but I kept saying no, then he wanted my phone number so I gave it to him because I thought that was harmless enough. Then the party ended and he left and I thought that was that, I'd never hear from him again, he was just one of those flirty types.'

'But you did hear from him,' said Hallie.

'He started sending me these texts. Not *those* kind of texts.

Just, like, really funny and sweet messages. And after a few days he asked me out again and I suppose I was just curious . . . so I ended up saying yes.'

'And you had a good time.'

'Oh God, we had the *best* time. There's just something about him that makes me feel . . . you know . . .' Bea clapped her hand to her chest. 'But I felt so guilty, because I knew you liked him too . . .'

'I didn't really,' said Hallie. 'I liked talking to him, that was all. He's pretty to look at but really not my type. I promise you, it's fine. I'm not jealous or upset or anything like that.' She smiled. 'He's all yours to enjoy.'

'Oh God, that is *such* a relief. I've been dreading telling you.' Bea threw herself down on the bed, arms outstretched, legs kicking in the air. 'It's been horrible this last week, dying to talk about him and not being able to. And you're right, he's *so* pretty to look at.'

Outside the open window, a dog barked and a woman's voice said, 'Daley, no, stop that!'

Jackknifing into a sitting position and bouncing off the bed, Bea peered out and waved down at Christina. 'Hey, we're up here! What's Daley doing?'

'Hello! Oh, he's being naughty and trying to chase the ducks. Daley, *sit*. Behave yourself, wicked boy. How's Hallie?'

'She's good. Everything's great.'

'It's quiz night at the pub this evening,' said Christina. 'Are you coming along?'

'Ooh, that's an idea. We could make up a team between us. Brilliant,' Bea said cheerily. 'See you later.' She waved again, then jumped back on to Hallie's bed. 'That'll be fun, won't it? And Luke's dead clever, so we might even stand a chance of winning. Are you completely sure you're OK with me seeing Ross?'

'Absolutely.' Hallie offered her the bag of toffee eclairs and this time Bea took one.

'Well he could come along to the quiz then, couldn't he? He's clever too. We can be an unbeatable team of five!'

Hallie hesitated. In due course, if her intuition told her anything, handsome charmer Ross would inevitably move on to the next girl in his life, leaving Bea in pieces and vowing never to fall for such a handsome, charming bastard ever again. For now, though, she was in the midst of that giddy, swooshing-with-adrenalin honeymoon stage. And Hallie wasn't sure she felt like being the odd one out at a table of ecstatically happy couples.

'I don't know. To be honest, I'm not feeling that great.' Was it tempting fate to get out of it by pretending to be iller than she was? Rubbing her throat and looking poorly-but-brave, she coughed a bit and said, 'I think I might be coming down with something. Probably best if I stay in tonight.'

'Oh no, poor you! Shall I cancel Ross? If you want me to stay in and keep you company, I will.'

She would, too. Hallie smiled, because Bea was a good friend, and she loved her. She shook her head. 'No, don't cancel him. I'm going to have an early night. You all have fun at the pub and win the quiz as an unbeatable team of four.'

Arriving home from work, Tasha found Rory asleep on the sofa, looking sicker than ever. OK, this was the fourth day now. No more excuses. She gently shook his shoulder until he opened his eyes.

'Hmm? Oh, hi. How was work?'

'Never mind me. How are you? Did you make that appointment with the doctor?'

Rory grimaced and shook his head. 'There's no point. It's just flu.'

'Maybe, but you need to get checked out.' A warning signal was niggling away inside her. She flipped open her phone. 'I'm calling the surgery now.'

'I don't need to see a doctor. You're just making a fuss over

267

nothing. Give me a couple more days and I'll be fine.' As she began to make the call, he protested, 'I won't go.'

'OK, now listen to me. You're *ill*.' Tasha gave him a look to show that this time she really meant business. 'You either see someone at the surgery, or I get one of the doctors to come here.'

Rory closed his eyes in defeat. 'OK, OK. Make an appointment. I'll go.'

'Thank you.' Exhaling with relief, Tasha disguised her growing concern with a weak grin. 'It's like a miracle – man agrees to see GP. I'll alert the media.'

'Very funny,' croaked Rory.

'Luke? Before you go, Dr West wants a word.'

Luke nodded at Susie on reception. 'OK, thanks.'

It was telling that everyone else in the surgery called each other by their first names but he was the only one brave enough to call Jennifer Jennifer. And it still didn't come naturally. He was sure she'd probably rather be referred to as ma'am.

'Come in,' said Jennifer when he knocked on her office door. 'Ah, Luke. Sit down. I have something to tell you.'

'OK.' Was there a problem of some sort? Had there been a complaint made against the practice? Jennifer's customary brisk manner and general lack of warmth meant it was impossible to tell.

She removed her reading glasses and blinked in that intense bird-of-prey way of hers. 'I'm leaving Carranford, leaving the surgery. Leaving the UK, in fact.'

Crikey.

'Wow,' Luke said aloud.

'Yes, yes.' Jennifer waved her hand in a dismissive fashion. 'I'm sure you'll miss me terribly. Anyhow, you clearly need to know, which is why I'm telling you now. I've tendered my resignation and obviously need to work my three months' notice. We'll have to find a suitable replacement, of course.'

'Of course,' murmured Luke. A less terrifying one, with a bit of luck.

'And by mid September I'll be gone.'

He was still struggling to take in the news. Somehow he'd assumed Jennifer would be here until the day she retired, efficient and soulless to the very last.

'You haven't asked me why,' said Jennifer.

'Sorry. Why?'

'I'm sick and tired of having to deal with people who aren't properly ill.' She crossed her thin legs and shook her head. 'Men complaining that they're overweight but refusing to exercise or eat less. Parents bringing their children to me because they stay up past midnight playing computer games then can't be bothered to get up for school. Women wanting me to refer them to cosmetic surgeons because they don't like the way their jowls sag. And don't even get me started on the ridiculous twenty-something girls wanting boob jobs and Botox.'

'That's not *all* of our patients, though,' said Luke.

'It's enough of them to drive me to distraction.' Jennifer pursed her lips. 'Anyway, I've decided there's more to life. To be honest, everyone talks about this village being such a friendly place to live, but I can't say I agree; I haven't found that at all. Half of the villagers are whingeing hypochondriacs and the rest just drink too much.'

Was there any point in attempting to explain why she might not have made too many friends during her time here? Luke decided on balance there probably wasn't.

'So, you said you're leaving the UK? Do you know where you're going yet?'

'Of course I know where I'm going, Luke. If I didn't, I'd be a complete moron. Africa.' Jennifer's tone was crisp. 'Specifically, Uganda. I've volunteered my services at a hospital there. Can't wait. I'll be using my skills to treat patients who genuinely need my help.'

Luke's phone buzzed to signal the arrival of a text, and he felt rather than saw Jennifer's momentary eye-roll as he glanced at the screen: *Hi, just put salmon in oven. Home soon? Also, don't forget quiz tonight – we're teamed up with Bea and Hallie! Xx*

It was Christina, waiting for him at the cottage. The mention of Hallie and Bea gave him a jolt.

'Well, you're obviously busy.' Straightening a pile of papers on her desk, Jennifer continued, 'Anyway, now you know what's going to be happening. Please don't mention it to anyone else at the moment – there's no need for it to become public knowledge just yet. And another thing, when the time does come, I really don't want one of those ghastly surprise leaving parties.'

'Right, got it. I won't let that happen.' Luke nodded seriously and somehow managed to sound sincere. 'But well done on the voluntary work. It sounds very worthwhile.'

'I'll be making a real difference,' Jennifer agreed. 'Treating the Ugandans and educating them in health matters.'

She would too; she was a fine doctor. Luke said, 'Good for you.'

And good luck to everyone in Uganda.

Chapter 43

The Tiffany ring had been tight before. Now, just ten days later, it was loose. Tasha turned it around and around her finger, counting the number of times the diamond reappeared. It wasn't as sparkly as it had been. She took it off and held it up, viewing it against the background of the fluorescent ceiling light.

'Everything OK?' said the nurse.

'It used to be sparklier than this. It's gone all dull.'

The nurse pointed to the antiseptic hand gel dispenser. 'That's what's done it, endlessly putting that gunky stuff on your hands. Give it a good scrub with detergent and an old toothbrush and it'll be as good as new in no time.'

As good as new in no time.. If only they could say the same about Rory. Tasha swallowed and leaned forward in her chair to study his half-closed eyes, those beautiful light green irises and the long dark lashes she loved so much.

Except it was unfair to single out the eyes; she loved every aspect of Rory, every last detail of him. From his toes to his shoulders to his ear lobes to the silky-soft skin on the insides of his wrists . . . she loved *all* of him.

Reaching for his hand and easing her fingers between his, she gave them a squeeze and felt the tiniest squeeze in return.

271

Just at the moment it was all he could manage, the limit of his strength. *Dear God.*

It still seemed completely unbelievable that this could happen to someone like Rory. After a lifetime of daredevil antics and deliberate risk-taking, how was it possible that a tiny, *microscopic* virus could lead to a situation like this?

But it had. The bug had turned out to be real flu after all, then niggling discomfort in Rory's ribcage had grown into severe chest pain and breathlessness. Always super-fit, he'd become too exhausted to take more than a few steps at a time. By the time Tasha had succeeded in persuading him – typical man – to see his GP, the virus had worsened and so had the chest pains. Urgent admission to hospital had followed and the diagnosis had been made.

Most people caught viruses and felt a bit unwell for a few days, then the body's wonderful immune system magically dealt with the virus and everything returned to normal. But in Rory's case, the virus had ruthlessly attacked his heart muscle. It was a rare complication, but it occasionally happened and he'd been one of the unlucky ones.

Rory had myocarditis, and not the mild kind. His signs and symptoms were severe, including a fast, irregular heartbeat, tiredness, shortness of breath and pyrexia. Following admission to hospital, he'd undergone a torrent of chest X-rays and blood tests, an echocardiogram, ECGs, and an endomyocardial biopsy. As the results had come in, the medical staff's expressions had grown more sombre. This was serious, far more so than they'd initially thought.

And it just kept on happening, like the worst kind of nightmare you couldn't wake up from. Tasha, desperate to lean on Rory for support, had to manage on her own, because Rory was so ill it was as much as he could do to lie there in the bed and carry on breathing. Pain medication and sedation meant that most of the time he didn't have the energy to speak. His body was covered in wires and tubes, and surrounded by hospital machinery. Other people in the cardiac ward were similarly accessorised; some awake, some not. Most of them were older than Rory.

And then there were the hospital staff, all incredibly hard-working and kind. They explained everything they were doing and encouraged Tasha to take regular breaks and look after herself. They were lovely, but the one thing they couldn't do was promise her that everything would be fine and Rory would make a full recovery.

Which was really the only thing she wanted to hear.

Tasha swallowed; it wasn't only her who wanted to hear it. Everyone who knew Rory was willing him to get better. His parents might be dead, but his Aunt Mel, the one who had broken her leg just before Christmas, was beside herself and visiting daily. As was Joe, who had been an absolute rock and would be here again – she checked her watch – any minute now. Initially the staff had been reluctant to allow him on to the unit, until Joe had said with feeling, 'You let brothers in? Well, we're more than that; we're closer than any brothers. You have to let me see him.'

Truthfully, she didn't know what she would have done without Joe. His support meant so much. Her mother was always there at the end of the phone, but the many animals she cared for at her home in France, with no one else available to look after them in her absence, meant she was unable to fly over to be with her during this horrible time.

And here was Joe now, being buzzed into the ward, washing his hands in the sink next to the entrance, then drying them and cleaning them again with a squirt of alcohol gel. There were whole new routines to learn in a hospital, that seemed weird to begin with but within days became unthinking second nature. You didn't take any chances when one slip could be fatal.

Then Joe was giving her a brief hug and Tasha breathed in the clean outdoors smell of him.

'How's he doing?'

'I don't know. Same, I think. Sometimes the heart thing gets more irregular.' She pointed to the electronic readout on the machine opposite them. 'They're waiting for more test results before they decide what to do next.'

Joe nodded and clasped his big hand around Rory's wrist. 'Hey, it's me. I'm here with Tash. Are you awake?'

After a couple of seconds Rory nodded, just slightly.

'You OK?' Joe kept his gaze fixed on his friend's face.

They waited, then Rory licked his lips and whispered, 'Never better.'

'You'll be out of here soon. I'm going to take you heli-skiing,' said Joe. But this time there was no response; Rory had drifted off once more.

In all the times she'd seen the two of them together, the laughter and joking around had been virtually non-stop. Now it was absent. Joe had never looked more serious. Tasha watched the muscles tighten in his jaw as he stroked Rory's forearm with the backs of his fingers, silently letting him know he was still there.

'Have you eaten anything?' said Joe.

She shook her head. 'No.'

'You really should, you know.'

'I can't. Not at the moment.' The irony of having jokily vowed to diet in order to make the engagement ring fit wasn't lost on her. She'd lost eight pounds since then, through sheer panic and inability to swallow food. For now, she was existing on coffee from the vending machine outside the unit.

'You need to keep your strength up.'

Tasha shrugged helplessly. *What strength?*

'He's right.' The nurse was back to do Rory's observations.

'You need to eat. Keeling over in a heap isn't going to help anyone.'

'Come on,' said Joe. 'I'm taking you to the café.' He reached for Tasha's hand and stood up. 'We'll be back in half an hour.'

'Good idea.' The nurse, who was probably sick of the sight of her, beamed encouragingly. 'You do that.'

Chapter 44

'What's going to happen to him? Is he going to start getting better soon?'

'I don't know the answer to that,' said Joe. 'Nobody knows the answer.'

'Oh God.' They sat facing each other across the orange Formica-topped table in the hospital cafeteria. Tasha picked up a chip, dipped it into mayonnaise and attempted to summon the enthusiasm to eat it.

'Are you sleeping?'

'Not really. I wish I could just . . . take out my batteries and wake up twelve hours later.'

Joe said, 'You could ask for a couple of pills to help you with that.'

'But I don't want to miss anything important. What if something happened while I was asleep?'

He nodded to show he understood. 'I know. Same. You're being very strong, though.'

'I don't feel strong.'

'You're doing so well.' He paused. 'I haven't seen you cry yet.'

Tasha shook her head. It simply hadn't happened, not even when she was at home. All her efforts were taken up with concentrating on getting Rory well again. Breaking down in tears might detract from that.

Besides, she had to be there for him. Stay strong.

'I'm not much of a one for the soppy comments,' said Joe, 'but he loves you so much. He really does.'

Tasha nodded. 'I know. I love him too.'

'Are you going to eat any more of these?' Joe nudged the plate towards her.

It was the last thing she wanted to do. But he was right: Rory needed her and she in turn needed – somehow – to keep on going. Swallowing the lump in her throat, she braced herself and picked up another chip. It didn't matter that they didn't taste great. She looked at Joe, 'Oh yes, I'm going to eat them all.'

Returning to the unit, they found Mel there, sitting beside Rory's bed. She jumped up and met them at the entrance. Since the staff preferred there to be no more than two visitors at any one time, Joe said, 'I'll head off and come back later.'

'No, don't. The consultant just called the ward to ask if we were all here. He wants us to wait and he'll see us as soon as he arrives. They're expecting him at around five o'clock.'

'Why does he want to talk to us?' said Joe.

'I don't know.'

'Is it good news or bad news?' The moment she'd uttered the question, Tasha wished she hadn't. She felt a surge of nausea.

'Oh darling, I don't know.' Mel's face was drawn with worry. 'We'll just have to wait and see.'

For the next hour Tasha talked to Rory, holding his hand, trying to persuade herself that he was looking better.

Except he wasn't, she knew he wasn't. Just as she knew that the consultant cardiologist was unlikely to have phoned ahead and asked the three of them to wait so he could personally inform them Rory had turned a corner and was on the mend.

Basically, there had to be a perk to the job, but she doubted it was that.

The clock on the wall, typically, had slowed right down now. Five o'clock came and went, each minute passing with interminable slowness. Was it her imagination, or were the nursing staff avoiding her gaze? Did they know more than they were letting on?

Oh God, *oh God*.

At five forty-three, the consultant swept into the unit and Tasha's knees began to judder with fear. She pressed them together and straightened her spine. Surely whatever it was he had to say couldn't be too bad, could it?

'Hello, hello, so sorry to keep you waiting. Traffic was awful.' Dr White had kind eyes, a long bumpy nose and an air of calm authority about him. He shook hands with each of them in turn. 'We have the latest test results in and I'd like to discuss the situation with you.' Glancing over at Rory, whose eyes were closed but who could still be listening, he beckoned to them. 'If you'll follow me, we can talk about it in the office.'

'I just can't believe it,' said Carmel two hours later, back at Tasha's flat. 'I mean, Rory. Of *all* people.'

'I know.' Dr White and the nurses had insisted she leave the hospital and come home to get some sleep. Tasha couldn't imagine sleeping, but she'd known they were right. As with the eating, she had to keep herself as healthy as possible in order to support Rory.

She'd let Joe drive her back here, and Carmel had arrived shortly afterwards. If Rory's condition altered during the night, the staff had promised to phone straight away and let them know.

It felt odd, being at home. Then again, everything felt odd; normality had ceased to exist. Tasha counted the ways:

There was a glass of red wine on the coffee table in front of her and she had no desire to touch it.

She'd just received a text begging her to fly to Barcelona to work on a video shoot starring one of the world's most mega-successful female singers and had turned the job down without a second thought.

Oh, and Rory's heart was failing. His other organs were starting to shut down. His condition had deteriorated to such an extent that he was now on the list for a heart transplant.

Really and truly. *An actual heart transplant.*

Most horrifying of all, this was actually the best-case scenario. Because if he didn't get a heart transplant, he would die.

'You're not going to drink this wine, are you?' Carmel picked up the glass to take it back out to the kitchen. Evidently desperate to help, she said, 'Tell me what you want and I'll get it for you.'

I want a new heart for Rory.

But they already knew that, and saying it wouldn't help anyone. Tasha forced herself to consider the realistic options. 'I think there's a tin of custard in the top cupboard. Could I have some of that?' She was almost certain she could manage a small bowl of custard.

Carmel nodded. 'Cold or warm?'

'Warm. Please.' She'd loved tinned custard as a child, had never tired of it.

'Joe? Anything for you?'

He shook his head. 'No thanks, I'm OK.'

Watching them reminded Tasha of the first night Joe and Carmel had met, of the way they'd taunted and teased each other. The next moment, with vivid clarity, she remembered Joe assuring a suspicious Carmel that Rory wasn't a player, that he was genuinely smitten with Tasha. Whereupon Carmel, defending her oldest friend, had warned him, 'If he gives her any grief, he'll have me to answer to.'

And Rory, with his arms around Tasha and his breath warm against the side of her face, had murmured in her ear, 'I wasn't planning on giving you any grief.'

Which had made her shiver with delight.

Except he hadn't stuck to that plan, had he? This was more grief than she'd ever expected.

Tasha silently marvelled at the vicissitudes of fate. After all these years of expecting the worst to happen, now it *had*.

And since crumbling wasn't an option, all she could do was face it head on and deal with the situation as best she could.

Chapter 45

'This must be what it's like being famous,' said Zander out of the corner of his mouth. 'Everywhere I look, people are staring at me. I feel like Brad Pitt.'

Flo grinned, because it was true: he was definitely the centre of attention here today. And when old people were interested in someone, they didn't bother making any secret of it.

'They've been waiting months for this, ever since they first heard about you. Sorry they aren't being terribly discreet.'

'It's OK. You did warn me.'

'They don't get out much. And they do love to gossip. You're big news.'

'Afternoon, Flo. So is this the boyfriend?' Eunice Allsopp came up behind Zander and attracted his attention by prodding him in the back with the end of her ebony walking stick. 'Come on then, let's have a look at you.'

With good grace, Zander waited while Eunice chose the correct spectacles from the selection strung around her neck. Putting them on, she peered suspiciously at his face. 'Are you wearing mascara, young man?'

'No.' Zander's mouth twitched. 'No, I'm not.'

'Hmm.' Clearly not convinced, Eunice looked over the top of her spectacles at Flo. 'Is he gay?'

'He isn't gay,' said Flo. 'He's my boyfriend.'

'So? He still could be. One of my husbands was gay. Lovely chap,' said Eunice. 'We got on very well together. It has its advantages, too. He didn't *bother* me all the time, if you know what I mean.'

'I do.' Zander nodded gravely. 'But I'm still not gay.'

'Oh look,' said Flo, before Eunice could launch into a full-blown interrogation, 'there's Margot, I promised to introduce you to her. She's dying to meet you!'

Nairn House always held a huge and impressive summer fair in order to entertain the current residents and hopefully attract future ones. It was advertised widely and all sorts of entertainment was provided throughout the day. Luckily the weather for this year's fair was perfect, drawing even more visitors than usual. The stalls were busy, the grounds were immaculate, the pink and white striped tea tent was bursting with customers and a ballroom dancing display was proving popular, the visiting troupe currently enthralling their audience with a racy tango.

'Hello, darling,' said Margot when Flo and Zander caught up with her at the jewellery stall. 'And hello *you*.' She eyed Zander with interest. 'If you haven't already heard the old dears gossiping about you, the general consensus is that you're quite the dish.'

'Thank you,' said Zander, shaking her outstretched hand. 'So are you.'

Was there anything nicer than observing two people you liked being introduced and instantly getting on well together? Secretly glowing with pride and satisfaction, Flo examined the jewellery laid out on the velvet-covered trestle tables and listened to Zander and Margot chatting easily to each other. She was distracted for a few minutes by one of the residents asking for help with a bracelet clasp. When she turned back to Flo and Zander, she saw them waiting for her.

'Right, we're having a competition to see which of us knows you best.' Margot indicated the table beside her. 'We've each chosen the necklace we think you'd prefer. Now you have to decide.'

'OK. And which one did you choose?'

Margot shook her head. 'Come on, I'm not going to tell you that.'

'So I'm going to end up offending one of you.'

'You won't,' said Zander, 'because we're grown-ups.' He nodded at the necklaces. 'Go on, choose.'

The one on the left was composed of midnight-blue and silver stones, a double strand that caught the light and swung elegantly from her hand. Flo put it back down and picked up the one on the right, shorter and rounder in shape, made up of clusters of tiny seed pearls interspersed with white glass beads.

'OK, I love them both. But I love this one more.'

'Ha!' Margot clapped her hands. 'Good!'

'I chose yours?'

'No, mine was the blue one. I'm glad you prefer Zander's.' Her eyes bright, Margot said, 'Shows he knows what he's doing, proves he's the right man for you. Now, what's that stall over there? Is it Splat the Rat? Excellent!'

For the next hour they toured the plant, cake and bric-a-brac stalls, and watched small children on the old-fashioned round-about and older ones throwing themselves around the bouncy castle. A steel band played calypso music, a girl sang Celine Dion songs, a juggler juggled with vegetables, then a street-dance troupe put on a break-dancing display. Zander won a coconut on the coconut shy. They drank rum punch and ate home-made cakes. 'Whoops,' said Flo in an undertone as two people, one young and one old, made their way past them.

'Who's that?' Zander murmured.

'The old one's Beryl and the embarrassed-looking one is her granddaughter Julia. She's the one who's been having that torrid affair with you behind my back.'

283

'Ha.' He smiled at Julia as she glanced across at them. 'Poor thing, her neck's gone all blotchy.'

Annie rushed up to them. Her spiky bleached-blond hair was quivering around her head, and she was wearing a leopard-print tank top, tight white jeans, fluorescent pink lipstick and giant hoop earrings that jangled as she spoke.

'Oh my God, I've just seen the fortune-teller! She told me I was going to go on holiday somewhere hot beginning with B and meet the man of my dreams in a nightclub! And where am I off to next week? Only Benidorm! On my life, she's the real deal!'

'That's brilliant,' said Flo.

'I know! I can't wait to get there now – about time I found myself a decent bloke! Have you been to the fortune-teller yet?'

'Well no, I—'

'Oh but you *must*. Seriously, go now while there isn't a queue. Come on, she'll tell you everything you need to know!'

Annie practically dragged her over to the tiny yellow and white striped tent, and Flo found herself being unceremoniously bundled inside.

'I'll take your handsome young man over to the tea tent and get to know him better.' Annie linked a proprietorial arm through Zander's and waved goodbye. 'Come and find us when you've finished, if we haven't run off to Benidorm by then!'

Inside, the walls of the tent were draped with black velvet and the small circular table had been covered with crimson satin. Madam Zara, in her sixties at a guess, was wearing red and black robes, lots of costume jewellery and plenty of black eyeliner.

Actually, rather more on one eye than the other.

'Now then, my darling, that'll be ten pounds for a reading,' she said. 'You've got a lucky feeling about you, I can tell that already.'

Ten pounds to sit in a stuffy, overheated tent and be told a lot of twaddle by someone who was just making it up. Honestly, what a rip-off. But she was trapped now, there was no escape. Flo breathed in the heavy, spicy scent of the woman's perfume and wished she hadn't splashed on quite so much of it.

'Let me see your hand, lovey. Oh I say, you are having a nice time at the moment, aren't you? Lots of good stuff going on in your life just now.'

'Mmm.' Shrugging in a non-committal fashion, Flo wondered how much of this was related to Annie's mention of Zander being her handsome young man.

'You've got a lovely dog,' said Madam Zara. 'A black one.'

'No I haven't.' Flo glanced down at herself to see if one of Jeremy's dark hairs had attached itself to her top.

'Ah, so it hasn't happened yet.' Zara nodded wisely. 'You're *going* to have a lovely dog. He'll be such a wonderful companion you'll wonder how you ever managed without him. And I see a happy partnership ahead of you too. There's a church and a beautiful wedding. Three bridesmaids.'

'Oh.' Flo looked disappointed. 'Only three?'

'Three little ones,' said Zara. 'And a couple of bigger ones too. All wearing lovely blue dresses.'

'Any idea where we'll go for our honeymoon? Will it be Venice?'

'Oh yes.' Zara nodded firmly. 'Definitely Venice. You'll have one of those trips in a gondola and it'll be *so* romantic . . .'

'And will we have children?'

'Definitely. Two,' said Zara. 'A boy and a girl. I'm not going to tell you their names though, lovey. Don't want to spoil the surprise.'

'True,' said Flo. 'I'd rather wait until they get here.'

'You're all going to be so happy together, that's in no doubt at all.' Zara nodded. 'It's as clear as day. I quite envy you.'

Such a load of old tosh, Flo knew that. But there was no getting away from it, being told this by a fortune-teller – even

285

if she was a complete fraud – was giving her a warm glow in the pit of her stomach.

Because you never knew, it might come true.

But ten pounds didn't go far these days. Her time was evidently up. Madam Zara said, 'There you go, my darling, that's you done. Can you tell the next one to come in on your way out?'

Flo was mortified when, emerging into the daylight, she discovered that rather than going to the tea tent, Annie and Zander had been standing outside shamelessly eavesdropping the whole time.

And, needless to say, finding it absolutely hilarious.

'Blimey, you didn't waste much time,' Annie cackled. 'You were like Jeremy Paxman in there! Seriously, I had no idea you were going to start interrogating her like that. Especially about the wedding!' Never one for discretion, she gave Zander a comedy nudge. 'Ding dong, eh? Looks like I'm going to need to buy myself a fancy hat!'

It was seven in the evening and plenty of people were out on the Downs, sharing picnics, firing up barbecues, playing games or just admiring the view of Clifton Suspension Bridge strung across the Avon Gorge. Below them, the river twisted and turned, a silvery ribbon of water reflecting the still blue sky. Above them, hot air balloons drifted lazily across from Ashton Court, taking advantage of the perfect flying conditions. Dogs leapt up and barked indignantly as the balloons floated overhead, and the gas burners intermittently roared like dragons, startling small children.

'I've never been up in a hot air balloon,' said Zander.

'Would you like to?'

'I would.'

Flo filed away the information for future use. Zander's birthday was at the end of August. If they were still seeing each other then, a balloon ride would make a great surprise present. That was, if he hadn't dumped her by then and cut off all contact with the crazy spinster with the one-track mind.

'Sorry,' she said, not for the first time since they'd left the summer fair.

Not even for the tenth time, probably.

Zander smiled and shook his head. 'Will you stop apologising?'

'It's still bothering me.'

'Don't let it.'

'I can't help it. Every time I think about it, I just want to die of shame.'

'OK, now listen.' He turned to face her and took her hands in his. 'I'm glad I heard you asking those questions. You know how it feels when you really like someone but you're scared to let them know in case they don't feel the same way?'

Flo gazed up into his steady blue eyes and felt her mouth go dry. She nodded. 'Yes.'

'Well, that's been me. Wanting to say stuff but not wanting to frighten you off.' He paused. 'Like, there's an idea I've had that would help us all out, but I don't want you thinking I'm only suggesting it because it would benefit me. Because that's not why I thought of it, I swear.'

And that was when she knew, because it was the exact same solution she'd been too afraid to voice, for fear of seeming overkeen.

She nodded, feeling suddenly brave. 'Lena stays in your flat and you move in with me.'

It wasn't until Zander exhaled that she realised he'd been holding his breath. 'That's the one.'

'I've been wanting to say it too.'

'Really?'

Oh, those dark eyebrows. 'Really.' Braver still, Flo said, 'I do quite like you, you know.'

'I was worried you'd think it was too soon.'

'Same.' Was it too soon? It honestly didn't feel that way.

'I love you,' said Zander.

'I love *you*.'

'I can't think of anything I'd like more than living with you.'

'Me neither.'

He took another breath. 'And . . . it's not something I've ever considered with anyone else, but seeing as the fortune-teller brought it up, I can definitely see myself wanting us to have babies.'

'Wow,' said Flo.

'One girl, one boy. Sounds good to me. In your own time,' Zander amended with a lopsided smile. 'Not necessarily straight away.'

As he said it, another hot air balloon, this time a chequered purple and green one, sailed by overhead. Two small children raced after it, waving and screaming with delight. Flo felt as if she could float with happiness. After all these years, the perfect man had come along and she knew he wouldn't let her down. Together they could overcome the problem of Lena.

And having Zander's flat all to herself, even if it wasn't the flat she most wanted, might hopefully, in turn, go some way towards easing the way Lena felt about Flo.

'So is this it?' Flo wrapped her arms around Zander's waist. 'All sorted? You're going to pack up your things and move in with me and Jeremy?'

'If you think Jeremy'll be OK with that. Maybe you should check with him first.'

'He likes you. It'll be fine. He'll welcome you with open paws.'

'Well,' said Zander, 'I call this a result.'

Together they made their way back across the Downs to the car.

'Hang on a second. I never remember to do this and I really should.' Pausing, Flo pulled out her phone and held it up to take a photo. She framed the two of them on the screen with the dramatic gorge and the suspension bridge behind them and a huge orange hot air balloon drifting overhead. *Click* went the camera, and the moment was captured forever.

'Years from now, we'll show that picture to the kids,' said Zander. 'What are we going to call them, by the way? Any ideas?'

'Already sorted,' said Flo. 'Gaviscon and Petunia. Those are their names. We'll tell them this was the day we decided to have them.'

He gave her shoulder a squeeze. 'All in all, it's been a pretty great day.'

Flo put her phone away and blew him a playful kiss. 'Better still, it's not over yet.'

Chapter 46

Dear Rose,

My three things are:

I am the cleverest person I know.

I compile cryptic crosswords for fun.

It annoys me when people think they know better than me, especially when I know they don't.

My best friend Sally is driving me mad. We've known each other since we were children and we're both now twenty-six. For the last ten years she's chosen all the wrong boyfriends, but each time I tell her this, she refuses to listen. But I'm always right. Why won't she believe me? I could save her so much heartbreak.

Sincerely,

David

Dear David,

People need to be allowed to make their own mistakes, otherwise they'll always be convinced their choice was the right one. We always think we know best – that's just human nature. If Sally really liked someone but didn't go out with them because you'd told her not to, she would forever be convinced that this one would have been the big love of her life.

But I do sympathise. Yes, of course it's frustrating, but in her position you'd feel exactly the same. All you can do is be there for her when the wrong boyfriends let her down. And hopefully one day your best friend Sally will meet the right one, who won't.

Love,

Rose

PS I do wonder if you're secretly hoping you might turn out to be the right one? Maybe you will, but be prepared to accept that this might not happen

Poor David, in love with his best friend and unlikely to find his somewhat regimented feelings returned. Sally might be his best friend but was he hers? Hallie uploaded her reply and guessed that it wouldn't satisfy David; short of *demanding* that his views be listened to and obeyed, nothing would.

Oh well.

She sat forward on the sofa to relax her back and shoulders. Last week's session with the musculoskeletal physio had helped to ease the pains brought about by the effort required to breathe, but she still ached. On the up side, she was feeling less woozy today, had managed to stay awake after doing her meds and had put on almost two kilos, which was a great achievement. Struggling to gain weight was the bane of her life.

And now she'd updated the website too. Good going, after the last few days of feeling rubbish.

Her phone began to ring and she answered it.

'Hey,' said Bea. 'Where are you?'

'In Tanzania, in a hot air balloon floating above the Serengeti. Honestly, you should see it,' said Hallie. 'It's amazing. There are herds of wildebeest sweeping across the plains—'

'You've been watching *Fawlty Towers* again. Are you at home?'

'Yes.'

'Good, open the door then. You've got visitors.'

Plural. Bea and who?

Thirty seconds later, she found out.

'Hallie, lovely Hallie. These are for you, from me.' A blast of designer aftershave, a crackly flourish of cellophane, and the biggest bouquet she'd seen for some time briefly filled her field of vision.

'Surprise!' said Bea, as Hallie found herself being air-kissed on both cheeks by Ross. 'We thought we'd come to see you!'

At a guess, so they could get the first-time-as-a-couple awkwardness out of the way. Amused, Hallie took the flowers. 'Wow, thanks, these are amazing. How lovely! Nice to see you again! Come along in.'

They went into the living room and Hallie hooked herself back up to the oxygen supply. The flowers really were amazing, exotic and wildly extravagant; it was sheer bad luck that the arrangement included so many lilies, whose sickly scent reminded her of death.

Never mind, it's the thought that counts.

'Wow, you're looking *great*.' Ross said it with rather too much enthusiasm.

Hallie, who knew she wasn't, said, 'Thanks, so are you.' Which *was* true; in his leaf-green designer-of-course shirt and navy blue trousers, and with his dark glasses perched on top of his head, Ross was tanned and glowing with health. Next to him, Bea was visibly besotted.

'We've just been over to Abingdon for lunch with Ross's parents,' said Bea. 'They're so great. I loved them!'

'And they loved you too. Don't forget about those theatre tickets, by the way,' Ross reminded her. 'As soon as you know you can go, tell Mum and she'll book them.' He turned to include Hallie in the conversation. '*Les Miserables* in London. Not my cup of tea, but Mum loves it.'

Hallie smiled. *Les Mis* was the musical she had always most longed to go and see. After Suze's death, she'd vowed to make it happen, to experience it on Suze's behalf, but like so many overambitious plans, it had fallen by the wayside.

Belatedly realising this, Bea exclaimed, 'Oh, that's your favourite. You could come too!'

But Hallie was already shaking her head. 'No, I couldn't cope with it all . . . and I'd only cough during the show. No one likes a cougher in the audience, do they?' This was true; much as she'd love to see it, she wouldn't want to ruin the show for everyone else. 'But you must go with Ross's mum, then you can come back and tell me what it's like.'

When they left an hour later, Ross gave Hallie a long, sincere look. 'It's been great seeing you again. Really. You look after yourself now.'

As if she were a ninety-year-old great-grandmother. The playful tone and flirtatious eye contact between them had evidently been banished for good. Which was only appropriate, of course, now that he was seeing Bea, but it still made her feel barely human.

'I will, and you look after Bea. If you mess her around, you'll have me to answer to.'

'Wouldn't dream of it.' He grinned in that way some men did when they were perfectly well aware that they would be messing their girlfriend around because it happened every time without fail.

Then he went on ahead, leaving Bea to say her goodbyes.

'Well, what d'you reckon? He seems keen, doesn't he? Do we look like a proper couple? He's so much nicer than Phil . . .'

Which, seeing as Phil had cheated on her with at least four other girls during their six months together, wasn't the most encouraging endorsement in the world.

But Bea's eyes were shining, her optimism boundless.

'He is nice, and you look great together.' Hallie hugged her on the doorstep, taking note of her own Dear Rose advice. 'Have fun. I'll see you soon.'

Chapter 47

Zander's heart sank when he saw his sister's name flash up on the phone on Sunday night. Would it ever *stop* sinking? That was the million-dollar question. Personally he doubted it.

'Go on, answer it.' Flo, sensing his reluctance, was reassuring. 'She might have just locked herself out again.'

As ever, Flo was right. Spending the next couple of hours wondering what the problem might be was worse than getting on and dealing with it.

He lay back against the pillows, pressed Answer and said wearily, 'It's midnight, Lena. What do you want?'

'Zander, I need you to come and pick me up.' The words tumbled out in a rush. 'Can you come straight away?'

'What? No, I can't. Where are you, anyway? What's going on?' He could hear voices in the background, raised in anger.

'OK, it totally isn't my fault, right? Giles's wife was meant to be away for a few days, taking the kids to see her mother in Plymouth, so Giles invited me over to stay at the house while it was empty, except they came home early and she had a complete *head fit* when she found out I was there . . . and then she called Giles's mother over and they both started on at me . . . I'm telling you, you wouldn't believe the things they've been saying, it's a complete nightmare and I haven't even done anything *wrong* . . .'

Zander briefly closed his eyes. Nothing ever really changed.

One of his earliest memories was of their mother attempting to apologise to an inconsolable school friend of Lena's because Lena had ripped the arms off her favourite doll.

'Listen to me, where are you exactly? Give me the full address.'

Lena told him and added, 'Hurry up please, before I slap them both.'

'Just wait there and don't slap anyone. I'm calling a cab to come and pick you up.'

'No, no cab, I don't want a cab!'

'And I don't want to get out of bed to come and fetch you.'

'Zander, please!'

'Why can't Giles drive you home?'

'Because he's had a couple of bottles of wine and his bloody mother won't let him.'

Zander briefly considered saying he'd been drinking too, but Lena always knew when he was lying. He tried again: 'A cab can be there faster than I can; just let me call them and—'

'Oh for God's sake, why are you being so *difficult*?' wailed Lena. 'OK, OK, I'll tell you what happened. I accidentally broke a clock and if you don't come over here and give Giles's mother two hundred pounds, the old witch is going to call the police!'

There it was, the reason he was going to have to get out of bed after all. Taking a stand and letting Lena bear the consequences of her actions, he knew from experience, would only end up making life *more* difficult for all concerned.

Zander felt a hand rest on his arm and turned to look at Flo, who had heard everything. She nodded, gave him a sympathetic smile and mouthed: *You'd better go*.

He experienced a surge of relief; girlfriends in the past hadn't been nearly so understanding. Which was, essentially, the reason why they were in the past.

And why Flo would be with him in the future.

'Right, I'm on my way,' he told Lena. 'I'll be there in twenty minutes.'

'Quick as you can,' said Lena. 'These bloody squawking women are driving me loopy.'

Four minutes later, dressed in jeans and a black polo shirt, he leaned over the bed and kissed Flo on the mouth. 'I'll be back by one, hopefully before that.'

'It's OK, I'll still be awake.'

He loved the way her eyes danced when she looked at him. 'You don't have to wait up.'

'Maybe I want to,' said Flo.

Now it was his turn to smile. They both knew why; there was unfinished business of the bedroom kind still waiting to happen.

'See you in a bit, then.' Zander gave her one more kiss for luck.

'Don't forget to stop off at the cashpoint. Jaaahls's mum might not accept credit cards,' said Flo.

A light warm drizzle was falling as Zander withdrew two hundred pounds from the cashpoint and climbed back into the car. At this time of night, it wouldn't take him more than fifteen minutes to reach the address Lena had given him.

He headed out of Clifton across the Downs and through north Bristol. Along Cribbs Causeway, over the motorway junction and down the hill towards Easter Compton. The road was clear and the car was running like a dream. Zander switched on the CD player and smiled to himself as Flo's choice of music burst out of the speakers. It would always remind him of her, he knew that. To look at Flo, who would guess that her all-time favourite track was David Guetta's 'Titanium'?

Needless to say, the moment Lena climbed into the passenger seat and heard it, she would recoil in horror and say, 'What's that godawful racket? Turn it *off*.'

But for now, it could be as loud as he liked. Zander upped the volume and let the track wash over him. If this business was all dealt with quickly, he could drop Lena off at her flat and be back in bed with Flo by one o'clock. And tomorrow, when the dust had settled, he would tell Lena that he was going to be moving in with Flo. With a bit of luck she'd realise—

The fox raced across the lane just as he rounded the bend, and Zander simultaneously jerked the steering wheel to the left and tried to slam on the brakes. The rain had made the road slippery, and there was an ear-splitting squeal of tyres on the tarmac. In the slowed-down microseconds before impact, three things went through Zander's mind:

Shit, I was going too fast.

Lena's going to be so mad when I don't turn up.

And finally, because he knew it was going to be bad: *Oh Flo, I love you, I'm sorry . . .*

Then, like a high speed tank, the car slammed head first into the dry-stone wall.

Flo was making tea and toast when the phone rang.

'Right, what's Zander playing at? Where the bloody hell is he? Because if he thinks it's funny keeping me here, let me tell you it *isn't*.'

'What? He left ages ago.' Flo put down the butter knife and checked her watch. 'He should be there by now. Try his phone.'

'Oh please, what do you *think* I've been doing? It's ringing and ringing but he's not picking up.'

'Maybe because he's driving the car,' said Flo. 'And he might have had trouble finding a cashpoint that works. He needed to get money out, remember.'

Two hundred pounds, in fact.

'Well he needs to get a bloody move on,' Lena declared, 'because I'm telling you now, I'm sick of this pair of witches giving me grief.'

This was crazy. Flo's fingers shook as she dialled Zander's number yet again and heard it begin to ring. Yet again. *Why* wasn't he answering? He couldn't still be driving, surely? Should she call a taxi and see if she could find him, or would that be—

She jumped as the ringing abruptly stopped. At *last* he'd picked up. Awash with relief, Flo said, 'Zander? Where are you? Oh God, I was really starting to get worried . . .'

But when she heard the male voice at the other end of the line, the fear came rushing back with a vengeance.

Because it didn't belong to Zander.

The rain was heavier now, falling steadily from a slate-grey sky. Flo, staring out through the waiting-room window, heard two nurses in the corridor outside attempting to calm Lena down.

She closed her eyes for a second as the realisation of what had happened washed over her once more. There had been an accident and Zander was lying unconscious in the intensive care unit. The police had contacted Lena and driven over to Giles's mother's home to collect her and bring her to the hospital. Another officer had finally answered Zander's phone when Flo had rung it for the twentieth time to find out where he was. She'd called a taxi and arrived here an hour after Lena.

Now it was seven o'clock on Monday morning and Lena appeared to be blaming the nurses for the fact that her brother was in a coma.

Luckily they were adept at coping with difficult relatives.

'Right.' Lena threw open the waiting-room door. 'I'm tired, I'm going home to get some sleep. What are you doing?'

'I'll stay here a bit longer.'

'Well obviously I would stay a bit longer but I'm *exhausted*.'

'I know, it's fine. I'll speak to you later.'

Lena picked up her cream jacket. 'Text me as soon as he wakes up, please. I asked the nurses when it was going to happen and they refused to tell me.'

'That's because they don't know when he's going to wake up,' said Flo.

Lena rolled her eyes at the nursing staff's incompetence. 'Well they *should*.'

After Lena had left, Flo sat beside Zander's bed and watched him sleeping. OK, he wasn't really sleeping, but he looked as if he was. The head injury was a closed one, so there was no visible damage. His ultra-straight glossy dark hair still fell over his forehead, his high cheekbones were as beautiful as ever. His eyes were closed; he was breathing with the aid of a ventilator. To look at him, it seemed entirely feasible that he could wake up at any minute. Yet the doctor had just been in to tell her that he would shortly be taken down to the neurosurgical operating theatre to have a burr hole drilled into his skull and a device installed to monitor his intracranial pressure.

Because at the moment, his condition wasn't looking good.

At eleven a.m. the theatre was ready for him and Flo prepared to leave the hospital. She needed to shower, change, feed Jeremy and arrange for someone to come in and keep a regular eye on him. Maybe doze for an hour or two if she could.

'I'll call you straight away if there's any news,' said the lovely nurse. Lowering her voice, she added, 'I know his sister is officially the next of kin, but she's upset at the moment . . . and excitable. Well, you know what I mean.'

Flo nodded. 'Oh yes, believe me, I know.'

'Bit of a handful, is she?'

'More than a bit.' Was it unfair talking like this behind Lena's back? Maybe, but she needed them to understand what Lena was like. 'It's just the way she is. She can't help it.' She knew it was illogical, but she didn't want the fact that Zander had an annoying sister to be a reason for them to take less good care of him.

As if reading her mind, the nurse gave her shoulder a consoling squeeze. 'Of course she can't. Don't worry, we know.'

Flo made it all the way back to Clifton and into the security of her flat before bursting into noisy tears. Jeremy, eyeing her with supreme disdain, stood there for several seconds before turning and stalking away. When he reached the kitchen, he sat down beside his empty food bowl and gave her one of his I'm-so-disappointed-in-you looks.

'I know, I'm sorry. I'm just so worried about Zander.' And now she was apologising to a cat. Rubbing her wet face with her sleeve, she set about washing and refilling the blue ceramic bowl. Once it was done and the fresh food was ready for him, she straightened up. 'There you go.'

Whereupon Jeremy turned once more and left the kitchen, the slow swish of his tail registering his disgust.

Four hours later, Flo was standing on the doorstep of Zander and Lena's flat, alternately hammering on the door and ringing the bell.

At last Lena answered, wearing a lilac dressing gown. 'What is it? You woke me up.'

'It's the hospital. We have to go back.'

Lena's pale forehead creased. 'But why? I was asleep.'

'Something's happened. They wouldn't tell me what. We just need to get over there.' Flo heard her own voice vibrate with fear.

'Why didn't they call me? I'm the next of kin.'

'They've been trying to ring you. You didn't answer.'

'Do you think he's woken up?' said Lena.

'I don't know.' But from the tone of the phone call, she didn't think that for one minute. 'Come on, put some clothes on and we'll go. I've ordered a taxi.'

'Shut up, what are you even *talking* about?' Lena's voice rose as she stared in disbelief at the doctor sitting on the other side of the desk. 'You're supposed to be making him better, not worse! You can't sit there and tell me my brother's going to *die*.'

Flo stared at the cheap, hard-wearing grey carpet and concentrated on the words the man had just uttered; it was important to take them all in, even when he was saying the unsayable.

'I'm so sorry, Lena, but sometimes we just aren't able to make people better.' The doctor's tone was compassionate but firm. 'The initial injury caused the haemorrhage, and the damage from that is too severe to be compatible with recovery. In such cases, there simply isn't anything more that can be done. All I can assure you is that your brother didn't suffer. He's been in no pain.'

'According to *you*,' said Lena.

Flo pressed her hands together between her knees and said, 'Is there any brain function at all?'

The doctor shook his head. 'No, there isn't.'

'He can't die,' said Lena. 'He just can't.'

But of course he could. Zander might be on life support, but he was, in effect, already dead. It was happening, whether they wanted it to or not.

'So what happens now?' Flo fought down the expanding panic in her chest. 'Do you turn off the life support?'

'Not just yet. The tests have to be repeated.' The doctor, who was in his fifties, with steel-grey hair and heavy jowls, paused for a moment, then said, 'And we also need to discuss another matter with you . . . I don't know if you were aware of how Alexander felt about organ donation . . .'

'What? Is that why you're so keen to switch off the machine? Oh no you don't,' said Lena. 'No, no, you're not having his organs. He's not donating anything to anyone.'

'Lena, I know how you—'

'No way.' Lena was shaking her head, vehement. 'Not happening. NO NO *NO*.'

'He would want to,' said Flo. 'We talked about it a few weeks ago. He carries a donor card in his wallet.'

'I DON'T CARE,' bellowed Lena. 'I'm not letting them do it. I don't want them cutting him up.'

301

'OK, let's leave this for now. It's fine, don't worry, we're not going to do anything you don't agree with,' said the doctor. 'That's a promise.'

Lena had the look in her eye of a cornered wild animal. 'It had better be.'

'This can't be happening.' Shaking her head, Lena pushed the mug of tea away.

It was midnight, and they were back in Zander's flat. Friends and colleagues from his place of work had been contacted and informed of what was going on. Understandably, they were shocked and horrified; something like this was everyone's worst nightmare.

Flo was exhausted but determined not to give up yet. 'I know. But listen to me.' She kept her voice gentle. 'If you needed a kidney and the doctors said they had one for you, would you take it? Or say no?'

'Don't start that again.'

'Lena, I have to, because there isn't much time. It's what Zander would want to happen. Refusing to let them take his organs isn't going to save him. And I know it helps the families who give their consent. They're always so glad, afterwards, that they let it happen, because it means that something good came out of . . . something bad. Just knowing that other people have been helped . . . well, it does make them feel better.'

Tears slid down Lena's thin white face and she made no effort to wipe them away. 'I don't care about other people.'

'I know, I know. But in years to come it'll make *you* feel better, that's what I'm saying. For now, the organs get used or they don't get used. Either way, it won't change what's going to happen to Zander.' Flo's voice caught in her throat at the thought of it. 'He's still going to die.'

'Stop it.' Lena shook her head like a child in denial.

'And if his organs aren't used, it's just such a waste.'

'I don't want his organs to be used,' sobbed Lena. 'I don't want Zander to die. I can't bear this.'

'I know, I know. Look, I'm going now.' Getting to her feet, Flo hesitated. But today had been the most unimaginably awful day of both their lives. At the front door, she turned and gave Lena a hug.

To begin with, Lena stiffened and leaned back; it was like putting your arms around a clothes airer. Then, with a huge gulping sob, she clung tightly to Flo and buried her face in her shoulder. For several seconds they stood together and held each other, both weeping for the man they loved.

After a while, Lena mumbled something unintelligible and Flo had to say, 'What?'

'The accident. It was my fault.' Utterly bereft, Lena choked out, 'If I hadn't phoned him, none of this would have h-h-happened.'

'Sshh, don't even think that.'

The tears were flowing faster. 'But everything would be all right if it wasn't for me!'

'Listen, you can't blame yourself. I didn't want him to get out of bed and pick you up,' said Flo. 'Don't you think I wish I'd tried harder to stop him? Of course I do! But does that mean it's my fault?'

Helplessly, Lena shook her head. 'N-no . . .'

'There you go then. And it wasn't your fault either. It just happened.' Her own heart breaking, Flo wiped away the tears sliding down Lena's face; she wasn't sure if she believed what she was saying, but she knew she had to say it. 'That's why it's called an accident.'

Dozing fitfully in her bed, Flo was woken at four in the morning by her phone. For a split second she thought it must be the hospital ringing with news of Zander – *No, please don't tell me he's died before I can say goodbye* – then she saw Lena's name flash up on the screen.

Although it still could be that. Lena *was* the next of kin.

Her mouth was dry. 'Yes?'

'Just so you know, I've spoken to the doctor on call. I told her I'll sign the forms so the organs can be donated.'

'Really? Thank you.' Weak with gratitude, Flo saw Jeremy's luminous green eyes gleaming at her from the foot of the bed. 'I promise you won't regret it.'

Lena's voice was croaky with grief and exhaustion. 'I hope you're right.'

Flo buried her nose in the pillowcase next to her and breathed in the faint, heartbreakingly familiar scent of the cologne Zander had always worn. How she was going to get through this, she couldn't begin to imagine. But somehow, because there was no other way, she knew she had to.

Exhaling slowly, she spoke with feeling. 'I know I'm right.'

Chapter 48

The moment Hallie saw who was calling, her heart went into overdrive. Jonathan was her transplant coordinator and it was eleven o'clock on Monday evening. All things considered, it was unlikely he'd be ringing at this time of night for a friendly chat.

Six minutes later, Hallie pushed open her mother's bedroom door.

'Mum? Would you be OK to give me a lift?'

Fay was sitting up in bed with her hair in squashy pink rollers, reading a book and eating her favourite crisps. She put down the book and looked puzzled. 'What? You mean *now*? Where on earth do you want to go?'

Hallie was trembling all over. 'To the hospital. Jonathan just called. They think they've got a match for me.'

'OH MY *GOD* . . .' Fay clapped both hands to her mouth. Crisps went flying and the book hit the floor with a thud as the duvet was thrown back and she scrambled out of bed. Then her arms were around Hallie and they were both shaking, unable to take in the fact that at last the call had come.

'It's not definite yet. It might not be a good enough match.' Hallie knew this was a possibility, but just now, she wasn't even considering it; deep down inside she was convinced that this was it, the surgery would go ahead.

'Oh my darling, I can't believe it's happening. After all this time. Oh my God, look at my *hands* . . .' Fay held them up so they could both see the tremor.

'Are you OK to drive? Or shall we get a taxi?'

'No, no, I'll be fine. Give me five minutes to get dressed . . . oh God, my brain, I don't know what to think. I'm in shock . . .'

'Oh Mum.' Hallie hugged her again and heard crunching underfoot. 'We're treading crisps into the carpet.'

'My beautiful baby girl.' As she held her tight, Fay whispered into her ear, 'I love you so much.'

It was over, it was really and truly over. And she'd been right about yesterday being the very worst day of her life, but Flo knew that harder days still – and many of them – were yet to come.

It was now early morning, the rain of the last few days had cleared and the sun was coming up over the rooftops of Clifton. As if sensing that she needed contact, Jeremy was in her arms, purring and gently kneading his paws against her chest.

And he *never* did that.

Across the square, Lena was in Zander's flat with Giles. Yesterday they'd somehow got through what had needed to be done, and everyone at the hospital had been wonderfully kind. A specialist nurse in organ donation had arrived from the transplant centre and arranged everything. She'd been lovely, patiently explaining each step of the procedure whilst organising the completion of all the necessary tests and investigations. Then, when the documentation had been taken care of and the last details arranged, Flo and Lena had separately said their final goodbyes to Zander.

After that, he'd been transferred to the operating theatre and the surgery had been carried out. From there, his body – oh God, that *word* – had been taken to the mortuary, and the specialist nurse, having personally packed the organs due for transplant, had arranged for them to be delivered to wherever they'd be used.

She couldn't have been kinder or more empathetic, and it had helped.

Well, as much as anything could.

Out there somewhere, other people were getting the chance of life.

Please God, let them appreciate it.

A tear slid down Flo's cheek and dripped off her chin. It landed on the top of Jeremy's head, causing him to twitch his ears. Then her phone beeped and with a yowl of irritation he wriggled free, leaping to the floor.

Flo unlocked her phone and read the email that had just arrived.

Oh my dearest darling girl, I've just heard the sad news about your lovely man. What a terrible tragedy, I'm *so* sorry. I know how hopelessly inadequate these words are, but the sentiment is heartfelt all the same. You won't be working for a while, understandably, but if you ever need to be with people who know how you feel, do drop by – most of us here at Nairn House have been through what you're going through now.

Much love, Margot xxx

Oh God, the pain was just unbearable. On Saturday afternoon they'd all met Zander for the first time. Now it was Tuesday morning and he no longer existed. How was she ever going to get through this?

Alone in the flat, crushed with grief and despair, Flo covered her face with her hands and wept.

'They've found a heart for Rory. All the tests have been carried out and it's apparently a good match. They're taking him to theatre in two hours.' Tasha met Joe at the entrance to the ward and saw his expression change as he took in what she was babbling at him. 'I know! Isn't it amazing? I mean, I'm terrified,

307

obviously, but it's his only chance. I didn't think it was going to happen . . . and now it *is* . . .'

'Thank God.' Joe's face grew flushed with emotion as they hugged, and she felt the tension in his body subside. 'Oh thank God.'

'Don't squeeze me too hard. I might be sick.'

'Sorry. I'm just so relieved.' He let her go, and she saw the glimmer of tears in his eyes. 'I never thought they'd find one in time either.'

Tasha nodded, overcome and unable to speak. Whilst hoping for the best, they'd both been forced to contemplate the worst-case scenario.

'And now they have,' said Joe. 'They've got a heart for him.' His voice was unsteady. 'Do they know where it came from?'

'No idea.' Tasha shook her head. 'Maybe they do, but they wouldn't tell us that.'

'Now, sign your name next to each of the crosses,' Jonathan instructed, 'and we're done.'

Hallie signed the form in front of her. Since arriving at the hospital in the early hours, she'd been settled into her room and had loads of blood samples taken from her by various members of staff. Swabs had also been taken from almost every section of her body. After that, she'd been showered, shaved and washed again with pink chlorhexidine liquid. Then they'd waited . . . and waited . . . while the rest of the tests were carried out.

Finally the news they'd been waiting for had come through. The transplant would be going ahead. And it wasn't just going to be lungs, either; she'd be receiving a new heart too.

It wasn't that much of a shock; Hallie had heard of this happening to other people before now. Basically, it was easier for the surgeon to transplant a heart and lungs than a pair of lungs on their own. And in turn, she would donate her own heart to someone else who needed it. This was known as a domino transplant. Her lungs might be damaged by the cystic fibrosis, but her heart was as healthy as anyone else's.

If anything went wrong after the operation, though, you weren't allowed to ask for your old heart back.

She'd just signed away her rights to it for ever.

Unexpectedly, the earlier fear and anxiety had receded. Thirty minutes from now, she would be wheeled into the operating theatre; all they could do was hope for the best outcome. It was what they'd been waiting and praying for for years.

Hallie smiled up at Jonathan and handed him back the ball-point pen. 'Thanks. Tell them to take good care of it.'

'Don't you worry.' Jonathan winked reassuringly as he prepared to leave the room. 'I'll make sure they do.'

And then she was alone again in the small grey and white medical-smelling room. Her mum was outside making phone calls to everyone she knew, despite the fact that it was only six thirty and most of them were still asleep with their mobiles switched to silent. Hallie had left messages with her own friends and had also uploaded to her website the confession she'd written earlier. In this brave new electronic world, followers of www.threethingsaboutyou.com from around the world had already begun to respond, sending lovely comments and wishing her luck. And yes, most of the messages might have been sent by strangers, but each one still felt like a tiny supportive hug. They might not know her in real life, but their kind words were heartfelt nevertheless.

And they helped, they really did help.

A text came through at that moment, from Luke: *Hey, just heard the news. Good luck. How are you feeling?*

Short and to the point, but Hallie gazed at her phone and pictured him saying the words. Where was he right now? Still in bed? Downstairs in his kitchen, waiting for the kettle to boil? Was Christina there with him?

Whichever, it didn't matter. It was just nice of him to have

309

sent the text. Feeling warm and cared for and unbelievably lucky, she pressed Reply and typed: *Thanks, everything's great. Can't wait for it to happen. Today's the first day of the rest of my life.*

She paused, smiling, imagining the worried look on his face. Then added: *Really, I'm fine. Xxx*

All the other texts she'd sent this morning had ended with three kisses. It wasn't until she'd pressed Send that Hallie realised she'd done it again.

Whoops. Oh well, maybe another time it would be more embarrassing. But today, frankly, she had other, more pressing issues on her mind.

Chapter 49

Flo made her way along Princess Victoria Street in Clifton, moving sideways to avoid an overweight man with a whippet on a red lead. Passing the florist's shop, she waved and mouthed hello to the friendly girl who ran it. The mingled scents from the galvanized-silver buckets of flowers reminded her of something she really didn't need reminding of, seeing as it would be imprinted on her brain for ever. This time two weeks ago, she'd been standing outside the crematorium after Zander's funeral, gazing at the rows of wreaths and cellophane-wrapped bouquets, while fretful spots of rain had fallen and grey clouds had scudded by overhead.

Today, in contrast, the temperature was up in the eighties, an unrelenting sun was beating down and Flo's hair was sticking to the back of her neck. She'd finished her shift at Nairn House and now needed to pay a visit to the supermarket. She'd initially thought she might take a few weeks off, but it hadn't worked out that way at all. Sitting at home with nothing to occupy her mind had turned out to be akin to solitary confinement in prison. Keeping busy was the answer, and going back to work had been a lifesaver, especially since – as Margot had so wisely pointed out – the majority of the residents of Nairn House knew just what she was going through. Nobody minded if she had a bit of a cry. They understood that she wasn't going to be as cheerful as usual. They also kept offering her biscuits she didn't have the appetite to eat.

Anyway, supermarket. At least there'd be air-conditioning to look forward to. Flo took a couple of deep breaths and paused to pull the small bottle of water out of her bag. She uncapped it and took a swallow. Eurgh, warm. Even more eurgh, shoals of little black dots were starting to cloud her vision and a woolly sensation had begun to invade her brain.

Oh God, don't say she was going to faint; this hadn't happened since she was a teenager during an overlong morning assembly at school. Panicking, she ducked into relatively empty Waterloo Street and leaned against the pink-stuccoed outer wall of an antiques shop. But the black dots were expanding, the buzzing in her ears was growing louder and the bones in her legs appeared to be turning to Play-Doh . . .

The next moment, opening her eyes, she was flat out on the cobblestones with the contents of her handbag scattered around her and the now-empty plastic water bottle lying in the gutter. Someone was holding her head and simultaneously reaching for her turquoise purse.

'Oh please don't take it . . .' Flo tried to sit up and stop them; the money wasn't important, but the purse had been a present from Zander. 'Please.'

'I'm not stealing your purse, I'm putting it back. Have you ever fainted before?'

'At school, when I was thirteen.' Staying where she was and woozily recovering her bearings, Flo watched as the man collected up the rest of her belongings and returned them to her bag. His other hand was supporting the back of her head, keeping it off the stony ground. It took a few seconds before the penny dropped. 'Oh, it's *you*. Hello.'

She might not know his name, Flo realised, but he was no stranger. Since the fateful tomato soup incident back in January,

312

she'd seen him a few more times, though he no longer sat outside the pub on Princess Victoria Street.

'Hi. I'd ask how you're feeling, but that would probably be a silly question.'

'Well, I've had better days.' She managed a brief smile in return. 'Actually, not so bad now.'

A woman from the antiques shop came out with a glass of cold water, and Flo drank it down gratefully in one go.

'Where do you live?' said the man.

'Caledonia Place.'

'OK, can you stand? Let me help you home.'

Flo took a few deep breaths. Once she was on her feet and fairly sure she wasn't about to collapse again, they made their way carefully around the corner.

'Thanks,' she murmured as they walked. 'Sorry I'm being slow. My head's still a bit muzzy.'

'You'll probably feel rubbish for a while. Wiped out. Take it steady.' He held her arm as she wavered. 'I'm Jason, by the way.'

'And I'm Flo. Haven't seen you around lately.'

'I've got a job.' Jason announced it with pride. 'Washing up in the new Italian restaurant down the road. Sorry, do I sound smug? That's because I am.'

She smiled. 'That's brilliant. Well done.'

By the time they reached the flat, Flo was perspiring and feeling light-headed again, and needed Jason's help up the staircase.

'This is really kind of you,' she said as he guided her across the living room and over to the sofa. Legs wobbling, she collapsed on to it in the nick of time. Oh, the relief of sitting down.

'No problem. Can I get you anything?'

Her mouth was like cotton wool. 'I'd love a cup of tea. Two sugars, please.'

He was back from the kitchen thirty seconds later, holding

the almost empty litre carton of milk from the fridge. 'This has gone off, I'm afraid. It's sour.'

'God, sorry. Yes, I knew that.' Life at the moment was full of too many things to remember; it was a constant battle to stay afloat. 'I was on my way to the supermarket when I fainted.'

'Was that the list that fell out of your handbag? There's no way you're up to shopping now,' said Jason. 'Would you like me to go to the supermarket for you?'

She hesitated. 'I don't want to put you out.'

'Honestly, not a problem. Happy to help. Here.' He passed over her handbag and Flo gave him the list she'd compiled, then opened her purse. When she paused for a second, Jason said, 'It's OK, I promise not to run off with your money.'

'Don't even say that.' Unable to remember what she'd written down, she handed him three twenty-pound notes. 'There, that should be enough. Thank you so much.'

'My pleasure.' Was he secretly wondering why she was looking so awful? If he was, he didn't ask. Glancing at the items scribbled on the shopping list, he said, 'I'll be back in half an hour. You stay where you are.'

The weakness and wooziness had receded by the time the doorbell rang twenty-five minutes later. Flo buzzed him in and said, 'Really, thanks so much for this,' as he carried the bags past her into the kitchen.

'Stop it. Do you have any idea how good it makes me feel, being in a position to help someone else?' Jason was in his forties, thin and wiry, with well-muscled arms and a scar across his left temple. But his voice was gentle, his expression compassionate. 'You helped me out. I'm just glad to have a chance to return the favour.'

As he spoke, he was efficiently unpacking the three supermarket carriers on the table. She'd pretty much run out of all the essentials, so there was fresh milk, bread, butter, eggs, coffee and tissues, along with ham, Marmite, two packets of liquorice allsorts and three bottles of Tabasco.

'OK, all that chilli sauce isn't for me.' Feeling the need to explain, Flo said, 'I work at Nairn House, and one of the residents asked me to get it for her. She likes to keep a good supply . . . *oh.*'

Her voice faltered as Jason took the last item out of the carrier bag and said mildly, 'Is this for one of the residents too?'

Flo sat down at the kitchen table and felt her own heartbeat thundering in her ears. She'd compiled the shopping list during her lunch break, sitting outside in the shade with Annie and Bridget. Annie, as nosy as ever, had peered over and said, 'Two packets of liquorice allsorts? *Really?*'

'I've eaten most of Margot's, so I'm replacing them. And the other bag's for me.'

'Didn't think you liked liquorice allsorts,' said Bridget.

Flo had shrugged. 'I just fancied them for a change.'

And Annie, never backward in coming forwards, had said bluntly, 'Oh love, you're not pregnant, are you?'

It was a completely ridiculous question. For a couple of seconds the possibility skittered through Flo's brain . . . They'd been careful, hadn't they? And her period was late, but after the shock of the accident, that was only to be expected. Oh no, the prospect was too terrifying to contemplate; she shook her head rapidly, let the idea scurry away and said, 'No, of course I'm not.'

But while she'd been adding Tabasco to the list, she'd been aware of Annie and Bridget exchanging significant glances.

It couldn't happen. She wasn't even going to think about it.

Now, her hand trembling slightly, she said, 'Can you pass me the shopping list, please?'

There were all the items she'd written down in blue ballpoint. And there at the bottom of the page, in Annie's handwriting in black felt-tip pen, was: *pregnancy testing kit.*

Subtle as ever.

'Sorry.' Jason followed the direction of her gaze. 'Was I not supposed to buy that?'

'No, it's fine. You were.' Oh God, and she'd fainted; was that another sign?

'Right.' He pulled a face. 'Thought for a moment it was some kind of joke.'

'It wasn't.' The effort of not thinking the unthinkable was making Flo's mouth dry and her jaw ache. 'Thanks for getting it.'

'Caused a few raised eyebrows, I can tell you.' Reassured, Jason broke into a grin. 'They all know me in that super-market, and you know what Clifton's like for gossip. Mary on the checkout whispered, "Oh dear, good luck, love," when she put it through the till. Anyway, here you go.' He'd reboiled the kettle and made her the promised mug of tea. 'I'll be off now. Want me to carry this into the living room for you?'

'Thanks.' Flo followed him across the hall and settled herself back on the sofa.

'You're still not looking well,' said Jason. 'Might be an idea to see your doctor. Especially if you're . . .' He gestured awkwardly in the vicinity of his own flat stomach.

'I will.' Flo nodded and saw him notice for the first time the sympathy cards lined up on the mantelpiece.

He turned and said with compassion, 'Oh dear, poor you, looks like it's all happening at once. Who died?'

Poor Jason was unprepared for the answer she was about to give him. 'My boyfriend,' said Flo.

'Here we are.' Flo held up the bottles of Tabasco. 'Did you think I'd forget them?'

'Honestly?' said Margot. 'Yes, I did. Not that it would have mattered a bit,' she went on as Flo lined up the bottles on the

316

kitchen worktop. 'And I wouldn't have blamed you if you had. After Yves died, my memory was like a smashed mirror. I could barely remember my own name.'

'Same here. That's why I wrote a list. And I bought these for you too.' Flo produced one of the packets of liquorice allsorts. 'To make up for eating the last lot.'

'Oh darling, you didn't need to do that.'

'Well I thought I should. This way I'll be able to pinch a few more while I'm working.' She paused. 'I never used to like liquorice.'

'Didn't you?'

Flo shook her head. 'When I told Annie I'd started eating it, she asked me if I was pregnant.'

Margot put down her iPad and removed her reading glasses. 'And?'

'I took a test last night.' It had taken her until midnight to pluck up the courage to do it.

'And?' said Margot again.

Just say it. Flo took a deep breath. 'And . . . it turns out Annie was right.'

'Oh goodness. Oh my darling.' Margot reached out to clasp her hand. 'It's not often I'm at a loss for words, but this is one of those moments.'

'You're the first person I've told.'

'And how are you feeling about it?'

'Shocked. Scared. Overwhelmed.' Flo paused, eyeing the packet of allsorts on the worktop and yearning to open it. 'Confused. That was last night. Then I went to bed, thinking I wouldn't get any sleep at all. But I *did* sleep, better than I have since the accident. And when I woke up this morning, it suddenly seemed like a good thing, a perfect present from Zander. And I'm just so glad it's happened, I really am.'

Margot nodded with satisfaction. 'In that case, come here . . .' She threw her arms around Flo and hugged her. 'It *is* a good thing, I promise you. The best surprise present you could have. Congratulations!'

'Thanks.' It wouldn't be easy, Flo knew that, but it felt right and she was going to give it her very best shot.

'I've just thought of something,' said Margot. 'That ridiculous fortune-telling woman at the summer fair who got everything wrong . . .'

'I know.' The irony of it hadn't escaped Flo either.

'Didn't she say you and Zander would have two children?'

How they'd laughed at hopeless, incompetent Madam Zara with her wild guesses and her wonky eyeliner.

Flo pulled a face. 'I'm not sure I could cope with twins.'

Chapter 50

It was the last week of September, and the first signs of autumn were making themselves known. Through the windows, the leaves on the trees outside were starting to turn, various shades of green edging into ambers, pinks and browns.

Hallie's phone began to ring. She saw who was calling and pressed Answer. 'Hi.'

'Hey,' said Bea. 'Where are you? What are you doing?'

The questions her oldest friend had been habitually asking her for years. 'Oh, nothing much. Just finished a 5K run. I'm going to dive into the pool next, probably swim twenty or thirty lengths. Then after that I'm planning to head over to the restaurant and have a nice lunch with this friend of mine, I forget her name . . .'

'Her name is *Bea*, and she's wondering if you've happened to notice the guy over to your right.'

'Which guy?'

'The one on the cross-trainer. Black vest, gorgeous biceps. Gorgeous *everything*.'

'I *may* have noticed him . . .'

'Yay!'

'No, not yay.' Twisting round to survey Bea over by the rowing machines at the other end of the gym, Hallie said, 'I also noticed his wedding ring.'

'Oh bum, that's a shame. You could have asked him to join us for lunch.'

'Will you stop trying to set me up? If I wanted a man, I'd organise it myself.'

'OK, fine. How are you feeling, anyway?'

Hallie smiled, because she'd just told Bea she'd completed a 5K run on the treadmill and it had been true. 'I'm great.'

And this was true too. It hadn't all been plain sailing, of course. The first few days following the transplant had passed in a muggy haze of sedation, discomfort and tubing, peppered with endlessly being woken up when she'd far rather be asleep. But from day one the hospital staff had informed her that the surgery had been a success, and even in her drugged-up state, Hallie had been aware that breathing was easier, that the endless weight of the cystic fibrosis in her lungs was gone.

She'd been lucky not to succumb to any infections. After the initial post-op period, recovery had been smooth and utterly miraculous. The fog had cleared, physiotherapy had intensified and eventually visitors had no longer needed to be masked and gowned-up when they came to see her.

A stranger's heart and lungs were now functioning beautifully inside her chest, and somewhere, hopefully, her own heart was beating inside another person's body. It was just the most extraordinary thing . . . yet it didn't *feel* extraordinary; it just felt normal and right.

Two and a half weeks after the surgery, she'd been discharged from the hospital. And yes, she still had plenty of tablets to take and regular tests to undergo – that went without saying – but it didn't *matter*; it was a tiny price to pay in return for the unbelievable gift she'd received.

And now, three months on, Hallie found herself appreciating each day more and more, jogging and cycling and amazing everyone with her achievements. This was the new life she'd never truly expected to get the chance to live, and she wasn't going to waste a moment of it. In due course she planned to do all the things other people took for granted – get a proper job, take foreign holidays . . . even having a baby at some stage was now a possibility.

Basically, who knew what the future held?

As they drove back to Carranford later on that afternoon, Bea said, 'I was reading some of the problems on your website last night.'

Since Hallie had outed herself on the night of the transplant, it had become common knowledge that she was Dear Rose; even Carranford's least internet-savvy inhabitants now knew about threethingsaboutyou.com. Hallie said, 'Oh yes?'

'There's something I feel really bad about.'

Mystified, Hallie looked at Bea. 'Go on.'

'There was a message from a girl called Fran who had loads of scars after a car accident. She was in love with her best friend's boyfriend but knew he'd never be interested in her.'

'I remember.'

'And you said you knew exactly how she felt.'

'Yes.' Hallie nodded. She remembered that too.

'And I saw the date you replied to that message. It was the night of Marilyn's party at the pub,' said Bea. 'When you first met Ross and he didn't know you were ill.'

'Right.' Baffled, Hallie tilted her head. 'Why are you being weird? What's he got to do with anything?'

'Because you told me you didn't fancy him, but when I read that, I realised you must have done . . . and it just made me feel terrible all over again . . .'

Hallie started to laugh. 'Well you can stop feeling terrible, because I wasn't talking about *Ross*!'

Then she abruptly stopped laughing, because Bea had done a double-take and was now raising her eyebrows in Miss Marple fashion.

'No? So who *were* you talking about?'

'No one. Just not Ross.'

'Come on, I heard the way you said it. You weren't just telling me it wasn't anyone, you were stressing that Ross wasn't the one. You emphasised his name,' Bea pointed out. 'Like, it wasn't *Ross*, but it was definitely someone else.' Her eyebrows were still up. 'See? I know I'm right. I'm not stupid.'

God, she was like a ferret when she got her teeth into an idea. To change the subject, Hallie said, 'Although we did lose the last pub quiz because you thought the capital of Azerbaijan was Baklava.'

'And now you're trying to change the subject.' Bea was triumphant. 'But it won't work. Because I'm not going to give up until I find out who it is.'

'Well good luck with that.' Hallie surreptitiously wiped her palms, slick with perspiration, against the sides of her jeans. 'Because there isn't anyone. I just made it up to make the girl feel better.'

'Don't believe you.' Narrowing her eyes, Bea tapped her nails against the steering wheel as she gave the matter some thought. 'OK, is it Brendan?'

Brendan ran the hotel across the river from the pub.

'Yes, it is.' Hallie nodded.

'Shut up, it isn't. How about Den Simpson?'

'Yes, it's Den Simpson.'

'OK, it's not him. Is it Steve from the rugby club?'

'Yes, it's definitely him. All these years I've been secretly in love with Steve Biggins.'

'No you haven't. You don't like his ears.'

Was it any surprise, seeing as they were as weird and curly as cooked snails?

Hallie said, 'Maybe I was only pretending not to like his ears. Maybe I actually find their curliness completely irresistible.'

'Don't you make fun of me. I'll figure it out sooner or later.

Ooh look, there's Christina.' Driving past Luke's cottage, Bea tooted and waved as Christina and Daley emerged from Christina's car. 'Anyway, are we going to the pub tomorrow night? It's Luke's thing, remember.'

Luke. Hallie inwardly jumped, bracing herself for yet more suspicious questioning, but it didn't happen. Bea's interrogation had concluded; this time the subject really had been changed and she'd moved on to tomorrow's meet-and-greet.

'We should go.' Hallie nodded in agreement. 'Everyone else is. And I know Marilyn's doing food.'

As she'd guessed they would, her friend's eyes lit up.

'Brilliant. I wonder if there'll be Scotch eggs?' said Bea.

Luke was in the living room, checking emails on his computer, ensuring that the changeover would be smooth. Yesterday Jennifer, his ex-colleague, had left Carranford and was at this moment aboard a flight to Uganda. Tomorrow evening her replacement at the practice would be introducing herself to the villagers by way of an informal get-together at the White Hart. Which might not be standard GP practice but seemed like a pretty good idea all the same.

Dr Tess Hannigan was about as far removed from her predecessor as it was possible to be. The other week Jennifer West had pursed her lips and said, 'Hmm, I'm not sure, is she really the kind of person you'd want working here?' Whereupon Luke had replied with great firmness, 'Oh yes.'

Tess was in her forties, happily divorced, chatty and friendly, with a frizz of chestnut hair, crimson lipstick and oversized jewellery. Plump, curvy and given to bright outfits and elaborate shoes, she was extrovert but also evidently extremely bright, incisive and hard-working. Most importantly, Luke knew the villagers would like her.

He pressed Print on the computer, and the printer next to him trundled into life.

He'd left the front door on the latch, and now it creaked open as a small, determined animal pushed its way through the gap. Luke turned as Daley came skittering across the floor and launched himself on to his lap.

'Hey you, hello! Where've you been then? Careful now . . .' He swung round in his chair before Daley's enthusiastic tail-wagging could send flying the sheets of paper that were being rhythmically churned out by the printer. Then he tickled the dog's ears and paddled his paws in the air. 'Look at you, who's a good boy?'

'Hi,' said Christina, watching them from the doorway.

Luke smiled at her. 'Hi.'

'What's this?' Crossing the living room, she picked up one of the printed sheets.

'That's Tess. It was her idea to put up a few photos of herself, then people would know what she looked like. So I took some of her this afternoon.'

Christina eyed the end result. 'Hmm. Thought she'd be prettier. I mean, I suppose she's not bad, if you like that sort of thing. Not exactly stunning, though.'

'She's a very nice person,' said Luke.

'You're looking forward to working with her, aren't you?' There was a slight edge to Christina's voice.

'I am.' Luke nodded, outwardly calm. Inside his brain, however, a switch had been flicked, the decision made. The time had come; he simply couldn't do this any more. Once his mind was made up, that was it. 'OK, we need to talk.'

'About what?'

He looked at her steadily. 'Come on, you know the answer to that. This isn't working out, is it?'

She froze. 'Is it her? *Tess?*'

'No. Absolutely not. And it's not your fault either. It's no one's fault,' said Luke. 'We tried our best, but it isn't happening. Be honest, you know it as well as I do.'

All the tension slid from Christina's shoulders and she nodded slowly. 'Oh God, I suppose you're right.'

'Sorry,' said Luke. He meant it, too; since getting back together, they'd both been doing their level best to pretend that everything was fine, but the basic central premise – the bit where genuine love was called for – simply wasn't there. They'd hoped they might be able to recreate it, but it hadn't happened.

'It's all right. I thought I was making such a grand romantic gesture, turning up at Marilyn's party that night.' Christina's slim fingers fiddled with the rolled hem of her pistachio silk scarf. 'I think I thought it would make you love me more. But all it did was railroad you into going along with the whole thing. You didn't want everyone to see me make a big fool of myself, so you pretended to be happy about it.'

'That's not true.' Luke shook his head. 'Don't put yourself down. I didn't pretend to be happy. I genuinely thought it might work. We both gave it our best shot.'

'But it wasn't enough,' said Christina. There was sadness in her voice, but also acceptance.

'No,' he reluctantly agreed. 'It wasn't.'

'Shame.' She managed a brief smile. 'Oh well, at least we tried. Shall I tell you what's ironic?'

'Go on.'

'Last time you finished with me, it was partly because you didn't like my beautiful snakes.' Christina glanced at Daley, still lying happily against Luke's chest. 'And this time I'm pretty sure you stuck it out a bit longer than you wanted because you like my beautiful dog so much.'

She was pretty much spot on; he knew he was going to miss Daley more than he'd miss Christina.

'You don't need to say anything,' she continued wryly. 'Look at the way you greet him when we turn up. Then look at the way you greet me.'

Feeling bad, Luke apologised again. But in truth, the overwhelming sensation was one of relief. He'd said it at last; the deed was done.

'Never mind, can't be helped. I noticed you've been a bit more distant over the last few weeks.' Christina's sleek hair fell forward as she took another look at the photo in her hand. 'Sure it isn't her?'

The early evening sun was streaming in through the windows, reflecting off the glossy photographic paper that bore the image of Dr Tess Hannigan with her frizzy hair, beaming smile and plump pink cheeks.

'I promise you it isn't,' said Luke.

Silence, followed by one last disparaging glance at the photo.

'Well, good,' said Christina. 'Because she's definitely not your type.'

Chapter 51

If Luke had imagined he'd need to make a welcoming speech and introduce Dr Tess Hannigan to the villagers who'd come along to this evening's get-together at the pub, he'd been wrong. Tess had stood up on the stage and made her own speech, welcoming herself to Carranford and expressing her joy at being here. She'd then gone around and started introducing herself to everyone present, pausing to chat to each person in turn. It had been a triumphant PR exercise; within minutes even the most dubious potential patient had been visibly charmed and won over.

Approaching the bar for a refill, Luke found himself next to Hallie. 'Well?' He indicated Tess at the other end of the room. 'What's the verdict?'

'She's fantastic, so warm and friendly.' Hallie gave him a sympathetic look. 'And to think you used to be the popular one. You do realise what's going to start happening now, don't you?'

'You mean all my regular patients are going to abandon me and want to become her regular patients instead? I know.'

'Think of all the extra free time you'll have.' Hallie's eyes sparkled. 'You'll be able to take up golf.'

Luke smiled, because she knew how much he hated the idea of golf; it had been a running joke between them for years. 'You're looking well.'

'Thanks. Feeling well. Still getting used to being out and about without my oxygen. I keep doing this.' She mimed adjusting a set of nasal specs and tucking the plastic tubing behind her ear.

'You're doing brilliantly,' said Luke. Appearance-wise, the difference was dramatic: the dark shadows beneath her eyes had vanished, her eyes were brighter, her hair shinier. She exuded new-found energy and *joie de vivre*.

'I ran 5K on the treadmill at the club yesterday, and swam twenty-five lengths. I'm very smug about it.' Hallie paused for a second. 'We passed Christina outside your place yesterday. I thought she might be here tonight. Will she be along later?'

Luke prevaricated; was now the time to say it? 'No . . . she won't. Not tonight.'

'Oh, OK. It's just that she wanted to watch the *Les Mis* DVD and I said I'd lend her my copy.' Hallie unzipped her shoulder bag and rummaged around in its depths. 'That's why I brought it along with me. But if I give it to you, you can pass it on to her, can't you? You can watch it together!'

Looked like he was going to have to say it after all.

'Actually, not much point giving it to me.' He shook his head as she finally, with an air of triumph, produced the DVD from her bag. 'I won't be seeing Christina for a while . . . well, for quite a while . . . um, probably never, to be honest.' *Oh yes, that was cool, handled like a pro. Well done you.*

Hallie was staring at him. 'What? Why?'

Because she's tied up and locked away in my attic. Aloud, Luke said, 'It didn't work out. We . . . broke up.'

'Oh no! That's a real shame. I'm sorry.'

She sounded as if she meant it. He shrugged. 'It's OK. I mean, things weren't great.'

'Oh right, I didn't know.' Her gaze was focused on his face, switching from his eyes to his mouth as if searching for clues. 'We all thought you two were . . . you know . . .'

328

Luke wiped a dribble of condensation from the outside of his glass. 'Yes, well, turns out we weren't.'

'Are you upset?'

'Honestly? No.'

'That's all right, then.' A flicker of a smile. 'Shame about Daley, though.'

'I know.' He nodded. 'I thought that too.'

'He loved you.'

As she said it, there was a burst of laughter from a group of people over by the window. For a split second, Luke thought she had said *I love you*. The logical part of his brain kicked in almost instantly, but the whoosh of adrenalin had already set off around his body. He swallowed and cleared his throat. 'I'm going to miss him. A lot.'

Hallie did the automatic tucking-the-oxygen-tubing-behind-her-ear gesture, then caught herself and took a swallow of wine instead. 'Maybe it's time to get a dog of your own.'

Luke hesitated. This was a possibility that had crossed his mind earlier. 'That'd be great, but I don't know if it'd be fair, what with the hours I have to work.'

'Well, if you ever decide to go for it, I'd be happy to help out with dog-sitting and walks. Ha, listen to me,' Hallie marvelled, shaking her head. 'I can't believe I'm saying that, offering to take a dog for walks. I still can't get over being able to go for walks myself . . . it's like a miracle.'

Her eyes were bright, the corners of her mouth lifted. How he longed to touch her face.

'Thanks, I'll bear it in mind if—'

'Oh for God's sake, can you believe it?' Bea bounced up to them, huffing with frustration. 'Ross just called. He's not able to make it tonight after all. Some stupid client can only view the property at nine o'clock this evening and he wants Ross to show him round.'

Hallie looked sympathetic. 'That's a pain. Couldn't Ross say no, book it for another night?'

'It's a three-million-pound Georgian manor house in Winchcombe.' Bea pulled a face. 'At that price, the customer calls the shots. Ah well, can't be helped. Work comes first, I guess.'

Hallie didn't want another drink, but buying one for Bea gave her a minute or two's leeway in which to think. It was hard to concentrate on what her best friend was saying when her brain was in a complete flat spin with the news that Luke and Christina had broken up.

'Here.' She handed Bea a big glass of Pinot Noir. 'Shall we go and get some more food? Have you had any Scotch eggs yet?'

'No. Oh, who am I kidding? It's the third time it's happened in two weeks.' Bea heaved a sigh, slumping on to a stool and abandoning the pretence. 'He says he's coming over, then cancels at the last minute.' Now that Luke had moved away and it was just the two of them, she could admit the truth. 'I've checked his company website, too. They don't have a Georgian manor house in Winchcombe on the books.'

'Oh dear.' Poor Bea; Hallie felt for her. It wasn't the first time this had happened to her.

'Shall I call him back?'

OK, it wasn't the first time *this* had happened either. Hallie shook her head. 'No, don't.'

'I could get a taxi and go over to his place.'

Yet another familiar ploy. As if it had ever worked before. 'Listen to me,' said Hallie. 'It wouldn't be a good idea.'

'But—'

'Really.' It was time to get firm. '*No.*'

'OK, this is a teeny-*weeny* bit embarrassing,' said Bea.

'It is?' Tess Hannigan looked intrigued. 'Why's that, then?'

Hallie deftly slid a couple of empty glasses out of the way before Bea and her alcohol-fuelled arms accidentally sent them flying. It was now ten thirty, and their turn to have a chat with the new doctor.

'Because I've had a few drinks and I'm a little bit tipsy . . .' When she was like this, Bea had a habit of blinking like an owl; she was doing it now. 'And you've come over to talk to us and you've never met us before, so now you're going to think I'm the village drunk, but I promise you I'm not. It's true, isn't it?' She turned to Hallie for confirmation. 'I'm a very moderate and sensible drinker as a rule, but tonight's been a bit crappy, to be honest. I expect you've already heard about Hallie and her brand-new heart? Well, mine's old and broken.' Bea clapped both hands over her left breast. 'Right here. Shattered into little pieces. By my boyfriend. Well, ex-boyfriend now. *Bastard*.'

Hallie pulled an apologetic face at the new doctor. It was her own fault; if she'd confiscated Bea's phone, Bea wouldn't have been able to lock herself in one of the toilet cubicles and call Ross. Hallie, on the other side of the cubicle door, had heard Bea say shakily, 'Ross, just tell me the truth, are you seeing someone else?'

Hallie had held her breath until the ensuing pause was broken by Bea declaring, 'Oh I *knew* it.'

After that, the drowning of the sorrows had begun in earnest. And now, fairly predictably three sheets to the wind, Bea was earnestly informing the new doctor that she really *didn't* have a liver the consistency of a bath sponge.

Bea finally reeled off into the garden, leaving Hallie with Tess Hannigan.

'She's telling the truth,' said Hallie.

'I know, I can tell.' Tess nodded easily. 'It's OK, I'm here to help people, not judge them.'

She really *was* different from her predecessor. Hallie relaxed. 'That's good to hear.'

'And you're Hallie Kingsley. I've obviously heard all about you from Luke.' Tess paused and smiled. 'You're looking very well.'

331

'Thanks. Feeling it too. It's quite weird, getting used to not being ill. I mean, like now, look at me.' Hallie gestured to her legs. 'Standing up! No oxygen, no wheelchair, no endlessly having to clear my lungs. I've been so lucky. It's like a miracle.'

'A whole new life ahead of you.' Tess's voice was warm.

'Yes.'

'Boyfriend?'

'No.' Hallie shook her head.

'Love life's been pretty rubbish, has it?'

'You could say that. Well,' she managed a rueful smile, 'it wasn't exactly a priority.'

Tess's grey eyes sparkled. 'So that's something else to look forward to. It's all going to start happening for you now. Anyone you might have your eye on?'

Honestly, talk about up front. Definitely not backward in coming forwards. Praying she wasn't going pink, Hallie said, 'Not yet, no.'

'Ah well, plenty of time,' said Tess.

By eleven forty-five, everyone had left the pub. Luke and Tess made their way outside to Tess's car; she'd offered him a lift home.

'Well that was a success,' said Luke as she drove out of the village towards his cottage. 'They all loved you.'

'That's because I'm a fabulous person.' Tess swung the car expertly around a hedgehog that was ambling across the road. 'I'm also a perspicacious one.'

'Perspicacious?' It was an impressively long word for this time of the evening. Amused, Luke said, 'In what respect?'

'Body language. Micro-expressions. Bit of a speciality of mine. I notice things other people don't see. Left or right?'

They'd reached a fork in the road. 'Left,' said Luke. 'And that's my cottage up there . . . the one with the blue gate.' He waited until she'd pulled up outside the cottage, then added,

'Go on then: this perspicacity of yours. So what is it you've noticed?'

Tess smiled slightly. 'I was watching you and Hallie earlier, talking to each other. There's quite a connection between you two.'

Luke tensed. 'I'm her doctor. She's my patient. Hallie's been through a lot. And she never complains.'

'She's a lovely girl.'

'Nothing's ever happened between us.' He felt the need to come straight out and say it. Tess wasn't making idle conversation here.

'But you have feelings for her.'

God, this was embarrassing. There was such a thing as being *too* perspicacious. Stiffly, Luke said, 'I'd never do anything that might jeopardise my career.'

'Oh Luke, relax, I'm not accusing you of anything! I'm just saying you like her. I mean, really like her.' Tess paused, then added, 'And she really likes you too.'

He did a double-take; this was something he hadn't expected to hear. 'What?'

'Come on, you heard me. The interest is mutual. Did you genuinely not realise that?'

'No.' He shook his head, numb with shock. 'Are you making this up?'

'Absolutely not. Like I said, body language and micro-expressions. It's all there, as plain as day. To me, anyway.' Entertained, she added, 'Clearly not to you.'

'Shit, shit. But no one else has ever spotted it. And I know they haven't,' said Luke, 'because if they had, trust me, it wouldn't have stayed a secret. Not around here.'

'They've all known Hallie for years. They're used to her being chronically ill. It isn't something that's ever occurred to them to consider. Whereas I'm a fresh pair of eyes,' Tess explained. 'Plus, like I said, I have my magical observational

333

skills.' Her eyes danced. 'Sometimes it's an interesting talent to possess.'

'God, I had no idea. Are you sure?'

'Oh yes. Everything you feel for her, she feels for you. It's right there, I promise.'

Luke couldn't speak; he was still mentally reeling. His chest felt as if it were trying to contain far too much emotion. He looked across at his new colleague. 'I swear I didn't know.'

'Then I'm happy I told you. Maybe I could take over her care. Then you wouldn't be her doctor any more. And when the time feels right . . . well, you can broach the subject with her.' Tess pulled a face. 'God, sorry, *broach the subject* sounds unbelievably stuffy and legal. It can be far more romantic than that.'

'What if she turns me down?' said Luke.

'Life's all about taking risks. You're an adult. You'd get over it. But in my opinion, I sincerely doubt that would happen. The feelings you two have for each other are mutual. Have a little faith,' said Tess with a broad smile. 'And trust me. I'm a doctor.'

Chapter 52

Luke's heart was racing. OK, this was crazy, but taking the plunge now felt easier than waiting and plucking up the courage to say it at some unknown point in the future.

And since sleep currently wasn't an option, he might as well do it now.

It took fifteen minutes to walk back into the village. The sky was clear, a crescent moon hung above the church spire and the stars were out in force. Hallie was still awake. Luke knew this because he could see that she was currently chatting on Twitter to a female friend in Tempe, Arizona.

No one else was around as he crossed the ancient stone bridge and approached Hallie's house. He looked up and saw that the light was on in her bedroom window.

On his phone, he saw that she was still exchanging messages with her friend. He tapped in: *Hi, I'm outside. Wondered if I could have a word about something?*

Five seconds later, Hallie's face appeared at the window. Spotting him, she waved and beckoned for him to come to the front door. The next moment his phone pinged with the reply: *Of course! Come on in.*

Luke mentally braced himself; the next few minutes could either turn out to be the very best of his life, or the worst so far.

God, Tess Hannigan and her self-styled intuitive skills had better be right.

Hallie briefly checked her face in the mirror, raked her fingers through her hair and brushed a couple of biscuit crumbs off the front of her T-shirt. It was half past midnight; why on earth did Luke want to see her now? Not that she was unhappy about it – the thought of seeing him was having its habitual adrenalin-inducing effect on her bloodstream.

As she skipped down to answer the door, taking the stairs two at a time, it occurred to her that maybe he was here to talk about Christina. Perhaps he was having second thoughts with regard to the break-up . . . he might be wanting Hallie's advice on whether he and Christina should get back together . . .

Urgh, please don't let it be that.

Then she pulled open the front door and her heart did that little dolphin flip of joy. Even though it was a different heart, it had instinctively learned to react in exactly the same way towards him. She beamed and said, 'Hello!'

'Is this OK?' Luke looked worried. 'Not too late?'

'It's fine, I'm wide awake. And Mum's staying over at Pete's, so it's just us.' She gestured for him to follow her into the kitchen, adding flippantly, 'So we can play wild music and dance and make as much noise as we want.'

'Well I wasn't planning on that, but it's an idea.'

'Drink? Tea, coffee? Scotch?'

Luke hesitated, then nodded. 'Scotch would be great, thanks. No ice.'

Hallie sploshed some of her mother's Glenfiddich into a tumbler. Turning to hand it to him, she saw that her fingers were trembling. In order to distract Luke from noticing, she said hastily, 'So is this about Christina?'

He said, 'No,' then shrugged and went on, 'Well, not really. More about Tess.'

'Oh.' Tess? Good grief, where was *this* going?

'We had a chat this evening. About various . . . things.'

'You and Tess.' Hallie was still having trouble assimilating this scenario, springing as it had out of nowhere.

'I think she's great,' said Luke. 'Don't you?'

There was a new light in his eyes. Oh my *God* . . .

'She is great.' Hallie nodded, bracing herself for yet more disappointment. It looked like Luke wasn't intending to hang around. First Christina, now this. And she hadn't imagined Tess would be his type.

Except . . . why was he looking at her like that, as if there was something still more significant that he needed to say?

And do I even want to hear it?

'She thinks you shouldn't be my patient any more,' said Luke.

'What?' Confused, Hallie attempted to make sense of the statement. Was Tess Hannigan pathologically jealous? Was she claiming ownership of Luke and declaring that from now on he would only be allowed to see patients who were either male or over seventy?

Luke raked his fingers through his hair and said with a touch of desperation, 'She feels it would be better if you only saw her from now on.'

Because she was a complete bunny-boiler, by any chance? Bursting with the injustice of it, Hallie said, 'She's allowed to just make those decisions, is she? And you're happy to go along with them?'

He shook his head. 'It isn't a decision. It's a suggestion. Tess was watching us earlier, when we were talking together at the party. She thought there was something . . . you know, like a connection between us. Apparently she has a talent for noticing things like that.'

337

Hallie's mouth had gone dry. Luke was watching her and she didn't know what to do with herself. Embarrassed, she blurted out, 'Well, it's not true.'

'Isn't it?'

'I mean, I *like* you, of course I do, but not in the way she's saying.'

'Right.' Luke nodded, then shook his head once more. A muscle was jumping in his jaw. 'OK.'

'So she isn't interested in you herself?'

'What? God, no!'

Got that one wrong, then. Phew. 'But she looked at us and thought I was keen on you?'

'She thought we were both keen,' Luke said evenly. 'On each other.'

Was Tess right? Could there actually be a connection between them that didn't just exist in her mind? Was it possible that it was – had always been – mutual?

Hallie's knees began to tremble. All this time she'd kept to herself the reality of how she felt, because these were feelings that could never be acknowledged.

But now . . . oh *but now* . . . from the way he was looking at her, was there a possibility that something could be about to happen after all?

'And what did you think when she told you that?' She couldn't quite believe she was asking the question.

Luke paused, took a big gulp of Scotch and swallowed. 'I hoped she was right.' He briefly rubbed his jaw, then fixed his gaze on her and said, 'I really hoped it was true.'

Was there the sound of electrical humming in the air, or was it only inside her head? Hallie could feel the wooden back of one of the kitchen chairs against her spine, possibly holding her upright. If he'd taken the plunge, so could she.

'I could never say anything.' Her voice was unsteady.

'Nor could I.'

'I wanted to, so much.'

'So did I.' He nodded.

'For *ages*.'

'Me too. Can I just ask one question?'

'Anything.'

'You and Nick.'

'What about me and Nick?'

'Do you still have feelings for him? I mean, do you still wish . . .' Luke hesitated, clearly not sure how to word the question he wanted to ask. 'Is there . . . unfinished business between the two of you?'

So that was what was bothering him. Nick had mentioned briefly meeting Luke while she'd been asleep upstairs on the afternoon of his flying visit. She shook her head. 'Nothing happened that day. He offered, which was kind of him, and I turned him down. He'll always be a friend, but I'm over him now. We're completely finished business.'

Luke nodded and exhaled, clearly relieved. 'Well, that's very good to know.'

Her new heart was thud-thud-thudding in her chest. 'And you're sure it really wouldn't be a problem if I wasn't your patient?'

'Really not a problem,' said Luke.

'I can't believe Tess saw it and no one else did.'

'Including me.'

'And me.' Hallie half smiled. 'Maybe she's a witch.'

'If she is, I'm glad. Otherwise we could have carried on indefinitely, neither of us ever saying anything.' He moved towards her, reached for her hands. 'And that would've been terrible.'

Zing-zing went the synapses in Hallie's arms, in response to the touch of his warm fingers against hers. *Oh my God* went the voice inside her head as the gap between them closed and she kissed Luke Hilton for the very first time.

In real life . . .

It could never have happened before, but it was happening now. And it felt perfect.

Oh yes, some things were definitely worth the wait.

Chapter 53

'Where are we going?' Next to him in the passenger seat, Tasha's head swivelled like a meerkat's. 'This isn't the right way.'

Rory shrugged, looking innocent, and carried on driving in the direction he'd taken. It was Christmas Eve and he had a plan. At his side, Tasha, wearing a silver-grey faux-fur coat and a red velvet scarf over a cream wool dress, was looking amazing as always. As far as she was aware, they were due to be attending a dull but necessary lunchtime drinks party with his dull but unavoidable ex-boss and his wife.

He loved the way, despite the tedium of the event, she'd still made the effort to look her best. He also loved the way she'd individually wrapped home-made rum truffles in silver paper for two people she'd never met before and would probably never meet again.

Basically he loved everything about Tasha Sykes, his fiancée, the girl he wanted to be with for the rest of his life.

It was six months now since the transplant, and the first few weeks hadn't been easy. Unaccustomed to feeling even slightly unwell, he'd found the endless setbacks hard to bear. Being grateful to still be alive was one thing, but his road to recovery hadn't been smooth. There had been adjustments to make, both mental and physical, as well as problems getting the complicated new drug regime properly balanced.

Eventually, with the help of the cardiac rehabilitation programme, recovery had kicked in and he'd felt better able to cope with everything that had happened. Physiotherapy had begun in earnest and he'd regained his strength and stamina. The future had started to seem like a challenge he could conquer.

And throughout it all, Tasha had been there at his side, supporting him every step of the way. Nothing fazed her; she understood when he had down days and encouraged him with unfailing patience and good humour.

Now that the scariest part was behind them, they were both back working full time and the future was bright; having been given a second chance at life, he didn't intend to waste a day of it.

'Are you going to tell me where we're going?' said Tasha again.

Rory gave her knee a squeeze. 'Don't be so impatient. You'll find out soon enough.'

'Oh my God.' Tasha started to laugh. 'I don't believe it.'

Rory had parked the car and led her through a rabbit warren of back streets. It wasn't until they'd entered a shop via the back entrance, emerged through the front door and come out on to the main road that she realised where they were and why he'd brought her here.

The scene was exactly the same, the sound of Christmas songs being played was the same; the crowds were the same too. Only the first flakes of falling snow were missing, twelve months on.

Rory held her hand. 'This is where we met, exactly one year ago.'

'It is.' Touched, Tasha leaned against him and kissed the side of his jaw.

'Here's our bin. It'll always be our bin.' Leading her over to it, Rory said, 'If it wasn't for this bin, we would never have met.'

Tasha pointed to a KFC carton, visible on top of the pile of rubbish. 'Fancy a chip?'

'Hmm, maybe not. Wouldn't say no to a coffee, though. Excuse me . . .' Rory turned to speak to a middle-aged man who was making his way past them. 'Could I ask you a quick favour? Would you just take a photo of me and my fiancée?'

The man stopped and took the phone from him. 'Move away from the bin, then.' They were standing either side of it like proud parents of a beloved only child.

'It's fine, we want the bin in the picture,' said Rory.

Seeing the bemused expression on the older man's face, Tasha gave the cast-iron lid an affectionate pat. 'It's the whole reason we're here,' she explained.

'He thinks we're mad,' said Rory when the man had taken the photo, handed back the phone and hurried off.

'Who cares? Look at it.' Tasha gazed down fondly. 'Our lovely bin.'

'Shall we get that coffee now? Remember the café?' Leading her towards it, Rory said, 'This is where I was when I first saw you rolling up your sleeves and digging around amongst the rubbish.'

'Coleslaw and cigarette ends. Cold coffee and ketchup dripping from my hands. I'll never forget it,' said Tasha.

He pushed open the door of the steamy café, indicating for her to go in ahead of him, and Tasha saw Carmel and Joe sitting at the table by the window.

Holding hands.

Actual hands.

She stopped dead in her tracks and Rory bumped into her. She pointed. 'Look!'

'What?'

'It's Carmel and Joe!'

'So it is.'

'But . . . but . . . they're holding hands.'

'So they are.'

He wasn't sounding surprised. Tasha realised she'd been royally set up. Turning, she said in disbelief, 'You *knew* about this?'

'About what?'

'The hands!'

'Joe told me last night.'

Joe and Carmel were watching her, laughing at the stunned expression on her face. Crossing the café with Rory, Tasha said, 'OK, tell me everything.'

'We thought we'd come here to share your anniversary,' said Joe.

'And this?' She indicated the hands.

'It's our coming-out day.' Carmel was wearing the biggest grin. 'We're officially a couple.'

'Finally! *Hooray.*' Tasha hugged them both. 'About time too!'

'She's a lucky girl,' Joe agreed.

'And you just decided last night!'

'We did.' Carmel turned to Joe. 'Didn't we?'

'Oh yes.'

'Amazing,' said Tasha.

'Mind you,' Joe added, 'we've been sleeping together for months.'

'*What?*' Tasha stared at them both. 'Are you *kidding* me?'

'I kept asking her out, she kept turning me down.' Joe winked. 'As you know. For some reason she wasn't sure she trusted me.'

'I didn't think it would work out,' Carmel explained with a shrug. 'He's not my type.'

'But in the end I wore her down. She couldn't resist the lure of my body.'

'Except I still didn't want a relationship,' Carmel rejoined.

'So we settled for friends with benefits instead. Which suited us both,' said Joe.

Tasha shook her head, marvelling at their subterfuge. 'And you kept it a secret all this time?'

'You had enough to worry about. Besides, I didn't expect it to last,' said Carmel. 'I mean, it wasn't a proper relationship. It was never meant to become one.'

344

Joe said, 'Plus it was quite fun having it as a secret. Just between us. And of course I won her over in the end.'

'With his legendary modesty and charm.' Carmel was pretending to roll her eyes, but in reality she exuded happiness.

'Not to mention my stupendous sexual technique.'

She gave him a nudge. 'Yes, definitely best not to mention that.'

'This is so brilliant.' Sitting down next to Carmel, Tasha grinned at Joe and Rory across the table. 'I can't believe you didn't tell us, but it's made my day.'

'It's my cheapskate way of giving you a Christmas present that doesn't need wrapping up,' said Joe.

Carmel leaned against Tasha. 'Shall I tell you what really did it? It was the way he looked after Rory in hospital and during the weeks after the op. He was just so lovely to him, it completely won me over. I realised what a good person he was. Kind. Patient. Nicer than I'd always thought.'

'I'm going to have that carved on my gravestone,' said Joe. 'Here lies Joseph James. Nicer than you thought.' He paused. 'And great in bed too.'

The middle-aged waitress, arriving to take their order, pointed at Rory with her pencil and exclaimed, 'Got it! I've just realised who you are!' Rory looked up at her.

'You think he's Ryan Reynolds, don't you?' said Joe. 'Sorry, he isn't. But I am Brad Pitt.'

'And I'm Angelina Jolie,' said the waitress. She turned her attention back to Rory. 'This time last year. There was a girl over by that bin out there . . . we were all watching her search through it and you went out with one of our bin liners to help her find whatever it was she was looking for.'

'She'd lost her credit card,' said Rory.

'A gang of teenage boys on skateboards were giving her a hard time. You sent them packing. Then when she finally found

345

the card, you made her wave to us over here in the café! And we all waved back!'

'You did.' Rory nodded. 'I remember.'

'And then you both headed off in separate directions and everyone in here went *Aaaahhh* because we wanted you to go off together, like in one of those lovely Christmassy films on the telly. But you didn't,' said the waitress. 'We were *so* disappointed.'

'Ah well, never mind,' said Joe. 'He managed to find himself a girlfriend in the end.'

'Of course he did, handsome chap like him. And you look lovely too, dear.' The waitress's lit-up plastic antlers waggled as she nodded and beamed at Tasha.

'Thanks.' Tasha held up her left hand. 'We're engaged!'

'I say, that's a sparkler! Just goes to show, it was all for the best – you're the one he was meant to be with after all.'

Tasha smiled, unoffended; her hair was far longer now than it had been a year ago. She was also blonder. Plus, the waitress had only ever seen her from a distance.

'This one's called Tasha,' Rory told the waitress. 'Ask me how we first met.'

'Ooh, was it romantic? Go on, do tell.' She gave him an encouraging nod. 'I love stories like that.'

'Well,' said Rory, drawing out the moment, 'it was Christmas Eve, Tasha was out doing some last-minute shopping and she lost her credit card in a litter bin . . .'

'Oh my goodness!' The woman's mouth had formed a perfect oval of delight. 'Really? It was *you*?'

'It was me,' Tasha agreed.

'That's why we call her Bin Girl,' Joe added helpfully.

'That's why *you* call her Bin Girl.' Carmel gave him a nudge. 'The rest of us use her real name.'

'Well I never, this is fantastic.' The waitress was enthralled. 'Oh, but frustrating too – I want to tell all the other people who were in here last year that the two of you *did* end up

346

getting together, and I can't because they're not here. Well anyway, you've made my day. That's just wonderful. No wonder you both look so happy.' Her antlers bobbed as she beamed at them. 'This must have been the best year of your lives.'

Tasha pressed her foot against Rory's under the table. They smiled at each other. Aloud, she said, 'Oh it definitely has.'

Chapter 54

'OK, now *push*,' ordered the older, slightly bossier midwife.

'I don't want to. It *huuuuurts*.'

Flo gasped and grabbed the bed rail as another great wave of pain squeezed her insides with a tightening iron grip.

'Come on, nearly there now, you can do it.' The younger midwife was stroking her arm, taking on the good–cop role and being encouraging.

'I can't, I can't.' Flo shook her head as perspiration trickled down her temples into her ears. But she knew they were right. It might seem physically impossible, but somehow, in the next few minutes, she was going to have to give birth to a baby.

The older midwife was checking the monitors. 'Here we go, here comes the next contraction. Let's do it now.'

Gathering herself, willing herself on and clutching the younger midwife's hand, Flo took a huge breath and embarked on the task of squeezing an actual human being out of her own body . . .

And then, in a sweaty blur of noise and lights and hands and pressure and unbelievable pain, it happened in a whoosh of slippery wetness and an outraged wail of just-born dismay.

'Oh my God . . .' Flo's voice cracked as the older midwife cut the cord, gave the baby a brisk wipe with a towel and placed it on her chest. Tears sprang to her eyes and a great sob escaped her lungs, but she was laughing too, overwhelmed with the emotions she'd been warned would swamp her, but which she hadn't been prepared for because how could you know they'd be this overwhelming?

'Well done.' The older midwife was smiling, no longer bossy. 'You did it. You've got yourself a beautiful baby girl.'

And now Flo was crying and laughing in earnest, because the mixture of emotions was truly extraordinary, but the over-riding one was joy. Several people had told her over the course of the past months that Zander would be with her in spirit when she gave birth to his child, but they'd just been trying to make her feel better. In reality she couldn't feel his spirit. He would have loved to be here, but he wasn't. She still missed him dreadfully, but she would cope alone without him. She wasn't the first to find herself in this situation, nor would she be the last. But she had Zander's baby and that was a miracle. In so many ways she'd been incredibly lucky.

And what was breathtaking was the resemblance to Zander. As they gazed intently at each other, Flo was struck by more and more similiarities . . . from the long, dark, spiky lashes to the shape of those cobalt-blue eyes, from the precise angle of the dark eyebrows to the curve of the upper lip.

'Hello,' Flo whispered, her mouth brushing the baby's forehead as she held her close. 'You're my baby and I'm your mum.' She breathed in the smell of her daughter's newborn skin and examined her tiny, almost translucent fingers. 'Look at you, you're *perfect*.'

The room off the main ward contained just two beds. Flo suspected she'd been allocated it in order to make her feel less left out when visiting time came around and all the fathers trooped in bearing flowers, helium balloons and presents for their wives or girlfriends.

Instead she was sharing with a pretty, down-to-earth single

mother of three who'd been let down yet again by the father of her newest baby.

'Swear to God I thought I'd found a decent one at last,' Ceecee had already confided. 'He was good with the other kids, didn't like football . . . even had a job, which made a nice change, I can tell you. He seemed to be happy enough when I fell pregnant with this one. I was made up, reckoned he was a keeper. Then last month he started going out every night . . . not ideal, but I didn't nag him about it.' She pulled a face. 'But two weeks ago he went out and didn't come back. Sent me a text the next day saying it was over and he was seeing someone else. Not even a sorry, cheeky sod. So here we are, back to square one again, just me and the kids coping with it like we always do. Still, they're the important ones, aren't they? As long as they're happy, that's all that matters.'

'True.' Flo nodded, impressed by Ceecee's sanguine attitude. Life might not work out as you'd want it to, but you just got on with it anyway.

'Look, sorry about your chap,' said Ceecee. 'The nurses told me what happened, probably to stop me sticking my big foot in it and saying something awful without realising.'

'Thanks.'

'Have you got a photo of him so I can see what he looked like?'

'I have.' Flo reached into her bag for her phone.

'I'll show you mine and you can show me yours.' Taking out her own phone, Ceecee began scrolling through a sea of pictures, then came and sat on Flo's bed, next to her. 'There he is, that's Matt.'

Matt was lying across a leather sofa, wearing a pink polo shirt and jeans, grinning cheekily into the camera and making a peace sign. Flo in turn showed Ceecee the photo she'd taken of her and Zander up on the Downs with the suspension bridge behind them and the hot air balloon drifting overhead.

'Ah, that's lovely. He looks really nice,' said Ceecee. 'What d'you think of mine, then?'

What could she say? 'He looks nice too,' said Flo.

'You reckon?' Ceecee gave her a cheery nudge. 'Ha, looks like a no-good cheating bastard to me.'

'Oh my darling, look at you!' Margot entered the side ward like a queen, on the arm of one of the nursing staff. 'You are *glowing*.' She gave Flo a gin-scented kiss on the cheek before settling herself carefully on one of the visitor's chairs. 'Now, let's see this baby of yours. Oh I say, hello, Alexandra. You're a beauty! Can I have a hold?'

Flo passed Alexandra over to her. There was something particularly lovely about seeing a newborn baby being cradled in the arms of an octogenarian. Her heart expanded with love and pride as Margot admired her daughter, now twelve hours old.

'How did you get here? By taxi?'

'No, Patrick brought me. He's gone to park the car. Everyone from Nairn House sends their love, of course. You'll get all manner of strange knitted items sent to you, I'm sure. But seeing as I don't knit, I thought Alexandra might like these from me.'

Flo opened the faded leather jeweller's box. There, nestling amongst the folds of ivory satin, lay a pair of diamond stud earrings, small but perfectly formed. 'Oh my goodness, Margot, you can't give me these!'

'They're not for you, they're for her. And I insist.' Margot's dark eyes softened. 'Give them to her on her eighteenth birthday. I'll be dead long before that, but it's nice to think of them being worn again by a pretty young girl. My parents gave them to me when I was twenty-one. I wore them when I was presented at court. No, don't look at me like that. I want your daughter to enjoy them. And please don't try to argue with me, because we both know you won't win.'

'Well in that case, thank you. They're beautiful. It's the nicest present anyone's ever given her.' Flo leaned over and hugged Margot again.

'And how are you feeling, my darling?'

'Happy and sad. I'm doing OK.'

'You'll be fine, I know you will. You're a coper,' Margot pronounced.

'Here's Patrick.' Flo waved as he hesitated in the doorway. 'Hi, come on in.'

She'd seen Patrick a couple of times at Nairn House before going on maternity leave. His relationship with aerobics instructor Jade had run out of steam before Christmas, and Patrick was now unrepentantly wearing his untrendy trousers and favourite old shirts once more.

'Congratulations. Here's a little something for the baby.' He handed Flo one of the smart cardboard bags from the shop. 'Sorry it's not diamonds.'

It was a tiny pink and green woolly hat with knitted roses and leaves attached.

'That is gorgeous,' said Flo, touched. 'Thank you so much.'

'And I did buy you a bunch of tulips on my way over to Nairn House, but I left them on the roof of the car when I was fiddling with my keys. Next thing I knew, I was heading down the dual carriageway and they'd fallen into the road behind me.' He shook his head sorrowfully. 'Got run over by a Tesco delivery truck.'

'Never mind. It's the thought that counts,' Flo said with a smile.

'Well?' Margot was holding Alexandra up so he could admire her. 'What do you think?'

'She looks like a baby.'

'That's not good enough, Patrick!'

He winked at Flo. 'She looks . . . lovely. Well done.'

'Typical man,' Margot tut-tutted good-naturedly. 'Now come along, take lots of photos of us so I can show everyone when I get back. I feel like a proud grandmother.'

Patrick said to Flo, 'How was the . . . you know, the whole giving-birth thing?'

'Pretty excruciating. Would you like me to describe it in revolting technicolour detail?'

He winced. 'Maybe not.'

Thirty minutes later, Lena arrived. She looked from Margot to Patrick and said, 'Who are you?'

'They're my friends,' Flo explained patiently. 'Margot lives at Nairn House. Patrick's her nephew.'

'Right. Well I was going to buy something for the baby, but I didn't know what. So I didn't get anything.'

'That's fine,' said Flo.

Lena, catching the look Margot was exchanging with Patrick, said, 'What did you get for it, then?'

'Diamond stud earrings,' replied Margot easily. 'From Cartier.'

'Well that's just barbaric.' Lena's eyes narrowed. 'Babies shouldn't have their ears pierced; it's a ridiculous idea.'

'You must be Lena.' Patrick reached across to shake her hand. 'We've heard all about you.'

'Oh. Well if she's said anything bad, just ignore her. It's not true.'

Flo said, 'Would you like to meet Alexandra?' because so far Lena hadn't so much as glanced at her new niece.

'Who? Oh, the baby. Let's have a look at it then.'

'It's a girl,' Flo reminded her, tilting Alexandra towards Lena so she could see her properly. 'Would you like to hold her?'

'No thanks. Bit small. Might drop it.' Lena turned and gazed at the baby for several seconds. Finally she said, 'No need for a DNA test, then.'

Had she seriously been planning one? Then again, with Lena, anything was possible.

Gently, Flo said, 'There was never any need for a DNA test.'

'Suppose not.' Lena heaved a sigh. 'Go on then, I'll hold her for a bit.'

Flo passed the baby over and showed Lena how to support the back of her head. 'There you go. Don't worry, you're doing fine.'

Lena's expression softened. 'She looks just like Zander.'

'She really does.'

'I miss him so much.' A tear was glimmering now in her eye.

'I know.' Flo nodded; it had been tough for Lena too. She'd known and loved Zander for six months, but he'd been Lena's brother for thirty-four years.

'I've never held a baby before,' said Lena. 'It feels quite nice.'

Smiling, Flo said, 'It does, doesn't it?'

'Who's looking after Jeremy while you're in hospital?'

'Sarah from the downstairs flat.'

'You could always ask me to keep an eye on him, you know. I'm not a cat murderer.'

Let's hope not.

Aloud, Flo said, 'I know, but Sarah's right there. It's easy for her to pop in. And I'll probably be going home tomorrow.'

It had come as a terrible shock to Lena when she'd first learned from Mary, the solicitor, that Zander's baby would now be inheriting his estate. But to her credit, she'd slowly come round to the idea. Flo had agreed that she could carry on living in Zander's flat, and she seemed grateful for that. As Mary had crisply pointed out during their meeting, she was lucky to still have a roof over her head.

Lena nodded. 'OK. What time do you two think you'll be leaving here this evening?'

She was addressing Patrick, who pushed back his sleeve and checked his watch. 'Another half-hour? Visiting ends at eight.'

'So would you be able to give me a lift back to Clifton?' said Lena. 'I had to catch a bus to get here this evening. It was awful.'

Amused by her shudder of distaste, Patrick nodded. 'That's fine, it's not far out of our way.'

'Thanks.' Lena was now looking askance at his shirtsleeves. 'Your cuffs are *frayed*.'

Patrick kept a straight face. 'I'm afraid they are. Frayed.'

'But why would you wear them like that?' Lena was evidently horrified. 'You look like a tramp! Why don't you buy a new shirt?'

'I like this one.' Neither remotely bothered nor taking offence, Patrick added, 'It's my favourite.'

'But looking good is important. Trust me, when this baby's old enough to wear proper clothes, I'm going to make sure she looks stylish. These things *matter*.'

He shrugged. 'To you, maybe. Not to me.'

'You should make more of an effort,' Lena retorted.

'You sound like my ex-wife,' said Patrick.

Flo, sitting up in bed with Alexandra cradled in her arms, loved the way Patrick refused to be intimidated by Lena. She exchanged a secret smile with Margot.

'I'm just saying what everyone else is thinking,' said Lena.

'And I don't care. So if you don't want to catch that bus back to Clifton,' said Patrick, 'it might be time to start keeping your thoughts to yourself.'

Oh yes, he knew how to handle her all right.

Chapter 55

'OK, I'm off. Busy day. Some of us work normal hours.'

Tasha opened her eyes and smiled sleepily up at Rory. It was seven fifteen and he was already showered and dressed for work. She lifted her head for a kiss. 'Serves you right for having a normal job. I don't have to get to mine till midday.'

'Lucky you. I'll be home by six.' Another kiss. 'See you later.'

'Bye.'

When he'd let himself out of the house, Tasha texted Sandra, the photographer she was booked to be working with today. One of the better tabloids was running a feature in its Sunday magazine and they were often chosen to do jobs together. *Hi, just double-checking. The Carrick Hotel in Chelsea at noon, right?*

A minute later, Sandra texted back: *That's it. See you there x*

The Carrick Hotel was on Park Lane, with amazing views over Hyde Park. Red London buses, black cabs and thousands of cars made their way past in an endless stream. Over in the park itself, people were jogging, strolling, walking their dogs and . . . yes, picking up dog poo.

Hallie marvelled at the busyness of the scene. You could stand here at this window on the fifth floor and spend the entire day just gazing down at everything going on. It was a far cry from

Carranford, that was for sure. Yet here she was, in the capital, amongst the craziness of it all.

And by herself, too. Up until a year ago, the very idea of going anywhere on her own would have been completely unthinkable. But life, thankfully, was very different now.

It was the last week of May, coming up to a year since the miraculous transplant. When the invitation had arrived from the newspaper to come to London in order to be interviewed and photographed for a feature in their Sunday supplement, she'd been excited, because it *was* exciting to be put up in a fancy hotel and have a bit of a makeover into the bargain.

Luke hadn't been able to accompany her because he was working, as were her mum and Bea. But that hadn't mattered; she'd simply made the trip on her own. Like a normal person! Later this evening she would make her way back to Carranford, to the cottage she now shared with Luke. Also like a normal person.

And she'd brought three different outfits with her to be photographed in. That was completely normal too!

An hour later, following a phone call from reception to let her know that everyone was here, Hallie opened the door to greet the photographer, the make-up artist and the journalist who would be interviewing her for the piece. The journalist, a woman in her fifties called Jean, wandered out on to the balcony to speak on her phone.

'This is amazing.' Hallie beamed as the make-up artist, whose name was Tasha, opened her case and began setting out a mind-boggling assortment of brushes, bottles, sponges and cosmetics. 'I've never had this done to me before.'

Tasha carried on unpacking the case. 'Well I hope you like the end result!' she said cheerily.

'I don't usually wear much make-up.'

'Don't you worry.' Tasha's smile was reassuring. 'I won't do a drag-queen job on you. I'm going to make you look just like yourself, but even more fabulous.'

For the next ten minutes she expertly applied base, then primer, followed by different shades of foundation, explaining it all as she went. It was far more complicated than you'd think. Hallie watched in the lit-up mirror as Tasha moved around in front of her, bending and straightening, then standing back to assess each stage of her work. She was in her late twenties, at a guess, her honey-brown hair skilfully highlighted and fastened up in a topknot. Her eyes were very blue, her complexion flawless, and she was wearing a light lemony perfume.

'I know about your website, by the way,' she told Hallie. 'One of my clients used to read it.'

'Ah, thanks.' Hallie saw Jean end her phone call on the balcony and come back into the room. 'It's taken off a bit in the last year. Well, that's how the newspaper got interested, of course.'

Jean was surveying them with her head on one side. 'So you two haven't worked out yet what it is you have in common?'

'Sorry?' Eyebrows raised, Tasha lifted her head and looked at her. 'No, what is it?'

'Hallie had a heart and lung transplant last year.'

'What? You did?' Tasha turned back to Hallie. 'Really?'

'Well, yes.' It was clearly significant, but Hallie was at a loss as to why.

'My fiancé had a heart transplant too!' exclaimed Tasha.

'Wow.' OK, that explained it. Hallie shook her head. 'What a coincidence!'

'Not that much of a coincidence,' said Jean with a wry smile. 'The picture editor was going to book someone else to do the make-up for today's shoot, but I suggested she choose you instead, seeing as you'd kind of been through it with your chap.'

'Well it's still pretty amazing.' Hallie was touched that they'd thought of it. 'There aren't that many of us around. How's he doing?'

'Fantastic. Well, you know, bit of a rough start, but everything's

358

great now. He's back at work, obviously still having regular checks . . . it's coming up to a year now . . .'

'Me too,' said Hallie. 'Not quite a year. Eleven months.'

Tasha was gazing at Hallie's reflection in the mirror. 'Rory had his transplant on the twenty-fifth of June.'

The words shimmered and reverberated in the air between them. Their eyes locked and stayed locked. Hallie gripped the sides of the chair she was sitting on and murmured, 'Me too.' Her heart was clattering, her mouth bone-dry, her brain reeling at this revelation.

Jean glanced up from her phone. 'Well *that's* what I call a coincidence, two people both getting new hearts on the same day! I mean, what are the chances of that happening, eh?'

The photographer, whose name was Sandra, paused in the process of setting up the lighting system for the shoot and said, 'Wow, weird! If it'd been kidneys, they could have both come from the same person. But it's not as if anyone's got two hearts to give away!'

Hallie was lost for words. Time was kaleidoscoping, simultaneously speeding up and slowing down. Tasha was still watching her in the mirror. And she knew. Of course she knew. The vast majority of the population might never have heard of the domino transplant procedure, but she and Tasha were only too aware of it.

Oh my God . . .

'So I wonder if there was some huge traffic accident with loads of people involved?' Her eyes bright and beady, Jean said, 'That could make an interesting angle to the piece. Is there any way we could find out?'

Whoa . . .

'No.' Hallie was firm. 'They don't tell you who your donor is. It's all very strict. Any letters are exchanged via the transplant coordinator, and you might never even hear back from your donor's relatives.'

'They generally say to leave it for a year before writing to them.' Tasha joined in.

'So has your chap written to his donor's family yet?' asked Jean; being a journalist, she clearly had a nose for a story.

'Not yet,' said Tasha.

Hallie shook her head. 'Nor me.'

Somehow Tasha managed to pull herself together and resume applying foundation to Hallie's face. The secret seemed to enclose the two of them in a transparent bubble. Only when Sandra was otherwise occupied and Jean was out on the balcony taking another call did Tasha risk giving Hallie's shoulder a squeeze and murmuring, 'This is crazy.'

Hallie said, 'I know.'

'We'll talk when they've gone, OK?'

'OK.'

Then Jean came back in to begin the interview, Tasha carried on with Hallie's hair and make-up and Sandra began taking test shots. Together they chose the best outfit for the shoot, selecting Hallie's thin navy top and matching flippy skirt and teaming them with her new fuchsia sandals.

'I can't decide between the scarf and the necklaces,' said Sandra, 'so we'll take some shots with each of them, and some without.'

'I prefer clean lines.' Jean was blunt. 'You don't need accessories. Her face is enough.'

'I know, but we'd better give the picture editor something to choose from,' said Sandra, evidently a diplomat.

God, being photographed by a stranger was weird; smiling became unbelievably complicated. Answering Jean's questions required concentration. Hallie perched beside the window, then sat cross-legged on the king-sized bed and pretended to be typing out replies to people who'd sent their problems in to threethingsaboutyou. com. Finally she submitted to close-ups and sat backwards on a chair with Sandra moving around, getting shots from all angles.

All the time she was willing it to be over . . . *Please, that's enough now, time for the rest of you to leave . . .*

Finally it was done. Sandra had taken hundreds of photos. The interview was complete. As she was leaving, Jean said, 'It's been wonderful to meet you. We'll be running the feature at the end of June. And listen.' Taking a business card from her bag, she handed it over. 'If you ever do get in touch with your donor's family, we'd love to do a follow-up piece. Just let me know.'

'Thanks. It was great to meet you too.' They shook hands and Jean left. Now Sandra was packing away her equipment. As, very slowly, was Tasha.

'Oh, I forgot, you wanted me to show you how to put on false lashes.' Holding up a plastic box, Tasha added brightly, 'I don't have to rush off. Shall I give you a lesson now?'

'Fantastic,' said Hallie. 'Let's do it.'

Sandra, with cases of equipment slung over both shoulders, said a cheery goodbye and let herself out of the hotel room.

And then they were alone.

'Oh my God, three whole hours.' Tasha clapped a hand to her mouth. 'I can't believe we managed it. I thought I was going to *explode*.'

'What's Rory's blood group?' said Hallie, just to double-check.

'He's O.'

Hallie nodded. 'Same.'

'Come here.' Tasha wrapped both arms around her and held her tight. She whispered into Hallie's ear, 'This is amazing. You gave Rory your heart. He'd have died without you.' A hot tear spilled out of her eye and trickled down Hallie's cheek. 'Thank you *so much*.'

'It's not me, though. We both have the family of the other donor to thank. I sent them a card a while back, through my transplant coordinator, but I was waiting for the year to be up to write a proper letter.' Hallie knew it would be the most

361

difficult letter she'd ever have to compose. 'And they might never write back . . . there are no guarantees.'

'But in the meantime, we've found you. Oh God, I still can't believe it!'

'I'm going to call Jonathan, my coordinator, and see if he can confirm it's Rory.'

Five minutes later, she ended the call and said with a grin, 'Well, he can't.'

'You're still smiling, though.'

'I've known Jonathan long enough to know when he's holding back. He knows,' said Hallie, 'but he isn't allowed to confirm it. He said we need to get Rory to ask *his* transplant coordinator.' She shook her head with amusement. 'Poor Jonathan, he's always so calm and in control. But this time he was definitely shocked.'

'So what happens now?' said Tasha.

'I think Rory needs to make that call, don't you? Do it like Jonathan says, just to keep everyone happy. And after that, what time does he finish work?' said Hallie. 'I think I'd like to meet the man who has my heart.'

Chapter 56

'Oh will you look at her little face? Hello, lovely girl! Are you going to give me a smile?'

It was one of those could-go-either-way moments. Flo held her breath and willed it to go the right way. Luckily it did. Her daughter, now twelve weeks old, was less fazed than most babies by geriatric faces looming in front of her in a manner that could, admittedly, give a bit of a fright to some adults. Alexandra broke into a huge beaming smile and waved her little hands at ninety-eight-year-old Esme Carpenter, currently the oldest resident of Nairn House.

'Ah, look at that, she's a bonny one! Flo, you've got yourself a little angel there. I love it when you bring her in to see us. Makes my day, it does. What a gorgeous wee girl she is.'

While she was still on maternity leave, Flo had taken to visiting once or twice a week with Alexandra in tow. It was nice to keep up with the goings-on at Nairn House, and seeing everyone's delight at being able to interact with Alexandra was a joy. Today, she was sitting out on the terrace with several of the residents. To her left was Esme. To her right was Margot, busy taking photos with her iPad.

'Pretty girl,' boomed Thomas, who was sitting opposite them. 'Far too thin, though. Needs to eat a few pies. Not like you,' he retorted as Bridget trundled past with the tea trolley. 'You've had more than your share.'

Thomas was the newest resident, a retired naval captain with a loud voice and a robustly unreconstructed opinion on everything.

'Any more of that and I'll be cutting off your beard while you sleep,' said Bridget, unperturbed. 'Anyway, who's the pretty girl? Are you talking about Flo?'

'No, of course not. I meant this one!' Thomas jabbed a finger at the magazine he'd been reading.

Peering over at the page, Bridget said, 'Oh she *is* pretty. Not too thin at all.'

'Hmmph. I don't hold with this transplant malarkey,' Thomas snorted. 'It's all wrong, if you ask me, meddling with nature. Doctors thinking they're God, playing around with people's lives just because they can.'

Flo exchanged a glance with Margot, who shook her head and said in a clear voice, 'Thomas, does it *ever* occur to you to think before you open your mouth to speak?'

'What? Oh, don't you start on at me again, woman. You're as bad as my second wife.' With a huff of annoyance, Thomas levered himself out of his chair and grabbed his walking stick.

'I'm luckier than her,' Margot observed. 'At least I didn't have to be married to you.'

Grumbling under his breath, Thomas made his way back inside. Bridget rested a hand on Flo's shoulder. 'Just ignore him. Give us another week or two and we'll have the old sod whipped into shape.'

'It's fine.' Flo nodded at the magazine Thomas had left lying open on the wrought-iron garden table. 'Could you pass it over so I can take a look?'

'And is it my turn with Alexandra?' Putting down her iPad, Margot took the baby from her as Bridget handed the magazine over to Flo.

The feature was headed: *Three Amazing Things About Hallie.*

Several seconds later, Flo exclaimed, 'Oh my goodness, it's Dear Rose.'

'What is?' Margot glanced over at the double-page spread.

'This girl. Her name's Hallie. She's the one who set up that website. She was always anonymous, remember? Nobody knew who she was.'

'Of course I remember,' said Margot. 'We used to read the problems every week. Then my iPad needed resetting and I lost all the bookmarks to my favourite websites.'

'She had cystic fibrosis.' Still reading, skimming through the words, Flo felt her breathing quicken. 'She had a heart and lung transplant almost a year ago. It saved her life.'

'Well isn't that just wonderful? To think the whole time she was helping other people, she was going through all that.' Ever the multitasker, Margot was holding Alexandra securely with one arm and scrolling through pages on the iPad with her free hand. Within seconds she'd found the same article online and was reading it herself.

'You don't think . . .' Flo knew that Zander had helped a female, but that was the extent of the information she'd received. The recipient had sent a beautiful thank you card to Lena, but as far as she knew, Lena hadn't replied. And since Lena was the next of kin, there was nothing more she could do about it.

'Well that's annoying; it doesn't say the exact date.' Margot was ahead of her; she had now found the threethingsaboutyou website and was scrolling back through the entries. Then, abruptly, she stopped. 'Here it is. Oh sweetheart, look . . .'

Her heart thudding crazily, Flo looked at the entry. Her gaze skittered over the words . . .

1. I'm twenty-eight, I have cystic fibrosis and I never actually expected to live this long.

2. The hospital transplant coordinator called two hours ago – they have a new pair of lungs for me.
3. I've never been so scared in my life . . .

. . . Thank you, thank you, THANK YOU to the wonderful family of the donor for giving me this gift, this incredible chance. I hope you know how amazing you are. Your courage, kindness and generosity will always be remembered.

Flo took in the date, although by now she already knew. Tuesday the twenty-fifth of June.

'It's her. It's *her*. She's the one. I can't believe it. Look at her.' Breaking into a wobbly smile, Flo studied the photograph in the magazine of a pretty, healthy-looking girl with short dark red hair, huge bright eyes like Bambi and a dazzling smile. She was wearing a dark blue outfit and a striking scarf with splashes of colour like cascading fireworks across a night sky.

At that moment, a thud of recognition hit Flo in the chest. She stared into the brown eyes of the girl in the photograph, then at the scarf once more.

'Can you go back to the magazine piece?' she asked Margot.

Margot obliged and handed her the iPad. Flo expanded the photo and stared again. The scarf was inky blue, with explosions of fuchsia, lime green, purple and gold.

It was a one-of-a-kind scarf.

It had cost more than the girl wanted to pay, but she'd been unable to resist, returning to the stall later on that afternoon to buy it.

Flo briefly closed her eyes, conjuring up a mental image of the girl in the wheelchair, with her striking pallor and those deep violet shadows under her eyes, and the plastic tubing delivering oxygen from a cylinder into her poor diseased lungs. Yet despite her obvious ill health, she'd been cheerful, good-natured and likeable. Basically, the kind of person you'd instinctively want to be friends with.

Above the sound of Alexandra's babbling, Margot leaned across and said, 'Are you OK, darling?'

Nodding, Flo felt her eyes swim with tears, but for once they were happy tears. 'I'm fine. I can't believe we found out this way, but it really does make it better.'

'She looks lovely. Sounds it, too.'

'She is,' said Flo. Wait until she told Patrick about this. 'And guess what? I've already met her.' Her hand shook slightly as she pointed to the photo. 'In fact, I sold her that scarf.'

Chapter 57

Dear Rose (yes, I know you're Hallie, but you'll always be Rose to me!),

I have an update for you.

You probably won't remember, but last year I wrote to you with my problem. Basically, I loved my cats but my wonderful boyfriend hated them and wanted me to get rid of them. And you told me he wasn't a wonderful boyfriend at all.

Well, I cried when I saw your reply, but eventually realised you were right. He couldn't believe it when I ended our relationship, and the following months were pretty miserable. I will admit that I began to wish I hadn't done it.

But in September I went along to our local cats' home to see the new kittens and got chatting to a man called Paul who was there for the same reason. We ended up adopting one each from the same litter.

And guess what? Paul turned out to be a far nicer man than my old boyfriend. We kept in touch at first so we could compare our sibling kittens (their names are Bo and Marvin) and then we fell in love. We now live together – with all our cats! – and I've never been happier in my life.

So *thank you* for your kind words and excellent advice. You were definitely right, and Paul and I are both hugely grateful!

We're also very glad to hear that your own life is so much better now too. You are amazing!

With love from

Maggie xxx

Well, hooray for Maggie and Paul. Hallie flagged the email so it wouldn't get lost in her inbox. Updates were always welcome, but those with a happy ending were far nicer to read than the other kind.

She took a slurp of tea, a bite of toast and a moment to appreciate the fact that she was lazing in bed through choice rather than because she didn't have the energy to get out of it.

OK, it was ten in the morning. Soon she would get up and drive over to collect her mum and Bea, and together they'd head into Oxford to spend the afternoon shopping. The fun to be had from actually visiting lovely shops and experiencing objects with all your senses, rather than buying almost everything online, was a thrill that was yet to wear off.

She finished her mug of tea and opened the next email.

Dear Hallie,

Firstly, here are the three things about me:

1. I have a beautiful daughter who is twelve weeks old and the light of my life.
2. You and I have actually met once before, but I've only just realised this. It's a nice coincidence. I think you'll like it.
3. Being able to write this message to you today makes me very *very* happy. Hopefully you'll feel the same way when you find out why.

Now, here we go. My name is Flo Fenwick and I live in Bristol with my baby girl, Alexandra. Almost eighteen months ago, I was lucky enough to meet and fall in love with a wonderful man. We were very happy together and looking towards the future when sadly he lost his life in a car accident and my happy new world, as I knew it, ended overnight.

I've just read that feature about you in the magazine. You look and sound so lovely. I used to read the letters people sent to Dear Rose, and your brilliant replies, but I confess that following my boyfriend's accident, I rather lost interest in other people's problems. So it was cheering to read the feature and discover that you were in fact Dear Rose.

In it, you also stated that you would love to be able to get in touch with the family of your donor, which is – as I'm sure you've guessed by now – why I am writing to you today. I may not strictly be family, but Zander was the most important person in my life. And following his death, I discovered I was pregnant with his child.

Anyway, I just wanted to let you know that I couldn't be happier to learn that the transplant was such a success. If you'd like to see photos of Zander, I'd love to send you some. (As a proud new mum, I have plenty of his daughter too!)

I hope this is a nice letter to receive, and that it hasn't come as too much of a shock to you. The last year has been pretty hard, but things are starting to get easier for me now. Finding out about you has definitely helped.

Oh, and if you're wondering about that time we met before, cast your mind back to last year and Denleigh Horse Trials. The stall where you bought your scarf? The woman working on the stall who was forced by her boss to wear a purple trilby? Yes, that was me. (You missed Prince Harry, by the way – he called in not long after you'd left. Really!)

So there we are then, I'll give you time to catch your breath and digest this information. When you've recovered from the shock, it would be lovely to hear from you.

Love and best wishes,

Flo xxx

Wow. *Well.* Sitting back against the pile of pillows, Hallie slowly reread the letter from the beginning. Flo sounded wonderful. And she wasn't even aware yet of the other half of the story . . .

When she'd gathered herself, Hallie began a fresh email.

Dearest Flo,

Thank you, thank you. Your letter has made me indescribably happy too. We have *so* much to talk about. Can I phone you? Would that be OK?

Also, when can we meet up?

Chapter 58

It had been an unorthodox way of going about things, but it had all worked out in the end. Hallie smiled at the memory of Jonathan's look of disbelief when she'd told him about her meeting with Flo. 'It's all meant to be taken very slowly and carefully,' he'd said, shaking his head. 'It's a highly emotive situation, best handled by professionals. That's why we're here.'

'I know, but we'd found each other completely by accident. It felt like serendipity.' Struggling to explain, Hallie had waved her hands. 'It felt right for all of us. As soon as I told Flo about Rory, she wanted to meet him too. So that was it, we arranged for all of us to go down to Bristol together. And we met up at Flo's flat in Clifton. It was the most amazing day.'

And it really had been. Rory and Tasha had travelled down from London. She and Luke had driven from Carranford. Together they'd introduced themselves to Flo, all aware of the miraculous connection between them. Hallie had taken Flo's hand and pressed it to her chest so she could feel the steady beat of Zander's heart beneath her fingertips. Then they'd both felt Hallie's old heart thudding away inside Rory's ribcage.

And all thanks to Zander. Well, Zander and Flo, who had been so completely determined that his organs shouldn't go to waste.

A bond had been forged between them on their first day together. Against all expectations, Flo had been as grateful to them as they'd been to her. By that evening, a friendship had been born and they'd stayed in touch ever since.

And now it was the twenty-eighth of April, a beautiful spring day and Rory McAndrew's birthday. They were on their way to the party being held at his and Tasha's flat, along with assorted friends and family.

Hallie said, 'We're in Hampstead. Nearly there now,' and experienced a squiggle of excitement at the prospect of seeing them again.

And then they were there, on the doorstep, ringing the bell and being welcomed by Tasha.

'Yay, you're here!' Tasha threw her arms around Hallie. 'Rory, look!'

Rory appeared. 'New-family! Come on in!'

He'd coined the phrase last year, linking them all together. Hallie hugged him and said, 'Happy birthday. You're looking fantastic.'

Rory's green eyes sparkled. 'You too. All good?'

Hallie, as had become their new-family ritual, pressed the flat of her hand against his chest and felt the bump-bump-bump of her own heart. 'All very good. Oh wow, I can hear her already!'

They both turned to see Alexandra beaming and crowing 'BABAAAGAADAAWOOOOO,' as Joe carried her into the living room on his shoulders. Catching sight of Hallie and Luke, she raised her volume to the next level and wriggled to be allowed to reach them.

'Here, you're welcome,' said Joe, as Hallie held her arms up to take her from him. 'She's bursting my eardrums.'

Now thirteen months old, Alexandra was a happy, noisy baby who rarely cried and who loved social occasions.

'Good to see you getting into practice,' Luke told Joe, because Carmel was now seven months pregnant.

'Tell me about it.' Joe grinned. 'By June we're not going to know what's hit us.'

Hallie, cuddling Alexandra, inhaled the amazing baby smell of her fluffy dark hair. 'Hello, beautiful! Look at you!'

'Gadaboo,' said Alexandra, reaching up to grab Hallie's silver hooped earring.

'Gadaboo to you too.' Hallie pretended to bite Alexandra's tiny fingers, making her squeal with laughter.

'Now, has anyone seen a baby around here? Noisy little thing in a red onesie?' Flo was threading her way across the crowded living room. 'Ah, found her . . . Hallie, hello!'

They embraced fondly and Hallie said, 'How are you doing?'

'Great. She's teething, by the way, so she might try to chew your hand. How was your holiday?'

'We had the best time, didn't we?' Hallie turned to Luke, who had whisked her away on a surprise break to Venice in March. 'It was brilliant; when Bea called and asked me where I was, I told her I was sitting at a café in St Mark's Square being served a drink by a handsome waiter. And it was actually *true*.'

'Ah, that's fantastic. How's work going?'

'Oh, I love it so much. I get to boss Luke and Tess around and squeeze in extra appointments when I think the patients deserve them.' Had it been nepotism, when the vacancy for a new part-time receptionist had come up at the surgery and she'd applied for the job? Ha, probably, but she'd made up for it since with dedication, efficiency and sheer hard work.

'And how's Bea?'

'Same as ever.' Hallie grinned, because they hadn't only got to know each other; they were starting to know each other's friends too. 'She met a lovely man at the gym, spent weeks flirting with him over the rowing machines, then eventually he asked her out and she was *so* excited . . .'

Flo was wincing in anticipation. 'Oh God, what happened?'

'She'd only ever seen him in workout clothes . . . you know, shorts or tracksuits. And that was great. Until they had their date and he turned up wearing bright pink chinos. Poor chap, that was it, kiss of death.'

'So Bea's on her own again.'

'For the moment. But she's found someone else to lust after, and this one's guaranteed to break her heart.'

'Is that really guaranteed?' Luke frowned. 'Who is it?'

Hallie smiled. Luke hadn't encountered him yet. 'The new barman at the pub. His name's Angelo, he used to work as a male stripper and he met his last live-in girlfriend when she hired him for her hen night.'

'Ah,' said Luke. 'OK, you win. He'll definitely break her heart.'

'I always win because I'm always right.' Hallie winked at Flo. 'And how are things with Lena?'

'You won't believe this, but not too bad at all. She's really making an effort to get herself together.'

Having heard all about Zander's sister, it wasn't difficult to guess the reason for the improvement: since it had evidently dawned on Lena that she no longer had her brother around to rely on and bail her out of every hole, she'd finally decided to make the effort to become a less selfish person. Hallie nodded. 'Well, good.'

'That's not all,' said Flo. 'She's even gone and got herself a job!'

This was definitely a bombshell. 'Blimey, doing what? Bricklayer? Carpet fitter? Milkman?'

'Ha, can you picture it? No, she's working in one of those posh art galleries where you sit behind a desk and chat on the phone to your friends all day because hardly any customers ever go in. But she's doing it, that's the main thing. It's the first time she's ever stuck at something for more than three days. I feel like a proud mum!'

Hallie gave her another hug, because Flo could so easily have given up on Lena but hadn't. 'And I bet it's all down to you. Where's Patrick, anyway?'

'He's had to go and pick up a consignment of chandeliers from a studio in Primrose Hill.' Flo's cheeks gained some extra colour as she said it. 'He'll be back soon.'

As the party continued, Flo glanced out of the living room window and saw Patrick's car reversing into a space between a grey Porsche and a white Fiat 500.

Her heart lifted as it always did at the sight of him. Patrick had made her so much happier than she'd ever imagined. True, he'd never be mistaken for a male model, but he was one of the kindest men she'd ever known. He was also wonderful with Alexandra. His easy manner and ability to laugh at himself had charmed her from the start. She'd felt better in his company, even during those difficult early months following Zander's death. After first getting in touch with Hallie and hearing back from her, the only people she'd wanted to tell had been Patrick and Margot. And after discussing it with Margot, she'd discussed it for even longer with Patrick.

In the months that had followed, their close friendship had become more. When she'd heard about the developing relationship, Margot couldn't have been more thrilled.

And now here they were in April, and it was all good.

Flo watched as Patrick looked up at the window and, seeing her, broke into a smile. Her stomach tightened and she did a little wave back. He wasn't better or worse than Zander; he was just different.

And different was fine. They would both rather be in each other's company than in anyone else's. Not counting Alexandra, of course. Patrick had disappeared from view now, as he entered the house and made his way up the stairs. Flo looked forward to hearing his voice when he came into the living room.

As, she knew, did Alexandra.

Really, who could ask for more?

'Here goes,' Rory murmured, touching Tasha's arm as Joe began to attract everyone's attention by tapping a knife against his glass. 'He warned me he was going to make a speech.'

'He warned me too.' Tasha squeezed his hand in return. 'First time ever. Any idea what he's going to say?'

Rory shook his head; did anyone ever really know what words might come out of Joe's mouth next?

'Ladies and gentlemen, may I have your attention, please? No chatting at the back, either. I'd like to say a few words, if that's OK.'

'And if it's not?' Carmel called out from the far end of the room.

'Well that's just too bad, because I'm going to go ahead and say them anyway,' said Joe.

Everyone laughed. Tasha whispered, 'Let's hope he isn't going to make us jump out of a plane again.'

Rory smiled and pulled her closer. Tasha truly was the love of his life. Would he have got through the last year without her? Probably, yes. But would he have been a fraction as happy as he was now? Definitely not.

'My best friend Rory is twenty-seven years old today,' Joe announced, to a roar of approval from the gathered crowd. 'And I think we can all agree, the last two years have been pretty eventful.'

Carmel, standing with one hand resting on her protruding stomach, said drily, 'For me too.'

More laughter. Rory caught Flo's eye and she smiled at him, her own fingers entwined with Patrick's. Next to them, Hallie was still holding Alexandra, whose tiny left hand was splayed across Hallie's chest. Here they were, his new family, complete strangers who between them had saved his life. He owed them everything.

'Anyway, I'm not going to bang on about it, because we all know the details,' Joe continued. 'But I just want to say, none of us knows how long any one of us has left. It could be fifty hours, could be fifty years. We're just glad we're here today. And we won't forget those who aren't.' He paused and raised his glass. 'To absent friends. Especially Zander.'

Everyone else joined in.

Then Rory felt Tasha disentangle her fingers from his. Stepping forward in a rustle of sapphire taffeta, she surveyed the gathering of guests. 'Rory isn't going to waste this chance he's been given. He didn't want to tell you because he was worried he might sound boasty, so I'm going to tell you myself. Next year he's going to be running the London Marathon. He's hoping to represent England at the World Transplant Games. And he's also planning to cycle from John O'Groats to Land's End, to raise awareness of organ donation. I couldn't be prouder of him, I really couldn't.' Tasha's eyes were bright as she turned to smile at Rory. 'He's amazing. He's never going to change and I wouldn't want him to.'

A lump sprang up in Rory's throat; for a moment he felt himself waver. *Oh God . . .*

'Don't make him cry, Bin Girl.' Typically, Joe came to the rescue. 'We'll never let him live it down if he does.'

'Here's to Rory.' Flo, stepping into the breach, lifted her glass.

When the toast had been made, Rory said, 'And to Hallie.'

Hallie in turn added, 'To Flo and Alexandra.'

Finally, moving towards them and clinking her glass against each of theirs in turn, Flo said simply, 'Here's to us.'

Read on for a glimpse in to the world of

Jill
Mansell

– where you can ONLY wear sparkly flip-flops and
becoming an agony aunt is just a dream away . . .

A Q&A with Jill Mansell

Hallie asks everyone writing to her about their dilemmas to tell her three things about themselves. Tell us three amazing things about Jill Mansell . . .

Oh dear, this is tricky because I'm really not very amazing. OK, here goes:

1. As a very plain little girl, I used to watch the Miss World contests on TV and dream of one day becoming a beauty queen. I secretly made myself a red winner's sash out of crepe paper and spent hours up in my bedroom practising my winning-beauty-queen walk in front of the dressing-table mirror. (All these years later, on occasions when I'm required to walk out on to a stage and I hear the audience applauding me, it feels a bit like my childhood dream come true. Ooh, maybe I should make myself another sash!)

2. I love handbags and make-up and jewellery, but I hate shoes. I last bought a pair about twenty years ago, but I've never worn them. I have three pairs of boots to wear in the winter and in the summer I live in sparkly flip-flops. (I have a LOT of sparkly flip-flops.)

3. My best feature now is my very long eyelashes, but when I was young I hated them so much I used to cut them off with scissors. (Funny how I never got to be Miss World.)

What inspired you to give Hallie the role of agony aunt? And how much research did you do for this element in the book?

I love problem pages. I've always loved problem pages. One of the very best things about the internet is that I can now scour newspaper and magazine websites all over the world for new and brilliant advice columns and agony aunts. And I always have my own answers at the ready too – I'd love to do it professionally. Maybe one day, if this novel-writing career of mine shrivels and dies, I could start up again as Dear Jill . . .

If you've ever written to an agony aunt, what was the question? And what was the response? (Maybe going back to Jackie *days?!)*

I have never written to an agony aunt. But I definitely remember reading the 'Cathy and Claire' advice column in *Jackie* magazine and paying especially close attention to their advice on how to get a boy to like you. ('Be cheerful and smiley – personality is the most important thing,' they lied to us!)

Oh, and I recently saw a message from a fellow writer online, in which she chirpily confessed to having been Cathy-AND-Claire. There were never two of them! I have to confess, a little bit of my teenage heart was broken . . .

Hallie has such a positive outlook on life; did you find it infectious as you were writing the novel? Do your characters and storylines influence your mood and the decisions you make in your own life?

I think it's the other way around – if I'm in a good mood I'll let my characters be nice. If I'm in a grumpy mood, they might turn out to be a little less cheerful!

What compelled you to write about organ donation in THREE AMAZING THINGS? Is it an issue that's particularly close to your heart?

I worked in a hospital for almost twenty years and part of my job involved testing patients for brain death prior to organ donation so I have always been passionately in favour of this procedure. I think a lot of people still feel that if they are ever unwell in hospital, having signed up to the organ donor register means they'll have their organs whipped out before they're properly dead. If this has ever crossed your mind, I can assure you it really *really* isn't true. The reason I feel so strongly about this subject is that people are dying every day because organs are being destroyed instead of transplanted, and it's just such a WASTE. It's like watching someone drowning in front of you but choosing not to throw them a lifebelt.

The other reason to sign the donor register is because if someone dies and their organs are used, their friends and family will feel SO good that a part of that person lives on. I know for a fact that people who have refused to allow their loved ones' organs to be donated have later regretted it. I have never heard of anyone wishing they hadn't given their permission for organs to be donated. I think everyone just needs to ask themselves one question: if you desperately needed an organ transplant in order to live, would you be happy to receive one? Because if your answer is yes, then you should be equally willing to donate.

There are some dramatic hospital visits in THREE AMAZING THINGS, and you've worked in a hospital yourself. Do you watch hospital dramas like CASUALTY and HOLBY CITY, and do you think they catch some of the atmosphere of real-life emergencies? Why do you think people are so fascinated by A&E?

I think hospital dramas and documentaries will always be popular with TV audiences simply because they remind us how fragile life can be, how cruel fate can sometimes be, and how none of us ever really know what could happen to us five days . . . or five hours . or five minutes from now. Accidents and illnesses can happen at any time and change our lives, possibly forever.

Rory and Tasha spend a lovely weekend in a dream hotel. Do you have a favourite hotel? What's the secret of a romantic getaway weekend, for you and your partner?

I have such a weakness for gorgeous hotels, especially those in the Cotswolds or down in Cornwall by the sea. I love to write about them because it's the next best thing to staying in them! When I wrote STAYING AT DAISY'S I based the hotel in that book on The Manor House hotel in Castle Combe, which is just the loveliest place to visit. The little illustration on the front cover of the hardback of THREE AMAZING THINGS is actually inspired by a particular corner of Castle Combe!

Hallie has a lovely time sharing her favourite movie, THE SHAWSHANK REDEMPTION, with Luke – until they're interrupted. Do you have a favourite movie or movies? And does your partner love it (or them) too?

Ah well, I have to say that THE SHAWSHANK REDEMPTION is one of our favourites. There are lots of films we definitely don't watch together – I like rom-coms, he loves sci-fi and LORD OF THE UNBEARABLY DREARY RINGS – but we do have a few we both really like. THE GREAT ESCAPE, THE COLOR PURPLE and RAIN MAN spring to mind . . . I can't think of any more. Oh, and THE GODFATHER. Only five – that's how hopelessly incompatible we are. Ooh, and E.T.!

Do you ever imagine the book you're working on as a film or TV drama? Do share your dream cast for THREE AMAZING THINGS.

I really can't answer this question – I couldn't even begin to imagine real actors playing the characters in my books! I think I must be a bit weird because all the other writers I know seem to have very clear ideas and actor wish-lists, but I have no clue what my characters look like and feel all squirmy with embarrassment at the idea of suggesting who might play them. Sorry! (But that doesn't mean I wouldn't LOVE one of my books – and preferably *this* one – to be made into a film or TV drama!)

Can you tell us a little about your writing methods? Do you like to plan everything down to the last detail, or do you let the characters surprise you?

I write all my books by hand, with a fountain pen. My daughter types them up for me and loves to point out any mistakes I might have made along the way. I start out with one spark of an idea and keep building it up from there, in a haphazard kind of way. I can't plot out an entire book from beginning to end because the characters would only start saying or doing something I hadn't planned and that would derail the rest of the plot. It's easier to wait until the different ideas come along, then incorporate them into the story as best I can.

And do you have charts and Post-it notes all over the wall, or some other method for keeping track of dates and names?

I Sellotape together a lot of A4 sheets of paper to create a timeline, then stick coloured Post-its along the length of it to remind me when certain plot points have to take place. I gradually fill up the timeline as the book progresses – the idea is to keep everything under control and not lose track of any of the characters, but it doesn't always work!

Can you list ten books that have influenced your writing or inspired you?

Ten? That's a lot! OK, RIDERS AND RIVALS by Jilly Cooper because she made me realise I could combine fun and humour with drama in a contemporary setting that is glamorous but also recognisable.

GONE WITH THE WIND by Margaret Mitchell. It's full of characters who are flawed but somehow still loveable. This was my first experience (as a teenager) of reading a huge, fat book and I clearly remember loving the fact that there was so much of it.

THE YELLOW PAGES. I always use it to find jobs for my characters.

THE BUMPER BOOK OF BABIES' NAMES. I use it to name my characters.

As a child I absolutely loved LITTLE WOMEN by Louisa May Alcott. I also adored the LITTLE HOUSE ON THE PRAIRIE series by Laura Ingalls Wilder.

ONE DAY by David Nicholls is so fantastic. I had no clue when I was reading it that the 'huge event' was about to happen . . . and when it did happen, I was just knocked sideways. I can remember that exact feeling, and I knew I wanted to try and recreate it for readers of my books, because it's a pretty amazing thing to be able to do just with words on a page.

WONDER by R.J. Palacio is a gorgeous little gem of a book and I'm forever begging people to read it.

84 CHARING CROSS ROAD by Helene Hanff. Wonderful, warm characters, a huge love of books and the most frustrating ending ever. I know it's non-fiction but I'd still like it to end more happily, with the two main characters eventually meeting up. Maybe I could sneakily rewrite the last couple of chapters – would anyone really mind?

Pssst . . . if you're already looking forward to Jill's next
novel, here's a sneak peak!
It's called

YOU AND ME, ALWAYS

Chapter 1

There he was, sitting in the sun outside the Star Inn. Lily slowed and parked the van outside Goldstone House, next to the pub. Dan saw her and waved, and her stomach tightened at the sight of him, as it always had done. There was just something about the languid angles of his body, those long legs in black jeans stretched out in front of him, the tilt of his head as he chatted on his phone and laughed at something that had been said.

The tightening didn't mean anything, though, Lily knew that. It had evolved as a kind of Pavlovian reaction, a habit that had become ingrained over the years simply because Dan Rafferty was so physically attractive. The good thing was, the fact that he knew he was attractive, and traded on it shamelessly with all concerned, meant the idea of an actual relationship with him was the very last thing anyone in their right mind would want.

And since she was in her right mind, thankfully she was safe.

'Lily, Lily.' Dan's eyes crinkled and he pushed his dark glasses to the top of his head as she jumped down from the van. 'My most favourite girl in the world.'

See? This was what he was like. 'And you're the most annoying boy.'

'I'm not a boy. I'm a man.'

He was twenty-seven, two years older than she was. Technically he might be a man, but when you'd known each other since childhood, it just seemed wrong somehow.

'You used to put frogspawn in the hood of my anorak,' said Lily. 'You'll always be a boy to me. Where's your car, anyway?'

'Over in Chipping Norton.' Dan had texted her earlier asking if she could give him a lift to go and pick it up.

'Why?' As if she couldn't guess.

'Best not to ask. The usual, basically. Good wine and bad women. Well, one bad woman taking shameless advantage.' He gestured to the still full cup of coffee on the table in front of him. 'Are you in a tearing hurry, or can I get you a drink?'

Lily checked her watch. It was twenty past six. She'd spent the last three hours delivering a marble-topped table and a set of Victorian chimney pots to a customer in Chippenham, but work was now over for the day and the rest of her evening was free.

'Go on then, I'll have a Coke.' She joined him at the table, unsticking the back of her T-shirt from her shoulder blades and flapping the front of it to cool down her ribcage while Dan disappeared inside to order the drink.

When he returned, she took the glass and said, 'Cheers, thanks. Why couldn't Patsy give you a lift back to your car?'

'She's out. Gone on a date. With a mystery man off the internet.'

Lily perked up. 'Ooh, what's he like?'

'No idea.' Dan grinned. 'That's the whole point of him being a mystery. She didn't want me to meet him.'

'Well, after last time with the chap from Chepstow, who could blame her?'

'Welsh William.' He shrugged. 'That wasn't my fault. He was the one who challenged me to an arm-wrestling match. He was just showing off, trying to prove how strong he was.'

'You could have let him win,' said Lily.

'Me?' Dan looked horrified. 'Why? He was an idiot. Patsy wouldn't want someone like him anyway.'

Which was true enough. Ah well, maybe this new one might be an improvement. Lily swirled the ice cubes in her glass and took a gulp of Coke, then paused as her attention was drawn to a stocky man on a bicycle heading along the main street directly towards them. He was wearing an orange cycling helmet that clashed with his red face and turquoise Lycra leggings. As his legs pumped the pedals, he appeared to be talking to himself.

By this time Dan had turned and was watching him too. It wasn't until the man had drawn closer that they realised he wasn't riding an ordinary bike; it was a tandem. Nor was he having a conversation with himself; he was loudly addressing his cycling companion behind him.

'. . . and in September of two thousand and thirteen . . . or it might have been the October come to think of it . . . anyway, that was when I cycled from Ravenglass to South Shields alongside Hadrian's Wall, and that's one hundred and seventy-four miles in total, so it's quite a trek, but the views were phenomenal . . . then the following March I did the Devon coast-to-coast, from Ilfracombe to Plymouth . . .'

'Whoops,' Lily breathed as the tandem drew nearer still and they were finally able to see who was on the back of it. Dan sprayed coffee and rocked forwards on his seat. Poor Patsy, clearly mortified as her companion continued at top volume, saw them watching and pulled an *Oh God* face.

And then they were passing the pub, their legs moving in unison as the pedals turned and the tyres made a dry swishing noise on the hot, dusty tarmac. Patsy's date was still facing forwards, talking loudly for her benefit as he informed her of the importance of keeping up a nice steady rhythm.

Which made Dan, predictably, crack up with silent laughter. As the tandem moved on, Patsy glanced over at them for a moment, shook her head in despair and mouthed the words: *Help me.*

Oh dear, but it was hard not to laugh. At the junction at the end of the high street, the traffic lights turned red and the tandem dutifully slowed to a halt. They watched as Patsy put her feet down and turned back to give them a look of mortification and misery, whilst her date continued his loud monologue.

'How does she get herself into these situations?' Dan marvelled. He gestured to his sister and mimed diving sideways off the bike.

Up ahead, taking her weight on her feet and raising her bottom from the saddle, Patsy let go of the handlebars. The traffic lights changed to amber, then to green. Her companion pressed down on the front pedals and the tandem moved off, leaving Patsy standing in the road behind it. Evidently still entranced by the sound of his own voice, and oblivious to the fact that he'd lost his pedalling partner, the man who'd been her date continued on down the road.

Dan took a quick photo on his phone before the tandem completely disappeared from view. He grinned at Lily and said, 'Ha, brilliant. That's this year's Christmas card sorted.'

Patsy stood in the centre of the road and watched as Derek energetically cycled off without her. She couldn't quite believe he hadn't noticed she'd gone.

Why did this kind of situation always seem to happen to her? Derek had sounded so *nice* in his emails. He'd given her no cause whatsoever to suspect he was a secret cycling fanatic with a deep and detailed knowledge of every single cycleway in the UK and a passion for sharing *all* this information with her in a maximum-volume never-ending monotone.

If she'd known, the entire relationship could have been nipped in the bud before it even had time to become a bud. Some women might not mind the idea of sailing through life on the back of a tandem, but Patsy definitely wasn't one of them.

She sighed and brushed away the loose strands of hair that were sticking to her forehead. And now Dan and Lily were beckoning her towards them, no doubt finding her predicament hilarious. What she should have done, of course, was to tap Derek on the shoulder, politely explain that they might as well give up now, then shake hands, say goodbye and wish him better luck next time.

That would have been the normal way, the dignified way to go about it.

Oh God, poor Derek. She really shouldn't have done that to him.

Then again, poor *her*.

Jill Mansell

THE UNPREDICTABLE CONSEQUENCES OF LOVE

In the idyllic seaside town of St Carys, Sophie is putting the past firmly behind her.

When Josh arrives in St Carys to run the family hotel, he can't understand why Sophie has zero interest in letting *any* man into her life. He also can't understand how he's been duped into employing Sophie's impulsive friend Tula, whose crush on him is decidedly unrequited.

St Carys has more than its fair share of characters, including the charming but utterly feckless surfer Riley Bryant, who is besotted with Tula. Riley's aunt is superstar author Marguerite Marshall. And Marguerite has designs on Josh's grandfather . . . who in turn still adores his glamorous ex-wife, Dot . . .

Just how many secrets can one seaside town keep?

Just *Heavenly*. Just *Jill*.

Acclaim for Jill Mansell's fabulous bestsellers:

'Bursting with humour, brimming with intrigue and full of characters you'll adore' ***** *Heat*

'You'll fall in love with the characters in this lovely tale' *Sun*

'A warm, witty and romantic read' *Daily Mail*

978 0 7553 5593 8

headline
review

Jill Mansell

Books

straight through your letterbox...

The Unpredictable Consequences of Love	£7.99
Don't Want To Miss A Thing	£7.99
A Walk In The Park	£8.99
To The Moon And Back	£8.99
Take A Chance On Me	£8.99
Rumour Has It	£8.99
An Offer You Can't Refuse	£8.99
Thinking Of You	£8.99
Making Your Mind Up	£8.99
The One You Really Want	£8.99
Falling For You	£8.99
Nadia Knows Best	£8.99
Staying At Daisy's	£8.99
Millie's Fling	£8.99
Good At Games	£8.99
Miranda's Big Mistake	£8.99
Head Over Heels	£7.99
Mixed Doubles	£8.99
Perfect Timing	£8.99
Fast Friends	£8.99
Solo	£8.99
Kiss	£8.99
Sheer Mischief	£8.99
Open House	£7.99
Two's Company	£8.99

**Simply call 01235 400 414 or visit our website
www.headline.co.uk to order**

Free delivery in the UK.
For overseas and Ireland £3.50 delivery charge.
Prices and availability subject to change without notice.